Taking a seat on the front steps, she bit into her pastry. *Custard.* Oh, she'd just known it would be custard.

It was a very good thing she'd not been tempted to purchase one until now, she thought. As it was, the treats would cost her . . . nothing, she realized.

They're a gift.

It was true, she hadn't any experience receiving gifts. Certainly not from men. Most certainly not from handsome men whose presence made her feel strangely restless, as if she wasn't quite comfortable in her own skin.

It was the oddest sensation, the way her heart had tripped and her skin had prickled when he'd unbuttoned her gown that morning, and it was both unsettling and intriguing to remember how pleasant it had been to lean against the rail of the pasture with him, laughing and talking and standing in companionable silence. There had been a pleasant tightening in her belly and an unexpected temptation to shuffle her feet closer until they were standing arm to arm. And she no longer had an excuse to deny the obvious.

Nearly a Lady

Alissa Johnson

BERKLEY SENSATION, NEW YORK

THE BERKLEY PUBLISHING GROUP
Published by the Penguin Group
Penguin Group (USA) Inc.
375 Hudson Street, New York, New York 10014, USA
Penguin Group (Canada), 90 Eglinton Avenue East, Suite 700, Toronto, Ontario M4P 2Y3, Canada
(a division of Pearson Penguin Canada Inc.)
Penguin Books Ltd., 80 Strand, London WC2R 0RL, England
Penguin Group Ireland, 25 St. Stephen's Green, Dublin 2, Ireland (a division of Penguin Books Ltd.)
Penguin Group (Australia), 250 Camberwell Road, Camberwell, Victoria 3124, Australia
(a division of Pearson Australia Group Pty. Ltd.)
Penguin Books India Pvt. Ltd., 11 Community Centre, Panchsheel Park, New Delhi—110 017, India
Penguin Group (NZ), 67 Apollo Drive, Rosedale, Auckland 0632, New Zealand
(a division of Pearson New Zealand Ltd.)
Penguin Books (South Africa) (Pty.) Ltd., 24 Sturdee Avenue, Rosebank, Johannesburg 2196,
South Africa

Penguin Books Ltd., Registered Offices: 80 Strand, London WC2R 0RL, England

This is a work of fiction. Names, characters, places, and incidents either are the product of the author's imagination or are used fictitiously, and any resemblance to actual persons, living or dead, business establishments, events, or locales is entirely coincidental. The publisher does not have any control over and does not assume any responsibility for author or third-party websites or their content.

NEARLY A LADY

A Berkley Sensation Book / published by arrangement with the author

PRINTING HISTORY
Berkley Sensation mass-market edition / June 2011

Copyright © 2011 by Alissa Johnson.
Excerpt from *An Unexpected Gentleman* by Alissa Johnson copyright © by Alissa Johnson.
Cover art by Lott Reps/Shirley Green.
Cover design by George Long.
Interior text design by Laura K. Corless.

ISBN: 978-0-425-24181-3

BERKLEY® SENSATION
Berkley Sensation Books are published by The Berkley Publishing Group,
a division of Penguin Group (USA) Inc.,
375 Hudson Street, New York, New York 10014.
BERKLEY® SENSATION and the "B" design are trademarks of Penguin Group (USA) Inc.

PRINTED IN THE UNITED STATES OF AMERICA

10 9 8 7 6 5 4 3 2 1

For Maamin,
because if we had been banished to Scotland,
she would have packed salami sandwiches for the trip.

Prologue

The Marquess of Engsly was not quite so bitter as to believe duplicity the exclusive domain of women. At the moment, however, he was just bitter enough to entertain the notion it was a realm inhabited *primarily* by women and ruled, most effectively, by the grand duchess of artifice herself, the Dowager Lady Engsly . . . his dear stepmama.

And if that idea held a touch more of the dramatic than was becoming for a man of his station, well, he rather felt he was entitled to the lapse.

It was hotter than Hades in that room.

In concession to the southern Italian sun, both he and his man, Kincaid, had stripped down to shirtsleeves and bare feet. They'd thrown open windows and doors, but the papers covering the small desk and littering the floor lay still, untouched by even a hint of breeze. It was heat alone that poured into the close room and had sweat beading on the marquess's forehead and sliding down his back.

"Have a look at this, Kincaid." The marquess wiped a damp hand on a handkerchief before holding up the letter of receipt he was reading. "Seventy-five pounds to St. Agnus's Asylum in East London."

Kincaid glanced up from where—after what the marquess was sure must have been a substantial internal battle between pride and practicality—he was seated on the floor, half buried in twenty years' worth of journal entries penned by a madwoman. "I am unfamiliar with that particular charity, my lord."

"Of course you are," the marquess replied. "There is no St. Agnus's Asylum in East London."

He tossed the letter aside and grabbed the next, the contents of which had him laughing despite the miserable atmosphere.

"Eighty pounds annum for the care of one Miss Blythe, daughter of Mr. Robert Blythe and legal ward of the Marquess of Engsly." He waved the paper in a flourish. "A *ward*. My father, who could scarce stomach the sight of his own offspring, agreed to take on a small girl? What an audacious lie. How is it none of us noticed the woman's perfidy before this?"

"Your father was quite enamored of your stepmother."

The marquess moved to toss the paper with the last. "As far as he was capable of such an emotion, at any rate."

"A moment, my lord. What was the child's name?"

The marquess frowned across the desk. "Miss Blythe," he repeated, certain Kincaid had heard him the first time. "Is the heat getting to you? Perhaps a brief respite—"

"A respite would be welcome but unnecessary. I was inquiring after her given name."

"Ah." He scanned the lists detailing the purchases associated with the clothing and housing of a small girl. All of them fabricated, no doubt. "Here we are—Winnefred. Miss Winnefred Blythe."

"Winnefred." Kincaid blinked, realization and a bright smile of humor lighting his aging face. "Freddie. Heavens, I'd quite forgotten."

"Are you telling me this child exists?"

"She does, or did a dozen years ago. The vicar's daughter, little Annabelle Holmes, wrote of her shortly after we left your father's house. Charming child, Annabelle. Such a developed sense of the absurd for one so young."

"And a favorite of my brother's for that very reason," the marquess added, remembering how Gideon had never seemed to mind having Anna follow him about the estate, peppering him with questions. But that had been before Gideon had gone to war. He was a different man now. A very different man. He would no longer welcome the adoration of a small child. "What did the letter say?"

"If I recall correctly, your father and Mr. Blythe were both in attendance at a large, and by all accounts very festive, hunting party during which a drunken guest set the stables on fire. Mr. Blythe was brave enough, it seems, to have charged in and pulled out the horses, and foolish enough to be mortally wounded in the process. Moments after collapsing on the lawn, Blythe made a deathbed request of the man standing nearest him, your father."

"To take his daughter as his ward," he guessed.

"Ah, no. To take his 'Freddie,' I believe were his exact words. Your father and Mr. Blythe were little more than acquaintances, you understand, and his lordship assumed 'Freddie' to mean a son. Apparently feeling magnanimous toward Blythe for saving his prized horseflesh, he agreed—in front of witnesses—to see the child cared for . . . There was quite a fuss when little Winnefred arrived on the front doorstep. His lordship flew into a rage, certain Blythe had purposely misrepresented the situation. It took your stepmother's agreement to personally see the girl settled elsewhere to calm him down."

"She was the only person who ever could, I'll give her that. I'm almost sorry I missed it." The marquess read over the numbers again. "Eighty pounds annum. If Lady Engsly followed her usual pattern of stealing half the funds from causes that actually exist, that would give the girl forty pounds a year. Not much, is it?"

Kincaid dug his way out from the journals to stand. "Payment would have ceased when Lady Engsly disappeared."

A sick weight settled over the room. "More than six months ago," the marquess said softly. "Bloody hell. There's an address here." He tapped the paper. "Murdoch House, Enscrum, Scotland. That's near the border, isn't it? I'll send word to Gideon. With any luck, the allowance was paid annually and Miss Blythe will still be in residence. We can make this right."

"Your brother is handling the estate in your absence. Perhaps it would be wise for us to return—"

"No." The word came out harsher than the marquess intended and had him dragging a weary hand down his face. "I beg your pardon. Between the heat and the lack of progress, I am a bit out of sorts. Gideon passed on the responsibly of the estate to our secretary almost before I requested he take on the task. He needs something to do. Something to accomplish."

Something, the marquess thought, that might lighten the shadows his brother attempted to hide behind a cheerful wit and careless smile. "Playing knight-errant will be good for Gideon."

Kincaid gave a slight nod in acknowledgment but hesitated before speaking. "Have you considered that . . . some of the information you seek might not be here?"

The marquess chose to ignore the obvious implications of what was being suggested. "If it is not, it is with the dowager marchioness. When we find her . . ." Then they would find everything the woman had stolen over the years. "When we find her . . . we'll find Rose."

When Kincaid spoke again, his voice was soft and laced with the compassion of an old friend. "It has been more than twelve years, my lord. Twelve years without word. *Please.* You must resign yourself to the possibility that Rose is not to be found. There is every possibility that the lady is simply gone."

"I'd know." The marquess refused to look up from the desk, refused to give in to the doubt that had sat side by side with hope since he'd discovered his stepmother's betrayal. "Rose is not gone. She is merely . . . lost for the moment."

Like Lady Engsly, he realized, and Miss Blythe.

"It occurs to me, Kincaid, that this family has an unfortunate habit of misplacing its women."

Chapter 1

"Move so much as a finger, and I'll blow a hole clean through you."

Well . . . Damn.

During the long, long ride from London to Enscrum, Scotland, Lord Gideon Haverston had envisioned his reception at Murdoch House playing out in any number of ways. By most accounts, he was an optimistic—occasionally even fanciful—man, and so it was only to be expected that the vast majority of those ways had included the barest minimum of recriminations and tears, and an astounding amount of gratitude and rejoicing.

Use of the word "hero" had not been ruled out.

Not once, however, had he imagined at the end of his journey to find a house devoid of life, a stable sheltering a brigand, and the phrase "blow a hole clean through you" being whispered in the dark while a gun muzzle pressed uncomfortably into the small of his back.

Still, he'd had colder welcomes.

"If it's money you're after, you'll find it difficult to obtain unless one of us reaches for my pocket. Although, they say there's a man in Russia who can move objects with mere thoughts. There's a fine talent. Perhaps you're familiar with it?"

A short silence followed that statement.

"You're a cold one, aren't you?" the voice finally hissed. "And I'm not the thief here."

Young, Gideon thought, very young, and afraid. He was well acquainted with the boyish habit of hiding fear with bravado. He'd heard it often enough on the deck of the *Perseverance*—the false deepening of the voice, the underlying tremor, and that quality of thickness as words forced their way past the ball of terror lodged in the throat.

'Fraid? Not me, Cap'n. Not me.

But they had been. He'd not suffered fools on his ship.

The lad behind him was running, like as not, and thought to spend the night in a pile of hay. Better all around if he was put down before he did something they would both regret.

Gideon shifted his weight to his good leg, pivoted, knocked the barrel of the rifle away with one hand, and threw his other out in a fist.

A sliver of moonlight cut through the open door, and in the space of a heartbeat he saw trousers, bosom, and a long braid.

A woman.

Instinct had him pulling his fist back before it connected with flesh. No good deed goes unpunished, and for this particularly stupid act of chivalry, Gideon's penalty was swift, painful, and humiliating. He doubled over when the butt of the rifle slammed into his stomach, yelped when a sharp knee plowed into his nose, then slipped into blackness when something hard bounced off his head with a whopping crack.

Is he dead, then? Did we kill him?"

Winnefred leaned over her friend Lilly, who, in turn, was leaning over the man they'd just done their best to beat senseless. As their best had proved remarkably successful, she couldn't help but feel a touch of smugness along with relief and lingering terror. He should have kept his thieving to the house, the blighter, instead of coming after the animals.

"Because if we did, we'll need to hide the body straightaway. What if someone comes looking for him?"

"Then they will no doubt wonder how his horse came to be in our stable." Lilly crouched down in front of the prone man. "And *we* did not kill him. *I* struck him with the pan. You merely kicked him about a bit."

Though it was too dark to be seen, Winnefred felt that comment merited a roll of the eyes. "I'll be sure to ask the vicar to make that distinction at our respective funerals. Hanged murderesses are allowed funerals, aren't they?"

"With any luck, we'll never know. He's still breathing."

"Oh."

Winnefred felt rather than saw her friend's gaze. "Your regard for the sanctity of human life is most touching."

"You're the one who thumped him about the head," Winnefred reminded her. "Besides, a dead body is easier to hide than a live one . . . Shall we tie him up, do you think?"

"I suppose. His coat feels . . . rather expensive."

"I imagine there are some monetary benefits to being an outlaw. Would you ever consider—?"

"No."

"Pity. No one would ever suspect you." With hands that still wanted to shake, Winnefred retrieved two small lengths of rope and set about tying the man's hands while Lilly worked on his feet.

"He's wearing good boots and trousers of superfine," Lilly said. "I want to see him in the light. Fetch a candle—"

"No. We've only a few candles left. I'll not waste one on the likes of him."

"Freddie."

"Grab his feet, then. I'll take his shoulders. We'll drag him outside."

Years of physical labor had left both women with strong

backs and capable hands, but it was an awkward business hauling a grown man out the stable doors. There was a great deal of huffing on Lilly's part, and no small amount of swearing on Winnefred's.

His feet hit the moonlight first, and Winnefred couldn't help but notice that Lilly had been right about the boots— they were very nice indeed. She saw the trousers next, then the tailored coat. At last his face came into view— dark hair and long lashes, aquiline nose and hard jaw. His mouth was wide with—

"Oh, sweet heaven!" Lilly's horrified gasp seemed unnaturally loud in the dark.

"What? What is it?" Winnefred hastily readjusted her grip as the man's feet slipped from Lilly's hands and fell to the ground.

"It's him. It's him. It's . . . Wait . . ." Lilly bent closer to his face. "It isn't him."

"For pity's sake, Lilly—"

"It's the other one. It's Gideon."

"Gideon?" Winnefred echoed. "Lord Gideon Haverston, do you mean? Brother to our generous benefactor? Here?" She bent forward for another, more narrow-eyed look at his features. Then let his head drop to the hard earth.

"Winnefred, what are you thinking?" To Winnefred's bemusement, Lilly hissed the words in a whisper, as if Haverston's condition had suddenly and miraculously improved from unconscious to merely sleeping.

"You're absolutely right. That was quite careless of me." She straightened and planted her hands on her hips. "I should have aimed for a pointed rock."

"Oh, no. Oh, no. What have we done?"

"Missed a fine opportunity, in my opinion. We could be planning his trip to the bottom of the loch right now, instead of . . . Why the *devil* are you untying him?"

"We'll explain," Lilly breathed, sounding a bit hysterical as she tore at the knots. "Terrible mistake. Two women alone—"

"Lilly, stop." Winnefred bent down again and closed her

hand over her friend's. "We've been alone for years and he's never concerned himself over it before."

"Perhaps he wasn't aware—"

"He was." Winnefred hesitated before she spoke again. She'd never planned to confess what she'd done, but she couldn't see a way around it now. "I wrote him last winter when you were so ill. I asked him to speak to his brother on our behalf."

"He never answered," Lilly guessed dully.

"Oh, he answered," Winnefred muttered. She would remember the scathing insult of that reply for the rest of her life. "We have to go."

She pulled Lilly to her feet and tugged her toward the gardener's cottage. "Pack what you can easily carry. We'll take his horse. With any luck, we'll be long gone by the time he gets himself untied."

"We can't just leave him."

Winnefred shoved Lilly inside and slammed the door behind her decisively. "We can, and we will. If I can leave Claire"—and oh, how that thought tore at her heart—"I can bloody well leave *him*."

"Claire is a *goat*, Winnefred."

"Nearer to human than a Haverston."

She threw open an old chest, pushed aside the two gowns reserved for trips into town, and dug out the leather pouch that held the coins she'd managed to scrimp together in savings. "Nearly a half pound," she whispered, jingling the pouch.

"Oh, well." Lilly let out a breathy laugh of disbelief. "We'll tour the continent in style, then."

"I should think it's preferable to touring a prison—"

"Wait." Lilly reached into the trunk and pulled out a gown. "I've an idea."

Chapter 2

*T*ake off your trousers, Freddie."

"What if we have need to run? My legs will tangle in all this material. You should put yours back on, Lilly."

Over the course of his one-and-thirty years, Gideon had woken to the sounds of a great many conversations on a great variety of topics. None, however, had been quite so strange, nor quite so entertaining, as the one he was currently overhearing. In deference to both curiosity and the painful throbbing of his head, he kept his eyes closed, his breathing even, and simply listened.

"Your legs will tangle whether or not you've trousers on underneath."

"But I can throw the dress off, can't I?"

"You look suspiciously lumpy."

"I feel suspiciously stupid. I can't believe I've agreed to this."

Gideon heard the soft rustle of skirts draw near and caught the faintest hint of lavender and hay. He found it a pleasant combination.

"He's very handsome. Shame he's such a rotter."

"*Hush*. Honestly, what if he should hear you?"

"Not much chance of that, I think. He hasn't moved for hours." Gideon sensed the woman bending over him, and then a rag, cool and damp, was placed on his brow with something approaching, but not quite reaching, gentleness. "Are you absolutely certain he's not dead?"

Because the young woman sounded just a mite eager to find her friend's assessment of his well-being in error, Gideon thought it might be best to open his eyes.

His vision was filled by the woman from the stable. The braid was gone, he noticed. Light brown hair with broad gold streaks had been pulled up rather inartfully to frame an oval face. She wasn't beautiful by society's standards. Her nose was a trifle too prominent, her lips a touch too wide, and the near explosion of freckles across otherwise creamy skin was certainly unfashionable. And yet, the overall effect held an indefinable appeal.

A different kind of beauty, he decided. Not more, nor less, than the ideal held by his peers. Simply . . . other. Only a fool would insist a qualitative decision be made between two varieties of beauty. One would always be found lacking when the other was used as a measurement. Like comparing a bouquet of hothouse roses and a nosegay of wildflowers. Or like comparing the proverbial apples and oranges. Why apples and oranges? he wondered.

"Why not grapes and cherries?"

The young woman reared back at the sound of his voice, and Gideon noticed three things in quick succession. One, that her eyes—previously directed at the top of his head in the obvious hope of finding blood seeping there—were as golden as the streaks in her hair. Two, that she was rather small for having bested him in a fight—embarrassing, that. And three, she was indeed lumpy under her gown.

"I beg your pardon," he croaked. He cleared his throat and manfully ignored the increased pounding it caused in his skull. "That wasn't quite what I had intended to say upon our first meeting. Then again, I hadn't intended to have you bash my head in either. Bit more excitement than either of us had planned for the day, I imagine."

The amber eyes widened, then blinked. "I . . ."

"Miss Winnefred Blythe, I presume?" He was relatively certain it was Freddie who'd been told to take her trousers off. "Or have I managed to terrify the wrong woman entirely?"

Her eyes instantly narrowed to slits. "You haven't managed to terrify anyone. Least of all me."

The young woman was hastily pushed aside by another, slightly taller woman with dark hair and wide blue eyes. She looked to be the elder of the two by only a few years. Gideon wondered if she'd helped her friend in the stable last night. He certainly hoped so. Being knocked unconscious by two small women was a degree better than being knocked unconscious by just the one.

"I am Miss Ilestone," the second woman began. Very much, Gideon thought, as if she had expected him to have already guessed who she was. "Please forgive Miss Blythe. We've had an unsettling night. What she meant to say is that we think you were set upon by a ruffian, or ruffians. We found you bound and unconscious in the stable."

He idly rubbed his wrist and felt the lingering burn of rope. "Ruffians," he repeated, not believing a word of it. "With tart mouths and long braids of hair?"

"Braids of . . . ? Oh, dear, I was afraid of this." Miss Ilestone placed a mothering hand to his forehead. "Head wounds can be so precarious. Only last year, Mr. Pirkle fell from the roof of his inn. When he came round again, he swore up and down it was Mrs. Pirkle who pushed him."

Ah, so that was their game, was it? "And why could it not have been Mrs. Pirkle?"

"She has been dead these seven years."

"That would certainly make her an unlikely suspect," he agreed. "I suppose my things were stolen, my—"

"Not at all. Isn't that fortunate? Winnefred and I must have frightened them away when—"

"Terrified them," Winnefred interjected.

Miss Ilestone shot her friend a quelling glance. "—When we came out of the cottage. We were making a tremendous amount of noise."

"You knew they were there?" He really shouldn't be encouraging them, but it was such a fun story, really.

"Not initially, no," Miss Ilestone said. "We saw you come from the house and enter the stable, and when we stepped out for a peek, we heard the sounds of a scuffle. We ran back inside, grabbed pots and pans and—"

"A rifle, by chance?"

"Heavens, no. Whatever would we do with a rifle? At any rate, we made a great deal of noise with the kitchen-ware, waited a bit, looked in the stable, and there you were."

What a marvelous bit of lying, he thought. He would've liked to have asked who had come up with it, and whether it had been a spontaneous sort of thing or something they'd worked on over the course of his incapacitation, but he could hear the fear again. Just as he had in the stable. Miss Ilestone's voice was smooth, but her hands trembled. Miss Blythe gently pulled her away from the bed and took a sub-tle step forward to stand in front of her in a protective man-ner. It would be faster, easier, and less painful, he decided, simply to let them think he believed the lie for now.

"Well, it would seem I owe you ladies a great debt of gratitude."

Miss Ilestone flushed, coughed nervously, and fixed her stare on the headboard over his shoulder. "It was nothing, my lord."

"Don't be so modest, Lilly," Miss Blythe said sweetly. "You were exceedingly brave."

"Winnefred—"

"Miss Blythe is quite right. If you . . ." He trailed off, blinked, and cocked his head on the pillow. "Why do you assume I'm a lord?"

"We've met before," Miss Ilestone explained. "I sup-pose you don't remember. It was years ago and it was only in passing. You were home from school—just the day, I think—and I was staying with my cousin, Lady Engsly, at your father's estate."

"Lady Engsly is your cousin?" Gideon sat up slowly, relieved when the room didn't revolve in one direction and his stomach the other. "Have you had word from her recently?"

"No, not for . . ." She thought it over for a moment. "Not for nearly two years now. We were never close."

"Why?" Miss Blythe asked. "Has something happened to her?"

He blew out a quick breath. Though he didn't share his peers' mortal fear of scandal, neither did he enjoy discussing a family embarrassment. In his opinion, life was too short to spend it atoning for someone else's sins. But a debt was a debt, and the Engsly estate owed Winnefred Blythe for a promise not kept.

"Lady Engsly disappeared, some seven months ago and with a substantial amount of money stolen from the Engsly coffers."

"Stolen?" Miss Ilestone echoed, her eyes going round.

"Whatever for?" Miss Blythe asked. "Your father was rich as Midas."

"Freddie," Miss Ilestone chided.

The younger woman had the grace to look a little abashed. "I only meant she hadn't wanted for funds."

"No," Gideon agreed. "She hadn't. My father was generous with his second wife, both in life and in his death. She received a sizable inheritance upon his passing last year. Why she felt the need to secret away more money we've yet to determine. In the meantime, the family is making an attempt to remedy the damage she has done. Hence my trip to Scotland."

"Damage?" both woman asked at once.

He nodded and once again pushed past the distaste of airing his stepmother's crimes. "One of the ways Lady Engsly diverted funds was to patronize fictional charities. Another was to double the total of an expense and keep the second half for herself."

"And which are we?" Miss Blythe challenged. "The charity or the expense?"

"That would depend, wouldn't it?" Gideon tilted his head at her. "Have you received any money at all from the Engsly estate?"

"Yes."

"Then you're the expense." He smiled broadly at her scowl.

"But we received the allowance from Lord Engsly," Miss Ilestone pointed out. "First your father, then—"

"Not exactly. The funds may have been in Lord Engsly's name, but they were dispersed by Lady Engsly and Mr. Lartwick—my father's late secretary, in case you're wondering, and Lady Engsly's cohort in crime. My father never knew of the pair's pilfering, and neither my brother nor I knew you were here until last month."

The women exchanged a quick look of surprise and skepticism. Miss Blythe opened her mouth as if to say something—something unpleasant if her expression was any indication of her thoughts—but closed it again when Miss Ilestone gave one, almost imperceptible, shake of her head.

"Is there something you'd like to ask?" Gideon prompted.

Both women looked to him uncertainly. Always the fear, he thought. "Why don't you think on it some, and while you're at it, give some thought as to what you would like to do with yourselves now."

"Do with ourselves?" Miss Blythe repeated. "You've come to evict us, then."

He couldn't fault the girl for her tone of resignation, even if it did rankle. "I've come, as I believe I mentioned, to right the wrong done to you by a member of my family. The allowance owed you will be paid in full, Miss Blythe, and a small bonus added as restitution. You may stay here as long as you like, or if you prefer, we can find another home more to your taste . . . Unless your tastes run to Buckingham Palace. If that's the case, I'm afraid you're out of luck."

He turned his attention toward the older woman. "As for you, I think . . . How is it you came to be here, Miss Ilestone? My brother's letter didn't mention you."

"It didn't? I . . ." A shadow crossed her face, but it was gone as quickly as it arrived. "I came with Freddie—Miss Blythe, that is—from your father's estate. My immediate family is gone, and Lady Engsly offered me the position of governess."

She couldn't have been more than seventeen at the time, he thought. "And were you salaried?"

"Well, there was Miss Blythe's allowance . . ." She trailed off, looking uncomfortable. "I was hardly qualified, at any rate."

"I see. Your back pay as well, then. Equal to Miss Blythe's allowance, I should think."

Ah, there now was the sort of reaction he'd been imagining during his trip. Miss Ilestone's face lit with pleasure and excitement. Her hand reached out and gripped Winnefred's.

"Twelve years? Twelve years of back pay? Are you certain? It's a considerable sum, and your brother—"

"Will be appalled to find you've gone without compensation for your work." He shot a quick smile at Miss Blythe. "I'm certain it was . . . challenging."

Miss Ilestone's soft laugh filled the room, but his focus was on Miss Blythe. Unless he was much mistaken, her lips twitched just a little.

"I was an angel," she informed him.

"Fallen, perhaps," her friend said dryly. She let go of Miss Blythe's hand to brush at her gown. "Well, you must be famished by now, my lord. I'll fix some breakfast and ready a room in the house. You mean to stay a day or two, do you not?"

"I do, but you needn't put yourselves out. I'll take a room at Mr. Pirkle's inn."

"Unfortunately, the inn was lost to fire a fortnight ago."

"Mrs. Pirkle again?"

"Mr. Pirkle," Miss Blythe said with a cheeky smile.

"And he was in it at the time. You'll want to be careful with that bump on your head."

"Mr. Pirkle was pulled to safety with time to spare," Miss Ilestone assured him. "Come along, Freddie, we've chores, and Lord Gideon needs his rest."

"I believe I am adequately rested," Gideon began by way of protest, but Miss Ilestone shook her head at him.

"Better to be cautious." She moved toward the door but stopped with her hand on the handle. "I wrote," she said softly, turning to face him once more. "Your father and brother both. I never received a reply."

Gideon thought this new information through carefully before speaking. "I cannot answer for my father. I'm afraid it is possible he received your letters and chose not to respond. But Lucien isn't one to ignore his responsibilities. It simply isn't in his nature. The most likely explanation is that your letters never reached him. At the moment, I very much doubt he is aware of your existence."

She absorbed that information silently, then nodded once and left.

Miss Blythe waited for the door to close before speaking. "Lady Engsly hid those letters, didn't she?"

"Someone obviously did," he replied after a moment's consideration. "It could just as easily have been Mr. Lartwick, or someone they had in their pocket. There's no telling, really, until we find Lady Engsly."

Winnefred nodded in a way that mirrored her friend's before moving toward the door. "I need to help Lilly."

"A moment, Winnefred. Do you mind if I call you Winnefred?"

"I—"

"Excellent." He cut her off for the simple pleasure of watching those golden eyes flash a little in temper. "Why is it you've made your home in the gardener's cottage rather than the house? It's lovely, mind you, but cramped for two people."

He was being truthful on both accounts. The stone walls of the building were freshly washed and the rough plank floors scrubbed clean. Cheerful, if inelegant, curtains dressed the four small windows, and the bed—which he currently occupied—was covered with a spread expertly embroidered in shades of blue and green. Shelves along the far wall displayed dishes, cooking utensils, medicinal supplies, and an array of knickknacks women everywhere—to the bafflement of men everywhere—felt compelled to collect and showcase: small figurines of bisque, dainty boxes of hand-painted wood, and an ornate teacup too delicate to be of practical use.

But the one-room cottage hadn't been designed to house two young women; it had been built for a single man. There was scarce enough room to maneuver around the furniture, sparse even as it was.

Winnefred tilted her head and watched his face as she answered. "We found the cottage easier to maintain on a limited budget."

The Murdoch House was hardly a vast manor, Gideon thought with a frown. It boasted no more than four bedrooms, two servants' quarters, a single parlor, dining room, and kitchen. Her funds were limited, no doubt, but adequate to keep the house open.

"Perhaps I'd have been able to keep us out of this cottage," she continued, "if I were a man and therefore capable of grasping the value of a coin well spent and a coin well saved."

He blinked at that, then laughed. "What a singularly bizarre thing to say. And I don't think you believe a word of it."

She didn't immediately answer, just continued to search his face. For what, Gideon couldn't guess, but it was disconcerting, the way those gold eyes stared without blinking. After a moment, she turned and walked to the shelves. She pulled down one of the painted boxes, took out what appeared to be an opened letter, and returned to stand in front of him once more. Her chin came up, her mouth opened . . . then closed again.

She balled the letter into her fist. "If this is a jest," she finally said, "it is a cruel one. And I'll see you pay for hurting Lilly."

Before he had a chance to respond, she marched toward the door and left.

What an odd creature, he thought, and not at all what he'd been expecting. He'd envisioned a retiring young woman—shy and mousy—perhaps living with an elderly couple hired from the village to see to her needs. He'd imagined soft voices, quiet manners, and an air of genteel poverty.

Well, he'd certainly gotten the poverty bit right. They were living in the gardener's cottage and wearing threadbare gowns a decade out of fashion. What the devil had they been doing with forty pounds a year?

A simple enough thing to find out. Resolved not to spend what was left of the morning lying about and wondering over questions he could easily have answered, Gideon hauled himself out of bed. He was forced to lean against the headboard when his battered system protested the sudden movement, but his body had taken worse beatings, and it wasn't long before he managed to right himself again. Then he set out to look for his cane.

Chapter 3

"Mad as a hatter."

Winnefred made the comment to no one in particular. Upon leaving the cottage, she decided on taking the long way to the house. The very long way that included the path around the vegetable garden, which, in all honesty, wasn't a way to the house at all. But she needed the time and space to think, and she thought best when her hands were occupied.

There was always something that needed doing, something that required her attention—a chore, a responsibility, an errand. Murdoch House and the land it sat on could scarce be called a farm. Besides the large vegetable garden, their only agricultural possessions were a cow, a calf already claimed by a neighbor, a goat, and a handful of chickens. But even those small trappings had been won with years of hard work and sacrifice, and now required constant care and upkeep. She and Lilly hadn't survived the last twelve years by indulging in idleness.

She stopped in front of the turnip patch, stooped to pull

at weeds, and methodically considered the events of the morning and the man that had set them all in motion.

Lord Gideon hadn't come to evict them, and he wasn't lying about his intentions. Of that much she was relatively certain. She'd watched him, very carefully, when she'd said she might have been able to keep the house open if she'd been capable of understanding the value of money. It had been, nearly word for word, a quote from the nasty letter he had sent her last year.

He hadn't recognized it. She'd seen the mix of confusion and humor in his black eyes.

"The man should be in an asylum, or kept by his family, not running amok in the countryside," she grumbled. Because if he couldn't remember letters he'd written, and honestly believed a house could be run on five pounds a year, he was stark, raving mad.

If he'd been anyone else, anyone other than a Haverston, she'd have pitied him, even put a concerted effort into making him comfortable while they searched for his family. But he *was* a Haverston—next in line to the marquessate, at that—and her compassion for his illness took a distant second to her concern for what that illness might mean for her and Lilly.

Twelve years of lost allowance, plus bonus, and Lilly's back pay. All at once. It wasn't a great fortune, but it would be enough to buy more calves, a few pigs, and put aside a substantial savings in the likely event of lean years to come. With careful planning, they would never need to go hungry again. Perhaps she could even purchase a few luxuries like a new pair of shoes for herself and a pretty bonnet for Lilly.

There was a great deal they could do with that money. Dreams of new livestock and comfortable shoes had danced into her head the very instant Lord Gideon had made the promise. In Lilly's as well, Winnefred thought. Well, perhaps not the livestock, but the bonnet certainly. Lilly had always held a yen for things like that: pretty bonnets and frilly gowns, silly teacups that didn't have a purpose.

Winnefred had seen her friend's eyes light with hope, and it had frightened her as little else could. What if Lord Gideon wasn't in any position to be making such promises? What if Lilly set her heart on a pretty new hat and Engsly's men showed up next week to take the mad lord away?

Then again, what if her letter, like those Lilly had sent to Engsly, had simply fallen into the wrong hands?

Or what if she was wrong about his honesty and he was simply a marvelous actor with a penchant for playing malicious tricks on the unsuspecting?

She should have shown him the letter. She should have made him read it and explain himself.

"Damn." She straightened from her weeding, caught her foot in the hem of her skirts, and nearly tumbled headfirst into a row of turnips. "Blasted useless waste of material."

She yanked the offending gown over her head, not hard enough to damage it—that would have sent Lilly into fits—just hard enough to gain a small amount of satisfaction.

"Well now, this isn't something a man sees every day." Lord Gideon's voice floated through the fabric of her dress. "Not in daylight, anyway. Pity you're wearing a shirt and trousers."

For a few awful seconds, Winnefred stood, stunned, with her arms above her head and her face hidden in the folds of her skirt. She'd seen a drawing of a turtle once, and had the ridiculous thought that she very much resembled one now.

"You might as well finish the job, Winnefred. I know it was you in the stable last night."

It was the laughter that cut it for her. She didn't mind being poked fun at by those she knew and trusted—one should never take oneself too seriously—but being mocked by Lord Gideon was asking too much of her pride.

She swore, pulled at the dress, and managed to tangle herself hopelessly.

"Oh, *blast*."

"Stand still a moment."

She felt him step up behind her. Large hands brushed past her hair and down to her neck. For reasons she couldn't or didn't care to name, the sensation sent pinpricks of heat along her spine.

"It would help," he said from somewhere above her, "if you undid a few buttons first."

She had only a moment to register the play of deft fingers along her nape before the dress came off with a whoosh.

"Ah. There you are."

She looked up . . . and up . . . then stepped back a foot and looked up again. Heavens, the man was tall. She'd known he was larger than average, but it was hard to judge size accurately in the dark or while a body was lying down. At a guess, he stood well over six feet.

And he was quite broad. Not pudgy like their neighbor Mr. McGregor, and not impossibly thick like the blacksmith Mr. Dowell, but notably muscled across the chest, and arms, and legs, and . . . everywhere, really. Like a soldier, she decided, or one of the gladiators she'd seen depicted in books.

Only soldiers and gladiators didn't have black eyes that twinkled as they watched her. Nor did they walk with canes. Ebony ones with carved handles she couldn't quite make out but looked to be some kind of fish.

"Do you need that?" she asked suddenly. "Or is it an affectation?"

He glanced at his cane. "I can walk without it, just as I did now to fetch it out of the stable, but it eases the discomfort of a weakened leg. Why?" He grinned at her. "Feeling ashamed, are you, for having knocked a helpless cripple to the ground?"

"I might have been," she admitted, looking over his substantial form. "But you appear capable enough to me. Do you mean to bring charges against us?"

He handed the dress to her. "No, I don't. To begin with, you had every right to protect yourself. Beyond that—what man would willingly announce he'd lost in a fight to a woman? In fact, I'll strike a bargain with you. You keep that bit of knowledge to yourself, and I'll keep mum the fact that Miss Winnefred Blythe runs about in trousers."

Winnefred frowned down at the brown material. "We only wear them when we work because they're practical," she said, feeling a little defensive. "And a sight more comfortable than this ghastly old dress. Any sane woman would toss it off at the first chance."

Her eyes rounded in horror at the realization of what had just come out of her mouth. She waited for him to scoff, or to sneer. Instead, a laugh, low and pleasant, rolled from his chest. "And what sane man would argue?"

Her courage bolstered by his reaction, she started to ask him if he *was* sane. But she hesitated—it seemed unforgivably rude. As a rule, she wasn't particularly concerned—or even particularly familiar—with good manners, but asking simply "are you mad by any chance?" sounded a bit too crude, even for her.

Torn, certain she'd lose the courage at any moment, she dug the letter out of her pocket and held it out to him with a hand that wanted to shake.

"Did you write this?"

Dark brows shot up as he reached for the letter. "Is this the letter you took from the cottage?"

"It is."

"And is it the reason you keep looking at me as if I have two heads and a tail, and why I heard you muttering something about asylums a few minutes ago?"

She swallowed, thought about it, then decided to be truthful. "Yes."

"Ah. Well, let's see what you have." He shifted his cane to unfold the letter, and she watched, nervously, as he read. The humor and curiosity that she was beginning to think were permanently ingrained in his features faded, and his countenance grew darker and darker the further he read. By the time he reached the end of the last page, his brow was furrowed and his lips pressed into an angry line.

"Why haven't you burned this?" he asked in a quiet voice.

"Did you write it?" She had to be certain, absolutely certain.

"I did not." He handed the letter back to her. "It's vile, and at a guess, penned by my stepmother."

She looked at the paper thoughtfully, then brought her eyes to meet his. "Will you give me your word, as a gentleman, that you never received the missive I sent you?"

"I will. What did it say?"

She felt a blush rise to her cheeks. Lilly had been ill, terribly ill, and they hadn't the funds to pay for a physician. She'd been desperate the day she'd written, and it had led her to an act she had always promised herself she would never commit. She had begged.

"It was a request for help," she mumbled, hoping the letter had found its way into a fireplace somewhere. She shrugged, pushing the memory of those dark days away. "As is happens, assistance was not required. It matters little now."

"I see." His hand, warm and rough, came up to cup the side of her face. He cradled it for a moment, a moment that held her transfixed and made her belly tighten and the air catch in her throat. And then one finger slid down to her chin and tilted her face up to his. "And I'm sorry."

For one terrifying moment, Winnefred felt tears gather at the back of her eyes. She blinked them back, surprised at her reaction to a simple apology and an easy, albeit improper, caress. Merely exhaustion, she told herself, brought on by a lack of sleep and an onslaught of fear, worry, and—perhaps most draining of all—hope. People did the oddest things when they were overly tired.

The fact that she'd been a great deal more tired, and a good deal more worried, in the past and never before felt the urge to leak like a sieve wasn't something she cared to dwell on.

She was on the verge of turning away and making a light joke to cover her confusion when he spoke.

"Do you have those freckles year-round?"

"Do I . . . ?" She blinked, tears forgotten. "Beg your pardon?"

He tapped a finger against her cheek and let his hand

fall. "There was a boy on my ship. Joseph O'Dell. His freckles would disappear in the winter and come back every summer. I'd swear they were different each time they emerged, but then, I never looked too closely. Unseemly, don't you think, for a man to be counting a boy's freckles?"

"I imagine so," she managed, caught somewhere between baffled and charmed. "Are you quite certain you're not touched?"

He shrugged. "One can never be completely certain, as one would be the last to know."

"That's not at all reassuring." But she found herself smiling at him all the same. "And this may be the most absurd conversation I've ever had."

"I'm told I have a knack for them. Are you going to answer my question?"

She couldn't think of any reason she shouldn't. "Some of my freckles fade in the winter. But I couldn't say if their positions alter from year to year as I've never troubled myself over their placement. What of yours?"

He started slightly and grinned. "Mine? Have I freckles?"

"Seven," she informed him, realizing belatedly it may be just as unseemly for a woman to be counting a man's freckles as it was for a man to be counting a boy's. She mentally shrugged off the concern. It was only the truth, and she'd hardly been staring—much. "You've three on the left and four on the right. They're very faint, but they're there. Perhaps they're only noticeable in the sunlight."

"I'm not in the habit of looking in mirrors out-of-doors, so you must be right." He grimaced a little. "I've always considered freckles an endearing characteristic. I'm not at all sure I'm comfortable with that description being applied to me."

She'd known him less than a day, but Winnefred felt the adjective "endearing" fit him rather well. And that didn't seem right at all. Men who looked like Lord Gideon should have words like "swarthy," "dark," and "dangerous" attached to them. Large men shouldn't laugh softly, black eyes shouldn't twinkle mischievously, and rough hands shouldn't feel gentle when they brushed along a woman's skin.

She looked away. "We should go in. Lilly must be finished by now."

"Have we cried pax, then?" he asked.

She considered it. He wasn't lying, and he wasn't mad. In fact, he was rather likable. There was still the issue of his believing a house could be run on five pounds a year. But then, sometimes those in possession of the greatest fortunes had the least understanding of their value. Lord Gideon was likely merely eccentric, and as long as that eccentricity didn't extend to making wild promises he wouldn't keep, she saw no reason to spend the next few days being at odds with him.

She nodded, resolute. "Pax."

*B*reakfast at the Murdoch House generally consisted of one of three ingredients: eggs, fish, or porridge. Winnefred caught and cleaned the fish. Lilly collected and cooked the eggs. Porridge, despised by both of them, was used only under the most dire of circumstances and prepared by whomever was hungry enough to go to the bother of making it.

Meals in general were eaten in the kitchen with a single fork and tin bowl each. So it was with some surprise that Winnefred discovered the small dining room table set with the few pieces of chipped china they'd discovered in the attic, and a small hill of eggs, bread, and cheese. It was several days' worth of food, and the sheer gluttony of it had Winnefred gaping.

"What in the—?"

"Do have a seat, my lord. *Winnefred.*" Lilly sent a look that somehow managed to both plead with Winnefred to say nothing and promise the most severe of consequences should Winnefred refuse.

Familiar enough with pride—and with Lilly's rare temper—Winnefred moved around the table to sit, only to have Lilly stop her with a quick grasp of her elbow and a low, furious whisper.

"What happened to your gown?"

Winnefred shook her head. "He isn't angry. I'll explain later."

Lilly looked as if she wanted to argue but settled for a scowl before letting go of Winnefred's arm and taking her own seat.

Gideon sat at the head of the table and looked over his steaming plate. "It looks and smells wonderful, Miss Ilestone."

Winnefred smiled knowingly and waited for him to take his first bite. Gideon scooped up a forkful of eggs and tasted. His eyes widened in surprise, then closed in overt pleasure.

"Sweet Mary," he murmured around the mouthful. He chewed, swallowed, and took another, larger forkful.

Lilly smiled and blushed. "I am delighted it's to your liking, my lord."

Gideon bobbed his head but waited until his mouth was empty before speaking again. "Extraordinary. Absolutely extraordinary. What did you put in here?"

"A little bit of this and that—cream, dill, and so on."

"Are all your meals this well prepared?"

"They are when Lilly cooks," Winnefred answered.

"Winnefred makes a very fine trout as well, my lord."

"Gideon, please," he invited. "I suppose this is why you've no one else to cook for you, then. What would be the point, really?"

"I'm afraid a cook just wasn't possible with the funds Lord . . . I suppose I should say *Lady* Engsly sent us," Lilly replied.

Gideon stopped eating. "How is it two intelligent, practical women are unable to keep a small house and . . ." He trailed off as if just considering something. "How many pounds, exactly, did Lady Engsly send you?"

"Five," Winnefred answered around a mouthful of eggs. "I thought you knew that."

"Five," he repeated dully. He set his fork down, dragged a hand down his face, and swore under his breath. "As in, five-decimal-point-zero?"

"Yes, of course," Lilly answered with a small laugh.

He swore quietly again. "I beg your pardon. I'd rather hoped you were speaking in hundreds."

"Hundreds?" Winnefred would have laughed herself, but the cold shock on Gideon's face had a trickle of nerves dancing along her skin. "Lady Engsly didn't steal half, did she?"

"No." He blew out a hard breath. "Your allowance was set at eighty pounds annum."

There was a simultaneous gasp of breath and clatter of silverware. Lilly stared, openmouthed and wide-eyed. Winnefred moved her mouth to speak but found she was unable to form sound.

"There's the bonus, as well," Gideon reminded them. He scowled at his plate. "And given the extent of Lady Engsly's crime against you, whatever else you might like."

Winnefred's mind stayed eerily blank except for a repetitive echoing of Gideon's voice saying, "Eighty pounds annum. Eighty pounds annum. Eighty pounds . . ."

"I want a London season for Winnefred."

That sudden, decisive, and wholly unexpected statement from Lilly cut through Winnefred's mind like a sharp knife.

"What?"

Lilly ignored her in favor of addressing Gideon. "You said anything within reason, and I feel a season for a young woman of good birth is not beyond the realm of reasonable."

Obviously expecting an argument from him, Lilly straightened her shoulders and lifted her chin defiantly. She needn't have bothered.

"A season it is." Still scowling, Gideon picked up his fork and stabbed at his eggs. "Five pounds. It's a wonder the two of you survived."

Winnefred shook her head in bewilderment. "This is absurd. What the devil would I do with a London season?"

"Find a husband, I imagine," was Gideon's reply.

It only served to mystify her further. "What the devil would I do with a *husband*?"

"Obtain long-term financial stability," Lilly told her. "Something more reliable than sheep that can fall ill or crops that can fail."

"A husband can fall ill," she argued. "And I'd wager they fail their spouses regularly. Also, we haven't any sheep *or* crops."

"But we will, if you have your way."

"Well, what's wrong with that?" Lilly opened her mouth, ready, it seemed, to explain exactly what was wrong with that, and Winnefred tried another angle. "I'm nearly six-and-twenty. I'm too old."

"For a traditional debut, yes, but not a simple season." Lilly leaned forward, excited. "Think of it, Winnefred. The opera, the shops, the balls and soirees, rides in Hyde Park and trips to Bond Street. You could have that life—" She cut herself off, obviously remembering with whom she was speaking. "You could have a husband with enough funds to keep you knee-deep in sheep and soil for the rest of your life."

Winnefred considered her friend. It was impossible to miss the way Lilly's eyes lit up as she spoke of visiting London. "You should have the season," she decided. "You'd enjoy it far more, and make better use of it as well."

Gideon responded before Lilly could. "A fine idea."

"My lord, the expense, the trouble . . ." Lilly protested.

"Isn't something you need concern yourself with," he finished for her. "The Engsly estate can well afford it, and I've a great-aunt who would like nothing more than to introduce two lovely young ladies into society."

"She'll need to content herself with just one," Winnefred said, adamant she would not, absolutely *not*, be going to London to indulge in a silly game of husband hunting.

Lilly pressed her lips into a thin line. "I'll not go without you."

"Lilly, that's unfair."

"Fair or not, you know very well I won't leave you here alone."

"I . . ." She looked to Gideon for help, but the man had gone back to glaring at his eggs and mumbling about the five pounds. She gave a brief thought to picking up her fork and winging it at his head but managed to restrain herself. "I'll be fine, Lilly, honestly. I'll—"

"Come to London with me, or the both of us stay here."

Winnefred balled the napkin in her lap, met her friend's determined stare, and wondered how she could possibly say no. Lilly had always wanted more than what could be had at Murdoch House or purchased with their very limited funds in the nearby village of Enscrum. She had never complained, never shied from the hardest chores. She'd gone hungry with a smile, worn cast-off clothing without a hint of protest . . . and accepted, with open arms, a child that no one else would have.

But sometimes, at night, when they were too cold, or too hungry, or too frightened to sleep, she would speak in dreamy tones of her brief time in London—of the opera and soirees and those trips to Bond Street.

Winnefred tossed the napkin on the table, swore—fluently enough, it seemed, to pull Gideon's attention away from his eggs—and stood. "Fine. We'll go."

"Thank you. Freddie—"

"I've a fence to mend."

*G*ideon watched Winnefred stalk from the room. Considerable temper on the woman, he mused. Not the nasty and potentially violent sort his stepmother possessed, but formidable all the same. He found it, and the woman, more appealing than was comfortable.

He turned to Lilly and saw that she was pale, tight-lipped, and red-eyed.

"I suppose you think me very unkind," she said softly.

"On the contrary, I think you very clever and uncommonly selfless." He had looked up from his plate long enough to see the painful longing in her eyes when she'd spoken of London. She had risked what she wanted most for what she thought was best for her friend. "You're doing what's best for Winnefred."

"What's better, at any rate." Lilly picked up her fork and poked at the food left on her plate. "She's content here, and she'll never look for more than that unless she is bullied into it. I want her to have a chance at real happiness."

"And she'll find it in a London season?"

She surprised him by laughing. "Oh, heavens, no. She'll be miserable, like as not. But she needs the comparison, doesn't she? And there is always the chance she'll fall madly in love with a gentleman of means." She sighed wistfully. "Wouldn't that be lovely?"

As Winnefred didn't strike him as the romantic sort, he decided against comment. "Forgive my bluntness, but do you think she's adequately . . . prepared for polite society?"

"She is capable of basic civility," Lilly assured him. "She simply chooses to ignore it. Breaking her of that and providing the rest of her grooming can be accomplished within a few weeks. We'll be late for the season, but it can't be helped."

Gideon wondered if a few weeks would be several years too short a time to polish the girl up, but he thought it best not to voice that concern. "We should leave for London as soon as possible if you wish to employ a decent modiste, find a dancing master, and so forth. How long will it take to find someone to care for your livestock, do you suppose, two, three days?"

"Days?" Lilly shook her head. "Oh, no. We couldn't possibly bring Winnefred to London in three days. Her habits are more ingrained than that. I'll need three weeks, at the very least."

He set his fork down.

"That's not possible." The words came out quickly and, admittedly, a bit rudely. But *three weeks*? He'd come to Scotland with the intention of finding Miss Blythe, delivering her lost allowance, and making certain she was comfortably settled. In all, he'd scheduled no more than two days in her company. He was flexible man, and willing to add a day or two under the circumstances, but three weeks under his sole care was out of the question. That kind of responsibility was exactly the sort he'd made a habit of avoiding since the war.

"I'm certain you can manage in London well enough," he added in what he hoped was a bolstering tone. "My aunt will—"

"Lord Gideon," Lilly interrupted patiently, "Winnefred came here a child of thirteen raised by a series of indifferent governesses hired by a careless father. That was twelve years ago and one of her most recent brushes with polite company."

"The village must have something to offer in the way of social gatherings."

"The vicar and his wife, Mr. and Mrs. Howard, hold reign over Enscrum's small claim to society. We have never been welcomed to join their select group of friends."

"Why not? Surely, when the two of you first arrived—"

"Because in our first week here, when Mrs. Howard came to visit, Winnefred informed her that the vicar could not expect to see her sitting on the wooden pews come Sunday."

"Did she say why?"

"As I believe she explained it—she had read the Bible from cover to cover, and nowhere between those covers was there a passage indicating that admittance to heaven was dependent upon a person having spent every Sunday of her life with a sore arse."

He struggled with a reluctant smile. "In Winnefred's defense, there's not."

Lilly gave him a bland look. "She needs the time to properly train."

He tapped his finger against the table. "Why is it you ladies always make the season sound like a competitive sporting event?"

"For an unmarried woman, that's exactly what it is."

She lifted her eyebrows in an expectant manner. "Will you give us the three weeks?"

As he'd just given his word they could have whatever they liked, he couldn't very well say no now. Not without relinquishing all claims to honor and the right to call himself a gentleman.

He had, in essence, been neatly boxed in, and suddenly Winnefred's response to her friend's demands didn't seem quite so outrageous. In fact, he found the notion of swearing loudly rather appealing just now.

Unfortunately, he hadn't an excuse for such a grievous breach of manners.

He nodded in acceptance, made his excuses, and left to comfort himself with a long walk.

Chapter 4

Winnefred stood in front of a fallen fence rail, Claire the goat at her side, a hammer clenched in her hand, and aggravation etched clearly on her face. After conceding to Lilly's demand of a London season, she'd gone straight from the house to the tool bag stored in the stable, and from there, straight to the nearest broken patch of fence. Never mind it was a part of a pasture they rarely used, she was absolutely determined to pound on something.

Given her current mood, there was a high probability that she would pound that something into tiny slivers. Realizing as much, she tossed the hammer down with an annoyed grunt. She wasn't in the habit of destroying things in a fit of temper. Nor did she indulge in tantrums when something failed to go quite the way she liked.

But honestly—a London season?

"Grown men and women, parading about like a flock of peacocks," she grumbled.

She *detested* peacocks. She'd visited a grand manor with her father once, during one of the rare house parties where children had been allowed—not encouraged, mind you, but allowed—to attend. There'd been six peacocks there, and each one more determined than the last to out-screech, out-plume, and out-bully anyone unfortunate enough to blunder into its territory.

She imagined behavior amongst the ton wasn't too dissimilar.

"Goats are better," she announced to Claire. "Smart, loyal, entertaining—practical animals to have about. Don't you think?"

Claire trotted over to nose the hammer, then, apparently coming to the conclusion that it was inedible, trotted back to lie down.

"Smarter than peacocks, anyway," Winnefred murmured.

She leaned down to pat the goat on the head, then stood and turned her face into the soft wind. She breathed in the warm air, closed her eyes, and remembered the long-ago trip that first brought her and Lilly to Scotland. She'd been a girl of thirteen, grieving, afraid, and wondering what manner of cold welcome waited for her at the end of the journey. That there might be a warm welcome waiting hadn't occurred to her.

No one was ever particularly pleased to see Winnefred Blythe.

Her father, during his infrequent visits between hunting trips to whatever run-down residence they were currently letting, had always greeted her with an air of puzzlement and disappointment, as if he couldn't quite fathom how he had come to shoulder the expense of a small girl.

Her governesses had eyed her with impatience. Lord Engsly had met her with open hostility, and Lady Engsly with false smiles when others were present and unconcealed contempt when they were alone. Even Lilly had been initially—and understandably—overwhelmed with the sudden weight of a new charge.

How would the master and mistress of Murdoch House see her? As a burden? An intruder? Something to be endured or forgotten? Of the opinion that despised was worse than forgotten, she'd hoped for the last.

And, in a way, had been granted her wish.

There'd been no one to meet them when they arrived. Nothing had awaited them but fields that had gone fallow, outbuildings that had gone neglected, and a quiet stone house that had been stripped of most its furnishings.

Lilly had searched from room to room in a daze, as if she expected someone to leap out from behind dusty curtains at any moment and admit to it all being a grand joke.

But Winnefred had stood outside in the dying afternoon light and heard what Lilly did not.

The welcome in the silence. The silent plea for life. What was a farm without livestock and crops? A house without light, and sound, and voices?

She'd been a child yet, still in possession of that unique ability of the very young to seamlessly blend fantasy and reality, and she had imagined she heard Murdoch House whispering to her in the wind.

Welcome. Welcome.

Stay.

They had, and though they'd had no real choice in the matter, and surviving on a farm with virtually no funds or experience proved a great deal more difficult than she'd expected, Winnefred had never wished for a chance to leave. She was proud of what they had accomplished, excited by what they could do now.

They had come so very far. They had made a home. And now Lilly had set her heart on leaving it behind in favor of a house in the city and a woman who may or may not welcome them in.

Gideon walked the Murdoch House property, working his weak leg and contemplating the intricacies of promises.

He had heard men make all manner of solemn oaths in the heat and gore of battle. Some attempted to make pacts with God. They vowed, in exchange for their lives, to let off drinking and gambling, to attend church every Sunday, to treat better their wives or mistresses—or in the case of several officers, their wives *and* mistresses.

Some had made promises to themselves. He recalled a conversation he had heard between two of his men during battle. Christopher Weathers and Ian McClay, thick as thieves they'd been and always ready with a laugh. They'd shouted to each other over the whistle of shot, the boom of cannon, and the screams of men.

"If we survive, Ian, and make it to port, I'm going to buy the prettiest whore I can afford! Get stinking drunk with what's left over!"

"Are you daft, man?! Get drunk first and buy a cheap lass! I promise, you'll never know the difference!"

In the end, McClay had drank and whored for the both of them.

Gideon had made one promise and one promise only.

Never again would he be responsible for the well-being of another person.

In the two years since he'd left the *Perseverance*, he'd managed well enough. He'd sworn off marriage, bucked tradition and eschewed the services of a valet. He'd even refused to have live-in staff at his town house, preferring to eat at his club and relying on a maid to come during the day.

He wasn't a hermit. On the contrary, he sought out and enjoyed the company of others. But at the end of the day, he had only himself to look after.

So how the bleeding hell had he gotten himself saddled with a pair of young women for three weeks?

And what the devil was he supposed to do with them?

It took him a few minutes of worry and frustration, but eventually he decided he wasn't going to do anything with them at all—he was going to hire someone else to do something with them. In fact, he was going to hire a great many someone elses. He was going to cram Murdoch House so full of staff, provisions, diversions—more than two women could ever think of needing—that his presence there would be superfluous. Then he was going to hide himself away in a room and pretend he'd never thought to play hero in Scotland. It was illogical, cowardly, childish, and absolutely necessary for the retention of his sanity.

Feeling better about the current state of affairs, he turned from his path along a small pond and followed a fence line separating what appeared to be an unused pasture from an unplowed field. He topped a small rise and saw Winnefred standing with her back turned not thirty yards away.

Her hair, which he noticed earlier had begun to fall, was once again in a long braid. The gold streaks, brightened by the midday sun, wove in and out of the darker tresses like ribbons. She was doing something with the fence and talking to what appeared to be a rough-coated, black-and-white dog.

"I'll talk her out of it. There must be something else she'd like. I've responsibilities here, don't I? The animals need to be cared for, don't they? The garden has to be tended, wood gathered and chopped for winter. There are more rails like these, ready to fall with the slightest provocation. What if we forget and put Lucien here? Where will we put the new calves . . . ?"

Gideon stopped listening when she bent to inspect a fallen rail. Trousers, it suddenly occurred to him, should be required attire for every young woman. Why hadn't men— lords and masters that they were—not yet insisted upon it? They left a little less to the imagination, it was true, but imagination could only take one so far.

Then again, sometimes it took one a bit too far. Erotic images danced gleefully in his head. Standing perfectly still, he saw himself step up behind her quietly and run a hand down her strong back. He heard her gasp of surprise and purr of pleasure, saw the answering spark of heat in her eyes as she turned her head. He bent her over further, his for the taking, for the having. A quick work of buttons, a pull at trousers, and . . .

And devil take it, what was *wrong* with him?

After years at sea, he was no stranger to unbidden

dreams of very pretty women doing very wicked things. But never before had those fantasies included an innocent who—no matter how far he attempted to remove himself from the idea—was essentially under his care.

This was the very reason he should never be given the responsibility of another's well-being—he couldn't be trusted with it.

Calling himself a dozen different kinds of cad, he stood where he was, near to praying she wouldn't turn around, and concentrated on making himself presentable. It took several long, steadying breaths, and one singularly un-arousing image of the last time he'd seen the Prince Regent—half naked and pawing at his current mistress— to manage the task, but manage it he did.

Feeling in control of himself once again, he moved toward Winnefred and the odd-looking dog. Upon closer inspection, Gideon could see the animal had a boxy head, floppy ears, and a short, pointy tail. A goat. An enormous goat looking very un-goatlike, in Gideon's opinion, as it sat serenely in the grass, watching Winnefred and listening sympathetically to her complaints. Or it could just be begging for something in her pocket, he supposed.

"Do goats beg?" he called out to her.

Winnefred glanced over her shoulder briefly before hefting the rail that had been on the ground onto her knee, which certainly made a strong *practical* argument for the trousers.

Before he could reach her, she'd used her leg and both arms to lift the rail between two crossbeams. Stubborn, he thought, or so used to doing for herself she wouldn't think to ask for help. She reached in her pocket and pulled out a napkin full of scraps.

"Claire does," she told him, tossing the food at the goat, who gobbled it down greedily before turning slavish eyes to her mistress once more.

He propped his cane against the fence and leaned a hip against the wood. "You did a very kind thing for your friend this morning," he told her, mostly because she looked as if she needed to hear it.

She kicked at a rock and frowned as it went tumbling through the grass. "I didn't do it very graciously."

"Not graciously, no, but you accomplished it all the same." He bent his head in an effort to catch her eye. "Will it be so very terrible to spend a few months in London?"

"Yes."

The absolute conviction in her voice had him straightening. "Have you ever been to London?"

She leaned back against the fence next to him. "Isn't there anything you know you wouldn't want to do without ever having done it before?"

"Dying comes to mind."

One corner of her mouth hitched up. "That isn't exactly what I meant, though I suppose the principle is the same."

He tilted his head back in thought. "I shouldn't care to inherit the marquessate," he decided. "And not simply because I'm fond of my brother and his demise would be a prerequisite for the event. I just don't want the burden."

"Would it be so very terrible, being a marquess?" she echoed.

"Yes," he replied, chuckling. "Without question, *yes*. The land, the people, the politics—each and every one demanding one's time and undivided attention. I could name a few things I'd like less—like the aforementioned dying—but it would be a decidedly brief list."

She nodded in understanding, and he considered the rarity of that amongst the ladies of his acquaintance. Women of society generally considered a title one of life's greatest trophies, and obtaining one, one of the greatest accomplishments. Hoping to avoid one, he supposed, would be considered one of the greatest stupidities.

They stood in comfortable silence for a time—until, apparently bored, Claire uprooted herself from her spot on the grass to press her nose against Gideon's leg and huff loudly.

"Don't mind Claire," Winnefred told him absently. "She does that to everyone she likes. Though to be honest, that distinction seems to be made fairly randomly."

"I see." He frowned down at the goat, a little concerned she might try to communicate her sudden affection for him with a solid bite. "Interesting name for a goat, Claire."

"Hmm. The vicar has a nasty wife named Clarisse."

"Ah." He shook his leg a little in an attempt to dislodge his new friend. "And the Lucien I heard you mention?"

Perhaps it was coincidence that his brother's name was also Lucien, but he doubted it.

A half smile curved her lips. "Our calf—our neighbor's really as he's already paid for him."

He thought of the enjoyment he'd have informing his brother, the marquess, of his namesake. "Creative."

"Not very," she admitted. "We've only one calf a year, and it always goes to our neighbor Mr. McGregor. We name all the males Lucien—to keep from becoming attached, you understand."

"Perfectly. I don't suppose any of them manage to avoid becoming steers?"

"Not one."

"As I said, creative." He looked around the fields. "Is there a Gideon somewhere about I should be aware of?"

This time when she answered, it was with a bright grin that lit up her face and a mischievous sparkle in her amber eyes. "We've a cow named Giddy. She has the most enormous teats you've ever—"

She broke off at his laugh and tilted her head at him. "You cringe at the thought of being a marquess but appreciate having a cow named after you. I'm not certain if I find that commendable or absurd."

"A fine thing, absurdity," he replied, still chuckling. "Generally undervalued and overlooked. Yet it can be found in almost every situation. Even the darkest of circumstances often retain that small light of humor that we label the absurd—war, politics"—he winked at her—"London seasons. There's comfort in knowing that, don't you think? And a talent in being able to find it."

And sometimes, he thought, it was all that stood between a man and despair. Disturbed by the direction of his thoughts, he straightened from the fence and grabbed his cane. "Well, it's a lovely morning, but I've things to see to in town. I don't suppose you've a phaeton or the like hidden somewhere?"

She snorted at the mention of a phaeton. "There's an old one-horse cart behind the stable, but I can't imagine it still works."

"And will you ride to town with me if it does?"

"Thank you, but no. I've my own things to see to."

"Suit yourself. Anything you'd like me to retrieve while I'm there?"

She started to shake her head, then apparently thought better of it. "I shouldn't . . . I really shouldn't, but . . . will you wait a moment? I've money in the cottage and—"

"We'll settle later," Gideon interrupted. She'd need to become accustomed to someone else purchasing whatever she needed, but he thought it best to ease her into the notion. The habits that came from years of nearly complete independence weren't likely to drop away in a matter of hours.

"All right, if you don't mind." She grew excited, smiling and biting her lip at the same time. "There's a bakery, Mrs. Morrow's. She has the most amazing pastries in her windows. There's one I'd dearly love to have. It's fluffy and round and covered in some sort of glaze."

She made an attempt to form the shape of the treat with her hands. It helped him not at all.

"What's the name of this confection?"

"I've no idea, but it's filled with something, I think. It's too large not to be—fruit maybe, or some sort of custard." She sighed lustfully. "I sincerely hope it's custard."

She'd never had one, he realized. She'd wanted it long enough and well enough to sigh over the very thought—and she didn't strike him as a woman who made a regular practice of sighing—yet she'd never taken so much as a bite. What other pleasures, large and small, had been stolen from her?

"I'll be sure to bring it back." And he'd be sure it was filled with custard as well, even if he had to scrape out the fruit and stuff it anew himself.

"Could you bring two?" she asked with a hint of embarrassment. "One for Lilly? If it's too much—"

"Two it is."

*W*innefred spent the remainder of the afternoon and a good portion of the evening seeing to her chores. She skipped lunch, partially because they'd eaten a late breakfast but mostly because she wasn't quite ready yet to face Lilly.

Anger had passed, and so had self-pity. She was resigned not only to going to London but making the best of it. What would moping about do besides make everyone around her miserable? What she hadn't quite resigned herself to, however, were the preparations.

Winnefred was conscious of her shortcomings. She knew full well she wasn't adequately equipped for a London season, and she knew Lilly was, even now, making plans to rectify the matter. It needed to be done, and Winnefred was willing and able. She wasn't, however, anywhere near to eager.

And so she stalled out-of-doors, waiting until the sun had set and the last of its lingering light began to fade before returning to the cottage.

She found Lilly at the front door, holding a baker's box and a note and looking a bit dazed.

"We've a note from Lord Gideon. You just missed the messenger."

Winnefred looked down the road to see dust still hanging in the air. "What does the note say?"

"I don't know. I've not opened it yet."

"Why ever not?" A horrible thought occurred to her. "Do you think he doesn't mean to come back? Do you—?"

"What? Oh, no, nothing like that. It's only . . . well, we've never had a message delivered before . . . Twelve years and not a single letter besides the yearly allowance from Lady Engsly." She smiled broadly at the envelope. "And now look! We've a letter delivered by special carrier—and from a lord, no less. I believe this is one of the finest days I've had in years."

Because it was so like her friend to become excited over something so silly, Winnefred laughed and threw her arms around her, nearly crushing the note and box in the process. "I love you, Lilly Ilestone." She planted a kiss on her cheek. "I'm sorry I was so rotten at breakfast."

Lilly returned the kiss. "And I'm sorry I maneuvered you so unfairly into something you don't want."

"Sorry enough to—?"

"Not nearly."

Winnefred laughed and released her. "Well, open the note, then."

Lilly tucked the box under her arm and gently opened the envelope, careful not to tear the fine paper. "He couldn't find all that he needed in Enscrum and means to travel to Langholm. He'll return in the morning. He's signed it 'your servant always.' Isn't that lovely?"

"Exceedingly. Open the box."

Lilly ignored her and frowned at the letter. "Before he left, he asked if there was anything I'd like, and I gave him a small list. What if he's going through all this trouble because of me?"

"I shouldn't worry too hard on it, Lilly. Lord Gideon is capable of saying no." She smiled playfully and added, "Or perhaps he's too much the gentleman to deny a lady's request and he's cursing your name as we speak. 'Damn Miss Ilestone. Blasted irrational female, insists on apples when there's perfectly good strawberries to be found on every corner of Enscrum.'"

Lilly made a scoffing sound. "There are exactly four

corners of Enscrum. And very little to be found on any of them."

"Annoyed men tend to exaggerate." And so did Lilly. Enscrum was small, but it was charming, and it did have its own shops. "What's in the box?"

Lilly tugged the lid open. Nestled inside were a half dozen pastries.

"Oh, *heaven*." Winnefred sighed and reached in to pluck one out. She held it to her nose and drew in the smell of fresh cream and sugar. Treats were rare for her and Lilly, and treats extravagant as the ones in the box had been nonexistent until now. She wanted to savor every moment, to delight in and draw out every second of pleasure. Although—there were six in the box . . .

She furrowed her brow at the thought of what that would cost. "I only asked for two. Do you suppose the rest are his? I hadn't wanted to spend so much—"

"They're a gift." Lilly took a pastry for herself and, like Winnefred, breathed in the aroma. "Oh, my, that *is* nice, isn't it?"

"Are you certain?"

Still reveling in the sweet scent, Lilly blinked, a little lost. "That it smells nice?"

"That they're a gift."

"Of course." Lilly considered her a moment. "I forget, sometimes, how little experience you have with these sorts of things."

"What sorts of things?"

Lilly shrugged. "Men, gifts, being taken care of—"

Because it was a truth Winnefred found uncomfortable, she edged the conversation in another direction. "But the cost—"

"Oh, wait till you see what I asked of him." Lilly laughed. "Now take a bite. I'd prefer you in a pleasant state of mind when I tell you what Lord Gideon and I decided after you left this morning . . . In fact, why don't you take the box and indulge yourself while I see to dinner?" Lilly handed her the pastries and turned for the house. "I'll tell you of my plans while we eat."

Winnefred accepted the box with a worried frown. She hated to think what sort of plan required the fortification of half a dozen pastries.

Make the best of it, she reminded herself. Taking a seat on the front steps, she bit into her pastry. *Custard.* She sighed heavily around a mouthful of the treat. Oh, she'd just known it would be custard.

It was a very good thing she'd not been tempted to purchase one until now, she thought. She never would have been able to help herself from purchasing more. The half pound she had saved would have disappeared within a fortnight. As it was, the treats would cost her . . . nothing, she realized. The pastries cost her nothing.

They're a gift.

Winnefred took another bite and considered Lilly's words. It was true, she hadn't any experience receiving gifts. Certainly not from men. Most certainly not from handsome men whose presence made her feel strangely restless, as if she wasn't quite comfortable in her own skin.

It was the oddest sensation, the way her heart had tripped and her skin had prickled when he'd unbuttoned her gown that morning, and it was both unsettling and intriguing to remember how pleasant it had been to lean against the rail of the pasture with him, laughing and talking and standing in companionable silence. There had been a pleasant tightening in her belly and an unexpected temptation to shuffle her feet closer until they were standing arm to arm.

Lost in thought, she polished off her pastry and reached for another. She'd been weighed by a mountain of worries that morning and had been unwilling to add to them by giving more than a passing moment's consideration to her surprising physical reaction to Gideon. But now her heart and mind were resigned to a future much altered from the one she had always envisioned. And she no longer had an excuse to deny the obvious.

She was attracted to Lord Gideon Haverston.

The idea was more interesting than alarming. She wasn't a complete stranger to attraction. The fact that the butcher's son was quite good-looking had not escaped her notice, but the mild interest she felt on the rare occasions she had visited the butcher could not compare to what she felt in Gideon's company. She was drawn to him in a way she'd never experienced before. And it was disconcerting that such feelings had preceded the founding of trust.

She worked her way through the second pastry, eventually arriving at the decision that it was only natural a man as handsome as Lord Gideon had immediately captured her interest. She was human, after all, a member of the animal kingdom. A male specimen of superior physical quality would appeal to her just as surely as a fine bull appealed to Giddy.

Fortunately, she retained the ability to assess her physical state objectively. Gideon fascinated her, yes, but she had no intention of acting on that fascination . . . yet. Perhaps the feelings would pass, or perhaps the accumulation of trust would allow them to grow.

Either way, a wait-and-see approach seemed wise.

Satisfied with her decision, she swallowed her food and reached for another pastry.

Chapter 5

$\mathcal{G}$ideon returned the next morning as promised, but he didn't come alone. He brought a small army of servants and supplies with him—a carriage with two footmen riding in back, the driver and two grooms riding up top, and three maids riding inside. Behind them were two wagons full of food, linens, furnishings, a cook (he'd cleared the idea with Lilly first, of course), and three more servants he hadn't the slightest idea of what to do with. It hardly mattered to his mind, as long as they were there.

"Good heavens, what is all this?" Lilly stood on the front steps of the house and looked to be caught somewhere between delighted and stunned.

Gideon dismounted and held the reins to a groom who hopped down to grab them. "Didn't I mention I'd be going for help?"

"Well, yes, but . . ." Lilly watched him retrieve a pair of packages from the carriage. "Will *all* of them be staying?"

"That's certainly the idea." Gideon climbed the steps, shifted his boxes and cane, and took her elbow to usher her inside.

"But . . ." She craned her neck back once, twice. "But where will we put them? We've only two servants' quarters."

He led her into the parlor. "Two quarters will house four, the loft in the stable can house six, and the spare bedroom can be converted temporarily to house two more. We've plenty of space."

"But—"

"Would you like to see what I've brought?" He held one of the boxes he'd carried in. "Well, go on then, open it up."

She blinked at the box, recognizing what was in it by the size and shape. "But that's for Winnefred. I asked—"

"Winnefred has her own . . . but if you'd rather I brought it back—"

She snatched the box out of his hands on a laugh and tore open the lid. Inside was a gown of muslin, beautifully embroidered in vertical lines of pale blue. The color would compliment her eyes, Gideon thought, and the cut, while not quite as fashionable as those to be had in London, was a good deal more stylish than the one she had on.

"There are a few more like it," Gideon told her. "All ready-made, I'm afraid, so some alterations might be necessary. I've a modiste coming tomorrow—"

"It's perfect. It's absolutely perfect. I can take it up or in as need be." She pulled the dress fully out of the box and held it in front of her. "A new gown," she breathed, looking down at herself.

She twirled once and laughed again, a free and happy sound that made Gideon wonder if he and Lucien had missed out on a great deal by not having a sister to spoil and tease. "It pleases you, then?"

"Pleases me? I've my first new dress in a decade. I've new furnishings for the house, my own room, and people to see to the care of both. If it weren't unforgivably forward, Lord Gideon, I'd kiss you here and now."

"Gideon," he reminded her and bent down to offer her his cheek.

Lilly gave him a peck, then started when a crash, a yell, and several loud gasps sounded in the foyer.

"Who the devil are all these people?!"

Winnefred stumbled in looking breathless and flustered. Her clothes were wrinkled, her long braid of hair frazzled, and her face noticeably pale under the freckles.

"Are you ill?" Gideon demanded, something akin to panic skittering up his spine.

"No, I—"

"Of course she's ill," Lilly said pleasantly. "You sent those custard-filled pastries."

"Was something wrong with them?" Bloody hell, he'd poisoned the woman. "Can a person get sick from eating a stale pastry?"

"No," Lilly assured him. "But a person can get sick from eating six fresh ones."

"Six?"

"Five," Winnefred defended, still standing in the doorway. "And someone answer my question. Who are—"

"Our new staff," Lilly explained. "Isn't it wonderful? No more cleaning and cooking and washing and chopping and—"

"Yes, I know what a staff does." Winnefred glanced back into the hallway. "I thought perhaps you'd hire a person or two to see to . . . whatever it is a lord needs seeing to, but do you really need so many?"

"They're not for me, or not entirely," Gideon informed her. "They're here to provide for whatever you and Lilly might need."

Winnefred turned back to him, looking surprised. "But I don't really need anything. I—"

"Of course you do," Lilly said. "You need someone to care for the animals, the garden, the fences, stock wood for winter—"

"I can do that."

"You can, and you have, but now you've something else to occupy your time—you've lessons, remember?"

Winnefred winced. "I remember. I just assumed . . ." She trailed off and blinked at Lilly, who was running a smoothing hand down her gown.

Gideon took a step toward her. "Is something the matter?"

"That's a new gown," she answered in a dazed voice. "I hadn't noticed. I was distracted. I thought you were playing with a tablecloth, Lilly, or . . . I've no idea what I was thinking . . . You've a new gown."

Gideon may not have been raised with a sister, but he'd had his share of sweethearts and figured he could recognize hurt jealousy as well as the next man. He hadn't expected it of Winnefred, but then, he hardly knew the woman, really. He opened his mouth with the intent of pointing out the box he still held under his arm but got no farther than a quick indrawn breath before she turned to him and proved that perhaps he knew her rather well after all.

"You brought Lilly a new gown."

She smiled at him. And it wasn't a "where's mine, then?" sort of smile, nor the dreaded "I'm tragically disappointed, but I'll not admit to it" sort of smile. It was, without question, a "you are the dearest, cleverest, most wonderful of men" sort of smile.

Simply put, she beamed at him, and Gideon felt the power of it down to his toes. Her amber eyes lit up, her full lips parted, and her face flushed a lovely shade of peach. She looked, he thought, altogether too tempting.

He cleared his throat, pulled out the other box, and very nearly shoved it at her. "I've one for you as well, several for both of you, actually. One of the maids will put them in your chambers, I'm sure. Now if you will excuse me, I've some . . . some . . . correspondence to see to."

And with that singularly inelegant speech, he left the room with every intention of putting into action his plan of avoiding the ladies of the house for the next three weeks.

Particularly one Winnefred Blythe.

Gideon's departure was too swift for Winnefred to do more than stare after him, perplexed, and rather disappointed she'd not had the opportunity to properly thank him for bringing Lilly a gown. It had been such an act of thoughtfulness. One that very neatly, and very effectively, sliced through several layers of lingering distrust.

"Did I say something wrong?"

Lilly shook her head dismissively. "Not at all. I think our Lord Gideon is something of an odd duck. A man of his station is allowed his quirks. Aren't you going to open your box?"

"Hmm? Oh." She set the box down on a side table and pulled off the lid. Like Lilly's, her gown was white muslin, but there was no colored embroidery on the fabric, just a simple white-on-white vertical print and a touch of eyelet on the sleeves and hem.

Lilly smiled and nodded with approval. "An appropriate choice. You'll look lovely."

"I . . ." She trailed off as she ran a finger down the material. "Oh. It's soft."

Her old gown was coarse and scratchy; it pinched under her arms and cut into her sides with even the slightest movement. It wouldn't be so dreadful, she thought, to wear something that felt like this.

"Is it for London?" she asked.

"No, it is for you to wear here."

She snatched her hand back as if she were burned. "You can't be serious. We've weeks before we leave. What if I ruin it?"

"Then you'll be publicly flogged and left to languish in the stocks."

"I'm in earnest, Lilly. I wouldn't begin to know what to do with a gown as fine as this." She gestured at the dress. "I'll have it covered in mud in under an hour."

Lilly began folding her own dress. "Do you think you're the first woman to have occasion to walk on a muddy path?"

"Of course not, but—"

"Mud can be brushed out, Freddie."

"But I don't need a new gown now. I've the old one and my shirt and trousers."

Lilly replaced her gown in its box. "No, you don't need the old dress, shirt, and trousers now; you have new gowns.

We'll start your lessons tomorrow. No excuses . . . and no more sweets. Six pastries . . . honestly."

"Five," Winnefred reminded her. She rubbed a hand against her aching belly, sat down, and sighed. "And it was worth it."

Chapter 6

Winnefred's introduction into the complicated—and in her opinion, truly bizarre—ways of the ton began the next day and continued uninterrupted throughout the week. From dawn to dusk she was instructed in everything from proper dining etiquette, to executing the perfect curtsy, to how to address the various lords and ladies of Europe.

She found her new life and new surroundings in Murdoch House not unpleasant, exactly, but difficult. She and Lilly had shared a room since the first day they'd arrived in Scotland, for comfort in the beginning, then later for practical reasons. But now Winnefred went to sleep and woke alone, or with a stranger in the room stoking the fire. She hadn't yet decided which was more discomfiting.

She was dressed in fine gowns, served an abundance of fine food on fine china and silver platters, and instructed in the matter of fine manners. Everything, it seemed to Winnefred, was absolutely, unquestionably, and irritatingly *fine*.

She missed the muddy walks with Claire to the stream in the mornings. She missed the freedom of wearing what she liked, speaking her mind, doing as she pleased. She missed the sense of pride at having accomplished something tangible every day, whether it was catching fish for breakfast, or mending a broken stall door, or even washing the linens.

Lilly's lessons were challenging, certainly, but they weren't something Winnefred could point to and say, "I did that. I managed that quite on my own."

Of course, she *might* have been able to say that about the lessons . . . if she'd shown any talent for learning and remembering them.

"Is this really necessary, Lilly?"

It was the seventh day, and she and Lilly were sitting, straight-backed with their ankles crossed, in the newly appointed parlor. It was Winnefred's first lesson on the art of using one's fan, and her blasted bit of feathers and whalebone refused to cooperate. It insisted on folding when she fluttered it, sliding open when she tapped it, and molting feathers in a great cloud every time she snapped it shut. She'd pulled several out of her mouth now and was certain she had more sticking up from her hair.

"I believe mine's defective."

"It isn't; you're just being too rough with it. It's a fan, not a hammer to be swung about." Lilly leaned over to adjust Winnefred's grip on the handle. "And it *is* necessary. Communicating with one's fan has fallen out of fashion, but I'm sure the signals themselves are still recognized. What if you propositioned a man without realizing?"

"Is the man handsome?"

"That is not the point."

"It could be. It would be bold and daring and wonderfully wicked of me if he's handsome." She shrugged and bit the inside of her cheek to keep from laughing. "If he were homely, it would just be stupid."

Lilly heaved a great sigh and looked to the ceiling as if for inspiration. "To begin with, propositioning any man, for any reason, is nothing short of unforgivably forward and therefore *immensely* stupid. Secondly, a man's value does not rest solely in his appearance."

"But a woman's does," Winnefred scoffed.

"No. At least, not if that woman is well dowered and well connected. And last—don't shrug. It's vulgar."

Winnefred gaped at her. "I've seen you shrug *hundreds* of times."

"Not," Lilly replied with great dignity, "in the last week. I have successfully broken myself of the practice. You can as well."

There were a few things Winnefred would have preferred breaking at the moment—the ridiculous fan for one—but she'd made a promise to do her best, and she meant to keep it.

The lesson continued for another hour—another unbearably long hour to Winnefred's thinking—before one of the maids stepped in and announced dinner.

Lilly smiled at the younger woman. "Thank you, Bess. Will his lordship be joining us this evening?"

"No, miss. He's asked for his meal to be sent to his room."

Again, Winnefred thought, tossing her fan back into its box. She'd seen very little of the man since the morning he'd returned with the gowns. He was often away from the house, going to Enscrum for the day. And when he was in, he secluded himself in his room and made it perfectly clear to everyone that he didn't wish to be disturbed.

His continued absence only added to Winnefred's already troubled thoughts. She had come to the conclusion on the day he'd returned from Langholm that, despite the limited time they had spent together, she felt more than a physical attraction to the man. She felt a fondness. It had been so thoughtful of him to bring Lilly new gowns without being asked. And he'd been quite reasonable about the small misunderstanding in the stable. He'd made her smile when she'd wanted to pound her fence to splinters out of frustration, had sent those delicious custard-filled pastries, and had brought back from town the most wonderful of luxuries . . . chocolate. How could she help but be fond of him? How was she to ever discover if the way her belly tightened and her skin flushed whenever she caught a glimpse of him was something more than a temporary attraction and fondness if the man refused to speak with her? How—?

"Winnefred, are you listening to me?"

"I . . ." She blinked, then pulled herself away from her worries to find Bess gone and Lilly looking at her with an expectant expression. She offered an apologetic smile. "I'm sorry. I was woolgathering."

"You were fretting," Lilly corrected. "Which is the very thing I was commenting on. Why don't you take a walk after we eat? The air will do you good."

"Haven't we plans after dinner?"

"Nothing that can't be put off for one evening, and to make up for it, we'll have another extended lesson on dining etiquette at dinner."

Her pleasure at the thought of a solitary walk dimmed just a bit. "Of course we will."

*G*ideon turned a corner around a stand of pines and came to an abrupt halt. There, sitting on a rock by the stream that marked the boundary of Murdoch House land, was Winnefred, accompanied by her goat. Both of them oblivious to his presence.

His heart sped up of its own accord. It seemed to always do so when he caught sight of her. And he seemed to always be torn between turning his eyes and thoughts away and lingering to watch.

He'd chosen to watch only once, on the fourth day of his internment—as he had begun to call his stay in Scotland—when Lilly had taken Winnefred outside to practice walking gracefully, or so he gathered from the viewpoint of his window.

Intrigued by the notion a feminine walk was something that had to be accomplished through trial and error, he'd watched as Winnefred strode up and down the dirt drive with all the subtlety of a line of infantrymen marching to battle.

The woman lacked grace, there was no denying it. But neither was there any denying that he found the proud tilt of her head and those brisk, purposeful strides absolutely charming. He found everything about the woman charming. No, more than charming. One found fresh flowers and scruffy kittens charming.

Winnefred Blythe was an unholy temptation.

The sight of the gold strands in her hair being lit by the sun had made his fingers itch to touch, and the way the soft breeze had formed her thin muslin gown to her curves had made him recall how she'd looked in trousers, bent over to pick up a fallen rail.

He wanted her. Just as urgently and as painfully as he wanted to leave her alone.

He'd turned away from the window that day.

He wondered if there was any possible way for him to sneak away now. He'd become rather good at sneaking away over the last week—to Enscrum, to the fields, to his room, or just out the door or down the hall when one of the ladies suddenly appeared in his line of vision. Why did they forever seem to be appearing in his line of vision? For pity's sake, there were only two of them. How could it be that they were always in his path?

He took a step back, intending to make good his escape.

But then Winnefred sighed—not a wispy sort of sigh that indicated contentment, but a great heaving of shoulders and a long, hard breath that spoke of quiet misery.

Damn.

He couldn't walk away. Not now.

Resigned to at least offering a few words of support, or comfort, or whatever it was she needed, he coughed pointedly and stepped forward to close the distance between them.

"Claire isn't much of a guardian, is she?"

Winnefred glanced up from the water as Claire trotted toward Gideon. "She's better at being a companion."

Gideon sidestepped the goat's attempt to snuffle into his leg. "She is . . . amiable. What are you doing sitting out here by yourself? I'd have thought you'd be working with Lilly."

"I've been granted a temporary reprieve." She gave a small shrug. "We just completed another lesson."

"And how did it go?"

"Poorly." She bent down to scratch Claire's head in an obvious attempt to avoid eye contact. "I'm going to embarrass Lilly."

He took a seat beside her and caught the faint hint of lavender again. There was no scent of hay this time, and he found he missed it.

"I'm sure it's not as bad as all that," he tried.

"It is. Yesterday, I tried serving tea." She held a hand up, and for the first time, Gideon noticed a small white bandage on the palm.

Before he could think better of it, he reached out, took her hand in his, and rubbed the pad of his thumb where bandage met pale skin. He found a small line of calluses beneath her fingers. The feel of them made his stomach clench. He experienced the sudden, irrational need to smooth them away. He wished he could somehow go back twelve years and save Winnefred from the years of labor she had endured. When his time in Scotland was done, he decided, he was going to join his brother in the hunt for their stepmother. And when they found her, he was going to strangle the woman until the gnawing anger in his gut was appeased . . . or her eyes popped from her head, whichever came first.

"It isn't a serious wound," he heard Winnefred say softly.

He realized he was scowling at her palm. Surprised by his violent reaction to something as simple and common as a callus, he set her hand down on the rock carefully, as if it were something infinitely fragile and just as dangerous.

"You need to see a physician."

When he'd lifted his head, she'd been looking at him with frank curiosity and—heaven help him—expectant interest. Now she only looked shocked. "A physician? But it's nothing, little more than—"

"You'll have one all the same." Burns were painful. What if it turned putrid? What if a fever took hold? What if—?

She lifted her hand and pulled the bandage down to

reveal a very small reddened patch of skin with no signs of blistering. "I do *not* require a physician."

He frowned at the undeniably minor injury. "Perhaps not."

"Even the bandage is unnecessary, but Lilly—"

"You'll keep it on. And clean. And you will keep Lilly and me apprised of the healing process."

She dropped her hand to her lap. "Oh, for pity's sake. There is no need for—"

"Haven't you poured tea before?"

That question was greeted with narrowed eyes that held a hint of humor. "A change of subject on your part does not constitute an agreement on mine."

It did as far as he was concerned. "Would you rather continue the discussion of your injury?"

"No."

"Then tell me about the lesson."

She opened her mouth as if to argue, then shook her head and turned her eyes to the water. "I have poured before, but it's different now. It's not just Lilly and me sitting down in the parlor—it's the whole of London. That's how it feels to me. And instead of minding their own business, they're all paying attention to see if I splash, or fill the cups too full, or not full enough, or let the china clatter." She stood up but kept her eyes trained on the water. "It's only hot water and some leaves. I don't understand why the ton has to be so . . . so . . ."

She kicked at a small rock to send it tumbling into the stream.

"Ridiculous?" he offered. "Stringent? Pretentious?"

She blew out a short breath and smiled a little. "Yes, to all."

"Well, try to remember that you'll not be the only newcomer this season. Dozens of debutantes will be taking their first bows."

"And will any of them scald their guests with tea, do you think?"

"Doubtful," he admitted. "So you'll let Lilly do the honors when someone comes to call. There are all sorts of ways to get around things when it isn't just you trying to remember all the rules at once."

"And if I can't recall how to properly address a lord when introduced?"

"Try sneezing."

She pulled her eyes from the stream to blink at him owlishly. "I beg your pardon?"

"Develop a sensitivity to cats, or flowers, or whatever happens to be nearby, and excuse yourself in a fit of sneezing."

She choked out a noise that may have been a laugh but could just as easily have been a sound of surprise and disbelief.

"You can't be serious."

"Perfectly. You'll have to be suitably contrite about it, of course, and affect a considerable amount of suffering. Garnering sympathy for your plight will be key."

This time, it was clearly laughter. "I don't know that I could summon a believable sneezing fit on command."

"There must be something you're good at. Focus on your strengths, Winnefred. Do you play an instrument?"

"I'm afraid not."

"Watercolor, sketch?"

"No."

"Can you sing?"

"Not well."

"Do you know any French?"

A corner of her mouth hooked up. "A bit."

She cleared her throat. And then proceeded to recite a list of French invectives so extensive, so obscene, that she actually hit upon one or two he'd never before encountered.

He gaped at her for a moment. "It is a sad state of affairs, indeed, when a young lady can out-swear a sea captain. Or maybe just a curious one. I haven't decided. *Where on earth* did you learn those?"

"Here and there." Her grin spoke of pride and devilish delight at having shocked him.

"One does not pick up French curses here and there."

"One can if there's a prison not five miles away that used to have a wing filled with French soldiers."

"Ah, yes." He'd heard the townsfolk in Enscrum speak of the small and relatively new prison in terms both grateful and derogatory. They didn't care to have the dredges of society at their doorstep, but they certainly appreciated the coin it brought in. "I suppose a few choice French phrases were bound to escape into town. Do I want to know how you managed to pick them up?"

"I rather doubt it."

"I thought as much." He rose from his seat and, placing a finger under her chin, tilted her face up for consideration. The color was back in her cheeks, and the dullness gone from her eyes. "Feeling better?"

She went very still at his touch. Her eyes darted to his mouth. "Yes."

He shouldn't have touched her again. He knew it even before he'd reached out with his hand. But he'd been unable to stop himself. Just as he was unable to stop himself now from brushing his thumb along the edge of her jaw and imagining what it would be like to taste her right there, where the skin was soft and tight. The light kiss, the brief flick of tongue, the gentle scrape of his teeth along . . .

It took an enormous act of will to let his hand fall naturally to his side. The urge to snatch it away was almost as strong as the urge to wrap his fingers around the nape of her neck and pull her close.

"My pleasure." His voice sounded muted over the roaring of blood in his ears. "If there's anything else you need, you've only to ask."

He told himself the offer was little more than a formality. It was simply the sort of thing a gentleman said to a lady directly before taking his leave. The suspicion that he would agree to any request she cared to make in that moment was studiously ignored.

Winnefred said nothing, as if she hadn't even heard him. Her eyes, he realized with ever-growing discomfort, were still fixed on his mouth.

He took a full step back. "Well, if there's nothing . . ."

His imminent departure seemed to pull her from her thoughts. Her gaze snapped to his.

"What?" She frowned briefly and, to his immense relief, appeared to regain her composure. "Oh, yes, wait, there is something I should like, if it's not too much bother. Are you going into town tomorrow?"

"I could manage it." An errand several miles away. He could most certainly manage it. "Is there something you need?"

"Chocolate. I'd not tried it before you came, but now that I have, I can't seem to stop drinking it. I've never tasted anything so delicious in my life. I'm down to my last cup's worth."

"I'm afraid the little I brought was all Mr. McDaniel had in stock. His next shipment isn't due for another . . . fortnight, I believe he said."

"A fortnight? We'll be gone to London by then."

The disappointment in her voice tugged at him. She shouldn't have to wait until London. Not after waiting twelve years to start. "I'll make the trip to Langholm."

"For chocolate?" She laughed and waved her hand dismissively. "Don't be silly. I thank you for the offer, but I've not become *that* spoiled. I'll wait and save the final cup for a special occasion."

"Such as?"

"Well, I don't know yet, do I? Something monumental. My first gracefully executed curtsy perhaps." She watched him as he chuckled. When she spoke next, it was with enough hesitancy to make him nervous. "There is something else I should like to ask of you."

He hoped it was another errand. "I'm at your service."

"Would it . . . Would it be a great deal of trouble for you to attend meals now and again? I know you prefer eating in your chambers," she hurried on as if she could guess the direction of his thoughts, "but if Lilly were to have a distraction from time to time, it would help ease her burden, I think, as well as mine. With nothing else to do or think on, she's become a bit fanatical about our trip. I don't think it's healthy."

"She's devoted."

"She's nearing deranged. Lord Gideon . . ." She swallowed and looked at him with a hope he knew he wouldn't be able to deny. "Gideon, *please*."

It was just a meal or two, he told himself. Just an hour here and there, chaperoned and across the barrier of a sturdy oak table. He could do that.

"Certainly," he heard himself say. "I'll make a point of it."

She beamed at him. "Thank you."

"The pleasure will be mine, I'm sure." So would the torture. "If there's nothing else—"

"There is actually."

Oh, bloody hell.

He leaned on his cane, hard. "And what might that be?"

She shifted her weight and placed her hands behind her back as if to keep from fidgeting. "I realize this isn't the best time for me to mention this, not after you've been so gracious, but I've been meaning to speak to you of it for days, and I've not been able. You're so often gone or wishing to be left undisturbed." She grimaced at her own words. "I don't mean that to sound so much like a complaint, or a reprimand. It's only—"

"I understand." He *had* made it difficult, nearly impossible for her to speak with him. There was no denying it. "What is it you wish to say?"

"It's . . . I should like to start by saying that I've become rather fond of you."

Oh, bloody, bloody hell.

He nodded, slowly. "I'm fond of you as well. Winnefred—"

"I want you to understand that what I am about to say doesn't mean I'm not grateful for what you've done, or that I don't like you. It's only that I like Lilly more. She is, for all that we are not related by blood, my sister."

His nerves quickly turned to bafflement. He nodded

again, unsure of where she was taking the conversation.
"Of course she is."

"She is very excited about this trip."

"I've no doubt that's true."

"She has built enormous expectations around it."

"Only natural."

"She has . . . This trip has . . ." She pressed her lips
together in frustration. "She is now in a position of . . . a
position to be . . ."

"Spit it out, Winnefred."

"Right." She nodded once, tipped her chin up, and
stared him straight in the eye. "If anyone hurts or disap-
points her in London, anyone at all, for any reason at all, I
shall cut out your heart and eat it raw."

"Ah." He didn't doubt for a second she would try. He felt
the nearly irrepressible, and assuredly ill-advised, urge to
laugh. Not at her, but at his delight with her. She threatened
him almost begrudgingly. Not for herself, but for Lilly . . .
And not before she had asked her favors.

Lovely, clever woman.

"What makes you think I'd allow harm to come to
either of you?" Except for the obvious reason that he had
no intention of being responsible for either of them once
they reached London, he silently added. But she couldn't
know that.

"Nothing's made me think it. I just wanted you to be
aware that I am holding you personally accountable for
Lilly's happiness."

"That's a bit much to pin on a man, don't you think?"

She thought it over. "No."

"I see." He felt his lips twitch despite the effort to keep
them still. "Well, I'll do my best to ensure that Lilly has her
happiness and that my internal organs remain . . . internal."

She nodded, apparently satisfied. "Thank you. And I do
apologize for the necessity of the discussion."

"You are welcome, and forgiven." He turned and began
walking away but made it no more than three feet before he
gave in to his amusement and turned back again.

"Why raw?"

"Why . . . I'm sorry?"

"Why eat my heart raw?" he repeated. "It's such an odd qualifier, as if it were assumed I'd prefer it first be roasted and smothered in a fine plum sauce."

"Plum sauce?" Her mouth fell open, and a bubble of laughter escaped from her throat. "I think you *are* mad."

"I'm curious. Would the act of cooking really render the deed less barbaric? And what of the rest of dining etiquette? Is anything permissible? Silverware, for example, or napkins? A seat at the table and a glass of port?"

Her amber eyes began to dance with humor, and her lips trembled with suppressed laughter. "I'm going to take my leave now. Good day, Lord Gideon."

"Could there be side dishes and lively conversation?" He lifted his voice as she spun on her heel and walked away from him, Claire shuffling along at her side. " 'Pass the rolls, Mrs. Butley, and another helping of Lord Gideon's raw heart. No, no, just use your fingers, dear, he's being punished.' "

He heard her laughter echoing back to him. Unable to look away, he continued to watch her move away from him toward the house. Yes, it was going to be torture to see Winnefred Blythe sitting across the table from him every day, worse if he had to listen to that wonderfully low and free laugh of hers.

He made himself look away and begin a slow walk in the opposite direction. He'd attend breakfast, he decided. From what he could tell, breakfast was the shortest meal at Murdoch House. More important, performing his duty in the morning would give him the rest of the day to be alone.

He would not, under any circumstances, attend dinner. He would not end his day lying in his bed with the picture of Winnefred Blythe so fresh in his mind.

Nights, he thought grimly, were difficult enough.

Chapter 7

Gideon studied the wavering chart. He needed a plan. He needed to find a way to get them all out of this damnable mess.

But the chart kept shimmering in and out of focus. He couldn't read it. He couldn't think.

If the fighting would only stop for a minute, if the ship would be quiet for just one buggering minute, he'd be able to think.

"I can fight, Cap'n. Let me fight."

He looked up from the table. When had the boy come in?

"Get to the hold, Jimmy."

"But I can fight, Cap'n. Just give me a gun."

"You can't fight." He gestured impatiently at the boy's chest. "You haven't any arms for pity's sake."

The boy looked down at his bleeding injuries.

"Bugger me. So I 'ave'nt. Me mum's going to be right peeved."

Gideon blinked at the blood. That wasn't right, was it?

No, that wasn't right at all.

He needed to get the boy to safety. It was his responsibility to get the boy to safety.

"Get to the hold." Hadn't he told the boys to go to the hold? "Now."

"Nah." Jimmy shrugged. "Don't need me arms, really. But Bill's 'ead is gone. Could be a problem."

The cabin door swung open and young Colin Newberry came in with a hole the size of a dinner platter through his belly, and Bill's head clutched in his hand like a lantern.

"Found it! Where's the rest of him?"

"I'm losing you," Gideon heard himself whisper. "I'm losing you."

Lord Marson came in behind Colin. The left half of his upper body was gone, utterly gone, and blood flowed from the remaining half to pool on the floor. "What's the captain lost? Is that Bill's head? He'll be looking for it."

"Get to the hold! For pity's sake, I told you to get to the hold!"

Bill's head blinked at him.

"But, Cap'n, we just come from the hold."

As the figures before him blurred, a scream echoed in Gideon's head and strangled in his throat. He wanted to force it out. If, just for once, he could force it out, the agony of it would lessen. But nothing came from his lips but a long moan he heard as if from a great distance.

"Gideon. Gideon, wake up. Please, wake up."

Winnefred's voice floated to him over the waves of pain and frustration. Finally, *finally*, the scream began to die, slowly fading away like the final note of a violent symphony.

He saw her eyes first. It was so different to see something other than the ceiling or the bottom of a canopy when he woke from the dream, and for a moment he did nothing but stare while the last of the dream shrank away. It wasn't such a terrible thing, really, to wake to beautiful eyes filled with concern . . . and fear.

"Gideon?"

"Bloody hell." He pushed her away with shaking hands. "A moment. Give me a moment."

"Yes. Of course."

He sat up and reached for the shirt he'd tossed on the floor when he'd grown over-warm reading in bed. Pushing his arms through the sleeves, he rose, grateful that he'd fallen asleep with his trousers still on. Then he planted his hands on his hips and concentrated on settling his heart into a normal rhythm.

Only when he was certain he had regained a modicum of control did he turn to face Winnefred once more.

She was sitting on his bed, and he noticed for the first time that she was dressed in the rich cream night rail and wrap he'd purchased himself. The color had made him think of her skin. That skin was pale now, in sharp contrast with the spray of freckles across her cheekbones and nose. Her eyes were wide with worry and alarm, he realized with a sinking heart. He'd frightened her.

"I . . ." Disgusted that his voice came out rough and cracked, he cleared his throat and tried again. "I've frightened you. I apologize."

She shook her head and spoke softly. "I'm not afraid of you, Gideon. Only frightened for you when I heard you call out. You're not . . . You're not unwell, are you?"

"No, I'm not ill. I . . ." He trailed off, uncertain of what to say to her or do with himself. He settled for the blessedly mundane task of buttoning up his shirt. "What are you doing out of bed?"

She rose to stand, still watching him carefully. "I wished for a glass of milk. I was walking past your door and I heard—"

"You should have called for a maid."

"Oh. If you'd rather a maid come, I could wake Bess for you and—"

"No, for the milk . . ." He shook his head, irritated with himself and the situation. "Never mind. I'd like to be alone, Winnefred."

"Oh, yes. Right." She hesitated, turned around as if to

leave, then turned back again, her hands working nervously at the waist of her wrap. "I find it helpful, on occasion, to speak with Lilly of the things that trouble me. If you'd like to tell me of your dream—"

"I wouldn't." His voice was curt, but it couldn't be helped. The desire to accept what she offered, to tell her everything, nearly overwhelmed him. It was a new sensation for him—he'd never been tempted to tell another of his dreams, not even his brother—and it made him feel like a coward. The dream, and the cause of it, was *his* burden. He had earned it, and he'd bear the weight of it alone. "I don't wish to discuss it."

"If you're certain."

"I am." *For pity's sake, leave.* "Good night, Winnefred."

"Yes, well." She gave him a small smile. "Good night, Gideon."

She turned again and let herself out with a quick click of the door. For a long time after, he simply stood where he was and stared at it. It would be a simple thing, he thought at first, such a simple thing to call her back.

He considered this for several moments, until he was certain she would no longer be able to hear his voice if he gave in and said her name.

Then he thought of how easy it would be to slip from the room and catch her in the hall before she made it to her chambers.

Minutes passed and he began to envision what it would be like to walk quietly through the house to knock softly at her door. She'd let him in. She wouldn't give the impropriety of it a second thought. She hadn't thought of propriety when she'd come into his chambers, had she?

He was thinking of it now, of the door she would close, of the soft bed they would sit on as he told her of his nightmares. He thought of how understanding she would be, how sympathetic. How easy it would be for him to turn that sympathy to his selfish benefit. It was a fine thing, a comforting thing, for a man to lose himself in a woman . . . usually. With Winnefred, it would be something more.

And more was not something he had the right to take, nor the ability to give.

Still, he continued to stand where he was and torment himself by imagining what it would be like to seek her out. There was no telling how long he let his imagination run rampant, nor how long he might have continued to do so had a soft knock not sounded on his door.

Winnefred.

He should have known she wouldn't be able to take no for an answer. Should have known her stubbornness and innate desire to protect wouldn't allow her to back away.

He took a deep breath to steady himself and crossed the room to open the door, prepared to send her away once more.

She wasn't there. In her stead, a small tray lay at the threshold. It held a piece of toast, a note, and a cup of chocolate.

Dear Gideon,

Lilly insists upon my eating toast whenever I feel unwell. I, however, much prefer the chocolate. I do so hope one of them brings you comfort.

Yours most sincerely,
Winnefred

Her handwriting, he noticed, was atrocious. He stooped to picked up the tray and set it on his desk. Taking the cup, he stood in front of his window, stared into the darkness, and sipped the very last of Winnefred's chocolate.

Lost in a maze of thoughts, he didn't realize his lips were curved in the smallest of smiles.

Chapter 8

*W*innefred woke the next morning with a heavy heart and uneasy mind. For most of the night, she had lain awake, recalling again and again the fear she had seen in Gideon's eyes when he'd woken from the nightmare, and the misery she had seen after.

It had eaten at her to think of him alone and hurting. And more than once, she had envisioned returning to his chambers, pounding on the door until she gained entrance, and then . . . And then she'd recalled how painfully ineffectual her first attempt to comfort had been, and the determination to try again was lost.

She simply had no idea how to help.

The very few times Lilly had been out of sorts, it had been an easy, even natural, thing for Winnefred to provide what was needed to see her friend smile again. Lilly was fond of wildflowers, tea with honey, and an impromptu and well-executed limerick, preferably of a bawdy (not to be mistaken for vulgar) nature.

But Winnefred didn't know what sorts of things made a man such as Gideon smile.

Now, in the early light of day, she wondered if even her present of toast and chocolate had been childish, like a small girl offering her favorite toy to appease an adult's grief.

Grimacing, she rolled from bed and dressed without calling for a maid. It was early yet, and she wanted solitude, a long walk with Claire in the fields. For just a few hours, she wanted things to be simple again.

She found Claire in the stable, fast asleep in an enormous pile of fresh hay. Winnefred felt a small pain of regret that it had been someone else who had provided her companion with such a fine bed. Still, it was a pleasure to see Claire so well cared for. She crossed her arms on the top rail of the stall and rested her chin on her wrist.

"Look at you," she said softly. "Quite the princess . . . And the sloven, to be sleeping in your food."

Claire lifted her head, blinked twice, then promptly went back to sleep.

Winnefred laughed and uncrossed her arms to open the stall door.

"Have you taken to sleeping in as well, then? Lilly calls it keeping town hours, you know. Just a silly way to say sloth, really." She knelt down in the hay, reached into a pocket, and retrieved a napkin of scraps she'd taken from the kitchen. "Come here, darling. I have something for you."

The promise of scraps lured Claire from her bed and out the stable.

A little worried her companion might be tempted to turn back, Winnefred doled the treats out in stingy increments until they were out of sight of the stable.

"A very sad thing indeed that I should have to bribe you to keep me company," she remarked, stopping to offer the last of the food.

Unfazed by the censure, Claire inhaled her breakfast, then ambled off to inspect an old log.

Winnefred smiled and resumed her walk. The morning air was foggy, damp, and a little chilly, but the breeze that

caught at her skirts was warm, and the thin layer of clouds
held the promise of burning away by midday.

A perfect morning, she mused. And the very thing she
needed to clear her mind and lift her spirits. Though her
intention had been to use the time to work through her troubles, she resisted that task now, reluctant to weigh the lovely
scene with worries. She had time enough to think of Gideon.
An entire day, like as not. He would, as always, keep to his
room, or go to Enscrum for the day, and she would be kept
busy with Lilly's lessons. It was very unlikely they would
meet before dinner.

It was with some surprise that she rounded a small stand
of trees and saw him next to the pond, standing quiet and
still as a statue amongst the reeds. He didn't turn to face
her and gave no indication that he thought himself to be
anything other than alone—and content in his solitude.
She was too far away yet to see his face, but she imagined it was as serene, as unmoving, as the rest of him. He
was listening, she thought, to the birds, and the wind, and
the distant call of cattle. He was watching the early morning mist upon the pond, the gentle lap of water against the
banks, and the soft sway of the grass in the breeze.

She'd thought him handsome, that first night in the gardener's cottage, and charming the next day in the garden.
She'd viewed him as a man of power and wealth, wit and
fancy. Last night, she had thought him one of secrets.

But now, as she watched the mist roll off the pond to
wrap and swirl around his legs, she thought him simply
beautiful. And for the first time in her life, she wondered
what it would be like to have a man like that turn to her,
smile, and open his arms.

Instinct had her retreating back a few steps. It was one
thing to be attracted to a man, but it was an altogether different thing to want something more—something she may
never have. Pride and practicality had her stopping in her
tracks and moving forward again. She wasn't a coward,
and she needed to know if he was still suffering.

She cleared her throat to alert him of her presence, but

he didn't appear to need it. He glanced over his shoulder and gifted her with a smile, as if he'd known she was there all along.

"Good morning, Gideon."

"Winnefred. Claire."

She reached his side and stood there, with her hands gripped behind her back and her mind searching for something useful to say.

"Are you rested?" was the best she could manage.

"I am, thank you."

She stole a quick look at his features, but his expression revealed nothing.

She nudged a weed with her toe. "It's very early. I hadn't expected anyone else to be up and about."

"I always rose with the sun when I was at sea. I've found the habit difficult to break."

"Do you miss the sea?"

It was several moments before he answered. "I have very fond childhood memories of the coast. My mother often took Lucien and me to the ocean while my father visited London or his extensive collection of hunting boxes." He laughed softly and bent to pick up a smooth, round pebble. "No doubt my early perceptions of the sea were greatly colored by my father's absence."

Though he made the statement casually, Winnefred heard the edge of anger and sadness. She didn't know how to respond to either. "You do miss it, then."

"No, I do not." He skipped the rock expertly across the water. "Perceptions change."

Feeling at a loss, she wrapped her arms around her waist and bent her head to stare at her feet. She found the courage to speak, but the words were directed at her toes. "Gideon . . . Are you quite certain you are well?"

"Perfectly, I assure you."

"You don't seem it. Will you tell me of your dream last—?"

"You smell of hay again."

Her eyes snapped to his face at that startling non sequitur.

Was he attempting to be funny by poking fun at her? He didn't appear to be amusing himself at her expense. He was regarding her with a warm, inquisitive smile.

"I only just noticed it," he said, as if that somehow explained everything. "You smelled of lavender and hay the first time we met. But you've not smelled of hay again until now."

"I was in the stable this morning with Claire," she said, dropping her arms. "If the smell offends you—"

"It doesn't." He leaned toward her and sniffed. "Quite nice, actually."

She honestly didn't know what to say to that. The change of subject had been so abrupt, it left her reeling. And it wasn't every day a woman was complimented for smelling like a stall.

Gideon straightened and tapped the end of his cane against his foot in a thoughtful manner. "It's odd, don't you think, that we find so many scents to be agreeable and yet we'll wear only a few. Why does every lady want to smell like a flower? Why not roasted tenderloin or a filet steak? I've yet to meet the man who didn't appreciate a superior cut of beef."

She couldn't help but laugh a little at the image of a woman dabbing meat behind her ears. "The lady would go off."

"There is that. What of fresh-baked bread? . . . Or asparagus? I've a keen fondness for asparagus."

She gave up the notion of trying to have a serious discussion. Obviously, he had no intention of telling her of his dream or explaining his somber mood when she'd first come upon him. And since the silly conversation appeared to be restoring his good humor, she couldn't think of a good reason to try to change his mind.

"I don't know that asparagus is universally admired," she returned. "Or that it has a scent. Pumpkin might be nice."

"It would be. All this talk of food reminds me I've not yet had breakfast," he said suddenly. He turned his back to the pond and offered his arm. "Will you walk me back to the house and see that I'm fed?"

She took his arm with a smile and started them off at a leisurely pace. "I've special plans for breakfast. A picnic on the back lawn."

"A breakfast picnic?"

She ignored Lilly's rule and shrugged. "The weather has been unusually mild lately. Why shouldn't we take advantage of it?"

"Why indeed? I look forward to it."

"You mean to join us for breakfast?"

"A meal or two, as promised."

She'd been thinking of dinners when she'd requested he take meals with them, but after a moment's thought, she decided breakfast might work well enough. With a bit of luck, a relaxed atmosphere in the morning would cheer all three of them for the day.

"Is there anything special you should like Cook to prepare?" she inquired.

"Could we persuade Lilly to cook her eggs?"

She snorted at the very idea. "She would need to be persuaded from her bed first."

"Could it be done?"

"Not without cost."

He appeared to consider this for a moment. "How great a cost?"

"At the very least, you would require the aid of a sturdier cane."

He laughed, as she'd hoped he would. "I see. And has she always greeted the morning with violence?"

"On the contrary, she's quite cheery in the mornings." She took a deep breath of air, then let out a long dramatic sigh of content. "I *do* so love having a few hours to do with as I please this morning. I vow, if Lilly rises and I have to spend the next hour trapped in lessons instead of planning a picnic—"

"I am resigned to eating Cook's eggs."

"Delighted to hear it."

She told him of her plans for the morning as they walked, and when they reached the house, she took another look at his features. She noted with pleasure that much of his good humor had returned. "Would you like to help me with the picnic?"

He stepped forward to hold the door open for her. "I'm afraid I've no talent for planning meals, just eating them. I'll be in the stables if I'm needed."

"Oh. Well." She reached down to pat Claire good-bye but paused before stepping inside. She felt as if something else needed to be said or done, but when nothing came to her, she gave Gideon an awkward wave, turned, and headed down the hall.

"Winnefred?"

She turned back and found Gideon watching her from the open door. "Yes?"

"Thank you for the chocolate."

"You drank it, then." It had occurred to her at one point during the night that he might have simply rolled his eyes at the gesture and let the drink go cold.

"Naturally I drank it. It did wonders."

She smiled hesitantly as Gideon turned to walk away, letting the door close on its own behind him. Company, a bit of laughter, and a cup of chocolate—perhaps, despite her lack of experience in such matters, she had managed to provide a little comfort after all.

Or perhaps it was merely coincidence.

She wished Lilly would teach her something about lords and gentlemen besides how not to proposition one with a fan.

Chapter 9

Winnefred settled herself more comfortably between Gideon and Lilly on the picnic blanket and took in the sounds and smells of a waking Murdoch House. She heard Giddy's call, smelled the wood smoke from the kitchen chimney, and watched as Claire came trotting from the direction of the stable to investigate the strange happenings on the back lawn. The early morning clouds had burned away and the sunlight of midmorning cast a warm glow over the land.

It was, to Winnefred's mind, a perfectly lovely scene. She might have gone so far as to call it ideal, had the conversation about her now been of something—*anything*—besides the upcoming trip to London.

To give Gideon his due, he did make an attempt or two to steer Lilly toward other topics, but he gave up the effort when Lilly asked him to describe the Prince Regent. Less out of capitulation, it seemed, than a fondness for the task. Gideon had quite a bit to say about the man, very little of it flattering, a great deal of it shocking, and all of it undeniably amusing—particularly to Lilly.

Winnefred smiled as she bit into her toast. She might have been disappointed with Gideon's quick surrender, but the combination of food and lively conversation appeared to be so very effective in clearing the last of his dark mood, she couldn't be sorry for it.

She caught the familiar twinkle in his dark eyes as he began a description of the Prince Regent's drunken antics at a particularly merry ball, and she saw it brighten when Lilly broke into fits of laughter. He enjoyed that, Winnefred realized. He took considerable pleasure in making someone else laugh.

Lilly wiped tears from her eyes with one hand and pointed her fork at Winnefred with the other. "You mustn't speak of the Prince Regent in this manner to anyone else, Freddie."

Winnefred froze mid-reach for a second helping of ham. "I've not said a word about the man."

"I mean you are not to follow our example. A young, unknown, unmarried lady cannot disparage a member of the royal family in public."

"May I laugh if someone else is doing the disparaging?"

"That would depend on who."

"An elderly, popular, married lady," she drawled.

"Yes, certainly."

"I shall endeavor to remember that. Did you see the garden this morning? Something's got into the carrots."

Gideon chuckled at the less-than-subtle attempt to steer the conversation away from something resembling a lesson.

Lilly merely sighed. "I know you're not eager to go to London, but we have very little time left and a great deal to accomplish before we leave."

"Yes, I know." Worried she may have lessened her friends' pleasure in the morning, she put an effort into sounding cheerful. "I've no doubt seeing the Prince Regent will be quite memorable."

"There is more to London than just going into society, you know," Gideon informed her.

Winnefred nodded obligingly. "The opera and . . . other

things." She couldn't recall what other things Lilly had mentioned. "I'm sure it is all very exciting."

She wasn't excited, particularly, but she was intrigued by the idea of a night at the theater and thought that close enough.

"There's more than the opera as well," Lilly said. "There is Vauxhall Gardens and, though I cannot promise you will be allowed to attend, the Smithfield Market."

Winnefred experienced her first true flicker of anticipation at the mention of the massive meat and poultry market. "I should like to see that. What else?"

"Well, there's Hyde Park," Lilly continued. "The Royal Circus . . . Or is it something else now?"

"Surrey Theatre," Gideon told her before turning to Winnefred. "There's the British Museum as well, and—"

"Oh, your brother was so fond of the museum," Lilly cut in with a small laugh.

Gideon's gaze snapped to Lilly. "You knew my brother in London?"

Lilly faltered a moment, then suddenly found her toast exceptionally interesting. "We were childhood acquaintances. Will you pass the butter please, Freddie?"

"Lucien doesn't discuss his love of history with passing acquaintances," Gideon said.

"I suppose he was more forthcoming as a young man."

"Not as I recall."

"Oh, well . . . No doubt children pass through a great many changes of character. And a younger brother is probably not privy to an older brother's every minor alteration of character. Particularly not when they are both very young. The butter please, Winnefred."

Winnefred set the dish in front of Lilly, though what her friend thought to do with it, she couldn't imagine. Lilly had torn her toast into a half dozen pieces.

If Gideon noticed her agitation, however, he gave no indication of it. He simply nodded and reached for his drink. "You must be right. Were you in London long on your last visit?"

"A few short weeks. Not nearly long enough. I hadn't the opportunity to experience half of what I wished. I did so want to try Gunter's ices."

Winnefred only half listened as Lilly and Gideon began to once again list London's attributes. She poked at her eggs as curiosity and nerves poked at her. Lilly was hiding something. It wasn't difficult to tell when her friend was keeping a secret—the woman was not an accomplished liar—but it was impossible to demand an explanation in Gideon's company.

Under the assumption she would have to wait another hour or more to speak with Lilly in private, she was a little surprised when Gideon set his fork down five minutes later and pronounced himself done. His plate, which he had piled high with food earlier, was scraped clean. Winnefred gaped at it, wondering that he had managed to eat so much so quickly and still participate in the conversation. And then she wondered whether it was a skill she could acquire and put to use at dinner parties in London. Probably not.

"That was very quick," she commented and felt a pang of disappointment that he should be so eager to leave.

Gideon rose with his cane, his large form casting a shadow over the blanket. "I've some business to see to this morning."

She wanted to ask him what sort of business required he swallow his food without chewing, but she managed to restrain herself. She watched him bow and walk away, then she turned her attention to Lilly.

"What are you hiding?"

Lilly glanced up from her plate. "Beg your pardon?"

"You were lying just now, about London and Gideon's brother. What are you hiding?"

"Nothing, I . . ." Lilly sagged all of a sudden. "Oh, I am. I am lying. I'm sorry, Freddie. It comes out of habit."

"You're not in the habit of lying."

"I am about this. I didn't meet Lord Engsly as a young child." She exhaled loudly. "I met him at seventeen . . . We had an understanding."

Winnefred could have sworn the ground beneath her shifted. Had she been asked to guess the lie, an engagement would not have occurred to her. "You're not serious. An understanding? With Gideon's brother? With *Lord Engsly*?"

"It was not Lord Engsly at the time, and our understanding was never publically declared. His father and stepmother did not approve of our association."

"Why ever not?"

"Because I was the undowered daughter of a rural gentleman. There was nothing in the match for the Engsly estate. We kept our engagement a secret from all." She smiled slowly, remembering. "He called me Rose."

"Rose?"

"We were seventeen and twenty respectively, we met in a rose garden, and the contact between us was forbidden. We thought the use of a nickname quite clever."

"I see." She didn't actually, but then, her world at seventeen had been very different.

"We were foolish children," Lilly said quietly.

"It isn't foolish to fall in love."

"No, it isn't. But it was foolish to believe we could secure our future with nothing more than a silly nickname and a *tendre*. He bought a commission so we could live without his father's help and promised to return for me as soon as he could. He wrote every day for a month. And then he stopped. No reason was given, no warning. He just stopped."

Winnefred absorbed that bit of information and worked it over in her mind before speaking again. "Do you think Lady Engsly may have had something to do with that?"

"It seems likely, doesn't it? I suppose I might have the opportunity to ask him, if he returns to London during our visit." She exhaled loudly and straightened her shoulders. "But really, what does it matter now? It was such a long time ago."

It mattered, Winnefred thought. She knew Lilly well enough to see past the careless gesture and indifferent tone to know it mattered. She also knew her well enough to know when it was best to push and when it was best to allow some space.

Lilly brought her hand to her stomach. "Would you mind terribly if we put your next lesson off a half hour or so? I believe I overindulged."

Oh, yes, Winnefred thought, it most certainly mattered. She reached for her friend's free hand and squeezed gently. "Take a stroll, Lilly, or have a lie-down."

Winnefred watched her friend stand and leave. An understanding with the Marquess of Engsly. It was nearly impossible to imagine. How different Lilly's life would have been had the two of them not been separated. She would have spent every season in London, amongst those shops and theaters she adored. She would never have come to Scotland. Because a small selfish part of her was glad her friend had not become the Marchioness of Engsly, Winnefred put the matter aside, brushed off her skirts, and moved to stand. There was quite a bit she could do with another half hour of free time.

"Have you a minute more to linger, Winnefred?"

She started at the sound of Gideon's voice and spun around to find him coming out of the house once more. A tingle of pleasure danced up her spine. Perhaps he'd not been in such a hurry to leave her company after all.

"I've half an hour as it happens. Have you had a resurgence of appetite?"

"No." He gestured at her to resume her seat. "I've come to inquire after Lilly."

"Lilly? Why would . . . ?" She trailed off, her eyes widening. "Were you eavesdropping just now?"

His lips quirked into a smile. "No. But I was watching from my window."

"Whatever for?"

"I was not blind to her agitation at the mention of my brother," he said softly, taking a seat next to her.

"Oh. You didn't appear to notice."

"I assumed Lilly would be more comfortable discussing the issue with you."

She thought about that and reached down to pluck at a piece of lint on the blanket. "I have never before been put in the position of . . . Of having more than one friend. Nor having any friends with secrets."

Gideon nodded in understanding. "I don't wish to see you break a confidence, Winnefred. I only wish to know if there is something I ought to be made aware of."

"And if there is?"

"Then I will revisit the subject with Lilly."

That seemed reasonable. "No," she decided with a decisive nod. It hadn't been Gideon who had broken Lilly's heart, after all. "No, it has nothing to do with either of us."

"Lucien wasn't unkind to her in some way?"

"Is your brother the sort to be unkind to a lady?" she asked by way of deflecting the question.

"They met as children," he reminded her. "Even the best behaved of children can be cruel on occasion."

They hadn't been children, strictly speaking, but she couldn't see the sense in correcting him. "I'd wager you never were."

"You would lose that bet." He gave her a mischievous smile. "I pushed Miss Mary Watkins into a puddle of mud when we were both seven."

She found it very easy to picture Gideon as a small dark-haired, impish little boy, but she couldn't imagine him pushing someone to the ground. "Why?"

"She kicked at my dog."

Winnefred had never had a dog, but she rather thought her reaction would have been the same. "That's not cruelty, that's vengeance. And completely justified, in my opinion."

"She cried for a half hour after."

She sent him a pitying look. "And you felt badly, didn't you?"

"Not as badly as I was informed I should."

She laughed and pointed her finger at him. "Exactly, because you knew she deserved it. It isn't cruel if it's deserved. I believe I've won my wager."

"Ah, but what if I told you Miss Watkins had, until that

unfortunate day, been a sweet and gentle child, and later grew into an admirable young woman?"

"Did she?"

"No." He grinned when she laughed again. "But it might have happened."

"I suppose it might have," she conceded. "How does this sound? I can assure you that, to the best of my knowledge, your brother never pushed Lilly into a mud puddle or kicked at her dog."

"So, there is nothing I need to do for her, or could do for her?"

She thought of the life her friend had been denied and the life before her now.

"Yes, there is." She caught his dark gaze and held it. "You can keep your promises."

Chapter 10

The very next day, a pianoforte was delivered to Murdoch House, and Winnefred took her first dancing instructions from Lilly. To her great delight, she soon discovered one needn't necessarily be good at something to enjoy it. In fact, when it came to dancing, enjoyment seemed to increase in reverse proportion to the amount of skill a body was able to exhibit.

The house had no ballroom or music room to speak of, but the front parlor was large enough to accommodate the pianoforte and a pair of dancers once the furniture was lined against the walls. Lilly was the only person in residence proficient at the piano, and so Bess had been recruited as a dance partner for Winnefred. Unfortunately, Bess's familiarity with popular dances was only slightly more extensive than Winnefred's, and because the poor girl had no experience at all when it came to dancing in the role of a gentleman, she and Winnefred had spent the last hour bumping into, tripping over, and stepping on each other and the furniture.

Winnefred couldn't remember ever having so much fun.

"Stop. Stop." Lilly bent over the piano keys, choking

out words between fits of laughter. ". . . The pair of you . . . Like drunken marionettes."

Winnefred glanced at a sheepish-looking Bess. "I thought we were doing rather well just now."

They'd not collided more than twice in the last five minutes, which was a notable improvement.

Lilly took a deep breath and straightened. "Avoiding each other as if you fear the pox is not doing well. And you've been dancing as the gentleman again, Freddie."

"Oh." She considered this with pursed lips. The fewest number of mishaps seemed to occur when she was dancing as the gentleman. "I don't suppose there are any circumstances in which a lady—"

"No. It is never proper for a lady to lead."

Winnefred looked to Bess and winked. "Pity."

"'Tisn't Miss Blythe's fault," Bess offered. "I've no talent for dancing as a gentleman."

Winnefred grinned at Lilly. "You see? I was dancing as a gentleman because Bess was dancing as a lady. I believe that qualifies as having followed her lead."

"It qualified as a mockery of a perfectly lovely dance." Lilly sighed with frustration. "We need an actual gentleman."

"Perhaps I could be of assistance."

Winnefred turned to find Gideon standing in the open door of the parlor. No, not standing, she amended, but leaning comfortably against the doorframe. How long, she wondered, had he been there, watching?

He smiled, straightened, and stepped into the room. "Would you do me the honor of dancing with me, Winnefred?"

Winnefred shot Lilly a quick smug expression. She had suggested asking Gideon to be her dance partner, but Lilly had insisted that such a request would show a grievous lack of sensitivity. "I would be delighted. Can you dance with your cane?"

"No." He leaned the cane against the wall. "But I can manage without it for a time, provided Lilly slows the tempo a little for me."

"You won't risk exacerbating your injury?"

"Not at all."

"Even if I should trod on your foot?" It was practically inevitable that she would.

"The injury was not to my foot," he assured her as he crossed the floor.

"Oh. What was the injury to?" She pretended not to see the look of censure from Lilly. The question was indelicate, perhaps, but if Gideon wasn't troubled by the topic, Winnefred saw no reason why anyone else should be.

"The upper leg. So, if you could avoid swinging your arms about below your waist, or kicking your feet up above the knees, I believe we'll do well enough."

The image made her laugh. "I shall do my best."

Lilly shuffled the papers on the piano. "If you are ready, we shall try the same dance again, but slower."

As she took her place across from Gideon, Winnefred considered what a strange sensation it was to stand in front of a man, quiet and unmoving while the lilting strains of a piano filled the room. It was strange enough, in fact, that she lost count of the beats and stepped toward Gideon's side too soon. He caught her round the waist with his arm, lifted her off her feet, and set her back down again in her spot. "Not quite yet, Winnefred. And wrong side."

The words barely registered, nor did the sound of the music stopping and Lilly's groan.

"Good heavens," Winnefred breathed, "you're strong as an ox."

He stepped back to his own spot. "Perhaps you're just dainty."

"We start again," Lilly announced.

"Dainty?" Though Winnefred knew herself to be a woman of small build, the description "dainty" was one she never expected to hear applied to herself. She found herself grinning at the very notion. "Lace is dainty."

"Not the sort my grandmother used to wear," Gideon replied, raising his voice a little as Lilly began to play once more. "Lucien and I stole some yards of her lace once and fashioned a very fine rope swing for the lake."

"She must have been furious."

"We never admitted to the crime. Step forward now."

"What? Oh." She moved forward offbeat and remembered to take his hand only after he held it out to her, but she managed to refrain from trampling him as they turned a circle around each other, and she thought that a fine start.

"Swings aside, I'm not sure I care for the word 'dainty,' " she commented. "It implies fragility."

"A fitting description."

"Oh, you can't be serious."

"All life is fragile."

"Unless you're Mr. Pirkle falling from his roof," she pointed out and remembered just in time to switch hands with him and turn in an opposite circle. "Perspective, I suppose."

"Perhaps it is," he conceded. "Step to the right."

She did and nearly tripped over her feet in an effort to catch back up to the beat.

"Concentrate, Freddie," Lilly called out.

She shared a smile of amusement with Gideon but followed Lilly's advice all the same, forgoing conversation for the sake of paying attention to the music and the steps. And what she soon discovered was that dancing with an actual gentleman truly did make a difference. She'd been jesting about merely following Bess's lead earlier, but now that she had Gideon as a partner, it did seem quite a bit easier to step when and where she ought. Admittedly, it also helped that Gideon periodically reached out to steer her in the right direction.

It wasn't fun in the same way it had been with Bess, with the two of them dizzy with laughter. It was a completely different kind of pleasure dancing with Gideon. Every time they touched hands or stood mere inches apart, a warmth spread over her skin, her pulse beat a little faster, and her breath caught as if she'd been dancing with him for hours.

When the song ended, she felt giddy and light-headed, and more than a little disappointed it was over. Lilly, on the other hand, appeared ecstatic. She applauded with considerable enthusiasm.

"Well done, Freddie. Very well done. Much improved. Shall we try it again? Or something new . . . Oh, a waltz." She looked to Gideon. "I presume your aunt will see to it she gains permission—?"

"Naturally," Gideon cut in, "but I'm afraid I must decline."

Winnefred's disappointment grew. She was quite certain in that moment she could spend the rest of the day dancing, as long as it was with him. "I can't persuade you to try another?"

He tapped a finger against his leg. "Would that I could."

"Oh, I'm sorry."

"No need." He retrieved his cane from the wall and turned to Lilly. "May I request a respite for all parties? There is something I wish to discuss with Winnefred."

"Oh. Well." Lilly glanced at the clock on the mantel. "I suppose a few minutes wouldn't hurt."

*G*ideon led Winnefred from the room with his hand wrapped in a tight fist around his cane. He shouldn't have come to the parlor. He'd known it was a mistake the moment he peered into the room.

He'd taken one look at Winnefred, her face lit by laughter, and he hadn't been able to resist offering to dance. He wanted to be the one she was laughing with, the one she was stumbling into. He wanted to dance with her and knew he might never have another chance. A reel at full speed was more than his leg could manage, but the slow stop-and-go method of a dancing lesson was well within his capabilities.

It was a damn good thing two dance lessons had not been within his capabilities. Every smile, every intentional brush of the hand and accidental bump of shoulders had been exquisite torture. A torture he would have gladly continued had he been able. For the first time, he was grateful—albeit begrudgingly so—for a limitation set on him by his injury.

He'd heard it said that infatuation with a woman could make a man feel drunk, but he'd never before experienced the sensation. He'd been intrigued by women in the past, charmed by them, and certainly desired them, but he'd never been in jeopardy of losing his head.

Gideon glanced at Winnefred as they stepped outside into the sunlight, and he decided it wasn't like being drunk. It was like being tipsy—with just enough sense left to know one more drink would propel a pleasant headiness into outright inebriation, but not enough sense left to keep from reaching for the bottle.

He shouldn't have reached for Winnefred in the parlor. He'd known it would be a mistake to offer his services as a dance partner. He'd known exactly what he was doing and exactly what the consequences would be. And he'd done it anyway.

"You're very quiet all of a sudden, Gideon."

There was a thread of uncertainty in Winnefred's voice, prompting him to make a conscious effort to set aside his frustration and relax the hand gripping his cane. He'd brought Winnefred outside to surprise her, not worry her. "My apologies. I was woolgathering."

"Does it have something to do with the messenger that came this morning?" She reached for his arm. "It's not bad news, is it?"

"Not at all." He could feel the warmth of her fingers through his coat sleeve. "It's something I have been anxious to receive. Something for you."

"For me?" She dropped her hand. "But—"

"My first morning here, I told you, and Lilly, you could have anything you wanted from the Engsly estate as restitution for my stepmother's crimes. You asked for nothing."

"That's not true. I asked not to go to London."

"So you did," he conceded with a smile. "Well, I hope this makes up for the denial of your request."

"But I have plenty, Gideon. I don't need—" She broke off when he pulled a folded piece of paper from his pocket and handed it to her. "What is this?"

"Look for yourself."

She unfolded the paper and read the tidy script. It was, in essence, a deed to Murdoch House, or as close to one as an unmarried woman could hope to retain within the constraints of the law. It granted Miss Winnefred Blythe the letting of Murdoch House for the period of five hundred years, the amount due for such a time having been recognized by the Engsly estate as having been paid in full. In addition, the contract, and all rights granted within, was transferrable upon death to the inheritor of her naming.

She stared at the contract a long time without speaking.

"Does it please you?" Gideon asked softly.

She looked at him, back to the contract, then back to him again. Her expression was one of shock and marvel. "It's . . . When . . . Can you do this?"

"I can and have. I wrote to my brother's solicitor last week and requested he draft the lease immediately."

"It's mine," she breathed. "Murdoch House is mine."

"To do with as you please. The contract clearly states you are not required to answer to the Engsly estate for the condition of the land. You can restore the house and grounds, run a hundred sheep on the land, or you could burn the house to the ground and build a haberdashery in its place. The choice is yours."

"I don't know what to say."

"I would give it to you in full, if I could."

"No. This is . . . This is plenty. So much more than . . . It's more than I'd thought to even imagine." The stunned look faded from her face, and in its place came wonder and unbridled joy. She laughed suddenly and, to his considerable surprise, stepped forward to throw her arms around him. "Oh, thank you. *Thank you.*"

Gideon told himself it was simply instinct that made him wrap his arms around her in return. Instinct and a need to regain his balance—she had bumped his cane, after all. But even as he made the excuses, he knew them to be lies.

He wanted the feel of her. He wanted the warmth and smell of her. He wanted a moment to feel surrounded by something good and beautiful and innocent, and he wanted to enjoy that moment without envisioning turning it into something decidedly . . . less innocent. But that, apparently, was too much to ask. The smell of lavender teased at his nose, and he could feel the soft weight of her breasts pressed against his chest. Every muscle in his body tightened. Carefully, ever so carefully, he disentangled himself and held her at arm's length.

If she noticed his discomfort, it didn't show. She was looking at him just as she had the day he'd brought Lilly a new gown, with that wonderful wide mouth grinning, and those beautiful amber eyes lit with happiness. He dropped his arms and took a step back.

"I'm glad it pleases you."

She laughed and held up the contract. "You've given me Murdoch House. Pleased does not begin to describe what I am. Overwhelmed, perhaps, or . . . Oh!" She danced a little in place, and the silliness of it made him chuckle, easing his tension. "Oh, I have to show Lilly. May I show Lilly? Do you mind?"

"Of course not. Why should I mind?"

"I haven't thanked you properly. But I don't know how. I . . . Thank you." She laughed again, a girlish bubbling sound of pure joy that pulled at his heart. She stepped up to give him a quick kiss on the cheek. "Thank you."

She grinned at him once more, then spun on her heel and raced toward the house. Gideon watched her go and found himself grinning in return when she let out one very unladylike hoot of excitement at the top of the front steps.

He lifted two fingers to his cheek where the warmth of her kiss still lingered and told himself there was nothing wrong with having pretended to be a knight-errant for a few minutes. Hadn't that been his intention when he'd first come to Scotland, to play the hero?

Yes, it had been, and he'd been confident in his ability to fill the role because his only task had been to hand over an apology and a bit of coin. His responsibility had been to literally *play* the hero. As long as he refrained from trying to actually be one, everyone would remain happy . . . and safe.

Chapter 11

Winnefred lifted her hand to knock on Gideon's door, hesitated, then dropped her arm. There was a possibility, a very real possibility, the conversation to come would result in a disagreement.

Just the idea of it made her wince. She didn't want to argue with Gideon. It had been little more than twenty-four hours since he'd given her Murdoch House. The monetary value of such a gift was staggering, but it was the kindness of it that had made her chest tighten and the air catch in her lungs when she had read the contract. Gideon had handed her a dream, as sure as he was handing one to Lilly by taking them to London.

She could scarcely wrap her mind around the enormity of what he had given her. Now here she was, standing outside his chambers, about to ask for more. And willing to argue with him to get it.

She shuffled her feet, bit her lip, and told herself she wasn't asking for a *great deal* more. Just a small favor. One she was requesting only because Lilly had insisted upon it, and she was only nervous to do so because Lilly had made such a fuss to start.

"A few hours of time," she mumbled to herself. "It's nothing, really."

And there was no reason for her to feel ill at the possibility of disagreeing with Gideon. He had given her a gift for which she would always be immeasurably grateful. Gratitude, however, should not be mistaken for obligation. She would ask him the favor, and if he had a problem with granting it, he could take the matter up with Lilly.

Pleased, if not entirely confident, with her line of reasoning, she knocked on Gideon's door and let herself in at his answer.

She found him seated in one of a pair of seats before the window, an open book in his lap.

He looked up and frowned at her a little. "Something the matter, Winnefred?"

"No. No." She sincerely hoped not. She crossed the room to stand before him and decided to get straight to the matter at hand. "Lilly has decided it is no longer appropriate for me to walk alone to the prison."

Strictly speaking, Lilly had never been of the opinion that it *was* appropriate, but there'd hardly been a choice in the matter.

Gideon stared at her a long, long moment before speaking. "I cannot adequately express the number and ways in which I am currently in agreement with Lilly. Why the *devil* have you been going to a prison? *Alone?*"

In the interest of avoiding an argument, she met his shock with calm composure. "Some of the guards are willing to pay a nice fee for a well-mended shirt or coat, and Lilly has always been gifted with a needle and thread."

"There is no longer any reason for either of you to be sewing for money. If there's something you need or want—"

"The work was done before you arrived, Gideon. We'd simply forgotten about it during all the commotion. I can't very well keep them, can I?"

"Of course not. Send one of the footmen."

Exactly what Lilly had told her, and exactly what she didn't want to hear, let alone *do*.

"I'd like to go myself, if it's not too much trouble." She refused to give in to the urge to start fidgeting. "I've . . . other business there."

"Other business," he repeated slowly. "At the prison."

His tone rankled. It was one thing for him to disapprove of her past behavior, but it was something else altogether to speak to her as if she were a dim-witted child. She tipped her chin up. "I believe I just said as much. Now, will you take me, or shall I go alone and leave you to explain to Lilly why you couldn't be pulled from your . . ." She leaned forward and cocked her head to look at his book. ". . . *Tales in Verse*, by Mr. George Crabbe, to see me safely a few miles down the road? . . . Do you really read poetry?"

He shut the book carefully, placed it on a side table carefully, and spoke so very carefully, he succeeded in unnerving her a little. "On occasion. Now, have a seat, Winnefred, and tell me, exactly, what this business of yours entails. If I find it unsatisfactory, a footman will deliver the shirts and coats. If I believe you've adequate reason for going, I'll consider taking you myself. You may, if you choose, inform Lilly of whichever course of action I have decided upon. But let us be clear—I *explain* myself to no one."

She considered him quietly. He hadn't shouted, or cursed, or even snapped at her. His voice had remained perfectly even. But the authority—in the tone, in the words—was all but palpable.

She took the seat across from him, suddenly fascinated. "I've been *wondering* how you managed to captain a ship for all those years. I was beginning to suspect you injured your leg during a bout of mutiny."

"Delighted to have satisfied your curiosity," he answered in the same unforgiving voice. "Your reasons, Winnefred. I'll have them now."

She sat up straighter in the chair. "I am not a sailor

aboard your ship to be ordered about. And my reasons are none of your concern."

"On the contrary, and to my considerable frustration at the moment, you, and everything you do, are my concern until I deliver you into the care of my aunt."

The mention of frustration at having to care for her until he could hand her over to someone else made her heart stutter and the edges of her vision turn red. It was an irrational and disproportionate reaction to an offhand comment, she knew, but she was helpless to stem the anger. She'd had her fill of being delivered from one person to the next as a child.

Her eyes narrowed to slits. "I have no interest in being anyone's burden, Gideon. And I will not be passed between members of the Haverston family like an inconvenient head cold."

She rose from her seat and turned to leave, but Gideon stood and caught her hand before she could escape.

"Sit down," he said softly.

"No." She tugged her arm. "Let go."

"Winnefred, please."

She stopped pulling at his plea but didn't resume her seat.

Gideon gave her arm a gentle squeeze. "My frustration is with this particular conversation, not with you. I apologize for my poor choice of words."

"The conversation is with me."

"It is not our first disagreement." He gave her a disarming smile. "Can we not settle this one as we have others?"

"I haven't a rifle to hit you with."

"We'll make do." He let his hand slide away. "Will you sit?"

She didn't want to, particularly, but neither did leaving in a fit of temper still appeal to her. She sat reluctantly.

Rather than follow suit, Gideon rested on the arm of his chair. "I received a letter from my aunt this morning. She is looking forward to having two young ladies in her house.

I apologize for giving the impression neither she nor I care for your company."

"A poor choice of words, as you said." Because she didn't care to have it known how deeply his words had cut, she shrugged and strove for a light tone. "Heaven knows I've no ground to stand on when it comes to choosing the correct words—"

"You've a right to be angry."

"Yes, I do. But I don't wish to be angry with you."

"I'm grateful for it." He bent his head a little to catch her eye. "Are we friends again?"

They were only words, she told herself. "I would like to be."

"Excellent. Then why don't we try broaching the subject of the prison once more, and see if we can't work our way toward an agreement."

"How do you propose we do that?"

"By starting from the beginning. Like this." He made a show of taking a proper seat in his chair and then cleared his throat dramatically—a silly affectation that succeeded in making her smile. "Winnefred, *dear*, would you care to tell me your reasons—which I'm certain are fine ones—for wanting to visit the prison?"

She winced, fisted her hands in her skirts, and twisted. "No. I really wouldn't."

A pained laugh escaped from Gideon. "Oh, for—"

"I'm not trying to be stubborn, Gideon. I'm not. I . . . Couldn't we try starting somewhere else?"

"No."

She went from twisting to tugging. "If I agreed to tell you, would you promise not to poke fun or lecture?"

"I'll promise to do my best not to hurt or discount your feelings. Will that do? If, however, you're about to inform me you've been playing cards and drinking scotch with the inmates, I'm going to lecture. And if you tell me you've been instructing the men in the art of needlepoint, I am most certainly going to laugh."

A laugh was clearly what he'd been hoping to gain from

her with that small speech, but she remained silent, avoiding his eyes and tugging on her dress.

In the face of her reticence, Gideon went very still except for the rounding of his eyes. "Holy hell. Tell me you have not been playing cards and drinking scotch—"

"Certainly not . . . Not the scotch part, anyway."

He lifted a hand to jab a finger at her. "You are never, *never* again to step foot in—"

"There's a young man," she cut in, desperate to explain before he finished his ultimatum. "A young man I wish to see."

He dropped his hand slowly. "A young man you play cards with?"

"No. Well, once, but only as a means of gaining trust."

"Of course. Cards and trust," he drawled. "They're naturally suited."

"They can be, when one makes certain to lose a sixpence and pays the debt on the next visit."

"Five pounds a year and you lost a sixpence on purpose?" He shook his head in disbelief. "Who *is* this man?"

"His name is Thomas, and he isn't a man. He's hardly more than a boy."

Gideon blinked at this bit of news, then relaxed against the back of his chair with a bit more emphasis than she thought was strictly necessary. "A boy."

"He can't be more than thirteen years of age, though he would insist otherwise. I certainly do not believe he is the fifteen he claims."

"Even a boy of thirteen can be dangerous," Gideon said quietly.

"No doubt. But Thomas was caught stealing oranges from a vendor's cart in Langholm. Hardly the act of a vicious criminal. He's so very young, Gideon, and I thought . . . I thought perhaps, if he had a skill, or a bit of education . . . I've been teaching him to read."

There was a long pause before Gideon spoke again. "I see. Why did you hesitate to tell me this?"

"Well, it's not entirely acceptable behavior for a lady, is it?"

"I've seen you in trousers, swearing, and talking to a goat."

"Yes, but that was before. Before you and Lilly set your sights on seeing me . . . I don't know—reformed, I suppose. I didn't want you to think I'm wholly incapable of being educated, or that I'm ungrateful. And then there's the fact that most people would think it foolish to teach a common thief to read—a senseless expenditure of time and effort."

"What I think," he said gently, "is that there are two very different sorts of ladies and gentlemen in the world. There are those, like Lady Engsly, who hold the title by the questionable virtue of birth and marriage. And then there are those who merit it by virtue of their actions. Your willingness to help this young boy exhibits, in abundance, the very quality used to define what it means to be a lady—grace."

A flush of pleasure heated her cheeks and rendered her temporarily mute.

Gideon's lips twitched. "I take it you haven't yet had a lesson regarding the appropriate responses to a compliment."

"There are *lessons* for that?" She held up her hand and shook her head. "Never mind, I don't wish to know. Does this mean you'll take me, then? To the prison?"

"It would be my pleasure."

Winnefred didn't argue when Lilly suggested the carriage be used. It was only sensible, given Gideon's need to use a cane. She argued quite vehemently, however, when Lilly also insisted upon Bess accompanying them for the trip.

"I am going to a prison. A prison I have visited quite on my own a hundred times in the past." More important, she was distinctly uncomfortable having someone watching over her as if she were an ill-behaved five-year-old.

"A hundred is a considerable exaggeration," Lilly argued. "And this time, you are going as a well-bred young lady in the company of a gentleman. Bess will accompany."

"But—"

Lilly held a hand up. "Bess may ride up top with Peter, the driver, if she is amendable to idea."

"Is that permissible in London?" she asked, mostly out of curiosity.

"If I told you no, would you stop arguing?" Lilly sighed when Winnefred shook her head. "I rather thought not. A compromise this time, but you must learn to become accustomed to having a maid about. You've a reputation to consider now."

Winnefred, who had previously given her reputation only the minimum of consideration, rolled her eyes at this bit of reasoning but thought better of arguing further. Lilly had agreed to let her go, Gideon had agreed to take her, Bess would ride up top, and a solid two to three hours of lessons would be avoided.

One shouldn't look a gift horse in the mouth too often . . . Especially when that horse moved at an exceedingly slow pace, thus extending her freedom. Winnefred estimated she could have made it to the prison and returned half the mended clothes by the time the carriage was readied and its occupants settled.

She set her basket of shirts and coats on the floor as the carriage started down the drive with a jolt. "It would have been faster to walk."

Across from her, Gideon smiled. "But not as comfortable."

The carriage hit a large bump, forcing her to throw a hand out to the wall. "Doesn't feel particularly comfortable to me."

"When was the last time you rode in a carriage?"

"When I came to Scotland with Lilly." And if she remembered correctly, she hadn't found that an easy experience either. "I didn't care for it."

"It was a difficult time for you," he said softly.

"It wasn't just that." She frowned a little, remembering. "I wasn't feeling well. I had a touch of the ague."

"That would certainly leach the pleasure from a trip."

The carriage rocked over a series of ruts at the entrance to the drive and he added, "So can a very rough road."

"How did you find the roads on your way to Murdoch House?"

"In better condition than this one," Gideon replied and used his foot to keep the basket from sliding across the floor.

The movement served to emphasize how much of the small space was taken up by his large frame. He was so close, she could smell his soap. A few more inches and their knees would be brushing. Well, a foot, she conceded, but that still qualified as close.

Perhaps she would enjoy traveling. She hadn't given that aspect of their trip to London much thought until now. She would have days of sitting across from Gideon. There would be hours and hours to talk and laugh and ponder over what it was about the man that so thoroughly captivated her. Her eyes darted to his mouth, and she wondered what it might be like to lean over and press her lips to the very corner—

The carriage hit another rut, nearly unseating her and putting a quick end to the idea of trying to maneuver gracefully into a kiss with Gideon. Amused at the brief image she had of the two of them knocking heads, she swallowed a chuckle and took a firm grip on the front of her seat to steady herself.

"What shall we do to pass the time?" she asked.

"Right now?"

"No." She laughed. "On our way to London."

"Ah. Mostly, I'll be concentrating on staying upright in the saddle. It's a long trip."

"Oh." Deflated, and hoping he wouldn't notice, she made a show of looking out the window. "You'll be on horseback, then."

"For the most part." He pointed out the window as the carriage topped a small rise and the prison came into view. "That it?"

Because there was nothing she could do about Gideon's

decision to ride alongside the carriage instead of in it, she set the matter aside and wrinkled her nose at the hulking mass of dark stone. "Yes. Hideous, isn't it?"

Gideon leaned forward for a slightly closer inspection. "Not as ugly as Newgate. Newer as well, isn't it? I imagine it smells better."

She turned from the window to give him an incredulous look. "Smells better? That's all you have to say about that monstrosity? It stinks less?"

"A dubious distinction, I grant." He settled back against the cushions. "Except for those who have had the misfortune of spending time in both."

"I . . ." She hated to admit he had a point. "It's still a prison. No place for a boy."

"You'll have no argument from me on that score." He tilted his head at her. "How is it you met this Thomas? I thought you mended the shirts of guards."

"We mended the shirts of anyone able to pay for the service, including the prisoners."

"Interesting," he said in a cool tone, "that you should forget to mention that."

She hadn't forgotten. It just hadn't seemed wise to make a point of it. "Hmm. At any rate, one of the prisoners with funds enough to wear a decent shirt is named Connor. He's being held on charges of highway robbery, but I don't think he's guilty. He—"

"Highway robbery?" Gideon's face went blank for a split second before he lifted his cane and pounded on the roof of the carriage. "Stop!"

She scooted forward on her seat as the carriage slowed. "What? What are you doing?"

The driver's voice sounded from overhead. "Something wrong, my lord?"

"Yes! No! A moment, Peter!" Gideon dropped his arm and turned to her, his face a mask of stone. "*Highway robbery?* That is a hanging offense, Winnefred. What were you thinking associating with a man—?"

"I was thinking how much I needed the coin," she retorted

and was gratified to see his mouth snap shut. "I met Thomas because he was put in the cell next to Connor and his men."

"His men," Gideon repeated slowly. "Wonderful."

"They are, in fact. They've been very kind to Thomas."

"You believe they show the boy kindness for selfless reasons?" he scoffed.

"There isn't a selfless bone in Connor's body, that I can see," she admitted. "But an alliance with Connor, however selfishly offered, will serve Thomas better in prison than a handful of letters taught by me out of pity or—"

He held a hand up to cut her off, but it was a moment more before he spoke. She used that moment to watch a muscle work in his jaw.

"You're right," he finally ground out. "But on that point only. What do you think will become of Thomas when he is released?"

"I . . ." She shifted in her seat. "I may have offered him temporary shelter at Murdoch House."

He closed his eyes and took a deep breath through his nose. "Five pounds a year and you—"

"*Temporary* shelter. Only until he was able to find work and a home of his own." She shifted again. "What was I to do? He's only a child."

From the hard set of his features, she expected him to begin a very long list of things she might have done instead, but he said nothing. He simply sat there, studying her, the muscle still working in his jaw.

"Are we going to continue on?" she ventured after a moment.

"Yes, eventually."

"Well, what are we waiting for?"

"For me to decide whether or not I will allow you to step foot in that prison."

"What?" She gaped at him. "But you promised."

"I said I would take you to the prison, and so I shall." He hesitated, then lifted the cane to bang on the roof once more. "But you'll not meet with Connor and his men."

"Of course I will. I've a shirt—"

"You may give it to one of the guards to deliver."

"Thomas is in the next cell over. I can't possibly meet with him and not—"

"I'll see to it Thomas is brought to another room."

"You can't do . . ." She remembered he was Lord Gideon Haverston, brother to the Marquess of Engsly. "Very well, you can, but it's ridiculous, and I won't agree to—"

"You'll obey me on this, Winnefred."

Obey?

"Of all the high-handed, preposterous ultimatums . . ." She squared her shoulders and glared at him. "I will meet with whom I see fit."

If he was at all moved by her display of temper, it didn't show. "I understand you are accustomed to doing as you please, but I cannot allow you to continue to put yourself in danger."

"And I cannot allow you to continue under the misconception that you have any command over where I go and what I do. I requested your company today for Lilly's sake, nothing more. You are not my guardian, not my father, and not my husband—"

He jabbed a finger at her. "In about two seconds, I am going to be the man who hauls you back to Murdoch House and locks you in your chambers."

She sat back in her seat, folded her arms over her chest, and bestowed on him her most arrogant and defiant expression. It was, according to Lilly, a very impressive look indeed.

"Oh, do try," she challenged.

To her surprise, and considerable irritation, she saw his lips twitch. It made her want to hitch her skirts up and kick him in the shins. "You find this amusing?"

"A bit, yes. I've not had a woman lay a physical challenge at my feet before." The twitch grew into a smirk. "I'm twice your size, Winnefred."

"I'm spry," she ground out and looked at his cane pointedly. "And not above reaching for a weapon, you will recall."

To her mounting annoyance, he laughed at her. "You would beat me with my own cane."

No, but she hadn't any qualms about threatening it. She opened her mouth to deliver a scathing comment, but he stopped her by reaching out and tapping her gently under the chin with his finger. "Come now. It's a disagreement, not a duel. Put your anger away."

She pressed her lips together to silence the instinctive refusal sitting on the tip of her tongue. Though she felt her anger was warranted in light of his high-handed behavior, giving in to the urge to pummel the man wasn't likely to advance her cause.

"I will agree to put my anger away"—or try, at any rate—"if you will agree to letting me go into the prison without a fuss."

He shook his head and let his hand fall. "If I allow you to go in there and something happens to you, Lilly will never trust me again."

"Lilly has met Connor. She knows he is of no danger to me. He and his men are . . ."

"Are what?" he prompted.

"They're . . . not friends, exactly. But we are friendly."

"Friendly," he repeated. "You are friendly with highwaymen."

"Oh, do stop saying highwaymen like that. I told you, I don't think they're guilty." A new tactic occurred to her. "Besides, isn't protection the point of having a gentleman present? Surely you can keep me safe from a man behind iron bars."

His eyes flicked away. "I make a poor knight-errant."

She disagreed wholeheartedly, but it didn't seem the time to debate the matter. "I don't require rescuing."

"Not for lack of trying, it would seem."

She would not, would *not*, lose her temper again. There was nothing to be gained by it. "You should at least let me introduce them to you before you pass judgment."

The muscle began to work in his jaw again, and she wondered if that was a good sign, or bad. "Very well," he finally announced. "I will on one condition."

"What condition?"

"If, upon meeting these men, I decide you would be better off outside the prison—"

"It's a prison. Everyone is better off outside—"

"If I tell you to leave," he said coolly, "you will leave. Immediately. No arguments, Winnefred."

"What of Thomas?"

"I've given you my terms. Do you agree to them?"

She considered it. Naturally, ceding to his demands was not an option. If Gideon thought he had the right to limit her freedom, he was sorely mistaken. But they were even now pulling in front of the prison gates. If she refused, he would turn the carriage around and take them back to Murdoch House. Possibly, he would attempt to lock her in her chambers. Certainly, she would resist. It would all be very ugly.

"I think it's ridiculous, but I will leave today if you demand it." And come back, she silently added, another time.

Because his eyes narrowed as if he suspected the direction of her thoughts, she made good her escape from the carriage the very second it stopped.

"Miss?" Bess's voice called from atop the carriage, and Winnefred looked up to see the maid twisting a strand of strawberry blonde hair around her finger and eyeing the prison with obvious trepidation. "Am I to accompany you . . . in there?"

She had absolutely no idea.

"That won't be necessary," Gideon called out as he exited the carriage and handed Winnefred her basket. "You may stay here with Peter."

"Aye, my lord." Bess visibly relaxed in her seat. "Thank you."

Winnefred waited until a guard showed them through the gates before glancing over her shoulder at the maid.

"Why did you let Bess stay with the carriage?" she asked Gideon.

"Because I didn't fancy the idea of carrying her out if she fainted."

He took her arm and led her through the front door of the prison. The air inside was close and warm, despite the coolness of the day, and held the distinct scent of old straw, unwashed bodies, and mildew, none of which seemed to trouble Gideon in the least. He sniffed once and nodded.

"I was right. It smells better."

"I'll have to take your word on that." She smiled when a young man with a long face and earnest blue eyes emerged from a room off the main hall to greet them. "Mr. Clarkson."

Mr. Clarkson started and blinked at her; his eyes darted to Gideon, then back to her. "Miss Blythe?"

"As you see." She laughed, realizing for the first time what a surprise her alteration in appearance must be to those who were accustomed to seeing her in her old gown. "Lord Gideon Haverston, Mr. Ronald Clarkson. Mr. Clarkson is to thank for granting Lilly and I permission to visit the . . ." She trailed off as Gideon's eyes narrowed and Mr. Clarkson paled. "That is . . . How is your wife, Mr. Clarkson?"

"Very well. Very well, thank you. We have a son . . . Last week."

"Oh, that's wonderful."

"Yes, I . . ." He glanced at Gideon again, cleared his throat, and gestured down the hall. "I'll just . . . I'll just fetch someone to show you about, shall I?"

Winnefred turned to Gideon as Mr. Clarkson disappeared down the hall. "You frightened him."

"I didn't say a word to the man."

"You didn't need to." She gestured at him with her free hand. "You just stand there, looking . . . foreboding. I'm sure it can be very disconcerting for some."

"Can it?" He frowned a little in thought. "I find that surprisingly rewarding to hear."

She rolled her eyes and pushed her basket at him. "Here. If you cannot be pleasant, you can at least be useful."

Chapter 12

*G*ideon didn't feel useful quite so much as he did self-
conscious. There was something vaguely embarrassing about limping through a prison with a cane in one hand
and a basket in the other.

The guard Mr. Clarkson assigned to them, a taciturn
sort by the name of Mr. Holloway, led them down a series
of windowless halls and through a number of locked doors,
stopping here and there to allow Winnefred to exchange
shirts for coins with guards.

Gideon had considered suggesting she return the shirts
without accepting pay but knew she would refuse. Not
because she wanted the coin, but because she wouldn't
want to insult the men who had agreed to pay. He wished
now he had made an argument for it anyway. Every trade
of money for goods felt like salt on a wound. He couldn't
help but wonder how often she had done this alone, and
how often Lilly had stayed up late into the night, plying
her thread and needle by the dim light of a single candle.

"Here you are, my lord, miss." The guard unlocked
another door. It opened with what Gideon considered an

ominous creak of the hinges. "Just give a knock when you're ready to leave."

Gideon stepped through into a wide hall with three sets of long cells on each side. A narrow window, midway up the wall of each cell, let in stingy slivers of light. Men lounged about on the floor and in piles of straw. Some slept; a few paced the length of the cells. Those who spoke did so in muted tones.

Winnefred stepped in behind him and the quiet of the space was immediately lost. Men on each side stepped forward to greet her with good cheer and good-natured teasing. Winnefred greeted them each in return, but her attention, Gideon noted, was on the two cells on the far right. He assessed the occupants of the first with a quick but thorough glance. An elderly man sat lounging on a pile of straw. A middle-aged man with heavy jowls and a round middle sat in the cell's only chair, and a tall man near his own age with dark blond hair stood leaning against the wall by the window.

Gideon's gaze jumped to the second cell where a dark-haired boy with a cherub face stood looking out from the bars. It had to be Thomas, he thought. Winnefred was right—the boy was nowhere near to fifteen. He looked to be closer to twelve, and innocent with it. His enormous brown eyes reminded Gideon of his brother's bloodhounds. Thomas's bravado, however, reminded him of his boys aboard the *Perseverance*.

Thomas jerked his chin in Gideon's direction. "Who's that, then, Freddie?"

The tall man in the next cell smirked. "What's the matter with you, Thomas, don't you know a lord when you see one?"

"I know a mark," the boy answered with a grin. "He a nob like you, then?"

"No." The man crossed his arms over his chest. "He's not like me."

"Aye!" someone called jovially. "He'll no have his neck stretched for one—!"

"Shut up, MacCurry!" several people—Winnefred included—called at once and without much heat.

Winnefred turned to Gideon. "Lord Gideon Haverston, may I present Thomas Brown." She gestured at the boy, then motioned to the tall man in the other cell. "And Connor . . . er, Connor . . ."

"Connor will do," the man finished for her.

She gave him an annoyed look. "Fine. Connor Willdo. That's Michael Birch in the chair, and the gentleman sitting on the pile of straw is Mr. Gregory O'Malley. Gentlemen, this is Lord Gideon Haverston."

Gideon noticed she reserved the honorific for the elderly gentleman on the straw but refrained from commenting. He nodded his head in acknowledgment but kept his eyes on Connor. Of all the men in the hall, Connor struck him as the most dangerous. And the most out of place. Gideon had expected to find a man like all the others in that wing of the prison—poor, coarse, and rough of manner, but Connor had the speech of an educated man and the fashionable, albeit worn, clothes of a gentleman.

Gideon wondered if he was a man of good birth fallen on hard times, or if he'd stolen the clothes off someone's back.

Michael Birch leaned back in his chair. "Lord Gideon Haverston, is it?"

"Yes," Winnefred answered. "He is the brother of my guardian, Lord Engsly."

"Guardian," Conner repeated and flicked pale blue eyes at Gideon. "Bit late, aren't you?"

"Very," Gideon replied, uninterested in defending himself to a stranger. He gave Winnefred's elbow a soft nudge toward the next cell. "Don't you have a lesson?"

"Wait, lass." Gregory held his hand up, then moved to dig through his pile of straw. "Wait. Look what I made for you."

He stood up with a helping hand from Connor and stepped to the bars to present Winnefred with a small wooden carving of a woman with a young toddler on her hip. Gregory had captured perfectly the sleepy contentment of a well-loved child, but it was the woman who drew the eye. She held the child close, his head against her shoulder, her hand upon his hair in a gesture of love and protection. But her eyes stared at something in the distance. There was worry there, disappointment, and the very beginnings of fear.

"It's beautiful," Winnefred whispered. Gideon took hold of it through the bars and handed it to her. She held it carefully and turned it over in her hands. "Magnificent. You've outdone yourself, Gregory. Mr. McKeen would be a fool to pay you anything less than a half pound for this. Her face, her eyes . . . who is she? Is she real?"

"Sure and she's real. It was Connor who was noticing her first. Staring out the window of a Saturday, not bothering to tell the rest of us there was something worth looking at. Sweet on her, our Connor."

Connor acknowledged the small joke with a half smile that neither admitted nor denied the truth in what Gregory had said.

Gregory snorted, then winked at Winnefred. "And that's the most you'll be getting out of Connor on the matter."

"Is she the wife of one of the guards, do you think?"

"She's not, no. She visits the debtors' wing. Bringing the boy to see his da, I think."

"It's a fine piece," Gideon commented. And it would have taken a fine knife to fashion it. He took the carving from Winnefred and put it in her empty basket. "You'll want to begin your lesson with Thomas if you mean to be done before dark."

When she nodded and murmured an agreement, he took one of a pair of chairs by the hall door and set it in front of Thomas's cell for her, then he settled into the other chair to wait and watch.

Winnefred, he soon discovered, was a natural teacher—patient and encouraging. And Thomas was an exceptional student—interested, eager, and clever. Very clever, Gideon amended. For having only a handful of lessons under his belt, the boy had an impressive grasp of the written word.

He enjoyed watching the two of them, and because he did, he made no move to hurry her along as the thin beams of light from the windows stretched across the cell floors. It wasn't until that light begin to grow orange that he reminded Winnefred of the time.

She looked up from her work with Thomas and blinked as if she'd forgotten where they were. "Oh, yes, of course. Just . . . Just one more moment."

Winnefred handed a small stack of papers and a book back to Thomas and bent her head in the manner of someone about to begin a discussion of considerable import. Gideon listened to her explain her upcoming trip to London. "Please tell me you'll go to Murdoch House if you're released in my absence. I'll make certain the staff expects you. There's work for you there, Thomas, and a safe place to stay. I'll be back in the summer and we can begin our lessons again."

The boy lifted a shoulder, a perfect mimic of Connor's casual disregard, but even in the dim light of the prison, Gideon could see the flush of pleasure on his face. Murdoch House would have another mouth to feed soon enough.

Winnefred appeared far less sure of it. After trying and failing to gain a promise from Thomas, she walked away from the cell and said her good-byes to Connor and his men with a line of worry across her brow.

Gideon knocked on the hall door and bent to speak softly in Winnefred's ear. "You needn't worry over Thomas. He'll come to Murdoch House."

She looked both hopeful and skeptical. "Do you think so?"

"Wouldn't have said it otherwise."

The heavy door unlocked with a click and swung open. Winnefred held her peace until they were on the other side, following Mr. Holloway through the shadowy halls of the prison once again.

"But why wouldn't Thomas say so?" she eventually whispered.

"Because he is a boy in the company of men."

"Oh. I hadn't thought of that." She pondered that for a while before asking, "Do you think Connor will stand in his way?"

He shook his head. "He isn't dangerous to you, or to Thomas."

She didn't look surprised at his change of opinion so much as she did curious and expectant. "Oh, what changed your mind?"

"I think he took his men in out of charity."

"Gregory and Michael are not charity."

"They're certainly not highwaymen," he countered easily. "Gregory is an old man and Michael Birch looks as if he couldn't climb atop a horse if his life depended on it."

"I was hoping you would notice that." She looked decidedly smug. "Told you they weren't guilty."

"Of that particular crime, anyway."

*W*innefred decided to ignore Gideon's last comment in favor of relishing her small victories as long as possible. Thomas would come to Murdoch House, and Gideon had admitted—more or less—that she'd been right about Connor and his men.

She was smiling to herself as they stepped out of the prison into the dying light of the setting sun, and still smiling when Gideon assisted her into the carriage.

He climbed in behind her, settled himself on the seat, and quite out of the blue, asked, "Did you bring Gregory a knife?"

"What?" She put a hand out to the wall to steady herself as the carriage began to fight its way down the rutted road. "Where did that question come from?"

"Curiosity. Concern. Take your pick. Did you bring him the knife he used to carve that figurine?"

"No, of course not. I did see him with it once, though, and agreed to not say anything if he promised to keep it on his person at all times and only use it for his carvings." She shrugged. "I bring him the wood, and Lilly and I sell the pieces to Mr. McKeen in Enscrum. He has a small shop on the square."

"And what does Gregory pay you for your trouble?"

"It isn't any trouble."

"I thought so," he murmured. He studied her, his dark eyes unreadable, until she fairly squirmed in her seat.

"What?" She gave a small, uneasy laugh. "What is it?"

"How is it you came by Claire?"

She couldn't begin to imagine what Claire had to do with anything. "What on earth are you talking about?"

"You have a goat you neither milk, breed, nor show any intention of eating. In essence, a completely useless animal. Why?"

"Claire is not useless," she retorted. "She . . . grazes on the lawn. Keeps it quite tidy."

He didn't bother responding to that bit of nonsense. He just looked at her in silence until she caved.

"Oh, very well. We found her on the road to Enscrum. I imagine she belonged to a farmer passing through on the way to market, but no one returned to claim her so . . ."

"She's old, isn't she, no longer capable of breeding?"

"Yes."

"And yet you keep her."

"She has value to me."

She was a little afraid he would poke fun at her for the sentiment, but he merely nodded and said, "You've an extraordinary capacity for sympathy."

It was dizzying the way his mind jumped from topic to topic. "No different than any other's."

He tapped a finger against his leg, thinking. "You're right."

"I am?" She frowned at him, uncertain if she was pleased or disappointed to have won the argument so easily.

"It isn't your sympathy that's unusual," he explained. "It's your empathy."

Suddenly, she regretted having argued against his sympathy theory. "I did not empathize with a goat."

"The fact she was a goat had nothing to do with it. It was the fact she was lost."

"I've never been lost," she replied, deliberately mis-understanding his meaning. "I have a superb sense of direction."

"There are different kinds of lost," he said gently. "Even a superb sense of direction will get you nowhere if you have nowhere to go."

She knew he was speaking of her life immediately after her father's death. She wished he wouldn't. She was no more comfortable receiving sympathy from him than she was speaking of her own. "I had Murdoch House."

"Only after my father refused to take you in." He surprised her by chuckling softly and turning his eyes to the window. "I wonder what it would have been like, had my father kept his promise and cared for you himself."

"I'm sure the results would not have been the least amusing."

"A young girl with a penchant for bringing home every stray, wounded, and lost human and beast to cross her path? It would have had its moments."

"I don't bring home every stray I come across," she argued, mostly because she wanted to be done with the subject of being lost.

"Not for lack of wanting."

She smiled sweetly. "I wanted to drop you in the loch."

His gaze snapped away from the window. "Beg your pardon?"

"The night we dragged you out of the stable, I suggested to Lilly we drop you into the loch." Strictly speaking, she'd said it was a pity they'd missed the opportunity to send Lord Gideon Haverston to the bottom of the loch, but that was close enough.

He ran his tongue slowly across his teeth. "I stand corrected."

"To give your argument due, you weren't lost, exactly, and you weren't livestock."

If he had a comment for that, she would never hear it.

The carriage suddenly jolted violently, knocking her to the floor, and for a split second, it felt as if the whole of it would tip on its side. But after a few terrifying heartbeats, it slammed back down to the road and came to an abrupt stop.

Gideon's strong hands wrapped around her arms and pulled her up. "Winnefred. Winnefred, are you hurt?"

"I'm all right."

"You're certain?"

"Yes. Yes." Her knees stung a little from hitting the floor, but other than that she felt fine and oddly calm. "You?"

The moment he nodded, she reached for the carriage door and threw it open. "Bess! Peter!"

"Here, miss!"

Bess's voice came from the other side of the carriage, and Winnefred's calm disappeared in an instant. Bloody hell, the girl had been thrown from the top of the carriage.

"Oh, no." She scrambled for the door, but Gideon was the first to reach it and Bess.

She was sitting up, which was a relief, but her face was pinched with pain, and her hands gripped her leg above the ankle.

Gideon crouched down in front of her. "Here now, let me see."

"'Tis nothing," Bess said between gritted teeth. "Twisted my ankle, is all."

"I'm sure you're right, but let me see anyway." Gideon gently brushed her hands away. Winnefred saw that his own hands were steady, and his voice was reassuring, but his face was pale . . . much too pale.

"Gideon, are you certain you're unharmed?"

"Yes."

He didn't spare her so much as a glance; his attention was focused entirely on Bess. He inspected the ankle carefully, poking and prodding every inch of the injury. "Just a minor sprain," he finally pronounced, and Winnefred could have sworn she saw the color flow back to his skin. "A very minor sprain. You should be back on your feet in a day, two at most."

Bess nodded and adjusted her skirts. "Aye, my lord. The pain's easing already."

Winnefred blew out a hard breath of relief and took stock of their surroundings. The horses and carriage were still on the road and looked remarkably untouched, as if they'd simply come to a calm and steady stop and were merely awaiting their master's order to start again.

"What the devil happened?"

Peter gestured at something behind her. She turned and saw a deep, wide rut stretched halfway across the road.

"Oh."

"I'm sorry, my lord," Peter offered to Gideon. "We were set to miss it, but Samson there threw a shoe, stumbled, and pulled right into it. There weren't time to stop."

Gideon stood and gave Peter a quick, hard pat on the shoulder. "There's no blame in a thrown shoe. Let's see how he fares."

Winnefred peered over Gideon's shoulder as he inspected the horse's leg. "Is he injured?"

"No. Just has a bit of bruising, I suspect. Bad luck all around, eh, Samson? Free them of the harnesses please, Peter." Gideon stepped back and looked to Bess. "Can you ride a horse?"

"No, my lord."

He glanced at Peter, who nodded as he worked. "Aye. Well enough."

"Good. You'll take Bess back to the house on Odin, quick as you can."

"Aye."

"Miss Blythe and I will walk with Samson."

Bess's gaze shot from Peter to Gideon. "Begging your pardon, my lord, but Miss Ilestone is bound to have objections. It'll be dark before you—"

"Miss Ilestone may lodge her complaints with me upon my return, and after she's sent for a physician for you."

"A physician? But it's only—"

"No arguments." Gideon finalized the command by walking away to help unhitch the far horse.

Bess stared after him, then sent Winnefred a pleading look. Winnefred shook her head. "You were thrown from a moving carriage, Bess. You'll have to suffer being idle and spoiled for a few days."

Bess leaned forward to whisper, "But a physician, miss? It isn't necessary."

She was inclined to agree, but since she wasn't the one who would have to sit through the poking and prodding, it was easy for her to defend the idea. "Lord Gideon seems to think otherwise, and I trust his judgment."

Bess kept her peace until the horses were freed and she was set before Peter on Odin. She made one last attempt to argue for all of them returning together, but Gideon effectively silenced her by giving the horse a quick swat on the hindquarters, sending it off at a brisk trot.

Chapter 13

Gideon exhaled slowly. Bess would be fine. Her ankle might ache for a time, but she would heal.

There had been a minute when he'd seen Bess on the ground that he had imagined the worst and had imagined himself responsible. A thousand recriminations had run through his mind. He shouldn't have agreed to take Winnefred to the prison. He shouldn't have agreed to take Bess along as well. He sure as hell should not have agreed to Bess riding up top.

His reaction was irrational and he knew it. Horses threw shoes. Carriages fell into potholes and ruts. The top of the carriage was made to ride on. He hadn't even been the one driving, for pity's sake. But he'd not been able to completely shake his doubts until he'd assessed Bess's injuries for himself.

Winnefred stepped in his line of sight. "Are you all right, Gideon?"

He forced aside his uneasiness and smiled at her. "Well enough."

"Is it your leg? Will the walk be too far?"

"I can manage a couple of miles." His leg would pain him for it later, but that too could be managed.

"It's only that, just now, you looked . . ."

He grinned at her. "Lost?"

"A bit, yes," she replied with a smile of her own. "Shall I take you home?"

"I'd be grateful for it."

He grabbed a lantern from the carriage, took hold of Samson's lead, and set them off at a leisurely pace.

Gideon had always found long walks to be beneficial for clearing the mind, and with Winnefred for company, the trip to Murdoch House proved to be twice as effective in lifting his spirits. Every time he looked over at her, his mood improved, and so he told himself it was only sensible that he look over as often as possible.

She fit here, he thought. She looked natural strolling along a dusty road in the countryside, swinging her bonnet back and forth by the ribbons like a toy. She brushed at the strands of hair that had fallen from their pins, kicked idly at rocks until her hem and shoes were covered in red dirt, and pointed out plants and birds she recognized until the fields grew dim and silent.

"Where did you learn all that?" he inquired, stopping to light the lantern he'd taken from the carriage.

"From Lilly mostly. And a book we found in the attic." She took the lantern from him. "We may not need this. There's to be a full moon tonight."

He took her by the shoulders, gently turned her about, and pointed to the horizon where the moon was just appearing as a fiery golden orb. "And there it is."

"Oh, it's enormous," Winnefred breathed. "Like the sun rising all over again. Can one see the moon in London?"

He glanced at her in surprise. "Of course."

"Lilly says the lamps in Mayfair make the stars less vibrant."

"You can still see them," he assured her. "And the moon, though not quite so well when it comes up like this."

"I don't mind." She shrugged and turned to resume their

walk. "The countryside ought to have its own charms. Although, I should be interested to see what the night sky looks like from Hyde Park."

He considered that statement for a few minutes. "You do realize this sort of thing has to stop once we reach London?"

"Visiting prisons, do you mean?"

"Well, yes." He pictured Winnefred in the bowels of Newgate. "Absolutely, yes. But I was referring to midnight strolls with gentlemen."

She snorted at that, a small sound that was somehow both delicate and brash. "It's eight o'clock at the latest."

"It's dark, and if you were seen, you'd be ruined."

"And Lilly by association," she grumbled. "It wouldn't matter, I suppose, that we were stranded through no fault of our own."

"No."

"It's very unfair." She hopped over a rut in the road. "On the other hand, if it's dark, how would anyone see?"

"The lamps," he reminded her.

"Then it wouldn't truly be dark, would it? It . . ." She trailed off as they topped a small rise and Murdoch House came into view. The light of the moon reflected off the stone, and candlelight flickered in the windows. The entire house appeared to glow.

Winnefred stopped and set down the lantern.

"Oh, isn't it lovely. And mine, because of you." She turned to face him and smile. "Thank you."

Because she was there, because there was moonlight lighting her upturned face, and because he thought in that moment she was the most beautiful thing he'd ever seen, he bent his head and kissed her.

He managed, just for the time it took to lean down, to fool himself into thinking it would be a quick and simple thing. A harmless thing. But the second his lips met hers, the kiss became anything but simple and everything but harmless.

Her mouth began to move under his—with the innocence

of an untutored girl at first, and then with the irresistible
demand of an impatient woman, as if he was a new treat
she'd only just discovered. One she was determined to
devour in a single bite.

The effect was devastating. Desire, a smoldering ember
only moments before, leapt into flame. He let go of Samson's
lead and cupped the back of Winnefred's neck so he
could bring her closer and slant his mouth across hers at
the angle of his liking.

He had demands of his own.

He wanted to hear her sigh and feel her yield.

He drew his thumb along the underside of her jaw until
he reached her chin. Gently, he pressed until she opened for
him and he could slip his tongue inside the warm cavern
of her mouth. She tasted like heaven—unbearably sweet,
impossible to refuse.

She sighed for him then, a soft feminine sound that
fanned the flame into an inferno. It seared through his
belly and blistered his skin.

He was only vaguely aware of his own answering growl,
of dropping his hand to band an arm around her waist and
drag her hard against him. He felt the press of her soft
breasts against his chest and the hot puff of her breath
against his mouth. But it wasn't enough.

He needed the scent of her around him, the taste of her
inside him.

In his mind's eye, he saw himself dragging off her gown
and pulling her to the ground. He imagined her pale skin
glowing in the moonlight and shivering with anticipation
and helpless need in the cool night air.

He imagined taking his time with her, making her
wait while he stroked the smooth, lovely length of her with
his hands, while he laved the delicate skin of her breasts
with his tongue and teased her nipples taut with his mouth
and teeth. He imagined exploring every silken inch of
her at his leisure and watching her shivers turn to trembling
and her soft sighs to desperate moans. Then, when
he'd had his fill of tormenting them both, when she was lost

in the throes of passion, he would slip between her legs and
bury himself in the wet heat of her.

He could see it all clearly.

Much, much too clearly.

Winnefred reveled in the kiss, in the delicious feeling
of Gideon's arm banded about her waist and his hard
body bent over her own. His mouth moved over hers in
rough demand, and she was lost in the foreign sensations
of being overwhelmed and overpowered.

And then, suddenly, she wasn't—not overpowered, not
overwhelmed, and certainly not kissing. Gideon had pulled
away abruptly. One moment he was kissing her senseless
and the next moment they were standing a solid three feet
apart.

She stared at him, stupefied. Had she done something
wrong? Surely not. Surely kissing wasn't that complicated
a business. It was exhilarating and bewildering and had left
her decidedly muddled. But it wasn't something a person
could fail at, was it?

Nervous, she licked swollen lips and tasted him on her
tongue. "Gideon?"

"I apologize." His voice was rough and his breathing
ragged. "I'm sorry."

"I'm not." The words came without thought, but she saw
no reason to wish them back. It was only the truth.

Gideon made a pained sound in the back of his throat
and retreated another step.

She couldn't think of anything to say to that. She didn't
know what to make of it. Perhaps she *had* done something wrong. Something so terribly, terribly wrong that he
couldn't get away from her fast enough.

"I've never kissed a man before," she blurted out and
this time, rather wished she could take the words back. She
didn't mean to sound so obviously unsure of herself.

Gideon didn't immediately answer. Instead, he bowed

his head, leaned heavily on his cane, and blew out several long breaths. Finally, after what seemed an eternity to Winnefred, he lifted his face, squinted at her as if she'd been speaking in a foreign language, and said, "Beg your pardon?"

She gave a small, irritated sniff. "I just thought it was something you should consider before you backed into Samson."

"I . . ." Gideon glanced behind him to where the lame horse was grazing at the side of the road. "I don't follow."

"Look at you." She waved a hand to indicate how far away he was. "You'd not be running away, nor have pushed me away"—strictly speaking he'd pulled away, but she didn't feel like making the distinction—"if I'd not done something incorrectly or—"

"No." He took a large—and rather gratifying—step forward. "No. You've done *nothing* wrong. Nothing at all. Do you understand?"

That didn't address why he'd been quick to retreat, but he was so adamant in her defense that she found herself nodding anyway.

Gideon looked caught somewhere between relieved and pained. "It is unconscionable for a gentleman to have taken advantage of a lady in such a manner. I have no excuse for it. I can only assure you it will never happen again."

Was that all? But what if she wanted it to happen again? What if she wanted more?

She might have asked him that if Lilly's voice hadn't chosen that moment to sound in her head.

Propositioning any man, for any reason, is nothing short of unforgivably forward and therefore immensely *stupid.*

It seemed unlikely that propositioning a man after kissing him was *immensely* stupid, but since Winnefred remained unclear on the specifics of acceptable behavior for a lady, she decided to keep her question to herself. There would be time enough for her to explore her attraction to

Gideon. An isolated place like Murdoch House ought to provide plenty of opportunity for a gentleman and lady to find a few moments alone.

"I should hate for things to be uneasy between us because of this," she told him, and then, to make sure they weren't, she stepped over to pick up Samson's lead and hand it to Gideon with a smile. "I should also hate a lecture from Lilly about dawdling. Take me home."

Chapter 14

*I*n retrospect, Winnefred realized she should have known that what an isolated farm *ought* to provide and what it *will* provide are two entirely different animals. Murdoch House ought to have yielded a fine crop of carrots last year, and it ought to have given her another opportunity to kiss Gideon in the days since their trip to the prison. Neither of those expectations had been met.

Gideon attended one meal a day as promised, but immediately disappeared after, going to his room or into Enscrum. During the few hours of the day he did spend in her company, he acted as though nothing unusual had passed between them. He certainly gave no indication he desired for something unusual to pass between them again.

Once or twice, she had considered knocking on the door to his chambers with some excuse or other, but she'd not been able to gather up the nerve. It was one thing to kiss a man while standing in a moonlit field. It was something else altogether to imagine herself capable of re-creating that moment . . . without the fields and moonlight.

It occurred to her that he might be avoiding her on purpose, but she couldn't think of a single reason he should.

He'd kissed her, for pity's sake. That had to be an indication of *some* liking.

Didn't it? Lilly still had not expanded her knowledge of men, and Winnefred very much wished her own understanding of what went on between males and females extended beyond what she had gleaned from breeding Giddy. She was at a complete loss when it came to matters of the heart, even more so when it came to the courting rituals of gentlemen and ladies. Lilly *had* provided a few more do-not-evers in the past week, but there had to be more to it than that—subtle rules and signals she could only guess at.

She wondered if she'd given him an unintentional signal of disinterest, and she worried she might have missed one from him.

Just the idea of Gideon turning her away made her feel ill. She was no stranger to rejection, to the awful, crushing pain of it. The memory of that pain was enough for her to briefly contemplate putting her pursuit of Gideon aside. She might have done just that, were it not for three reasons. First, he *had* kissed her, which she was willing to take on faith indicated some interest on his part. Second, she had a difficult time backing down from a challenge.

Finally, and perhaps most important, she wanted him.

And if there was one thing she knew very, very well, it was how to fight for what she wanted.

Winnefred found this skill to be useful under a variety of circumstances. Including the morning Lilly stepped into the front parlor to announce they would be accepting an invitation to dinner at the Howards.

"This is absolutely ridiculous." Winnefred plucked the invitation out of Lilly's hand. "You loathe the Howards."

"That is patently untrue," Lilly countered. "I'm rather fond of the vicar. I just loathe his wife."

"Because Clarisse is a pretentious ninny and a right bi—"

"It is Mrs. Howard, Freddie."

"Certainly *now*, it's Mrs. Howard. You never bothered to call her so before."

"She wasn't of any use to us before."

Though she appreciated the honesty of that statement, it did little to sway Winnefred's opinion of Mrs. Howard. "I sincerely doubt she's been of use to anyone a single moment of her life."

"I suspect her children would disagree." Lilly snatched the invitation back. "We will be attending the dinner. You need the practice."

"I need to practice pretending to enjoy the company of someone I cannot countenance and who does not like me, all because that someone may be of use to me?"

"Yes. *Exactly*," Lilly exclaimed as if Winnefred had just successfully completed a particularly difficult lesson. "Oh, you are getting a grasp of things. Now, I think you should wear the green gown. The color is not so flattering as the peach, but the cut—"

"Wait. I've not agreed to go as of yet."

"You are going."

She had no doubt that was true, and she had to admit that Lilly's reasons for attending the dinner party were sound, but she had no intention of saying as much aloud . . . yet. "I will go, but I want something in return."

"And what might that be?" Lilly asked warily.

"A respite. I want a day, a full day, without lessons, without fancy dinners, without anything but you and I, and Gideon, if he can be persuaded to join us, simply having fun. We could go to town, or have a picnic and play games on the lawn, or . . . do anything really. Anything but speak of London or practice for London or plan for London or—"

"I gave you the afternoon to go to the prison just days ago."

"That wasn't a respite, that was a chore, and you weren't there. I want a day for both of us—"

"A full day is too long," Lilly cut in. "We can take a morning."

"A full day," she returned, folding her arms over her chest, "or I'll not go."

Lilly pressed her lips together, breathed loudly through her nose, and tapped her foot. All very positive signs.

"If I agree to this," she finally said, "you will attend the Howards' dinner, without complaint, and put every effort into being a pleasant and well-behaved guest?"

"It's not as if I'd planned to have a go at it with one of the footmen in the parlor."

"I want your word, Winnefred."

"Yes, all right," she groaned. "I promise to do my very best to behave as a proper lady."

Lilly switched tapping her foot for tapping her finger against the back of the invitation—an even more encouraging sign. "Very well, we have an agreement."

"Excellent." She unfolded her arms. "When is the dinner party?"

"Tonight."

"Tonight? And we've only just received the invitation?"

"No, it arrived two days ago. I just put off telling you."

Because she wasn't particularly surprised by that, Winnefred merely shrugged and said, "Still rather late." And a result, no doubt, of Mrs. Howard trying to decide if it was worth having two undesirables in her home for the sake of one brother to a marquess. "She probably hopes Gideon will go without us."

"There, you see?" Lilly shook the invitation at her. "A chance to thwart and disappoint Mrs. Howard. You should be thrilled."

Winnefred decided the most appropriate response was a noncommittal "hmm," followed by a prompt exit from the room.

In truth, she wasn't quite as resistant to the idea of Mrs. Howard's dinner party as she would lead Lilly to believe. It was a practical way to test her new manners. If she made a misstep at the party, it would be of little consequence, because if Mrs. Howard had any sort of influence in the ton, there would be no point in Winnefred preparing for a trip to London. Her name would already be ruined.

But feigning opposition allowed her to demand the day of respite, and she certainly hadn't exaggerated how little she was looking forward to an evening spent with the Howards.

She could still recall with perfect clarity the day Mrs. Howard had made her first, and only, visit to Murdoch House. She'd arrived full of probing questions, pompous opinions, and insufferable arrogance. Even at the age of thirteen, Winnefred could see how miserable and awkward the woman had made Lilly feel. The third comment on the deplorable lack of comfortable places in the house on which to sit had been the last straw for Winnefred. The moment the topic of Sunday service was broached, she had leapt at the chance to shock Mrs. Howard into an early departure. She regretted the action later, but not as strongly as she regretted ever having met Mrs. Howard.

Hours later, as the carriage rolled to a stop in front of the Howards' large Tudor home, Winnefred wondered how much she was going to regret agreeing to attend the dinner party.

Mrs. Howard could be seen standing on the other side of the open front door. She was wearing a dark orange gown that clashed painfully with her pale yellow hair and some sort of head wrap with what looked to be a very large peacock feather sticking straight out of the top.

"I hate peacocks," Winnefred muttered.

Across from her, Gideon lifted a dark brow. "What was that?"

"Nothing."

She pasted on a serene expression as she climbed from the carriage and up the front steps. Introductions, bows, and curtsies were exchanged, the latter of which Winnefred thought fairly well executed on her part. As expected, Mrs. Howard made a small fuss over Gideon, exhibited a reasonable politeness to Lilly, and strained her features into something roughly approximating a smile, but more closely resembling a snarl, when addressing Winnefred.

Despite the fact she had very rarely encountered Mrs. Howard over the years, Winnefred was quite certain that every time she saw the woman, her eyes had grown a little beadier in her head. Bird eyes, she thought and glanced at the peacock feather. How very fitting.

"Miss Blythe," Mrs. Howard said stiffly. "How fortunate you could join us."

"I am delighted to be here," Winnefred recited, just as she had, at Lilly's insistence, a dozen times on the carriage ride over.

There was a full five seconds of awkward silence following this exchange and likely would have been a full five more had she not been saved from further interaction by the arrival of new guests.

Lilly whispered into her ear as they moved from the front hall into the parlor. "Well done, Freddie."

Winnefred barely heard her, and she scarcely noticed the furnishings in the front hall and parlor. Her attention was focused on the guests. There were a dozen of them, most of whom she recognized as Mrs. Howard's dearest friends, along with two women she'd never seen before.

Not surprisingly, the two strangers were the only guests who did not, upon being introduced, eye her up and down like a yard of muslin they had no intention of buying.

She curtsied until her knees felt wobbly. And she recited the words "it is a pleasure to make your acquaintance" until her tongue felt wooden, and then she said a silent prayer of thanks when dinner was announced before anyone could draw her into an actual conversation.

Winnefred followed the other guests into the dining hall, very much hoping to be seated next to Lilly or Gideon or, if she were very fortunate, between them both. But she was placed in the middle of the table between an elderly gentleman with pungent breath and a name she could not recall and Mrs. Howard's mother-in-law, Mrs. Cress—a stout, gray-haired woman who used a walking cane and wore what even Winnefred knew was an unfashionable amount of lace about the neck.

Fortunately, the gentleman seemed disinclined to speak, and Mrs. Cress had been one of the guests who had greeted her with a warm and open smile. Winnefred thought perhaps she could attempt a civil conversation with Mrs. Cress . . . or simply keep her mouth closed for the duration of the meal.

Mrs. Howard had other ideas. "Miss Blythe. Miss Ilestone informs me you are to go to London. Such a reversal of fortune you have experienced, my dear. However did it come about?"

A dozen sets of eyes turned to her.

"I . . ." Winnefred swallowed and looked from Lilly to Gideon. How was she to answer such a question without embarrassing Gideon's family, or refuse to answer without embarrassing Mrs. Howard and, more important, herself?

Fortunately, Gideon appeared unperturbed by the question. "It is a long and complicated business," he informed Mrs. Howard. "We'll not bore you with the details."

"But you must tell us how you came to be acquainted with our dear Miss Blythe," Mrs. Howard insisted. "We'd no idea she had friends in London."

"Neither did she. Our friendship is a new one."

"Oh, do tell."

Gideon looked relaxed at present, but Winnefred clearly remembered his first day at Murdoch House and his obvious distaste for relating his stepmother's crimes.

She spoke quickly, before Gideon could. "The late Lord Engsly very generously left me an inheritance in memory of a brief friendship he shared with my father. Lord Gideon—"

"Upon his death?" Mrs. Howard cut in. "One should never look a gift horse in the mouth, of course, but why ever did he wait to see you settled?"

"He was not aware of my presence until very late. My father preferred to discuss matters of sport and horseflesh to family."

That confession was answered by a series of throat clearings and pointed looks between the guests.

Mrs. Cress seemed to be the only person oblivious to the silent conversation around the table. She chuckled merrily, sending the ruffles about her collar to waving. "My eldest grandnephews are very much the same. Gone to London these two decades and no word but at Christmas, and then but three pages filled with talk of their clubs and their horses. Such charming boys, but I vow, they would trade me for a matched set and entrance to White's, if the law allowed." She chuckled again and raised her cup in a mock toast to Gideon. "Ghastly creatures, you gentlemen. We ought have nothing to do with you."

"True," Gideon conceded. "But then you would be left dancing with each other and writing poetry to yourselves."

The guests laughed and soon the conversation turned into a lighthearted list of reasons ladies continued to keep company with gentlemen in the face of all good sense. Winnefred thought it rather silly that not one amongst them was willing to point out the obvious benefit of continuing the species, but thought it best to keep that opinion to herself.

The remainder of the meal passed without incident. The only oddity Winnefred noted in the next three hours was a tendency for Mrs. Cress to chew every third bite while staring at her. It came as no surprise, then, when the woman took pains to lead her away from other guests when the ladies retired to the parlor.

Mrs. Cress carefully lowered herself onto a small settee by the fire. "Do join me for a bit, Miss Blythe. I have wanted to meet you for some time."

"I . . ." Winnefred sat and brushed at her skirts, searching for an appropriate response. "I am delighted to finally make your acquaintance."

"It isn't often I visit my son and his wife." Mrs. Cress patted her right leg. "Twenty miles can be quite a trial for me, you understand. We are in dire need of more inns in Scotland."

She had no idea what to say to that. Fortunately, Mrs. Cress seemed not to require a response.

"But Mrs. Scarrow wrote to me stating that Mrs. Howard had written a letter to her indicating the possibility of

Mrs. Howard sending an invitation to you, and I could not resist the enticement of finally meeting you."

No wonder they had received the invitation so late. It had been approved by committee. "I hope the trip was not too taxing?"

"Not enough inns," she said again. "But the weather was lovely."

"I see."

Mrs. Cress tipped her head forward and whispered, "What do you make of my daughter-in-law?"

Oh, dear. "Er . . . Mrs. Howard has been very gracious tonight."

"Hmm." She straightened and eyed Mrs. Howard from across the room. "I do not care for the color of her gown."

"Umm . . ."

"Rumor has it the two of you had a very contentious first meeting."

"I . . ." *Oh, damn.* "I was thirteen."

"Oh, don't diminish your accomplishments by tossing about your age, girl. I hear you swore at her."

"Well, not *at* her."

"Pity. My daughter-in-law is a silly, ofttimes mean-spirited twit. A set down now and then would do her good." She looked at Mrs. Howard again and sighed. "But her affection for my son is sincere. A mother could not ask for more."

A mother who loved her son couldn't ask for more, Winnefred thought and found herself rather liking Mrs. Cress.

"The quail, however," Mrs. Cress added, "was quite dry tonight."

Winnefred couldn't keep her lips from twitching. "I confess I did not notice."

"No matter. The beef quite made up for it. Have you met Miss Malone?"

Winnefred glanced at a pretty young woman with pale blonde hair showcasing an inordinate number of ribbons and recognized her as the only other guest who had greeted her warmly. "We were introduced. She seems friendly."

"She has just returned to her family from school. The child is quite ridiculous but so lively of disposition one cannot help but enjoy her company. Her mother is an accomplished flutist, though her musical talents do not exceed Mr. Bate's gift of artistry. And his son is quite handsome, though his chin a bit overlarge . . ."

Winnefred made herself comfortable as Mrs. Cress began a very lengthy monologue on the various inhabitants of Enscrum and the surrounding countryside.

For a woman who so rarely visited the area, she had a surprising amount of information to impart about the people in the room. That information was given in leaps, fits, and starts, occasionally making it rather difficult to follow. Nevertheless, Winnefred enjoyed what she felt might loosely be termed a conversation. She could always find out later if it was Mrs. Ward who had the collection of vases and Mr. Gettle who pinched the servants, or the other way around.

Perhaps this was the way to ensure success at London dinner parties, she mused. She would find an individual of a friendly and chatty nature and spend the whole of the evening letting them talk at her.

She caught a movement out of the corner of her eye, and she turned her head to see Gideon making his way toward them. He looked particularly handsome tonight. He always looked handsome, of course, but she'd not had the opportunity to see him in a room full of other men until now. He did quite well in comparison. Quite well indeed. Though she knew it was foolish, she felt a small spark of pride at knowing he was the best-looking man in the room.

Gideon bowed when he reached them. "I beg your pardon for interrupting, Mrs. Cress, but might I have a word with Miss Blythe?"

At Mrs. Cress's assent, Gideon offered Winnefred his arm and ushered her across the room and out through one of the open glass doors leading to the side terrace. Light spilled from the parlor and there were torches scattered throughout the garden, but even so, the terrace was dimly lit compared to the parlor.

"Am I allowed to be out here with you?" she asked.

"As long as we remain in full view of everyone in the parlor." He answered in a soft and distracted manner, and when she glanced at his profile, she saw from his rather sober countenance that he'd not sought her out for light conversation.

"Is something the matter?" she asked.

He stopped and turned to face her, letting her arm slide free of his. "You lied to spare my father's name. Why?"

It took her a moment to figure out what he was talking about. "Oh, at dinner, you mean? I did no such thing." She shrugged and leaned against the stone balustrade. "I lied to spare you discomfort. Your father may go to the devil."

He smiled a little at that. "I thank you for the thought, Winnefred, but the deceit was unnecessary."

"So was the truth."

"Did you not consider that you may have done an injustice to your father?" he pressed. "He sounded a very callous man to have made no effort to see you were cared for."

"I have heard the story of how he died," she informed him, "and how Lord Engsly came to be my guardian."

"His last thought was for you."

Needing the time to sort through her feelings, she turned and began a slow walk down the length of the terrace, with Gideon falling into step beside her.

"It would be a lie to say that means nothing to me," she said at length. "It would also be a lie to say a moment's thought makes up for a lifetime of neglect. A good man, a good father, sees to the welfare of his children. He does not pass them off in the last minute of his life to the gentleman standing nearest." She stopped and met his gaze. "I may have painted a lighter picture of your father than he deserved, but I did not paint a darker picture of my father than he deserved."

Gideon gave a small nod of acceptance. "Then I will thank you again for sparing me from having to air my stepmother's sins and leave it at that."

She would have commented further, but she was distracted

by the discovery that their small walk had placed them in front of a six-foot section of wall separating the glass doors into the parlor. They were completely blocked from the view of those inside. Her initial instinct was to hurry back in front of the windows, but one glance at Gideon and that instinct disappeared as if it had never existed.

He looked so dashing in his evening attire. She was transfixed by the way the soft breeze tousled the locks of his dark hair, and the way the torchlight danced across his striking features.

And now, here, for the first time since their moonlit walk to Murdoch House, she had the opportunity to . . .

Her eyes fixed on his mouth, and she took a small step closer.

He took a larger step back. And then another, until he was right in front of the next set of glass doors.

"Did you see Mrs. Howard's hat?" he inquired.

She blinked at him, stunned at his retreat and the abrupt change of subject. Had he known what she was about? Had he backed away because he'd realized what she meant to do and didn't care for the idea? She searched his face, but all she found there was a sort of earnest curiosity.

"Her hat?" she echoed, not at all surprised that she should sound just as mystified as she felt.

"With the feather sticking out the top. Why do women wear headpieces with single feathers sticking out the top?"

She badly wanted to reach up and pinch the bridge of her nose.

"I do not know" was the best . . . No, the *only* reply she could come up with.

"They're like misshapen exclamation points."

She was not going to ask. Absolutely *not* going to ask.

"The women or the hats?" she asked. Because, really, what else could she do? Being present for one of Gideon's tangents was like finding oneself trapped in a bog. Struggling only made things worse.

"Both," he decided after a moment's consideration. "But it's worse when the hat is on a head."

"Why?"

"Because that makes them misshapen exclamation points *with legs*." He smiled and waited a beat, as if allowing time for the image to form in her mind. "You don't find that problematic?"

"I find this entire conversation problematic."

"It is a puzzler," he agreed. He winked at her and held out an elbow. "Shall we go inside and see what Mrs. Howard has to say on the subject?"

Wouldn't you rather step back into the shadows with me?

Oh, how she wished she had the courage to ask him *that*.

Because she didn't, she stepped forward and took his arm. And because she was preoccupied with thoughts of a missed kiss, and the amusing, albeit empty, threat to insult Mrs. Howard's hat, she failed to notice that the smile on Gideon's face slid away the moment they turned toward the doors. And she never heard the long, slow release of his breath.

Three hours later, Winnefred walked into her chambers at Murdoch House, tossed her reticule in the general vicinity of a chair, and promptly fell backward onto her bed.

She was exhausted. She'd done nothing but stand, sit, eat, and talk for hours, and yet she felt drained down to the very marrow of her bones. It was ridiculous, and if she'd had the energy for it, she would have been concerned. Was she to feel like this after every dinner party? How much worse would it be after a ball? She wasn't going to last a week in London.

And she wasn't going to last another week in Scotland wondering and worrying why Gideon had kissed her once and backed away from her twice.

She'd never found mathematics quite so depressing.

What the devil was she doing wrong?

Maybe it was simply that *she* was wrong. Maybe there were good reasons why people like her father and the Engslys had rejected her in the past. Maybe Gideon's tastes, like theirs, simply did not run to unsophisticated hoydens. Maybe she just wasn't likable. Maybe she wasn't worth the trouble . . .

She grimaced at the direction of her thoughts. The fears were old ones, and her response to them just as familiar. She ruthlessly shoved them aside and refused to give them further consideration. Feeling sorry for herself, and about herself, would accomplish nothing.

She stared at the plaster of the ceiling, instead, and had half convinced herself it was all right if she fell asleep in her clothes just this once, when Lilly threw open the door and flew into the room. She looked as happy as she had the day Gideon sent someone to deliver the note and pastries to Murdoch House, and twice again as energetic. She came to a stop in the middle of the room and performed a small, silly jig.

"Oh, you were brilliant tonight, Freddie. Absolutely brilliant."

Somehow, Winnefred found the energy to sit up and lean against one of the posters. "Was I?"

"Were you not aware?"

"I'm always aware of my brilliance in a general sense, but—" She stopped to yawn hugely while Lilly laughed. "But not tonight's brilliance, specifically."

"Your conduct was superior to Mrs. Howard's," Lilly said with relish.

"Oh, you jest."

"I don't. Upon our arrival, Mrs. Howard greeted you *after* me. That was very poorly done."

"Was it?" She frowned thoughtfully. "You are older."

"But, as the companion to the ward of the Marquess of Engsly, I am lower in rank."

"That is preposterous." She straightened from the poster. "You are not lower—"

"Not in your eyes." Lilly paused to give her a wink. "And certainly not in mine. But in the eyes of the ton, you occupy a loftier position in society. Mrs. Howard should have greeted you first."

"Oh." She relaxed again and thought that bit of information through. "Does that mean I can give her the cut direct the next time we meet?"

"No."

"Pity."

Lilly took a seat next to Winnefred on the bed and studied her face. "You look quite done in."

"I don't know why I should be."

"Nerves."

"I thought the same." But it was somehow more believable coming from Lilly. "Will it always be like this?"

"No." Her face a mask of sympathetic concern, Lilly reached up and gently tucked a strand of Winnefred's hair behind her ear. "It will get much, *much* worse."

"Oh, you *brat*." Winnefred gave Lilly's arm a playful shove as her friend howled with laughter. It was so rewarding, she thought, so wonderful to see Lilly being carefree and silly.

"What sort of governess are you?"

Lilly exhaled loudly and wiped at her eyes. "You've never really needed me as your governess."

"I have these past two weeks," she countered.

"That's true." Lilly leaned over to give her a peck on the cheek. "Well, you should get some rest. Good night, Freddie."

"Good night." She watched her friend stand up and practically skip toward the door. "Lilly?"

"Hmm?"

"I will always need you as a sister, and my friend."

Lilly's smile softened and her eyes grew bright. "Thank you, Freddie. I need you too."

Chapter 15

$\mathcal{F}$or the life of him, Gideon could not figure out how he'd been persuaded to join Winnefred and Lilly for a trip into Enscrum. Lilly had cornered him in the parlor before breakfast, that much was clear. She'd thrown words like London, shopping, necessities, and advice about, and the next thing he knew, he was walking across the modest town square with Winnefred, awkwardly hauling a small stack of packages under his one free arm.

He ought to have been annoyed, or at least stoically reconciled to having been pulled from his self-imposed exile, but it was impossible to retain a foul mood in the face of Winnefred's enthusiasm. She didn't appear to take any particular pleasure in the act of shopping, but she took obvious delight in walking about town, looking into the windows, and speaking of her future plans for Murdoch House.

Even the dreary gray weather couldn't dampen her mood. The sky was thick with clouds, the air cool and heavy, and a light mist clung to her eyelashes and hair in watery beads. He noticed the ends of her hair were beginning to curl in the humidity and he was suddenly grateful he was burdened with packages and a cane. He wanted to reach out and feel the damp locks with his fingers, and he wanted to bend down to taste the mist on her cheek.

She would smell of rain-washed lavender and her skin would feel like satin beneath his lips.

He dragged his eyes away and made himself think of something else, *anything* else. "We . . . Er . . . We should have brought a footman along."

Next to him, Winnefred shifted a small box containing a variety of hair ribbons. "Then who would have gone with Lilly to the booksellers?"

"The other footman."

"He's keeping Peter company."

He smiled at the ridiculous comment. "Peter does not require company."

"If you'd like me to carry more—"

"No, thank you." He'd been the one to insist on most of the purchases, after all. "You need to grow accustomed to having staff follow you about, you know."

"I'll never grow accustomed to it." She threw a quick look over her shoulder to where Bess trailed a ways back, carrying yet more packages, then pitched her voice into a low whisper. "It wouldn't be so disconcerting if we weren't literally being followed. I feel as if we're snubbing her."

"It's how it is done."

"I don't care for it . . . And I can feel her eyes on the back of my head."

"There are other things Bess finds of greater interest at the moment than the back of your head, enchanting though it is." He jerked his chin toward the carriage and Peter, who, in return, looked to be staring at Bess. It seemed a romance was in bloom. "We could disappear down one of these streets and be halfway across town before Bess noticed."

Winnefred's eyes lit with mischievous humor. "Really?"

"We are not trying it."

"Pity. It would be like . . ." Her voice trailed off when something in Mr. McKeen's shop window caught her eye. Since very little in the shop windows of Enscrum had

garnered much more than a curious inspection from Winnefred, Gideon was surprised when she stopped to stare at a
small gold locket and chain.

*D*espite her insistence otherwise on the day they'd
met, Winnefred was well aware of the fact she had
never been an angel. She'd committed her share of acts for
which she wasn't proud, but only two had actually been
nefarious enough make her well and truly ashamed.

Her first offense had occurred at the age of fifteen when,
hungry and tempted beyond endurance, she'd nicked a
sticky bun from Mrs. McAlister's shop while Lilly haggled
for a better price on day-old bread. She'd eaten the stolen
treat that night—in four selfish bites. And, unaccustomed
to the richness, nearly sicked it back up again. The guilt
had hurt worse than the ache in her belly, and she'd sworn
an oath to never, ever, ever, as long as she should live (she
was an adolescent girl, after all) steal again.

But there, in the front window of Mr. McKeen's shop,
was a locket and chain that mocked her as a liar.

She and Lilly had found it under a bed during their first
month at Murdoch House. Thievery not yet a consideration
in Winnefred's mind, she'd stuck it in a chest of drawers
and left it there. Until last winter when she'd nicked it, sold
it, and used the money to procure a doctor for Lilly.

"Do you like it?"

Gideon's voice sounded unnaturally loud in her ear. She
nearly jumped out of her skin. "What?"

"The locket." He gestured at the shop window with his
cane. "Do you care for it?"

It was on the tip of her tongue to say no—it was quite
the ugliest little trinket she'd ever seen. But a small voice
in her head—one that had begun sounding more and more
like Lilly with each passing day, she noticed—berated her
for the lie. She checked to make certain there was no one
else within earshot, and then, to her absolute shock and
horror, confessed all in a babbled rush.

"It's yours. Your necklace. Or your brother's, I don't know. I took it from the Murdoch House. Last winter when Lilly was so ill, and you sent that awful letter. Only it wasn't you, was it? But how was I to know? I'm sorry. I shouldn't have." A lady wouldn't have. A good woman, or at least a smarter one, wouldn't have. "I couldn't think of anything else to do. I tried selling Claire, I did, but no one would have her, and—"

"Winnefred, stop. Are you telling me you pawned that necklace?"

She swallowed past the dry lump in her throat. "Yes."

"And you are apologizing because . . . ?"

"Well, because I stole it." She'd thought that was fairly obvious.

"You didn't. You had my permission to sell anything you like from the house. You simply weren't aware of it." He gave her a disarming smile that went a very long way to setting her mind at ease. "Neither was I, come to that, but it hardly matters now—"

"Of course it matters. It wasn't mine to take."

He regarded her thoughtfully. "You're a moral creature, aren't you?"

"It is Lilly's influence," she grumbled.

"No. Not all of it, at any rate. How's this—which of your new belongings are you fond of?"

"Which . . . ? Oh, yes, of course." She would give up something of her own as payment for the locket. Granted, he'd purchased everything she owned, but in this case, it was the thought that counted. Hoping the thought would be enough, her eyes shot to the box containing a pair of new half boots. "I suppose—"

"I'm not taking your shoes," he interrupted a little impatiently. "Let me have the ribbons. You seemed excited about those."

"They're for Lilly."

"Why are you buying ribbons for Lilly?"

"Because she'll like them," she replied, thinking the answer was, again, rather obvious. "Why else?"

"Never mind. Tell me, did we purchase anything today that wasn't either strictly practical or a gift for someone else?"

She looked over the array of boxes. "There's the night rail. I don't need two. I don't really need any now that I've my own room."

He didn't immediately answer. Instead, he stared at her, and though she'd not have thought it possible for black eyes to go blacker, his did. His lids lowered, and his gaze traveled down . . . down . . .

The smoldering look alternately thrilled, discomfited, and confused her. She became acutely aware of her body, as if he had succeeded in undressing her with his eyes, and while it was gratifying to know the image of her without clothing was something he found intriguing, the sensation of truly being naked in front of Gideon was rather disconcerting.

Furthermore, she had no idea if he was seeing her, specifically, or merely a female form. Lilly had said most men were libertines at heart. And she knew too little of men to know if it was true.

She wanted to ask him if she would be expected to stand still and silent for every London gentleman who might care to picture her without her night rail but was a little afraid of what the answer might be.

"Gideon," she prompted.

His head snapped up.

"Keep the night rail," he said in a tight voice. "The bonnet. I'll take that."

She handed him one of the boxes she carried. "I don't even *like* that bonnet."

"And I'd never set eyes on that necklace before today. This makes us even."

"But—"

"We're even, Winnefred."

Chapter 16

The last days before the trip to London passed in a whirlwind of lessons and final preparations. Time seemed to fly by much too quickly for Winnefred. Though her confidence had received a considerable boost from the Howards' dinner party, there was still so much left to be learned. And there was a great deal left she wanted to do, including spending more time with Gideon. But try as she might, she couldn't find another opportunity to see him alone. He was present at every breakfast but, just as the days before the dinner party, made himself scarce directly after the meal.

She took what she could from those few short moments in his company. Any sort of conversation on topics of interest they might share was out of the question, as talk was almost exclusively of London. But she found pleasure in simply watching him as he ate and laughed and spoke with Lilly.

There were details about him she hadn't noticed before. He had a small, crescent-shaped scar on the underside of his jawline. His eyes were lighter in the morning sun than they were in candlelight or the bright light of midday. There was a lock of hair on his left side that had a propensity to curl up at the end. And he had a tendency to repeatedly flex and un-flex his hand when he was seated. She wondered if it was an attempt to relax muscles tired from gripping his cane.

She wondered a great deal about him—about his days as a sea captain, about the nightmare she'd woken him from, and most pressing to her, whether or not he was even half as fascinated by her as she was by him.

Given his propensity to isolate himself, it was easy to believe, despite the kiss, that her interest was not returned. But her study of him had left her in the position to notice every time he stole a glance at her while Lilly was talking. And she noted that he did so with some regularity. Once in a while, she didn't pretend to be preoccupied with her food and instead let their eyes meet and hold across the table.

He looked at her a little differently each time. Sometimes he sent her a friendly smile that warmed her heart. Other times she caught him watching her through hooded lids, and every nerve in her body would jump to life. And, once in a while, she saw a shadow of something heavier cross his face. She thought perhaps it was a kind of longing, or sadness, but it passed so quickly, she was never able to say for certain.

Granted, his frequent looks in her direction may have been a result of wondering why the devil she kept staring at him, but she liked to think it was something more. And though their eyes caught for no more than a second or two, for those few brief moments, she could almost believe they were the only two people in the room.

Almost. It was difficult to ignore Lilly's presence for long.

"I've made a list of things we must do during our visit," she was saying over the dining table. "The items are not in order of importance, mind you, but I did categorize them according to location and a few other variables."

Winnefred looked down at her breakfast to hide a smile. It was their last day in Scotland, and she was beginning to feel that might not be such a terrible thing. After all, once they were *in* London, Lilly would have to speak of something other than *going* to London. And that would be a fine change indeed.

"The first thing I should like to try are ices." Lilly stabbed a bit of egg with her fork. "Well, not literally the first thing, but as soon as I can, certainly."

"You've mentioned that particular desire before," Gideon said, looking up from his plate. "How is it you missed the opportunity to indulge when you were in London?"

"My visit was cut short due to my mother's illness."

"Visit?" A line formed across Gideon's brow. "I thought you were there as a child, and again for your debut."

"No, I was a child at my debut. Only days past seventeen."

"Seventeen? You were seventeen when you were in London? When you met my brother?"

"I . . ." Lilly picked up her toast. "Yes."

"That would have put my brother somewhere near to twenty. I was under the impression the two of you met at a much younger age."

"Yes . . . Well . . . Freddie, will you pass—?"

Winnefred passed the butter before her friend could mutilate her food.

Gideon tapped his fork against the table in a soft, thoughtful manner.

"Tell me, Lilly . . . Wait . . ." The line across his brow grew more pronounced. "Lilly," he repeated to himself. "Lilly . . . *Rose*." He stopped tapping his fork. His eyes widened to the size of saucers, and his mouth fell wide open, his lips curving up a little at the corners. Winnefred thought he looked very much like a man who had taken a sizable blow, and for some inexplicable reason, rather liked it. "Holy hell, you're *Rose*."

Lilly went still, butter knife on her toast.

"You are, aren't you?" Gideon pressed, leaning forward in his chair.

Lilly's continued silence was answer enough.

Gideon sent Winnefred a look of accusation. "You thought I didn't need to be made aware of this?"

Stunned by his reaction, she managed little more than a shake of her head. "I . . . She . . ." She tried to remember how Lilly had made the matter seem of less consequence. "It was a very long time ago."

"It was," Lilly finally said. She set her knife and toast down with great care. "And I hadn't realized Lord Engsly mentioned our friendship to anyone else."

"Mentioned?" Gideon ran a hand through his hair and laughed. "He's not spoken of another woman in the same manner before or since. He spoke of nothing but you in every letter."

"He did not speak of me for long, it would seem," Lilly murmured, "or you would have remembered my name."

"He never told me your name, out of respect for you."

"Respect?" Winnefred echoed.

"The ton does not look favorably upon broken engagements," Gideon explained before returning his attention to Lilly. "He was . . . He is so in love with you."

Lilly kept her gaze focused on the table. "As Freddie pointed out, it was a very long time ago."

"Until recently, he thought you married."

Her head snapped up. "What?"

"He thought you'd married a man named . . ." Gideon looked briefly at the ceiling, searching. "Thomas, Thompson, Townsend—that's it, Townsend. Jeffrey Townsend."

"I have never in my life met a man with that name. Why on earth would . . . ?" She closed her eyes on a quiet groan. "Lady Engsly. Oh, of course."

"In this instance, I'd not be surprised to hear she was aided by my father. They had very particular plans for Lucien."

Lilly shook her head slowly. Suddenly, her wide blue

eyes filled with a kind of horrified amusement. Her lips twitched, and a small giggle escaped.

Gideon tilted his head at her. "You're taking this rather well."

Winnefred rather thought so too. "Are you all right, Lilly?"

"I'm sorry," Lilly said, not sounding the least bit sorry. Another giggle escaped and then another. She put her elbow on the table and pinched the bridge of her nose. "Oh, it's just . . . It's all so much like something out of a torrid novel—villains and false marriages and stolen letters."

"It is a trifle dramatic," Winnefred murmured, mostly because she felt she ought to say something.

"My brother will know of your presence here," Gideon told her gently. "I sent a letter to him upon my arrival."

Lilly waved her hand in dismissal without lifting her head.

"He'll come to London," Gideon added.

"It's of no matter." Lilly heaved a heavy sigh and lifted her head. "Truly, Gideon, it's of no matter to me. It was so very long ago."

Winnefred wasn't surprised that after a moment's hesitation, Gideon nodded in acceptance and soon after changed the subject. Nor was she surprised when he excused himself from the table five minutes later.

He didn't believe Lilly either.

Winnefred listened for the sound of Gideon's distinctive footsteps to disappear down the hall before speaking again. "Are you all right, Lilly?"

Lilly flicked her eyes up from her plate. "Of course I am."

"It must be something of a relief," Winnefred tried, "to know your separation from Gideon's brother was Lady Engsly's doing after all. He didn't abandon you."

"No, he did not." There was a long pause before Lilly added, "Not initially."

"That's an odd qualifier."

Again, a long time passed before Lilly spoke. "He didn't

seek me out, Freddie. After being told I had married another, he didn't . . . He never came to me to ask why I had broken my promise."

"Nor you him."

"But I *would* have," Lilly returned, and for the first time, a hint of anger could be heard in her voice. "Had I the funds and the freedom, I would have gone to him and demanded to know why he had ceased to answer my letters. He was the only one with the wherewithal to fight for us, and he chose instead to believe in my betrayal."

Winnefred wanted to point out the obvious holes in that argument, but instinct told her that now was not the time for being reasonable.

"It was wrong of him not to fight for you." It would also have been wrong of him to seek out a married woman, but that was another bit of useless reasoning.

"Yes. Yes, it was," Lilly agreed, warming more and more to the topic. "Moreover, he had the luxury of nursing the heartache and misplaced sense of betrayal in the cradle of wealth and status, while we were here, nursing a fire without fuel and a sorry handful of turnips between the two of us."

"You're angry with him." And hurting, Winnefred thought. She could see the wounded feelings through the hard words well enough.

Lilly blew out a tight breath. "No . . . Yes . . . Perhaps a trifle disappointed, that's all."

It didn't seem a trifle to Winnefred. "Would you like me to recite a limerick?

The offer made Lilly laugh a little, just as Winnefred had hoped. "Not this morning, thank you."

Though she would have liked to end the conversation with Lilly smiling, there was one other question that needed to be asked. "Will it be uncomfortable for you, should Lord Engsly return from Italy while we are in London?"

"Certainly not," Lilly replied, and with enough emphasis to show she either truly meant it or very much wanted to. "I have known from the moment I requested we go to

London that the possibility existed we might meet with Lord Engsly. Have I given indication of being anything other than delighted to go?"

"No. Absolutely not."

And since there was nothing to gain by trying to convince Lilly that she *ought* to feel uncomfortable, Winnefred decided to entertain her friend with the bawdy limerick after all.

Chapter 17

*B*eset by excitement and nerves, Winnefred lay awake for most of her last night in Scotland. Images of Smithfield Market and Lilly on Bond Street danced alongside visions of tea-scalded guests and dance partners with broken toes. When she heard the clock in the parlor chime four, she gave up on sleep and climbed from her bed.

She took her time washing and dressing, and made her way to the kitchen to indulge in a leisurely breakfast of bread and cheese. By the time she stepped outside into the cool, dry air, the first soft light of dawn was breaking on the horizon.

She fetched Claire from the stable and began a long tour of Murdoch House land. Usually when she took a walk to ease her worries, she let her mind wander and paid little attention to her surroundings. But there was nothing she wanted more that morning than to drink in every inch of land with her eyes.

She knew every tree, every rock, every perennial bush and flower. She knew what to expect at the top of every rise, what would be waiting for her on the other side of every stand of trees. She knew where the stream would run slow and wide and where it would race narrow and deep. All around her was the familiar and the loved.

For the first time in her life, she was sorry she'd not taken up sketching or watercolors. It would have been nice to bring a picture of Murdoch House along to London. She picked a leaf she could press from a young silver birch instead. And then a second one when Claire nipped the first out of her hand and made a meal of it.

Winnefred sighed and rubbed her fingers along the leaf. She hated to leave, hated that she would miss the slow but steady transition from spring to summer. Then again, it was only for a few months, and a little time away might lend a new appreciation for everything . . . No, she thought with a small laugh, she hated to leave. Lilly, however, couldn't be more eager, and a brief trip to London was a small price to pay to see her friend so happy.

"I'll be back before you know it," she said aloud. Claire responded by making a grab at the second birch leaf.

Winnefred snatched her hand away on a laugh. "Greedy thing. Behave, or there will be no more scraps for you."

She tossed Claire a bit of bread and resumed her walk, following the stream to the pond. She wondered if she might see Gideon there and was disappointed when she reached the water's edge and found herself standing alone. They'd not spoken since breakfast the day before. She'd expected him to return and ask after Lilly, but he never did, leaving her with the assumption that he'd expected her to come to him if there was something he needed to know.

She'd rather wished there had been.

Lost to her thoughts, she lingered by the water, skipping rocks and feeding Claire the last of the scraps from the kitchen until the sun was fully up.

"Time to go," she called to Claire.

Lilly would be up by now and wondering where her charge was. Still, she took a meandering route home, and by the time she got back, Murdoch House had come alive. The front drive was a hive of activity. Footmen were loading trunks onto the carriage, maids darted in and out of the house, and to Winnefred's surprise, Gideon was standing with a pair of men from Enscrum, both dressed to travel and holding the reins of saddled horses.

He waved at her as she approached and left the group to meet her on the lawn.

"Good morning, Winnefred." Claire trotted over to Gideon to offer her usual greeting. He nudged her gently, but firmly, aside. "Claire."

"Good morning, Gideon." Lighter eyes in the morning sun, she thought with a stifled sigh. Worried the sigh may not have been as stifled as she'd like, she forced her mind to other matters. "What are those men doing here?"

"I hired them as outriders for the trip."

She craned her neck to look around him. "Both of them?"

"It's a long way to London. Why? Do they make you uncomfortable?"

"No, of course not," she answered, straightening. "It seems excessive, that's all. Two footmen, a pair of outriders, and yourself—"

"Nothing wrong with a bit of excess now and then."

"Excess in moderation is not sound logic."

He appeared to give that matter considerable thought, his face taking on a quizzical expression. "That's true. Makes one wonder if Aristotle really thought the matter through."

Winnefred wished her knowledge of Aristotle extended beyond how to spell his name.

"Perhaps you'd like to purchase of few of Mr. Howard's hounds to run alongside as well," she teased, hoping to change the subject before either her limited education or her embarrassment at her limited education became obvious.

"Mr. Howard has pugs," Gideon said.

"They're quite energetic."

"Mr. Howard also has funds enough to see him through

the year." Gideon subtly pointed in the direction of the outriders with his cane. "These men can use the work."

"Oh." She felt a little foolish for having made a fuss,
even if it had mostly been in jest. "Yes, you're right. Of
course—"

"Freddie!"

Winnefred turned to see Lilly come marching down the
front steps of the house and across the drive.

"Freddie, where have you been?" She took hold of Winnefred's arm and began pulling her toward the house before
Winnefred could even think of saying good-bye to Gideon.
"I've been looking everywhere for you. Do you not realize
how much we've left to do?"

*A*s far as Winnefred could ascertain, the vast majority
of what was left to do was worry over, check, and
double check all the preparations Lilly had worried over,
checked, and double checked the day before.

Despite Lilly's hovering, the carriage was packed with
remarkable speed, or so it seemed to Winnefred. With
every piece of luggage carried out the door, she felt a shiver
of nerves run up her spine. Oddly enough, the closer they
came to leaving, the more relaxed Lilly seemed to become.
By the time Gideon pronounced them ready to begin the
journey, Lilly appeared very nearly serene.

She took Winnefred's arm and led her down the front
steps of the house. "It is done, then."

"Done?"

"The preparations, the packing, and what have you."
Lilly sighed happily. "There's nothing more we can do now
but enjoy ourselves."

Winnefred forced a smile as her friend climbed into
the carriage. There were a great many things she might do
besides enjoy herself . . . Make a dreadful arse of herself
came to mind. She forced the thought aside and took her
seat next to Lilly.

The carriage started down the drive with a small jolt, and Winnefred twisted about for her last look at Murdoch House. She stared until her neck cramped and the house disappeared out of sight.

"You're not leaving forever," Lilly said softly.

Winnefred turned to find Lilly watching her with sympathetic eyes.

"I know. It's only . . ." She searched for the words to describe the riot of emotions she was battling.

Lilly found them for her. "Knowing isn't necessarily feeling."

"Yes. Exactly."

Lilly nodded and patted her hand. "Give this a chance, Freddie."

"I am. I will." She reached up to untie the ribbons of her bonnet. "I'm a bit out of sorts this morning, that's all."

"That I can understand. I didn't sleep a wink last night. I feel as if I haven't slept for days." Lilly chuckled and removed her own bonnet. "Like that time, not long after we arrived at Murdoch House, when we thought a wolf was sneaking into the chicken coop."

Winnefred laughed at the memory and felt some of her anxiousness melt away. They'd stayed up for days, absolutely certain—and really quite terrified—they would catch the thief in the act, only to be informed a few days later by a neighbor that wolves hadn't been seen in Scotland for more than fifty years. If their chickens were disappearing, they could be certain a fox was to blame.

"Why on earth did we presume a wolf?"

"You suggested it," Lilly reminded her.

"Oh, that's right," she murmured, recalling how loud the raids on the chicken coop had sounded. "However did we survive our first year?"

"I have asked myself this many times."

"And have you ever reached a satisfactory answer?"

"No." Lilly retrieved a small pillow from the seat next to her. "Though some credit undoubtedly goes to blind luck.

Would you mind terribly if I rested awhile? I feel as if I might fall asleep sitting up."

Winnefred shook her head even though she would have preferred the ongoing distraction of conversation. "I'll wake you when we stop to change the horses."

"Thank you." Lilly placed the pillow between her head and the side of the carriage. Her breathing fell into the shallow and steady rhythm of sleep within minutes.

Winnefred gave a passing thought to reaching for one of the books Lilly had brought along, but although the road to the south was in much better repair than the road they had taken to the prison, the carriage still rocked and jolted, making the idea of trying to focus on small print decidedly unappealing.

She turned her attention out the window instead and found her view of the countryside partially obscured by one of the men from Enscrum riding alongside the carriage. Pity Gideon had elected to ride behind the carriage, she mused. She would have much preferred to spend the day looking at him.

Still, with a bit of maneuvering, she was able to look around the outrider, and for a long while, she watched a small stream weave back and forth next to the road, cutting across pastures, disappearing into patches of trees and reappearing on the other side. It was the same stream that ran through Murdoch House land, and keeping sight of it felt a little like keeping sight of home.

She didn't remember falling asleep, and had no idea for how long she slept, but the moment she opened her eyes, she knew a drastic and alarming changed had occurred.

A painful ache had formed in her stomach, and when she shifted in her seat to alleviate the discomfort, she found the movement only caused the queasiness to worsen. A throbbing started in the back of her neck and began to spread, snaking its way up to her temples, across her forehead, and settling behind her eyes. She raised a shaking hand to her brow.

Was she feverish? Her skin felt hot and clammy, but having never suffered from anything more severe than a head cold and a touch of the ague, she had no idea what that might mean. She pressed her fingers to her eyes as fear began to grow. What if she'd caught something at the prison or from one of the guests at the dinner party? After all the preparations, all the work, was she to ruin everything by succumbing to illness?

She let her hand fall and inhaled slowly. No, she was not. She would not ruin Lilly's chance to visit London by falling ill. As if to mock her, the carriage hit a rut and sent her body into chaos.

Desperate, she forced another deep breath into lungs that felt squeezed and closed her eyes. She fought against the rising nausea, but with every jolt and sway of the carriage her stomach cramped and tossed until she was certain she couldn't stand it another moment.

Defeated, she lurched forward in her seat and pounded on the roof of the carriage. "Stop! Stop the carriage!"

She was vaguely aware of Lilly bolting upright. "Freddie? Freddie, what is it? What—?"

Winnefred threw open the door as the carriage slowed to a crawl, then stopped. She tripped and stumbled in her rush to get out.

"Freddie, please! Where—?"

"No. Sick. Let me alone."

She made it into a small wood, through the trees, and down a gentle slope that led to the stream. Then she fell on her knees and emptied her stomach into the water.

It was awful, simply awful, the way her body heaved and shook. And when it finally ended, she was left feeling only marginally better and twice as exhausted. She managed to rinse her mouth out before rolling onto her back and giving in to the overwhelming desire to close her eyes and rest.

She felt a cool hand slip under her neck and she swatted at it without thought and with even less force. She didn't want anyone there—didn't want anyone around her when she was weak and vulnerable. The hand moved to her forehead, and she batted at it again.

"Here now, enough of that."

Gideon's voice, unusually low and gravelly, came from somewhere above her. If she'd had the energy, she would have groaned at the sound. Why did it have to be him? There were a half dozen other people in their traveling party—if someone had to witness her humiliation, why couldn't it have been one of them?

"Go'way."

"Not quite yet." His hands moved to her throat and prodded under her jaw and chin. "Do you hurt anywhere, Winnefred?"

Did she hurt? Was he serious? "Everywhere."

"I know, darling, but anywhere in particular? Any sharp pains in your sides or chest?"

"No. Sick. Headache. Go'way."

He slipped something soft under her head and then he rose and stepped away. For a few moments, she thought he'd actually listened to her and left. A coldness swept over her skin and she shivered. Turning on her side, she pulled her knees up in an effort to fight the chill—and the sudden urge to call him back.

Don't leave me. Don't leave me here.

He didn't leave her, not for long. Within minutes he was back, gently laying something over her shivering form and tucking it between her and the cold ground.

She curled up tighter in the warmth. "I'm fine," she told him weakly. "I'll be fine."

"You will be," he agreed and brushed a cool rag across her overheated brow and cheeks. "Just rest for now."

He left the rag cooling the back of her neck and began busying himself with something else nearby.

It was soothing, the sound of him moving around her, and for a long while she simply lay where she was, listening to the leaves crunch under his feet. Though she knew it wasn't possible, she swore she could even make out his scent—soap and horse and man. She breathed deeply through her nose, comforted by the illusion. Slowly, the nausea and headache receded and her mind drifted in and out of a shallow sleep.

She didn't open her eyes again until she felt Gideon brushing the hair back from her face. "Wake up now, sweetheart."

She blinked, swallowed experimentally, and was relieved to discover the nausea had passed. But, *oh*, she needed something to drink.

"Thirsty," she rasped.

"I've something for that. Why don't you try sitting up." He slipped his arms around her, which she might have found agreeable if she hadn't been so miserable, and gently lifted her into a sitting position.

She tried to assist in the process, but her limbs were so heavy, the most she could do was grip the front of his coat and stare groggily at his loosened cravat.

Gideon released her with one arm to tuck her hair behind her ears. "Let's take it slow, shall we, and sit here a minute?"

She gave a small nod and was pleasantly surprised when her head didn't roll from her shoulders. Her neck felt as if it was fashioned of pudding. "Was I asleep for long?"

"Twenty minutes, more or less."

That was all? She felt as if she'd been lying on the ground for hours.

His hand moved in small, gentle circles against her back. "You gave Lilly quite a scare, you know. She tried to follow you when you hopped from the carriage . . . Not much of a tracker, is she?"

"Ghastly," she agreed softly. "Where is she?"

"Do you want me to fetch her for you?"

"No, she'll fuss."

Gideon chuckled. "I thought that might be the case. I asked her to wait by the road with the others . . . After I helped her find her way out of the woods."

It felt so good to feel her lips curve into a smile. "She has no sense of direction. She's not still worried?"

"Concerned now, but not worried. She sent this with me." He reached behind him and produced a toothbrush and toothpowder.

Too grateful to pay much heed to her embarrassment, she let go of Gideon with one hand to grip them as if they were made of gold.

Oh, bless you, Lilly.

"Think you could try standing?" Gideon asked.

"Yes." If it meant she could clean her mouth and get something to drink, she could try dancing.

He helped her up slowly and carefully, but the world still tilted and blurred.

Gideon tightened an arm around her waist when she wobbled. "Easy."

"I'm all right." Her legs were weak but steady. The dizziness was already passing. "You can let go."

He studied her with a line between his brows. "You're certain?"

She nodded, and he released her slowly, keeping a hand hovering a few inches from her waist. When she didn't immediately topple, he took a cautious step back. With his form no longer encompassing her entire vision, she noticed he had spread a blanket on the ground. A small array of food was set on top.

"What is that?"

He glanced over his shoulder. "A picnic, of sorts. We've bread, cheese, some aged apples and watered beer."

"But the others—" she began.

"Are enjoying their own outdoor meal, with the addition of pastries. I assume you're not feeling ready for that?"

"No, thank you."

"I thought not." He stepped around her and retrieved his overcoat from the ground. *That* was what had been pillowing her head, she mused. She hadn't imagined his smell after all.

With a small smile, she stepped away to clean her teeth. It felt like heaven, and by the time she joined Gideon on the blanket, another layer of discomfort had slipped away.

"Start with the bread," Gideon suggested and broke off a small chunk to hand to her.

"I don't think I can." That wasn't entirely true. She was sure she could eat. In fact, she was starving all of a sudden. But she wasn't at all confident she could keep the food down.

"Just a bite or two."

She tried and was surprised to discover it helped to further settle her stomach. Emboldened, she reached for more bread and a bit of cheese.

"Not too fast," Gideon cautioned. "Or too much."

She took a bite and spoke around the food. "It tastes like ambrosia."

"I am relieved to hear it."

An odd catch in his voice had her looking up. He looked a good deal more than relieved. "Are you . . . laughing?"

"Absolutely not." He lifted a fist to clear his throat, but she could see the smile behind his hand.

"You are," she accused. Offended, and just a little hurt, she set down her food. "Why the devil are you laughing?"

"I am happy to see you improved."

"Bullocks. You're amused. I could very well be quite seriously ill, and you're—"

"What you *are*, Winnefred," he told her with a grin, "is seasick."

If he'd told her she was the Queen of Sheba, she wouldn't have been more shocked. She gaped at him, absolutely speechless.

"Who'd have thought?" Gideon reached for her slice of cheese and ate it whole. "Our Winnefred has a delicate constitution."

She found her voice again. "Delicate."

"As the petals of an orchid," he crooned poetically and—in her opinion—stupidly. "As a single snowflake in spring."

Something like a laugh escaped her throat. "Snowflake."

"Precisely." He took a bite of bread. "The ton's chaises will certainly be put to good use this season. Lilly's explained how to execute a proper swoon, I hope? Because it won't do for you to go flipping over the backs of furniture haphazardly. There's an art to it—"

"I have never swooned in my life." Though it had been a near thing only a few moments ago.

"Looked to me as if it were a near thing only—"

"Have we anything besides watered beer?" she asked quickly.

"I'm afraid not. Unless you'd fancy a bit of the gin one of the outriders has stashed under his overcoat."

"No, thank you." The very idea made her stomach roll unpleasantly. She wrinkled her nose and shook her head. She took another bite of food, her brow furrowed in thought. "Are you quite confident it's only seasickness?"

Though she didn't care for the idea, it was much preferable to the possibility of scarlet fever or smallpox or some other horrendous and contagious illness.

"Strictly speaking, it's carriage sickness, but yes, I'm sure. I've seen it enough times to know." Gideon gestured in the general direction of the road. "It's the repetitive rocking."

She lost her appetite again. "We've days left before we reach London."

"There are ways to ease the discomfort," he assured her gently.

"You're certain?"

"I promise." He nudged the hand holding her food. "Try eating a little more."

Willing to take him at his word, she did as he suggested. They made an unhurried meal of their picnic, and Winnefred felt better with every minute that passed. By the time Gideon gathered the blanket and the remaining food, she felt almost human again. Almost.

"Do you want anything else before we go?" Gideon inquired as they made their way out of the woods.

Home. My own bed in the gardener's cottage. She bit back the words, hopeful the acute longing for the safe and familiar would pass with the lingering illness. "No. I'm feeling much improved, thank you."

Her confidence wavered as they reached the clearing on the side of the road. Just looking at the carriage made her feel woozy. She hesitated and reached for Gideon's arm without thinking. "I . . . I don't know if I can—"

"You won't have to," he said gently. "You'll ride up top."

Before she had a chance to respond, Lilly flew from the carriage in blur of blue skirts.

*G*ideon allowed Lilly to fuss over the state of her friend a little before assisting Winnefred to the top of the carriage. Rather than return to his horse, he settled in the seat beside her. Purely for reasons of safety, he assured himself. Winnefred was better off supported between himself and Peter—a bit of logic reinforced when Winnefred's head nodded and slid onto his shoulder within the first ten minutes.

But no matter how he justified his decision, a small part of him knew the truth. He wanted to be near her. He wanted to watch her sleep. He wanted the reassurance of her warm body next to his.

His world had stopped when he had found her on the ground next to the stream. When she'd whimpered in distress, it had started again with a slow, painful roll of his heart. He would have given anything in that moment to make her well again, anything she wanted. If she'd asked to return to Murdoch House, he would have turned the carriage around, and Lilly and his brother be damned.

And it hadn't been humor at her illness that had prompted him to laugh when she'd begun to eat. It had been relief, pure and simple.

The extent of his affection for her was unnerving, but he couldn't find a way around it, couldn't find a way to lessen the desire just to be near her. He'd tried. Over the last three weeks he'd tried nearly every distraction known to man . . . to the men in Enscrum and the surrounding countryside, at any rate. He'd even thought of finding a pretty, willing woman in Langholm, but he'd not been able to gather any enthusiasm for the idea. That revelation had been particularly disturbing. He had no intention of taking Winnefred Blythe to bed, but he'd be damned if he spent the rest of his life celibate.

Winnefred moaned softly and shifted against him. The blanket he had wrapped around her slipped to her waist. He replaced it carefully, tucking it gently around her shoulders and under her chin. Her skin, he noticed, was slowly losing the color it had regained during their picnic.

He spoke quietly over her head at Peter. "I seem to recall an inn not far from here."

"Aye, my lord. Not a mile down the road."

"We'll rest there for the night."

Gideon let Winnefred sleep until the inn came into view, then rubbed her shoulder softly and whispered in her ear, just once.

"Winnefred."

That was all it took. She woke with a start, bolting upright as if she'd been prodded with a hot iron. "What? What is it?"

He couldn't help but chuckle at her wide-eyed dishevelment. "You wake . . . quickly."

She looked at him and blinked eyes foggy with sleep. It was a few seconds before her brain seemed to process his words.

"Habit," was all she said.

His amusement vanished. Two women, alone for years on an isolated farm. Yes, he imagined it was a habit learned quickly and well. The muscles in his jaw clenched until he thought his teeth might crack.

Winnefred appeared unaware of his sudden change of mood. She shifted in her seat to look around her. "Why did you wake me?"

He cleared his throat and wiggled his jaw to relieve the pressure. "To keep you from becoming ill again. A bit of sleep is good for you, but keeping your eyes off the road for too long will bring the nausea back."

"Oh." She rubbed her stomach, as if testing his theory,

and looked around again when they slowed in front of the inn. "We're stopping. Are we changing the horses?"

"No. We're stopping for the day."

"For the day?" She squinted at the sun. "But we've hours of daylight yet. Is something the matter?"

"Nothing a leisurely meal and a good night's rest won't remedy."

"But it's so early. Why . . . ?" She turned and frowned at him. "I don't need to be coddled, Gideon."

On the contrary, he'd never met a woman more in need of coddling in his life, but he doubted she would appreciate the sentiment.

"You may not require a rest, but I do." He tapped a finger against his leg. "Extended periods of inactivity cause uncomfortable stiffness."

This was a complete and, in his opinion, entirely justified fabrication. It was also remarkably effective.

"Oh." She went from mulish to apologetic in the space of a heartbeat. "Yes, of course. I'm sorry. Why didn't you say something earlier?"

"It wasn't troubling me earlier." Or now, he added silently.

"But in the future . . ." she pressed.

"I will voice my dissatisfaction when necessary," he promised her, and in this, he was being honest. He intended to speak up every time she lost her color or looked tired or in any way distressed.

He intended to voice his dissatisfaction quite a bit.

Chapter 18

Winnefred spent the few hours before dinner finding ways to occupy her mind and keep her body awake. She could have slept. If she had crawled on top of the mattress and closed her eyes, she would have been dead to the world in under a minute. And because there was nothing worse than sleeping through daylight and being awake at night, she chose to read instead, and pester Lilly, and walk about the room until it was finally time to go downstairs for dinner.

The inn and tavern was a modest establishment, without a private dining room. As she took a seat with Gideon and Lilly at a table, Winnefred studied the scene around her. There were fifteen or so patrons scattered about in groups of twos and threes. Soft laughter sounded over the crackling of the fireplace, and a pair of barmaids in gowns cut low about the neckline wove expertly around tables and guests. The air smelled lightly of wood smoke and heavily of meat roasting in the kitchen.

She blew out a sigh of relief when her mouth watered

and her stomach tightened with hunger instead of nausea. "I am famished."

"I wish I could say the same," Lilly said meekly.

Winnefred looked at her friend and grimaced. Lilly was hardly a hothouse flower, but there was something about the heavy scent of roasting meat that sometimes put her stomach off.

"Shall we take our meals in our rooms, instead?" She willed Lilly to say no. After spending a couple of hours pacing the floor of the room she shared with Lilly, Winnefred found the notion of returning so soon distinctly unappealing.

Lilly shook her head. "I will take my meal upstairs. You may stay here with Gideon, if you like."

"Can I do that?"

Lilly nodded toward an elderly woman seated by the fire a few feet from the table. "The innkeeper's wife will make an acceptable chaperone. I'll speak with her."

To Winnefred's delight, the innkeeper's wife agreed to the arrangement. Better yet, she chose to perform her chaperoning duties from the continued comfort of her chair, allowing Winnefred and Gideon to carry on a conversation in relative privacy.

"Did you nap?" Gideon inquired from across the table.

She shook her head. "I slept in the carriage, and *on* the carriage. If I slept a minute longer, I'd be awake all night. It will be difficult enough, being in a strange place for the night."

"You've stayed at an inn before."

"Yes, on my trip to Scotland," she replied. "I had a dreadful time of it, trying to rest. I had a touch of the ague."

His lips curved into a knowing smile. "Are you sure?"

"Yes, of . . ." She trailed off, remembering the headaches and mild bouts of nausea, and how quickly she had recovered when they reached Murdoch House. "Oh. I hadn't considered it might be something else. I don't recall being nearly so ill as I was today."

"It was twelve years ago. There are things that affect us

more strongly as adults than as children. And vice versa, of course." He gave her a wink. "You've grown more delicate over the years."

She laughed but was distracted from commenting when a steaming bowl of stew and several slices of warm bread were set before her. The savory aroma wafted to her nose and set her mouth to watering again. She couldn't remember ever being so hungry.

For the next quarter hour, conversation all but ceased while she steadily made her way through the meal. When she finally looked up from the table, it was to find Gideon finished and staring at something behind her with his lips curved up at the corners.

She glanced over her shoulder but saw nothing out of the ordinary. "What are you smiling at?"

"Hmm?" Gideon looked at her. "Ah. Not what, who. I'm playing guess-the-secret."

"Guess-the-secret? Is it a game?" She set her spoon down, intrigued, and not the least surprised to find he was a grown man who still indulged in games.

"Of sorts. One of the young officers on my ship devised it during a particularly long voyage."

She stifled a yawn, sleepy now that her belly was full and the threat of further illness had been averted for at least a few more hours. "How does it work?"

"You pick people at random and guess their darkest secret, or which of their dark secrets they're most troubled about today. The second version worked best on the ship as one looks at the same people every day."

"Didn't you give your men enough to do?"

"They had free time now and then. Look there," he said quietly and jerked his chin at a portly middle-aged man in a worn coat. "He has pawned his deceased father-in-law's watch and chain to pay for his ale. He's frugal about it, though, and keeps the money hidden. He uses the funds to buy only one drink a week. See how he's nursing it? He wants to make it last."

"Could be he used an honest day's wage."

"Could be, if we weren't playing guess-the-secret. What about her?" He nodded toward one of the well-endowed barmaids. "What's her secret, do you suppose?"

Winnefred scowled thoughtfully at the maid. "She has an entire closet full of adequately fitting gowns that she neglects in the hopes of earning a larger wage."

"I'm not certain about the entire closet full of gowns part, but the rest is common knowledge. You'll have to do better. What's her secret?"

She pursed her lips, warming to the challenge. "The earrings she is wearing are from a lover. A very well-to-do lover. They're not something a woman employed at a tavern could afford. You see how she fiddles with them and smiles? But she doesn't look at the door. She's not waiting for him to come in. Because he's already in the room."

"Well done," he commented as she finally gave in to the urge to yawn. "You learn quickly."

"Some things," she murmured. "Now you. Which of these fine gentleman purchased the earrings?"

Gideon scanned the room. "The young man two tables over on your left. He's peeking glances and blushing and—"

"Married," she finished for him. "I wager he's married."

"That would be his dark secret. His wedding bed hasn't yet cooled and already he's warming another. He can't help himself. Her charms, her—" He broke off suddenly and cleared his throat. "Perhaps this isn't the most appropriate of games to be playing with you."

She rolled her eyes at him. "I've some idea what goes on between a man and a woman behind closed doors, Gideon." A very narrow idea, but it counted. "Giddy is bred every year, you'll recall."

"Nevertheless, it would be best if we moved on to other people. What about that man?"

Caught between annoyed and amused, she didn't even bother to look where he pointed. "He's not married, but he has two mistresses. In the same house."

He scowled at her. "The man in the blue wool coat by the fire."

"He likes his sheep for more than their wool."

"For pity's sake."

She laughed; she couldn't help it. But there was a dark edge to her humor, and a heaviness of heart she couldn't shake.

It had been only a week since she'd sat in his chambers at Murdoch House, worried he might think less of her for teaching a thief to read. It had seemed important to her then that he believed she could be taught to behave like a proper lady. But she found that wasn't what she wanted from him now. She wasn't interested in his approval of what she might become, or pretend to be for the short time she was in London. She wasn't sure she wanted to become a lady. There was very good reason to believe she might not even be capable of such a transformation.

In that moment, all she wanted from him was to accept her as she was now. And it chafed that he had to be reminded of who that was.

"Did you think a fine dress and some distance from my land would make me someone else entirely, Gideon?" she asked softly. "Have you forgotten how you found me? Who I am?"

He looked at her, his dark gaze searching her face for a long, long moment before answering. "I could never forget you, Winnefred."

She shrugged and traced her finger down the handle of her spoon. "Pity your family didn't feel the same."

"Yes, it is. A great pity."

She snatched her hand back from the table and winced. He'd been so thoughtful today, so wonderfully considerate, and she repaid him now by being disagreeable and petty.

"I apologize," she mumbled. "That was uncalled for. I don't know why I said it."

"Aside from the fact it is true," he replied with more kindness than she felt she deserved, "you said it because you are more tired than you are willing to admit."

She couldn't seem to lift her gaze above her empty bowl. "That is not an excuse—"

"And," he cut in, "you are taking this more to heart than you should for the same reason. Winnefred, look at me." He waited for her to comply. "You are a breath away from falling into your soup bowl. Go upstairs; go to bed. Things will look different in the morning."

Under other circumstances, she might have taken some offense at the insinuation she had difficulty seeing things as they really were. In fact, she *wanted* to take offense, which only went to prove his point.

She was exhausted. Her body felt leaded and her thoughts raced without getting anywhere. She knew she was angry still, but she couldn't decide if it was with him for thinking she ought to be a lady or with herself for not meeting his expectations. Probably, it was a bit of both, which made very little sense.

"Winnefred," Gideon said again. "Go to bed."

Giving up, she nodded and rose from the table to seek out her bed.

Chapter 19

The next morning, Winnefred stood at the front of the inn and watched as Gideon oversaw the harnessing of the horses to the carriage. She took a deep breath of the cool morning air and smiled. She felt herself again . . . Only better. Remarkably better. In fact, she felt very nearly exuberant.

It was the oddest thing. She'd gone to sleep worrying over her disagreement with Gideon and had woken in such a fine mood, she'd had no trouble at all addressing her troubles as she so often did . . . by pushing them away.

Gideon hadn't been angry when she had left. She wasn't angry now. And the rest could be worked through in time.

It all seemed so simple. Which, quite frankly, seemed a little strange.

How was it her body could still be battling a lingering weakness while her spirits practically soared? She contemplated this as Gideon walked across the yard to meet her. Then she contemplated how much she enjoyed watching Gideon walk across a yard to meet her.

He ought to seem ungainly, she mused, or less virile

somehow because of his injury. But he didn't. He moved with an unexpected grace, and the unmistakable command of a man confident in his physical prowess. She watched the sculpted muscles of his thighs bulge beneath the snug fabric of his trousers, then let her eyes wander up to the broad expanse of his chest and the quick bunch and release of his powerful shoulders when he leaned on his cane.

Oh, yes, everything about the man spoke of an uncommon physical strength. And everything about that had an uncommon effect on her.

"Feeling better this morning?" Gideon inquired when he reached her.

"Very much, thank you." Amused by the tenor of her thoughts—less so by the heat in her cheeks—she caught her hands behind her back and rocked on her toes. "You were right, you know. Things do look different in the morning. Dramatically so. I feel euphoric. It's the most bizarre thing."

He tilted his head at her. "You've not been ill before, have you?"

"I had a head cold once and the mild illness on the way to Scotland. Why?" She stopped rocking, a grim thought occurring to her. "Is euphoria a symptom of something more serious—?"

"No," he replied on a laugh. "Just a benefit of recovery."

"Oh." *How very nice.* "Does it last long?"

He looked at the carriage, then looked at her. "I'm afraid not."

"I'll take pleasure in it while I can, then," she decided. "Are we ready to leave?"

He chuckled and nodded. "I'll fetch Lilly."

An hour later, Winnefred noted with some disappointment that Gideon was also right about the life span of her euphoria. With every sway of the carriage a little more of her good mood slipped away.

She rode atop again, and though she found the movements of the carriage unpleasant, she also found plenty to distract her from her discomfort, and she wondered why anyone would ever choose to ride inside. There was so much to see, and the narrow view of the countryside to be had through a carriage window and around an outrider could not compare to the grand vista offered by an elevated seat. Better yet, Gideon had chosen to keep her company again, and he entertained her with tales of his travels and his youth. All of which he admitted to embellishing generously for the sake of good drama. She was delighted he did. She was delighted with *him*. Never before had she met someone capable of making her laugh and dream, wonder and want in the space of an hour, and then make her laugh and dream, wonder and want all over again in the next.

But what was most unfamiliar to her was the experience of being cared for by someone stronger than herself. With Lilly, there had always been companionship and cooperation. But with Gideon, she felt . . . protected. There was no other word for it, no other way to describe how it felt to be tucked up against his side, his large frame sheltering her smaller one. He steadied her with strong hands when the carriage rocked too hard, and the heat of his body permeated through her coat and gown, warming skin that wanted to chill.

She had always considered herself a person of independence, capable of caring for herself. But she could admit that there was a comfort, even a sense of freedom, in knowing she could rely on Gideon for a time. It was nice to know that, if just for a little while, she didn't have to be the strong one.

But even the frequent stops they made, the distractions of beautiful scenery, and the comfort of Gideon's company were not enough to hold off her illness indefinitely. By early afternoon, she was experiencing a persistent ache in her belly, and her limbs began to feel sore and heavy. She tried to stay awake, remembering what Gideon had said about the perils of keeping her eyes off the road for too long, but it was only a matter of time before her head drooped and she slipped into sleep.

She woke on her own, slowly and with the unsettling

notion that someone had stuffed a wool coat in her mouth during her nap. As she became more aware, she realized it would be more accurate to say that she had put her mouth on the coat.

She was drooling on Gideon.

Her head snapped up and off his shoulder fast enough to have her neck screaming in protest. "I'm sorry. I'm terribly sorry."

Oh, how mortifying.

"Quite all right," he assured her with a teasing smile. "You salivate charmingly."

She groaned and dragged the back of her hand across her chin. "Why didn't you wake me?"

"There was no reason for it. You've been asleep less than half an hour."

"My pride could give you a dozen reasons. All moot now," she grumbled.

"Exactly. So why worry yourself over it?"

"Easy for you to say." His dignity hadn't dribbled slowly out of his mouth for the last few miles.

"You'll make light of men and sheep, but throw in a little spit, and you color right up. You're a puzzle, Winnefred."

"I'm a terrific mess," she muttered. Her clothes were wrinkled and twisted, her bonnet was askew, and loose strands of hair whipped into her eyes. A headache was beginning to press against the back of her forehead and nausea continued its relentless assault against her system.

Gideon slipped out of his coat and draped it over her shoulders. "We'll be stopping for the day soon."

She wasn't cold, but the coat smelled of him, and she found that comforting. She smiled in thanks. "We don't need to stop yet. It's barely midday."

"It's nearing two." He pointed to a thick gray wall of clouds she hadn't noticed in the distance. "And we've heavy rain coming."

Not just rain, Winnefred thought, but a storm. The soft rumble of thunder could be heard, and the heavy sheets of rain extending from the clouds looked as if they could wash the road and everyone on it away in a matter of minutes.

She turned to Peter. "How far are we from shelter?"

"Ten miles back or nine miles forward, give or take."

She looked again at the brewing storm. "We'll not outrun it."

"No, we won't," Gideon agreed. "You'll need to get inside the carriage soon."

"No." She reached up and tied the ribbons of her bonnet more tightly. "Absolutely not."

"You'll be soaked."

She considered the alternative. "Then I'll be soaked."

"Winnefred—"

"I can't, Gideon. Not for nine miles. I just can't."

He looked as if he wanted to argue, but in the end, he simply nodded and tucked his coat more securely around her shoulders.

"You need this back," she said.

"I don't. And you'll keep it on, or you'll ride out the storm in the carriage."

She kept it on.

The rain began slowly, a mist of water brought in on the wind. It picked up, just as the wind did, and within twenty minutes, Gideon's prediction came true. She was soaked to the bone. The rain and surrounding air was warm, but the water drove against them in hard sheets. She kept her chin down and her eyes closed and didn't look up again until she heard a soft curse from Gideon and felt the carriage begin to slow.

"What is it?"

If anyone answered her, she didn't hear it over the storm, and it hardly mattered. She could see the trouble for herself. A large stream cut across the road. It ran fast, wide, and undoubtedly deep. And the wooden bridge spanning it had been built too low to accommodate the sudden influx of water from heavy rainfall. The rushing water buffeted against the side of the bridge, periodically lapping up and over the boards. Winnefred imagined that if it hadn't been for the howl of the wind and rain, one could hear the creaking and groaning of the wood. If the rain continued with such intensity, it would only be a matter of time before the bridge gave out.

The moment the carriage stopped, Gideon and Peter hopped down. Winnefred followed them, a little surprised Gideon neither insisted she stay nor assisted her down. If she hadn't known better, she would have thought he was completely unaware of her presence. He walked toward the stream without looking at her. And when the outriders moved to follow, Gideon simply stopped them with a distracted wave of the hand.

He stepped onto the bridge and looked down as another wave of water splashed over and onto his boots. It didn't quite pass his ankles. He didn't stand there long but backed off the bridge and rejoined her and Peter on the road. Winnefred waited for him to say something, but he simply turned around and stared at the water.

Peter lifted his voice over the storm. "Sound as rock, that bridge!"

Winnefred nodded and looked to Gideon. "Shall we cross?"

When he said nothing, simply stared at the bridge, she assumed he hadn't heard her over the wind and rain.

"Gideon, do we cross?!" she yelled louder, but still he didn't answer. He gave no indication he'd even heard her. A sliver of unease wound under her skin. "Gideon?"

The unease turned to fear when he remained still and silent. Swallowing it down, she turned and spoke to Peter. "Go wait by the carriage. Tell Miss Ilestone to stay inside. Lord Gideon and I will return shortly."

Peter glanced uncertainly at Gideon but ultimately obeyed. When he was out of earshot, Winnefred tried to maneuver herself into Gideon's line of sight, but he simply peered over her head at the bridge. He was too pale, she thought. His breathing was too heavy. Water ran down his brow and cheeks in rivulets, but he didn't appear to notice.

She took hold of his shoulders instead. "Gideon, what is it? . . . Gideon!"

He didn't look at her, but he spoke, finally, in a voice so soft she had trouble hearing him over the storm. "A minute. It just needs to stop for one bloody minute so I can think."

"What needs to stop?" The storm? The rushing water? He wasn't making any sense. It was as if he was trapped somewhere else, fighting a battle she couldn't see. But she knew torment when she saw it, and she recognized the pain in his eyes as the very same she'd seen when he'd woken from his nightmare.

"You can have all the time you want," she tried, her heart breaking for him, "just *look* at me."

It was as if she wasn't even there. She stepped back and brushed the rain from her face. Pleading with him wasn't working. Yelling at him wasn't working. She had to think of something else. She couldn't stand to see him so lost.

She looked at the bridge, at Gideon, and made her decision. She spun on her heel and marched toward the bridge.

Gideon was on her before she put a single foot on the wood. He grabbed her around the waist and dragged her back from the water before spinning her around in his arms.

"What the hell do you think you're doing?!"

His arms felt like bands of iron, and his features were hard as stone. He was furious. She hadn't known he was even capable of such anger. And all she could think was, *Thank heavens. Oh, thank heavens.*

She tipped her chin up and hoped the tactic she was taking was the right one. "Testing the bridge for myself. Someone needs to decide what's to be done."

"I will decide what's to be done!"

She reached up, gripped his face with both hands, and forced him to keep looking at her, and only her. "Then decide, Gideon. Do we cross, or do we not?"

He swallowed hard, but his eyes stayed on hers. "No," he said at last. "No, we do not."

"Excellent."

He nodded as if approving of his own decision, and as he did, the confusion and pain in his eyes began to fade. "The storm is moving quickly. We wait until it passes. The water will recede." He nodded once more. "We wait."

"We wait."

Delighted, relieved to the point of giddiness, she gave in to temptation and pressed her lips to his. He tasted of the rain, with the faintest hint of the gin he'd nipped from the outrider. She had just enough time to decide she rather liked the taste, and to register the feel of his fingers brushing lightly across her cheek, and then he was pulling away . . . Slowly, this time, and without a single backward step.

She could have kissed him again just for that.

Gideon had other ideas. "Get in the carriage," he said, his voice a little rough. "I'll fetch you when it's time to leave."

Chapter 20

Winnefred had no more than returned Gideon's coat and opened the carriage door before Lilly reached out, grabbed her arm, and yanked her inside. "What on *earth* is going on here?"

"Good grief," Winnefred gasped, pulling her arm free and taking a seat. "Give me a moment to right myself."

"You may right yourself as you explain."

Winnefred tried to take off her sopping bonnet, but the ribbons were tied into a hopeless knot. "There was a minor disagreement between Lord Gideon and myself. I thought it best to resolve the issue in private."

"Private? I could see you well enough from the window, Winnefred Blythe. There was nothing private about that kiss."

"Let it alone, Lilly."

"I'll not. You are my—"

"For now," Winnefred tried. "For now, let it alone. Please."

Lilly pressed her lips together, tapped a finger against

her knee—which was not quite so encouraging a sign as a tapping foot—then said, "No. Absolutely not."

Winnefred groaned. She should have known a spot of begging wouldn't put Lilly off. "I love you, Lilly. I do. But I'll not share a secret with you that is not my own."

Particularly when she hadn't the foggiest idea of what that secret might be.

"I'm not asking you to," Lilly returned. "I am demanding you explain that kiss."

"It was just . . ." She gave up on the knot and forcefully pulled the ribbons over her chin. "It was only a peck."

"I'm not blind. I saw how you were looking . . ." Lilly sighed and trailed off. It was some time before she spoke again, and when she did, her tone was sympathetic. "Are you in love with him, Freddie?"

Winnefred frowned in thought. She'd not considered the notion before, and she found now that no matter from which direction she looked at the question, she couldn't come up with a satisfactory answer. Worse, she couldn't work out how she even felt about the idea. She hadn't any philosophical objections to falling in love, but she did have some reservations, not the least of which was the notion of falling in love with someone who might not love her back.

She scooted forward in her seat, wrinkling her nose a little when her wet skirts bunched under her legs. "I don't know. What does it feel like to be in love?"

"It feels wonderful," Lilly replied. ". . . Until it doesn't."

"That's not at all helpful."

"The experience of falling in love is different for everyone." Lilly cocked her head. "How does he make you feel?"

"I just told you. I think I might be in love." Her eyes widened. "Oh, physically, do you mean? I find him quite attractive. Sometimes, when he looks at me a certain way—"

"*No*, that is not what I . . ." Lilly cleared her throat and carefully smoothed her hands down her skirts. "Yes, there are certain . . . corporal . . . er . . . indicators that certainly . . . indicate . . . Oh, dear."

Winnefred shook her head. "I've no idea what—"

Lilly closed her eyes briefly and raised her hand. "Let me try again," she suggested. "Does having him about make you happy?"

"Yes, very."

"And when he is not about, do you miss him?"

"I suppose I do."

"In a different way than you miss, let us say, Claire, or even myself?"

"Yes."

Lilly nodded. "Then there is a chance you are in love with him."

"Just a chance?"

"Only you can say for certain."

Winnefred slumped back against the cushions. If she were capable of saying for certain, she wouldn't have needed to ask. "What about . . . When did you know Lord Engsly returned your affections?"

"When he declared them to me."

"Oh."

Lilly laughed softly. "Give it time, Freddie."

"Do you approve, then?"

"Naturally, I do." Lilly leaned forward and gripped her hand. "For as long as he makes you happy."

She could have done without the second half of that statement. "Do you expect him to make me unhappy?"

"Not intentionally, no. And he does appear to be quite fond of you, but . . ." Lilly squeezed her hand again before letting go. "He *is* the brother of a marquess."

There it was, all her fears wrapped into one statement of fact.

She busied herself for a while, wringing out the water from the cuffs of her gown until she could gather the courage to voice those fears aloud.

"He reads poetry," she said quietly. "*Real* poetry, not silly limmericks. And he's traveled the world. He speaks of Aristotle, and he knows French. I wager he's never forgotten which fork to use at dinner." She worried her lip a moment. "Do you suppose . . . Do you suppose I'm just a diversion to him? Do you think he might see me as an amusing country bumpkin, and nothing more?"

"No," Lilly said, and with enough force for Winnefred to know she meant it. "Absolutely not. I have no doubt that what Gideon sees is a very clever young woman who is *learning* of forks and poetry, and will one day be as familiar with each as any other lady."

Winnefred tried, and failed, to produce a smile. By that logic, Gideon thought highly of the woman she might become, not who she was now.

Lilly spoke before she could. "And that's not what I was referring to when I spoke of Gideon's rank. I am sure he cares for you, but the brother of a marquess may very well have definite expectations placed upon him when it comes to his choice of wife. I shouldn't care to see you disappointed."

"Oh, *that*." She made a scoffing sound in the back of her throat and decided she was quite done investigating all the reasons she might not be good enough for Gideon. "He doesn't concern himself with those sorts of expectations, particularly. And it hardly signifies. I'm only *possibly* in love with him, and I'm not at all sure I want to be a wife to anyone."

It was difficult to see without sunlight coming into the carriage, but Winnefred could have sworn her friend paled a little. "You listen to me very carefully, Winnefred Blythe. If you intend to pursue your interest in Lord Gideon, you will do so *only* with the goal of marriage in mind. The consideration of any other romantic arrangement is unacceptable. Do you understand?"

"But—"

"No." Lilly didn't snap the word, but there was a finality in her tone Winnefred knew meant there was no point in further debate. "No other arrangement is acceptable. Do you understand?"

She bit back the urge to argue. "Yes."

"Promise me you will not even *think*—"

"I promise I will not enter into a formal arrangement with Gideon that does not meet with your approval." She wasn't any more interested in becoming someone's mistress than she was someone's wife.

"Good." Lilly narrowed her eyes. "Now say it again without the formal bit."

"Oh, look. The rain has stopped. That was very quick." She reached for the door handle, intending to make a fast escape.

Lilly threw an arm out to block her exit. "Winnefred."

She bit her lip, searching for a way to appease her friend without making promises before she'd thought through all her options.

"I don't want anyone to be disappointed," she said quietly. "Least of all you."

Lilly hesitated, then nodded and let her arm fall.

Stifling a breath of relief, Winnefred climbed out of the carriage and closed the door behind her. The air felt thick and the ground squished beneath her feet as she walked to where Gideon stood, his back to her, watching the stream. Already it was beginning to recede, she noticed. The water barely topped over the bridge.

She hesitated as she neared Gideon.

Are you in love with him?

How the devil was she to know? She had affection for him, yes. She was attracted to him, without question. She had respect for him and admiration and . . . And questions, she concluded. She had so many questions. About herself. About him. Now, however, was not the time to ask them. Not while he was standing alone under heavy gray clouds, his head bowed and the muscles of his broad shoulders visibly bunched under his coat. She set her own worries aside and stepped up beside him.

He spared her a brief glance and small smile. "Cold?"

"I'm not the one who stood out without a coat," she reminded him. "You're drenched."

And rather adorable with it, she thought. The dark locks of his hair were beginning to curl up at the ends.

He shook his head dismissively. "I'll dry out soon enough."

"The water is receding quickly," she commented, for lack of courage to say anything else. "Will we be able to cross soon, do you think?"

"Within the hour."

She pressed the toes of her foot into the rain-soaked ground and watched as the mud oozed around the leather of her boot. "Are you all right, Gideon?"

"Yes." He nodded and gave her a fleeting look. "Yes, I'm fine."

He didn't sound fine. He looked and sounded just as he had when she'd met him by the pond the morning after she'd woken him from his nightmare—tired, troubled, and distant.

She remembered that he hadn't cared to be pressed then, and that a silly conversation and a bit of laughter had seemed to make him feel better. The first she could manage, despite her raging curiosity, but for the life of her, she couldn't think of anything funny to say now.

Not until Gideon turned to her and said, "I imagine Lilly had a few questions for you upon your return to the carriage."

Oh, perfect. She smiled at him as if they were sharing a private joke. "About our disagreement and subsequent reconciliation? Indeed she did."

"A disagreement," he repeated, and just as she hoped, the first hint of humor tinted his voice. "Is that what happened?"

"Don't you recall? I am of the opinion that sheep raised in Scotland are the finest to be had in the world. You insisted they could not compare to English mutton." She tsked at him. "You were quite unreasonable on the matter."

He sent her a dubious glance. "Is that truly what you told Lilly?"

"She didn't ask for the particulars of our argument," she admitted and felt a blush begin to form on her cheeks. "It was the kiss that caused her some distress."

He closed his eyes and swore. "Bloody hell, she saw."

"Yes." She bit the inside of her cheek to keep from smiling. "She assures me you'll make an adequate husband."

His eyes flew open, and an abrupt choking sound emerged from his throat and was directly followed by the draining of all the color from his face. He garbled, "Beg your pardon," or something near to it, and then stared at her as if she'd grown a second head.

Stunned, she stared back. She hadn't expected him to believe the jest, but that was of minor concern compared to his severe, and decidedly unflattering, reaction to the notion they were betrothed.

He is the brother of a marquess.

Suddenly, she no longer needed to bite her cheek to keep her amusement in check. She did, however, have to fight to keep her feet in place as every fear of rejection, every doubt of her worth flooded to the surface. Her chest grew tight. Her eyes stung. She wanted to slink back to the carriage in defeat and give in to the sudden and humiliating urge to cry.

But not before she hit him. Hard.

Only the memory of how disoriented, how lost he had been only a half hour ago kept her from doing either. He wasn't quite himself. Some allowance could be made under the circumstances. Patience was warranted . . . Some patience . . . A little patience.

She couldn't let the insult pass completely unanswered, could she?

She forced her demeanor into one of mild interest.

"You look rather wan all of a sudden, Gideon. Are you of a delicate constitution as well?"

"I . . . What? No, Winnefred—"

"How fortunate we should have so much in common," she chimed sweetly. "Perhaps Lilly is right and we'll make a respectable go of it. I must confess, I did have my doubts."

Her saccharine tone must have filtered slowly through his panicked mind because it was a few moments before the working of his mouth was accompanied by any sound.

"You're jesting," he finally managed and blew out a quick, hard breath of obvious relief. "You're not serious."

"Clever as well," she said dryly. "What a lucky woman I am, to have landed such a catch."

"I . . ." He winced, twice. "I deserved that."

"Yes. You did."

He lifted a fist to his mouth and cleared his throat. "In my defense, it isn't often a gentleman obtains the hand of such an estimable lady with so little effort. I was quite overcome by the extent of my good fortune."

She tilted her head at him, unamused. "Too much for your delicate constitution?"

"Exactly so."

"We shall have to break the engagement, then, until you are able to comprehend the joy of it without tossing up your accounts."

He adopted a sheepish expression. "If I tossed them up now, would you forgive me?"

Despite the hurt and anger, that surprised a small laugh out of her.

"I could probably manage it," he continued. "The heart-break of having won and lost the hand of such a lady so quickly—"

"Oh, for pity's sake." The edge of her anger dulled, just a little, as the sound of his laughter blended with her own reluctant amusement.

He cocked his head at her as the laughter faded. "Does this mean I am forgiven?"

She wanted to say no. She wanted to demand he explain what, exactly, was so appalling about the notion of marrying her. But she couldn't do it. Not now, when he was finally sounding like himself again.

She swallowed her wounded feelings, but this time she couldn't completely ignore the heavy weight of them in her stomach.

"Forgiven," she agreed. But she would be wise not to forget.

Chapter 21

Winnefred tried and failed to stay awake for the remainder of the afternoon. It was still early when they reached the next inn, and after a change into dry clothes and a hot meal, she found the allure of a soft bed too powerful to resist. She slept through the rest of the afternoon and evening. When next she woke, the room was dark except for the dim glow of coals in the grate and silent but for the sound of Lilly's steady breathing next to her.

She closed her eyes and tried to will herself back to sleep but gave the effort up as futile after a few minutes. Resigned to being awake, she rose quietly from the bed and went to the window to peek through the drapes.

The light of a half-moon illuminated the yard outside, and she watched as a late arriving guest was relieved of his horse by a pair of stable hands. She felt the soft thud of the front door vibrate beneath her feet and wondered if the night would be so busy in London. Gideon's aunt lived in a house, not an inn, but that house sat on a city street, and there was no telling what sort of activity might run up and down that road.

Thoughts of late night parades outside her window were lost as the sound of a low moan filtered through the wall.

Gideon.

Winnefred glanced at the bed, half expecting the soft noise to have woken her friend, but Lilly remained still, her breathing shallow and even.

She chewed on her lip, uncertain what to do.

The memory of his horrified reaction to the news of their betrothal flashed through her mind. So did the memory of his fingers caressing her cheek as they kissed in the rain. She recalled how he had backed away from her on their walk from the prison and again at the Howards' dinner party. And she thought of how he had barely left her side for the last two days. He was thoughtful and generous and capable of such tenderness . . . And he had cut her deeply.

And the man said *she* was a puzzle.

Gideon moaned again, prompting her to action. She grabbed her wrap, pushed her arms through her sleeves, and headed for the door. She gave a passing thought to leaving a note for Lilly before discarding the idea. There was simply no way of saying, *Have gone to Gideon's room, be back shortly,* that wouldn't send her friend into a panic. She'd simply have to hope Lilly slept through her absence.

The hall was devoid of life, which was convenient. It was also devoid of light, which left her feeling her way to Gideon's door. She tapped softly at first, then with more force when she heard his groan through the wood followed by a single word.

"Cannons."

Then the groaning stopped and there was a long moment of silence.

She knocked again and wondered that the pounding of her heart alone didn't wake him.

"A moment." Gideon's voice was muted and distinctly annoyed. "Give me a moment."

She waited, listening to him move about the room. He stumbled over something and swore ripely, and then the door opened and he was standing before her in trousers and shirtsleeves. The soft glow of the fireplace flickered behind him and spilled into the hall.

"Winnefred?" He squeezed his eyes shut and opened them again, as if he couldn't quite tell if he was awake or asleep. "What are you doing out of bed?"

"The walls in this inn are thin. I heard you call out."

"You heard . . ." He trailed off and dragged a hand down his face. She'd never seen him look so tired. "Bloody hell."

He had sworn more today than in the entire time they had been acquainted, she thought sadly.

"Are you going to invite me in?" As she'd hoped, the bold request took him off guard. He released the grip he'd had on the door, and she pushed it open and brushed past him to step into the room.

He reached for her arm. "You can't be in here."

"I am in here," she returned, sidestepping him, "and unless you want someone to see me in here, I suggest you close the door."

It took considerable effort to instill a confident tone in her speech and manner. There were knots in her stomach and a flurry of doubts swirling in her head. Maybe she was taking the wrong approach by barging her way into his room, but she had to do something. She had tried giving him his privacy, and she had tried pushing him into action. It was the latter that had produced results at the bridge.

Determined, she stood in the middle of the room and waited until he closed and latched the door before speaking again.

"You had another nightmare."

"I'm awake now."

"As am I, and since we are both up and—"

"This isn't something you need to concern yourself over."

She chose not to dignify that comment with a direct response. "Are they dreams of war?"

"I beg your pardon?"

"I heard you . . . just now . . ." She gestured at the door. "I heard you say 'cannons.' Are they dreams of war?"

He was silent for such a long time that she was a little surprised when he opened his mouth to speak.

He snapped it shut again without saying a word.

Almost, she thought. Almost was a start. "Would you like me to fetch you some port or—"

"Thank you, no."

She shifted her feet, then wished she hadn't. "I'm sorry I haven't any chocolate."

"It's all right. Go back to bed."

"Wouldn't you rather—?"

"No. Go to bed."

She straightened her shoulders, battled back her nerves, and said, "No."

Dark brows rose nearly to his hairline. "No?"

She nodded, resolute. "I am not leaving."

He was still except for lowering of his eyebrows. "It was not a request, Winnefred."

"It was not mistaken for one."

"I see." He stepped back to lean against the door and fold his arms over his chest. "And what do you expect to accomplish by defying me?"

This was a mood she didn't recognize. There was a coolness to his speech that added to her nervousness, and a negligence in his manner she'd not seen from him before. He looked at her as if he found her interesting, but only a little.

"I expect nothing," she replied. "I hope to help. I have to try."

"Why?"

She refused to give in to the sudden desire to look away. "Because you are of importance to me. You are my friend. Because—"

"We've known each other less than a sennight," he reminded her with a curl of his lip. "Will you insist upon turning this into a comédie larmoyante?"

Hurt and temper fought for control while a thin but sharp blade of acute embarrassment worked its way under her skin. Because her hands wanted to shake, she gripped them behind her back, and to counter the sudden tremble in her jaw she raised her chin and met his eyes.

"I don't know what that is."

He blinked once, twice, then closed his eyes. "I'm sorry. Bloody hell, I'm sorry. There was no call for that."

She remained silent, uncertain of what to say.

Gideon unfolded his arms to draw a hand down his face. "I find I could use a drink after all."

"I'll fetch it for you."

"You won't. Stay here." He straightened from the wall, grabbed his cane from the side of the bed, stalked back to the door, and turned around again to scowl at her. "Stay *here*, Winnefred."

"Haven't I been arguing to stay here?"

His scowl briefly intensified before he turned and left the room.

Winnefred stared at the door as the sound of Gideon's footsteps echoed down the hall.

We've known each other less than a sennight.

Those words stung, but they didn't wound the way his behavior by the bridge had wounded. In part because she knew them to have been spoken in anger, but mostly because it wasn't a judgment of her. But the sentiment did give her pause. They reminded her that it often took more than hard work to obtain what was wanted. A person could tug on a carrot all day and not make it grow any faster or provide its bounty any quicker. One could water and feed and weed, but in the end, the need for time and patience could not be circumvented.

A man might be fond of a woman, be attracted to that woman, and yet be appalled at the notion of marrying her after only a few weeks' acquaintance. That made sense. It wasn't at all flattering, but it was reasonable.

She needed to be reasonable in return. She had been willing to fight for what she wanted; now she would need to be willing to wait as well, and accept that there was still a great deal for the both of them to learn of each other.

She could do that . . . Probably . . . Possibly.

Her store of courage was not infinite. She could push her fears aside as often as she liked, but they would always find a way to make themselves known—a way to eat at her resolve.

Whether he knew her for a sennight or a decade, she might never be the sort of woman Gideon would want to marry.

She wasn't beautiful, or educated, or charming. She wasn't a lady. She'd stolen a locket, and played cards with a thief, and kept company with a goat.

She wasn't the sort of person anyone had ever wanted to keep.

"Lilly did," she whispered in the empty room. Someone had wanted her before; someone could want her again. With a bit of time and work—and provided, of course, that it was still what *she* wanted—that someone might be Gideon.

Chapter 22

$\mathcal{G}$ideon wasn't in search of a drink . . . not exclusively. He wanted a few moments alone as well. He needed the time and space to rein in his temper, sort through his disjointed thoughts, and marshal his flagging determination to do what was right. He would apologize for his behavior, and then he would send Winnefred back to her room.

He found his drink in the tavern, where a few patrons sat apart from each other in moody silence. He wanted to join them, to take a seat by the fire and drink himself into oblivion. He purchased a bottle instead and took the first long drink in the stairwell on his way back upstairs.

Twice. *Twice* in one day he had lost himself in the memories of war. And twice in one day he had taken his troubles out on Winnefred.

It was a miracle the woman wasn't headed back to Murdoch House right now, eating his raw heart along the way.

He rubbed at his chest where an ache had been nagging since he'd realized how badly he had wounded her feelings by the bridge. She'd made a small, harmless jest about being betrothed and, like an utter bastard, he'd responded by nearly swallowing his tongue in horror.

Oh, she'd pretended not to care. She had affected a careless demeanor, and then she had laughed and forgiven him. But he'd seen the hurt in her eyes, and the way her skin had paled beneath the freckles. She hadn't been able to hide that. And he hadn't been able to find the words, nor the courage, to make things right. How could he explain his fears without explaining his reasons for them? How could he tell her a part of him, a small, selfish part of him, had indulged, just for a moment here and there, in the daydream of courting her, of *keeping* her? How could he admit to that and not tell her why the better part of him would never allow it to happen?

He couldn't. No more, apparently, than he could keep himself from being a bastard all over again. And this time, he'd not be able to smooth things over with a silly jest.

A comédie larmoyante. Bloody, bloody hell.

What had he been thinking?

His hand clenched around the bottle. He knew damn well what he had been thinking—that she had pulled him from the pain of his memories yet again. That she had looked as beautiful dripping wet and worried by the stream as she had laughing on a moonlit road in Scotland, and twice again as beautiful standing in his room with the light of the fireplace dancing along the gold strands in her braid. He'd been thinking that he had never wanted to grab hold of a woman so desperately in his life. And he'd been terrified what would become of the both of them if he did. He'd had to do something, anything, to make her leave.

And so he had cut her with careless words. She had stood her ground, but he'd watched her shrink before his eyes, which was equally effective in dousing the flames of ardor as it turned out.

He paused outside his room and thought about having another drink, but he pushed the temptation aside and opened the door. Oh, he planned on indulging in another drink or two, or possibly half a dozen. But he would face Winnefred sober.

He found her just as he had left her—standing in the middle of the room. Unable to bring himself to meet her gaze, he busied himself with locking the door behind him. When stalling failed to settle the gnawing in his gut, he caved and took the bottle to a small writing desk to pour a drink. Two would hardly render him drunk, he reasoned. It might render him something of a coward, but not a drunk.

"Why don't you sit down, Winnefred?"

"I've done enough sitting for one day, thank you."

He finished the liquid in a single swallow, blew out a long breath, and turned to look at her. She didn't appear to be angry or insulted as he felt she really ought. She looked heartbreakingly vulnerable . . . and very, very determined.

"You've been hiding a great well of patience," he said softly. "You should have slapped me and been done with it."

She gave him a tentative smile. "The temptation was there. But you looked to be adequately slapped already. I don't approve of kicking a man when he's on the ground."

He set down his empty glass. "Even when he deserves it?"

"No one deserves it."

"Oh, there are men who do," he assured her. And the fact she wasn't aware of that only threw the differences between them into sharper contrast. She shouldn't be here, he thought. He had no business dragging her further into the ugliness of his past. "I apologize for my behavior. There is no excuse—"

"I will accept your apology," she broke in, and to his considerable dismay, she crossed the room to stand before him, "if you will tell me what put you in such a state."

He shook his head and suddenly wished the desk was not set against the wall. There was nowhere for him to retreat. "I'm sorry."

"You've already said that."

"Your concern, and your patience, are appreciated, Winnefred, but—" Without thinking, he caught her arm when she would have turned away from him in obvious frustration. "I do not mean that to sound so much like a dismissal. I am grateful for your concern. I am, truly. But the dreams . . ."

He would have to tell her something, he realized. It was foolish and selfish to expect her to walk away now with nothing more than another apology and evasion. He let his arm fall and bunched his hand into a fist.

"You are right," he heard himself say. "They are dreams of war."

She nodded again. "Is it the same dream every time?"

"Yes. No." He didn't know how to explain. He'd never tried before. "It is the same battle, the same . . ." *The same boys.* The words hovered on the tip of his tongue. He bit them back. "It is the same people. The same day. The dreams change."

"Is it the battle in which you were injured?"

He shook his head and leapt at the chance to change the topic. "That came months before, in a small skirmish off the coast of Spain. Took six men to pull me out from under a yardarm."

She tilted her head at him. "You sound proud."

"I am, of my men." Here, at least, was one story he could tell. "They pulled me free in the midst of battle. Lord Emmeret lifted with one hand and used the other to pull out his pistol and fire a shot . . . I had fine men."

"It doesn't sound a small skirmish."

"It was, in the grand scheme of war."

"And the battle you dream of?" she asked softly. "What was it in the grand scheme?"

"Of the war? A moderate clash." In his life, it was everything.

"And the people you spoke of, they were lost in the battle?"

"Yes."

"And you cared for them."

His next words came without thought. "I should have done."

A line formed across her brow. "I don't understand."

And she shouldn't, he thought. She should never be asked to understand. He shook his head. "Perhaps another time, Winnefred."

He waited for her to argue, but she surprised him by stepping close and placing her hand against his cheek. "I am very sorry, Gideon."

He reached up, intending to draw her hand away, and found himself holding on instead. She looked at him with such kindness, such understanding . . . such beauty.

It was tempting, unbearably tempting, to lose himself in those soft amber eyes. If he thought of nothing but that, nothing but the beauty of her, he could pull her closer. He could bend his head and cover her warm mouth with his own. For a time, he could forget everything else, everything but her.

It would have been simpler if she had argued.

Through a force of will he didn't know he possessed, he drew her hand from his face, gave it a gentle squeeze, and let it go. "I'm sorry as well."

What happened in that battle? What did you see by the bridge today? Who did you lose?

A flurry of questions raced through Winnefred's mind, and she ruthlessly shoved each and every one of them away. She had come to Gideon's room determined that he would tell her something of what troubled him, and she had accomplished that. He dreamt of war and of the people who fought beside him. That was enough for one night.

Time and work, she reminded herself.

Still, she hesitated a second before she turned around and headed for the door. She'd never shied from work, but waiting on time had always been a problematic endeavor for her.

"Winnefred?"

"Yes?" She turned back to find him watching her with a steady, unflinching gaze.

"Thank you," he said softly. "You are important to me as well."

She let out a breath she hadn't realized she'd been holding, smiled, and left.

She had taken a chance tonight, pushing her way into his room and into his privacy, but the way her heart sang at the sound of those seven simple words told her it had been worth the risk.

Chapter 23

The following morning, Winnefred stepped out on the front steps of the inn to find the carriage and out-riders ready and waiting, and Gideon sitting on a small stone bench at the side of the yard. A large dog with a shaggy black coat, cropped tail, and floppy ears rolled about at his feet. Gideon bent over and indulged the animal with a hearty scratch of the belly.

"You can't take him home," she called out, descending the steps to meet him.

He straightened and looked at her, squinting into the sun. "Good morning, Winnefred."

"Good morning." She took a seat next to him and stroked the dog's head when he stood up to nuzzle at her knee. "How do you fare today?"

He gave her a wry smile. "That is the question I intended to ask you."

"Not quite as well as yesterday morning." The euphoria had returned but was markedly decreased in intensity. "But no doubt better than I shall this afternoon."

"We'll stop often. Whenever you like."

"Hmm."

A short, weighted silence hung between them until Gideon jerked his chin toward the dog and said, quite out of the blue, "Do you suppose his tail ever itches?"

Bemused, she looked at him, then the dog. "He's been clipped. There isn't much there to give him trouble."

"That's what I mean." He gave the dog another scratch, then sat up. "I have a friend in London, Andrew Sykes. He lost his arm to amputation and says the pain of it no longer bothers him, but the itch will drive him mad."

"I hadn't realized amputation causes itching," she commented, more than willing to encourage a silly conversation to make him feel better.

"It's the part that's gone that itches, only there's nothing to scratch."

"The part that's gone? How is that possible?"

"I've no idea."

"How awful." She frowned at the dog and leaned down to scratch at his tail. "I always feel a mite guilty knowing our bull calves are turned into steers. Now I feel dreadful. Although, given the physical composition of cattle, I suppose they'd not be able scratch even if we left—"

He broke into a roll of deep laughter that took quite a while to fade. "Damn if you don't do wonders for me, Winnefred."

No other compliment could have given her more pleasure. She grinned at him and decided she didn't care one jot that she'd not actually meant the comment to be funny.

"Delighted to be of service."

He chuckled again and reached for his cane. "As much as I hate to cut short such a pleasant interlude, we should be off."

"I'll fetch Lilly this time." She brushed her hands down the lavender skirts of her gown and rose. Then she hesitated and turned back.

"Gideon?" She spoke before she could talk herself out of it. "What's a comedy . . . lar . . . larm . . ."

"Ah." He grimaced and looked away. "Comédie lar-

moyante. It's an old kind of theatrical production. A maud-
lin comedy, for lack of better description."

"Oh. Well." She thought about that. "That's not so very
bad. In the future, however, you might wish to confine
your insults to terms readily understood by the intended
recipient."

He must have heard the amusement in her voice because
he looked at her again, and his lips twitched. "And why is
that?"

"To avoid the risk of finding yourself being treated in
kind." She gave him a sweet smile. "My knowledge of livestock physiology is quite extensive. Would you care to be
called a lippet?"

"What is a lippet?"

A word she'd made up on the spot, but she wasn't about
to admit to that. She smiled instead, winked, and walked
away.

*T*he day of travel passed peacefully, as did the days following, but their journey to London was a long one,
and the constant battle against illness left Winnefred a
little more tired each day. By the morning of the last leg of
their trip, she felt as if she'd been traveling for weeks and
sick for half her life.

It didn't help that the more weary she became, the more
difficulty she had staying awake on the carriage, and the
more she fell asleep on the carriage, the sicker she became,
and the sicker she became, the wearier she grew . . .

"Vile, endless cycle." She mumbled the words with her
eyes closed. Gideon had nudged her a few moments before,
and after countless naps against his shoulder, she no longer
troubled to check if she had drooled on him. She was simply too tired to care.

Just as she was too tired to open her eyes at present.
She needed to, she really did. Every second she waited
was another second for the illness to grow, but she couldn't
seem to concentrate long enough to get the job done. Her

mind wandered in and out of sleep until, finally, it wandered in and stayed.

She dreamt she was standing in a ballroom filled with people, only she wasn't dressed for a ball. She was wearing her trousers, which made sense, really—she always put them on when there was work to do. And pulling Claire away from the refreshment table took a considerable amount of work. The other guests didn't seem to appreciate her sensible attire, or her goat. They were laughing, and yelling, and pointing at her.

"There's no need to *shout* at me."

"What?" Gideon's voice sounded in her ear. "Winnefred?"

She woke with a start and might have toppled forward if Gideon hadn't reached out and caught her. "Winnefred. What is it? What's wrong?"

His words didn't register. Nothing registered, in fact, except for the realization that she had fallen asleep in one world and woken up in another.

"Good heavens, where are we?"

"We're in London. Have . . . I woke you ten minutes ago. Have you been sleeping sitting up?"

"Yes." She was too stunned by the unfamiliar scene around her to bother trying to figure out if he was amused or appalled.

She was surrounded by buildings. They were pressed right up against each other, and separated from the street by only the thin ribbon of a sidewalk. There were no lawns, no trees, no green of any kind that she could see. Just house after house, shop after shop.

And all of it was filled with people. There were hordes of people going in and out of the buildings, calling to one another, laughing with one another.

"You need a full day's rest," she heard Gideon grumble.

"What? Oh, no I'm fine, really." She wasn't, really. Her stomach was a knot of nerves and nausea. "How long was I asleep?"

"Including the last ten minutes? A full three hours."

"Good heavens." It was a miracle she didn't feel worse. "Why didn't you wake me sooner?"

"It's a steadier ride on cobblestone streets," Gideon explained. "I wanted you to rest a bit longer. Are you certain you're all right?"

"Yes, of course. I'm just overwhelmed, that's all. I can't believe we're here. In London. Oh, Lilly must be in raptures. I wonder—" She broke off, sniffed, and wrinkled her nose. "What . . ." She sniffed again. "What *is* that?"

Gideon chuckled softly. "That, my dear, is the aroma of civilization."

"Well, civilization could use a wash."

"In more ways than one." He produced a handkerchief from his pocket and handed it to her. "Breathe through this. The smell will improve once we reach Mayfair, I promise."

It didn't take long for Winnefred to discover this was true. Within a half hour, the streets began to widen. The shops disappeared and the houses grew larger and further apart. Finally, there were lawns and trees and gardens. And the smell improved considerably. There were less people about as well. Well-dressed men and women strolled along the sidewalks in groups of twos and threes.

It wouldn't be such a hardship to spend a few weeks in a place such as this, she thought.

The carriage began to slow, and for a moment she thought they were going to stop in front of a respectably sized house with cheerful green shutters on the front windows, but they turned instead and into yet another world.

The houses weren't respectably sized and cheerful here; they were enormous and daunting. And the carriage stopped in front of the largest and most daunting of them all—a three-story brick building that looked to take up a third of the block.

"Your aunt lives *here*?" Her voice sounded weak even to her own ears.

Gideon climbed off the carriage, turned, and assisted her down. "It doesn't meet with your approval?"

She honestly didn't know how to answer that. Fortunately, Lilly's emergence from the carriage meant she didn't have to try.

Grinning from ear to ear, Lilly practically skipped over to take Winnefred's hands in a viselike grip. "We are here. Can you believe it?"

"It does seem rather fantastical," she admitted.

"It seems marvelous," Lilly returned. She looped her arm through Winnefred's and fell into step behind Gideon when he headed toward the house. "What do you think, Freddie? Will it do?"

"It is not what I had expected," she hedged. It was all so much *more*. The house was bigger, the gardens more extensive—though they did not, she was relieved to note, appear to have any peacocks in residence—and the front door looked stout enough to keep out an army. When they were admitted into the house, she discovered that the front hall was large enough to fit the whole of Murdoch House, and quite possibly the gardener's cottage.

She'd never been exposed to such wealth before. Even the country manor she had visited as a child with her father could not compare to the extravagance of Lady Gwen's London home.

Even Lady Gwen herself wasn't what Winnefred had expected. In an effort to quash her fears about staying with a stranger, Winnefred had begun to picture Gideon's aunt as a short, plump woman with round, rosy cheeks and a friendly disposition. It seemed reasonable to assume she would have to be at least a little friendly to have agreed to sponsor two young women who were completely unknown to her.

Unfortunately, Winnefred's assumptions turned out to be so far off they would have been laughable, had they been at all funny.

Lady Gwen descended the wide stairs into the front hall with the physical bearing of a fair-haired Amazon and the dress and manner of royalty. She looked to stand somewhere near to six feet, and though Winnefred estimated a full three inches of that height was owed to the heavy mass

of hair that had been pinned up in thick curls and fat ring-
lets, the woman was still undeniably tall. And severe . . .
She looked to be very, very severe. Which is why Winnefred felt no desire to laugh.

Lady Gwen stopped before them, acknowledged their
curtsies and her nephew's greeting with a regal nod of her
head, and then proceeded to walk a slow circle around
her two new charges, eyeing them down the length of her
rather prominent nose in the same manner Mr. McGregor
eyed their yearly calf.

Winnefred glanced at Gideon, but he was too busy
speaking with the butler to notice. Tired, irritated, and
insulted, she clenched her jaw to keep from speaking out
and stared straight ahead until Lady Gwen had completed
her circle.

"Well, they certainly are not fresh misses, are they?"
Lady Gwen gave a quick nod of her head in approval.
"Thank heavens for that. Foolish business, wedding giggling infants before they have a chance to know their own
minds."

She stepped a little closer to Lilly. "The hair is too dark
for fashion, but I daresay the rest is more than adequate.
You are fortunate in your eyes, Miss Ilestone. That shade
of blue is not often seen."

"Thank you, my lady."

Lady Gwen harrumphed by way of reply before turning
sharp eyes on Winnefred.

"This one looks green."

Gideon cast a look over his shoulder. "Winnefred?
Didn't I mention this is her first season?"

"Not green, you buffoon. *Green.*"

He lifted one dark brow. "Of course, *green.* What was
I thinking?"

"I believe she means ill," Winnefred informed him
and immediately regretted having unclenched her jaw,
because now that she had allowed herself to speak, she
found she couldn't stop. She turned a haughty face toward
Lady Gwen. "I've ears, a mouth, and a reasonable grasp of

the English language, my lady. I'll thank you not to speak of me as if I'm deaf, mute, and stupid."

Lilly gasped. "Winnefred!"

"Ha! The gel has spine!" To Winnefred's shock, Lady Gwen nodded once more in approval. Then, somewhat less surprisingly, she immediately narrowed her eyes. "See that you do not confuse it with insolence, child."

Gideon stepped forward and grinned. "The sort of insolence that results in the daughter of a marquess marrying a mere baronet rather than the viscount picked out for her?"

"That was not insolence," Lady Gwen replied with a sniff. "That was shrewdness, which is always to be commended."

Gideon merely winked at Lady Gwen's glare. "Be merciful, aunt. The journey was a taxing one. Winnefred needs to rest."

"*Miss Blythe*," Lady Gwen said with enough emphasis to show her displeasure with Gideon's use of first names, "shall be shown up to her chambers directly."

"Excellent." Gideon slapped his gloves against his leg. "Then if you ladies need nothing further, I'll beg your leave."

"Where are you going?" Lady Gwen demanded.

"Home."

"When will you return?"

"I am at your disposal, naturally," Gideon said easily. "Send one of your footmen with word when you have need of me."

"A waste of time and staff. You shall stay here."

If it hadn't been unforgivably rude, Winnefred would have laughed outright at the appalled expression on Gideon's face. "I will not."

"Would you have the ton say Lord Gideon Haverston cares so little for his wards that he could not stand to be under the same roof with them?"

"They are my brother's wards," Gideon argued.

"I'm not anyone's ward," Lilly pointed out.

"I certainly don't want to be," Winnefred muttered.

Lady Gwen ignored all three statements. "Have your man bring what . . . You haven't a man, have you? I keep forgetting your propensity for living as a savage."

"A house in Mayfair and a day maid is hardly—"

"Never mind, a few of my staff can be spared this once to fetch what you need."

"Generous of you," Gideon drawled. "Aunt—"

"It is settled then." She motioned for a pair of maids to step forward. "Sarah and Rebecca shall show the ladies to their chambers."

Chapter 24

Winnefred followed Lilly and the maid upstairs, but the long walk went by in a blur. Her mind registered the expensive carpet under her feet, the elaborately framed portraits on the walls, and the passing of a seemingly endless number of doors and hallways, but she found it impossible to concentrate on anything but the growing knot of worry in her belly.

The house was too big. There were too many servants. She'd already forgotten the names of the maids she was following. Lady Gwen hated her. She shouldn't have agreed to come to London.

"You've the blue room, miss."

"What?" Winnefred blinked and noticed for the first time that they'd stopped.

Lilly reached out and rubbed her arm. "You look done in, dear."

"I feel ghastly, to be honest. Lilly—"

"Get some rest." Lilly gave her a peck on the cheek. "I'm only down the hall a little ways."

Winnefred nodded and sighed in relief. She'd rather

feared they'd be settled in different wings. But the small boost in confidence quickly diminished as she watched Lilly walk away with one of the maids. A little ways down the hall was not quite so little when that hall was very, very long.

"Miss? Would you like . . . ?"

"Hmm?" She turned and found the other maid holding open a door. "Oh. Right. Thank you."

Winnefred gave the girl a sheepish smile and stepped over the threshold and into the most enormous, most extravagantly appointed, and most . . . *blue* room she had ever seen.

"Good heavens."

"Shall I stoke the fire for you?"

Winnefred was only vaguely aware of nodding. She was overwhelmed by the size and hue of the room. Everything was blue—the canopy over the ocean-sized bed, the settee and matched set of chairs in front of the fireplace, the drapes over the long line of windows, even the yards and yards of carpet . . . The very fine and very expensive-looking carpet. She would spill something on it. She was certain of it.

She would have worried over that frightful inevitability longer, but a movement in the hallway caught her eye. Turning, she saw Gideon stop in front of her open door. He glanced both ways down the hall, then poked his head into her room.

"Will it suit you, Winnefred?"

"It is enormous," was all she could think to say.

"And blue," he added with thoughtful nod. "I've always thought this room too blue."

"Perhaps . . . Perhaps I could . . ." *Go back to Murdoch House.* Oh, but even the idea of climbing back on a carriage made her stomach roll.

"Do you want a different room?" Gideon prompted.

Yes. "No. Of course not. It was very generous of your aunt to . . . It's only . . . It's so big."

"Average for a house of this size."

"It's *colossal.* Look at all of this space." She spread her arms out, a small bubble of laughter catching in her throat. "Whatever is it for? Did the original occupant perform acrobatics in her bedchamber?"

The maid fumbled the poker, banging it against the metal grate.

Winnefred dropped her arms at the sudden realization of what might have been inferred from her comment. "I beg your pardon. I didn't mean . . ." She trailed off, felt color rise to her cheeks, and dearly hoped the maid would see only her embarrassment at the slip and not the laugh that wanted to escape. The laugh she was not going to allow to escape. Absolutely not.

A helpless giggle escaped, and then another. She slapped a hand over her mouth, disgusted with herself. Bloody hell, what was *wrong* with her? It was one thing to be crass in a remote tavern with only Gideon present; it was something else to be so in his aunt's home, in front of his aunt's maid.

Gideon stepped into the room. "Rebecca. I believe the fireplace in the sitting room requires attention."

"Yes, my lord."

Winnefred watched with increasing alarm as Rebecca opened a door she had assumed led to a closet. Her hands fell away from her mouth. She didn't want Gideon to know how awful she felt, how overwhelmed and out of place. But . . . "There's *more* to this room? Oh, this is . . . This will never work. I *knew* it wouldn't work."

"What are you talking about?" Gideon asked gently.

"This." She threw her arms out to indicate everything around her. "Me. In London. It was a dreadful idea. We've been here less than an hour and already I've been disagreeable to your aunt, made a very vulgar jest, *and* laughed at it. I should not have come."

"Sit down, Winnefred."

"I don't want to sit down. We've been sitting down for days."

"You're overwrought."

She wrinkled her nose in distaste. "Small children and silly woman become overwrought."

"So do sensible ladies who have spent days traveling and battling illness."

"I . . ." She hated that she knew he was right. "I'm not quite myself, it's true. But I don't think I can sleep, Gideon. I was so tired on the carriage, but now I'm much too . . ." She searched for the right word, but her whirling mind refused to provide it. "Too awake," was the best she could come up with.

"You don't have to sleep. Just lie down and close your eyes for a bit . . . An hour."

"Just lie down? For an hour?"

"I'll tell you a story to pass the time."

It wouldn't be such a terrible thing, she thought, to lie down awhile and listen to Gideon. Or perhaps it would be. She glanced at the open door to her chambers, then craned her neck to look into the sitting room.

"Are you supposed to be in here?"

Gideon shrugged. "The door is open, Rebecca is right there, you are ill, and until my brother returns, I am essentially your guardian."

She gave him a bland look. "Are you *supposed* to be in here?"

"Probably not, but my aunt is in the orangery and Rebecca isn't one for gossip. Now." He took her hand and led her to the bed. "Have a seat."

She sat on the edge of the mattress and nearly jumped out of her skin when Gideon knelt down in front of her and began to unlace her boots. "Don't. I can—"

She pulled her foot away, only to have him snag her ankle and gently pull it back. "Hold still . . . And quit arguing."

"I'm not . . ." She pressed her lips together to keep from arguing. When his fingers brushed bare skin at the top of her boots, she pressed them together to keep from shivering.

He pulled off one boot, then the other. "There we are. Into bed with you now."

She stifled a sigh, though whether it was one of disappointment or relief the task was done, she couldn't say. And to hide her confusion, she took a few extra moments rearranging pillows before lying back, her arms folded over her stomach.

"What sort of story are you going—?"

"The sort of my choosing," Gideon cut in. He picked up a small chair near the window and settled it, and himself, by the side of the bed. "And there will be no commenting from you. This is the telling of a tale, not a conversation."

She closed her eyes and smirked. "Aye, Captain."

"We understand each other. Now then, how would you like to hear the story of how Lady Gwen defied her parents and married a lowly baronet."

"Oh, very much."

"No commenting," he reminded her. "The story is as such . . . My aunt was promised at the age of six to Viscount Wunrow. A short, fat man with a tyrannical nature and a propensity to whistle when pronouncing the letter S. Envision a rotund, lisping Napoleon . . . Stop laughing," he chided. "You're supposed to be resting."

She bit her bottom lip and nodded.

"Thank you. Not surprisingly, as Lady Gwen grew into adulthood, she became less and less enamored of the idea of becoming Lady Wunrow. She requested a release from the engagement and was soundly denied by both her family and Wunrow. He was vehement they would marry and threatened to ruin her good name should she attempt to break the contract."

"Could he do that?"

"Not important. Rest." He waited for her next nod before continuing. "Now, you may have noticed that my aunt is unusually tall in stature."

"I did."

"Shush." This time, he waited for her to stop giggling. "What you do not know is that she was also unusually clever for her age, and patient. She was very, very patient. She began, at age sixteen, to place lifts in her shoes whenever Wunrow came to visit. Small ones to start, then gradually increasing in size. When larger ones were not to be had, she secretly paid a cobbler to add extra height to the heels of some of her shoes. By the time she was eighteen, she towered nearly a foot over Lord Wunrow. I'm told the sight was fairly comical. And all the while, she was encouraging the attentions of a man she did care for—an unknown, unconnected, and relatively poor baronet of respectable height."

"How do you know this?"

"Also not important. The result of her efforts is what matters. Wunrow broke the engagement—a scandal of insurmountable proportions by Haverston standards. The jilting of a viscount can mark a young lady as unsuitable for marriage, and in the eyes of the Haverstons, an unmarried lady is a useless lady, a burden."

"That's disgusting."

"Stop talking. It benefited my aunt in the long run. When her young baronet came to ask for her hand—and her immense dowry—with nothing to offer in return but his lowly title, my family was all too happy to accept."

"That's lovely."

"Shh. They honeymooned on the continent. Spain first, I believe. My aunt still speaks of the coastline. Golden sands and unpredictable waters. The sun shines more brightly there, or so she says. They went to Italy next . . ."

Winnefred's mind wandered as Gideon began to describe the travels of Lady Gwen and her baronet. Her limbs grew comfortably heavy. Soon, his voice became a low, soothing murmur in the background. She was only vaguely aware of him rising from his chair, of a warm blanket covering her, and of the soft whispering at the foot of her bed.

"Shall I help her to change, my lord?"

"No, let her rest."

And then she fell into a deep, dreamless sleep.

Winnefred did feel improved after a long nap—an exceedingly long nap as it turned out. It was half past eight when she rose. But as much as the rest did to improve her physical well-being, it was a visit to Lilly's chambers that lifted her spirits. She found her friend awake and sitting on the edge of a green bed in a decidedly green room.

"Good heavens." Winnefred laughed, closing the door behind her. "This room."

"Extraordinary, isn't it?"

That was one word for it. "Are they all like this, do you think?"

"I imagine so."

"But there are only so many colors to be had." With green and blue already taken, she wondered what color was to be found in Gideon's chambers.

"What do you find so amusing?" Lilly inquired.

"I am imagining Lord Gideon awash in a sea of pink."

"It does make for a novel picture," Lilly agreed, cocking her head a bit to the right.

Winnefred laughed and joined her friend on the bed. "I assume you're happy with your room."

"Oh, yes. Look." Lilly pointed at a thick rope hanging from the ceiling next to the bed. "It's a bellpull. It took Sarah twenty-three seconds to answer."

"Twenty-three?"

"I counted."

"You didn't." She could see from Lilly's expression that she had. "What did you call her for?"

"Mostly just to see if the bellpull worked," Lilly confessed with a giggle. "But I asked for a cup of tea. And look . . ." She jumped off the bed and opened a door into her own sitting room. "It's bigger than our parlor. Oh, and . . ." She practically skipped across the room to pull back the drapes. "Gardens. Well, it is too dark to see them now, but there are real gardens full of flowers. Not a vegetable in sight."

For some reason, Winnefred felt compelled to defend the garden at Murdoch House. "Some vegetables flower."

Lilly didn't appear to hear her. "It's beautiful. It's magical. I cannot believe we are finally here."

This, Winnefred thought with a burgeoning smile, was why she had come to London. To see her friend glow with excitement and delight.

And, admittedly, the idea of a functioning bellpull in her room was intriguing. She looked at Lilly's speculatively. "Could I ask for chocolate, do you think?"

"You may ask for whatever you like, Freddie. You're a guest."

Winnefred blinked at that. *A guest.* Not an intruder, or an unwanted burden, but a guest. Strange she'd not thought of herself that way until now.

"I suppose I am," she said softly. "I suppose we are."

She loved the idea of it . . . for as long as it took her to realize that a guest could be kicked out as quickly as an intruder. She went to stand next to Lilly by the window and lifted a hand to finger the drapes. "What do you make of Lady Gwen?"

Lilly shrugged. "She is rather imposing. But she doesn't strike me as being unkind."

"She looked us over as if we were livestock."

"It wasn't her intention to insult," Lilly replied easily.

"How can you be so certain?"

"Because a woman like Lady Gwen has better things to do with her time than bring two unknown young women down from Scotland just to insult them."

That made sense, but . . . "Could be she just finds it a happy side benefit."

Lilly smiled at that. "Give her a chance, Freddie."

She'd already decided to, but only because the woman was Gideon's aunt. And because she couldn't help but admire the way Lady Gwen had outsmarted Lord Wunrow.

"I will give her a chance," she agreed. "I only hope she affords me the same courtesy."

"She appreciates your spine," Lilly reminded her.

"That's true. And I appreciate hers. That's not such a bad beginning. Maybe in time—" She stopped talking, interrupted by the loud rumble of her own stomach.

"Good heavens." Lilly laughed.

"It seems my appetite has returned." She rubbed the heel of her hand over her belly. "Will it be long before dinner?"

"Another hour, but I saw Gideon in the hall a little while ago and he says you are to take dinner in your room. Breakfast tomorrow as well."

"Whatever for?"

"For the purpose of recovery. He said you are not to come downstairs until you are fully well." Lilly frowned a little, remembering. "Quite adamant about it, really."

"That's absurd. He can't banish me like some sort of—"

"Would you *rather* come downstairs for dinner?"

She opened her mouth, closed it, then shook her head.

"I thought not." Lilly looped her arm through hers. "Come along, let's get you something to eat. I want to try the bellpull in your chambers."

Chapter 25

*I*t was nearly a full two days before Winnefred felt quite like herself again. Well, it was really only a day and a half, but she stalled in fear of sitting down to a meal with Lady Gwen.

She might have procrastinated longer, but after a half day of feeling healthy and not being able to leave her chambers except to visit Lilly in hers, she was near to climbing the walls with boredom.

Also, she missed Gideon tremendously. She'd not seen him since he'd told her the story of Lady Gwen and her baronet. According to Lilly, he frequently asked after her condition, but he'd not come to her chambers again.

She very much hoped to see him at breakfast that morning, even though it meant taking a meal with Lady Gwen. After washing and dressing, she followed a maid's directions to the dining room and found Lady Gwen seated at the long table alone. A table, Winnefred could not help but notice, that was devoid of food except for Lady Gwen's plate. The alluring scent of eggs and meat and fresh bread emanated from the long sideboard against the far wall.

Oh, blast.

Lilly had told her of such arrangements being popular, but for the life of her, Winnefred couldn't remember if she was to make her own plate or wait for someone else to do it for her.

She hesitated in the doorway and had just decided to sneak back upstairs for Lilly when Lady Gwen looked up from her plate.

"Miss Blythe. You are looking much improved." She set her fork down and gave Winnefred a thorough looking over. "Very much improved, indeed. It is a pity about the freckles, but it would seem you are, overall, quite acceptable."

Winnefred was too preoccupied with trying to figure out her next move to trouble herself over the lukewarm compliment. "Thank you . . . I . . ."

Lady Gwen glanced over at the sideboard. "Ah. You may serve yourself this morning or request a servant do so for you. In the future, should a gentleman offer to bring you a plate, you may accept."

She blinked at the easy manner in which the woman explained what was no doubt, to her, a very simple matter. "Oh. Thank you."

Lady Gwen raised one brow. "You appear quite stunned, Miss Blythe. Have you been laboring under the impression Lord Gideon failed to inform me of the state in which he found you?" She dropped the brow and pursed her lips in obvious disgust. "Shameful."

Good manners or not, Gideon's aunt or not, Winnefred could not let that pass. "There is *nothing* shameful in what I and—"

"Settle your feathers, child. I refer to the behavior of Lord Engsly, not your own. The neglect of two young ladies is inexcusable." She pursed her lips again. "My brother always was a churl."

Oh, how she wished she had stalled in her chambers for longer . . . possibly until fall. "I apologize for the assumption."

"Unnecessary." Her eyes flicked over Winnefred's shoulder. "Ah, Miss Ilestone, your timing is impeccable . . . As is your attire this morning. That is a lovely shade of green, my dear. We shall have to see it on you in a gown of more fashionable cut. Now, do show Miss Blythe the proper way to fix herself a plate and have a seat. We have much to discuss regarding your come-outs, as it were. I do believe Lady Powler's ball next week will be just the thing."

*A*s far as Winnefred could ascertain, the preparations required for a ball that was to be "just the thing" were the same as those required for an upcoming London season, with two notable exceptions. To begin with, this time round, Lilly's responsibilities were not those of an instructor, but of a student. It was a role she fulfilled with aplomb. There wasn't a dance she couldn't master, a name she couldn't remember, a French phrase that didn't trip easily off the end of her tongue.

Winnefred's lessons, on the other hand, progressed much as they had in Scotland. She spilled the tea, forgot if the wife of the second son of an earl was a lady or a missus, and failed to impress the dancing master with her impression of an inebriated puppet. With every misstep, she felt a little more out of place. With every fumbled lesson, she grew increasingly worried that the upcoming ball would prove to be a disaster.

As a further blow to her confidence, Gideon became a regular witness to her failures, his presence being the other difference between the Scottish and London preparations. Lady Gwen insisted he take an active role in the tutelage of his charges—a responsibility he bore with varying degrees of enthusiasm. He managed to use the excuse of his weak leg to disappear while the dancing master was in residence, and she caught him nodding off while Lady Gwen read from *Debrett's Peerage* on the evening of the third day. But he did seem to enjoy accompanying them to Bond Street the next morning, and to her bewilderment, he took an inordinate amount of interest in the selection of her new wardrobe, even going so far as to repeatedly reject the choices made by his aunt. In fact, within a half hour's time of entering the modiste's shop, he was going through the fashion plates and selecting the gowns himself.

To Winnefred's further surprise, Lady Gwen ceded to the majority of his opinions without argument.

"I see nothing amiss with your selections," she commented as she and Lilly looked over the plates. "You surprise me, nephew. I would not have thought you a connoisseur of ladies' fashions."

Gideon looked slightly offended at the accusation. "I'm not. I employed a bit of common sense, that's all. Do you care for them, Winnefred?"

Though she appreciated that he would ask, her complete ignorance of fashion left her no criteria with which to judge the gowns other than the feel of the material. She fingered several bolts of fabric set aside for her. "Yes. They're lovely."

Lilly gently nudged a plate toward her. "You should look at the drawings before making a decision, Winnefred."

"I don't see the point," she admitted. "The three of you are far more qualified than I to choose new gowns."

Lady Gwen nodded. "I applaud the good sense you exhibit in deferring to those of experience, Miss Blythe."

Winnefred straightened a little at the small compliment. Praise was a rare thing from Lady Gwen—praise directed at her, at any rate—and while the good opinion of haughty, judgmental ladies was not something she wished to trouble herself over, she found herself reluctantly eager for the approval of Gideon's aunt. "Thank you, my lady."

"However," Lady Gwen continued, "it will not do for you to have so little knowledge of fashion. It is a common topic of conversation." She motioned Winnefred closer. "Come here, child. Gideon will explain to you the reasoning behind his choices while Miss Ilestone and I select fabrics for her own wardrobe."

Gideon's head snapped up from the plate he'd been examining. "Explain?"

"Yes, nephew. Explain. Come along, Miss Ilestone."

"I . . ." Gideon looked at Winnefred, at his aunt's retreating back, and once again to Winnefred. "Well . . ."

She would have helped him if she'd known how. Possibly. It was a rare and fascinating thing to see Lord Gideon Haverston so comically flummoxed.

He cleared his throat, twice, and gestured at the plates. "Well . . . pale colors are, of course, de rigueur for young unmarried ladies."

She was relatively certain she knew what de rigueur meant. "Of course."

"And the uh . . . The high . . ." He waved a finger in the general vicinity of the woman's bust. "The high cut of the waist is . . . also de rigueur."

"Is it really?"

He shot her a quick, threatening glance that had her stifling a laugh.

"Well, for pity's sake," she whispered, "even I know that."

"You were wearing trousers the first time we met," he reminded her.

"They didn't render me blind," she returned. "And I did own a gown, you'll recall."

"So you did, and do you know what marked that gown as outdated?"

"The fact that it was a dingy shade of ivory and had several patched holes in the skirt?" She leaned a hip against the table, remembered that a lady did not go about leaning on furniture, and promptly straightened again.

"No, that marked it as old," Gideon said. "The cut is what marked it as outdated. The waist was *too* high. The strict adherence to classical style has been tempered in recent years. Waists are lower these days."

"I see." He looked inordinately proud of himself for coming up with that bit of information. She suspected it was the only bit he had. "And is that what you looked for in these gowns? A fashionable waistline?"

"Well, *that*, and . . ." He frowned thoughtfully. "And

certain details that were uniquely suited to you. See this one? I bought a gown for you in Scotland this same shade of peach. I know by way of experience that it brings out the roses in your cheeks without accentuating your freckles."

She felt a flush of pleasure at the roses comment and pulled a face to hide it. "I do wish I hadn't the freckles."

"There is nothing wrong with freckles."

"Then why concern ourselves over their accentuation?"

"Because it is a matter of taste, and . . . And there is no accounting for taste." He smiled at her bland expression. "We just do, that's all."

"Mm-hmm." She reached over and tapped one of the plates with her finger. "You haven't an inkling as to why you chose those gowns, do you?"

"Certainly, I have. I chose them because they suit you, as I said." He drew a small stack of plates from the end of the table and showed her a pale blue gown with lace and ribbons and something very large and very odd attached to the back. At best guess, it was a badly tied bow. "This is the ball gown Lady Gwen insisted upon."

"Oh. How very complicated."

"Exactly so. You're not complicated. You're simple."

"Simple," she repeated dryly. "May I presume you will not be instructing me on the art of delivering compliments?"

"I see you've still not been instructed on how to receive them. Simple can be a very fine thing."

"So can manure in a turnip patch."

"Point taken," he said with a curve of his lips. "Let me try another avenue of explanation. You, Winnefred Blythe, are genuine. Wholly without guile or artifice. A conversation with you requires no interpretation, no search for hidden meaning. Being friends with you is effortless. That is what I meant by simple. These . . ." He gestured at the plates. "These layers of ruffles and lace and intricate patterns, they belong on a woman who would hide who she is. Not on you."

It was such a lovely speech, she hadn't the heart to point out how much of herself she hid by trying to be a lady of the ton, nor the heart to wonder if he truly realized it.

"Thank you," she murmured instead and, fearing a blush would be noticed by more than just she and Gideon, quickly changed the subject. "Is the ball gown as bad as all that?"

"No," he assured her, "or I'd have made a more determined argument against it. It's a very fashionable gown. And it doesn't hurt for a person to expand their tastes from time to time."

"That's true." She cocked her head at the plate. "It is a lovely shade of blue."

"I believe yours is to be pink."

"Oh. Well, I trust Lady Gwen knows what she is about. I trust you do as well, but I must say, none of this is going to help me discuss fashion with any sort of authority."

"You've an eye for color and feel for material of quality. Limit your input to those, and when in doubt, mention that your gowns came from Madame Fayette. The other ladies will be suitably impressed."

The sound of Lilly's soft laughter kept her from responding. She turned her head and watched as Lady Gwen gave a rare smile and nodded in approval of something Lilly said.

"She's wonderfully happy. Lilly, I mean," she added, turning to Gideon. "I've you to thank for that."

"Am I to retain my internal organs, then?"

She considered it, and the weeks of balls and dinner parties ahead of them. "Let us see how things fare at Lady Powler's ball."

His lips curved into a smile, but it wasn't one of amusement; it was one of understanding. "I'm sure my aunt was careful in her choice of invitations to accept, Winnefred. You don't need to be afraid."

She squared her shoulders, indignant at the implication. "I may grow nervous on occasion, but I am not *afraid* of anything."

Chapter 26

$\mathcal{F}$our days later, as the hour of Lady Powler's ball drew near, Winnefred stood alone in the middle of her chambers and admitted to herself that she was afraid.

In truth, she was terrified.

That hadn't been the case earlier in the day. She'd simply been too busy to be afraid.

She had bathed in rose-scented water, been helped into her pink ball gown, and sat through the lengthy process of having her hair pinned into a complicated array of curls. She wished the process had been a bit lengthier, because now she was left with nothing to do but think about how incredibly nervous she was.

She was going to embarrass Lilly.

She was going to humiliate herself.

No one was going to be fooled into thinking she was a lady.

In an effort to distract herself, she studied her reflection in the cheval mirror and, after moment's consideration, decided that her appearance, at least, was acceptable. In fact, she looked rather pretty. There was still the matter of her freckles, and skin that had, despite Lilly's best efforts over the years, become slightly browned in the sun. But the muted rose of the silk did a fair job of flattering her complexion, and the low cut of the neckline did an exceptional job of flattering her charms.

She looked down at herself with pursed lips. She'd never thought of herself as a woman with notable charms before. But there they were, pushed up, laced in, and practically spilling over the top of her bodice. What hypocrisy that she should be forbidden to acknowledge in the company of a gentleman what was being so blatantly revealed for the benefit of that gentleman.

Here, sir, what do you make of these? I should think them the finest bubbies at the ball.

Snickering nervously, she turned her head when a soft knock sounded on her door.

"Yes. Come in." And stay, she thought. She didn't want to be alone with her nerves.

The door opened a crack and Rebecca's head popped inside. "Lord Gideon would like a word with you, miss."

Oh, perfect. "Of course. Where is he?"

By way of answer, Rebecca entered the room with Gideon following behind her. He stepped inside, caught sight of Winnefred, and stopped. Slowly, his gaze trailed up and down the length of her, his eyes coming to rest at the low-cut bodice. She couldn't have asked for a more effective means of distraction, and she wasn't certain what she wanted to do more—blush, invite him closer, or laugh outright. Hypocrites or not, the ladies of the ton knew what they were about.

Rebecca cleared her throat delicately. "Shall I stoke the fire in the sitting room, my lord?"

"Hmm?" Gideon blinked and turned his head slowly as if waiting for his eyes to catch up. "Oh, right. The fire. Thank you, Rebecca."

When he looked at Winnefred again, his eyes had cleared and there was a smile playing at his lips. "It appears I was wrong about the gown. You look exquisite."

"Thank you." She bobbed a quick and much-practiced curtsy. Then, because it felt as if the movement had shifted the material lower, she tugged at the bodice. "It feels like a ton of bricks."

"I imagine it does." His gaze followed the movement of her hands a moment before snapping to her face. "Why bricks, do you suppose?"

She stopped tugging. "I'm afraid to inquire what you mean by that."

"If it's a ton of something, what difference does it make if it's a ton of bricks, or a ton of stone, or a ton of very fluffy pillows? They all weigh the same by definition."

"Is it absolutely necessary I spare thought for that?"

Gideon shook his head sadly and crossed the room to stand before her. "You display a distressing lack of curiosity."

"It's true, I do. And the shame of it weighs more heavily on me every day. Much like a ton of fluffy pillows."

"Well. I hope you'll not mind the addition of a few more ounces." He glanced into the sitting room and, seeing Rebecca occupied, pulled a small box from his pocket. "I saw this today and thought of you."

She looked at the box and groaned. This was not the sort of distraction she wanted. "Gideon, no."

He'd bought her presents every day for the last four days—bonnets and bracelets, earrings and fancy slippers. On several occasions, he'd had multiple gifts sent to her chambers. "You cannot keep purchasing such things for me."

"Why not?"

"Because it's too much, and they are inappropriate. Even I know a gentleman is not allowed to give a lady jewelry or articles of clothing. And a lady is not allowed to accept."

"As your acting guardian in my brother's absence, it is perfectly acceptable for me to purchase items necessary for a London season."

"It is acceptable that you pay for them, not buy them as gifts."

"The difference escapes me." He shifted his cane to his arm so he could open the box.

"It does not. It . . ." She trailed off, her eyes going round as he revealed a necklace fashioned of small, delicate pearls and ending with a moderately sized diamond pendant. It was beautiful. Simple, elegant, beautiful, and no doubt worth a small fortune. She felt her resolve to decline the present slipping away. "Oh, it's so lovely . . . I shouldn't accept this. I shouldn't accept any of your gifts."

"Why do you, if it bothers you?"

"Because . . ." She shifted her feet and bit her lip. "Because they're lovely, and . . . Do you *know* how many sheep I could buy with this? And the garnet bracelet? It could see Murdoch House through a drought, and . . . And I can't say no."

He bent his head and laughed softly.

"I shouldn't take this," she mumbled, looking at the box in his hand. She reached out and took it. "But I can't say no. I *could*—I'd not be tempted, if you would only stop offering. What must I do to persuade you to stop?"

His laugh faded, and when he lifted his head to speak, his dark eyes were somber. His voice was soft and edged with a sadness she didn't understand.

"Take them for granted," he said.

She shook her head. "What?"

"I want you to take these things for granted. I want you to be as sure of their existence in your life as you were of hunger and cold in Scotland." He reached out to tap the edge of the box with his finger. "I want to bring you a pretty, useless trinket and have you see a pretty, useless trinket—not a windfall, not its worth in livestock, and certainly not salvation from the hardship you seem to think awaits you in the future."

"You want to spoil me."

"I do, yes."

"And I want to be annoyed with you for it. It pricks at my pride." She looked down at the necklace. "But it would be foolish of me."

"*That*, Winnefred, is my very point. When you can turn away an expensive piece of jewelry without feeling like a fool, then I will curtail my gifting habits." He slipped the necklace from the box and handed her his cane. "Hold this a moment."

Before she could ask what he meant to do, he'd stepped behind her and reached around to settle the pearls and diamond against her throat. She barely registered the weight of the jewels on her skin. It was impossible to think of anything but how close he was standing. She felt the warmth of his breath against her hair and the brush of his wrists across her shoulders. Heat and a giddy sense of anticipation gathered in her chest then spread out in waves, until she was certain every inch of her was flushed. She wanted to turn around and tilt her face up to his, but Rebecca was still in the sitting room. And all too soon, the necklace was secured and Gideon was stepping away.

"Perfect," Gideon announced when she turned around. "Now for these."

To her astonishment, he pulled another box from his pocket and revealed a set of sapphire earrings.

"More jewelry?" Without thought, she reached out to touch.

Gideon pulled his hand away. "Becoming greedy already? That's a fine start." He snapped the box shut. "But they're not for you."

"Not for me? But . . ." She looked up and saw the familiar twinkle in his eyes. "For Lilly?"

"Indeed. Would you like to give them to her?"

She would have rather kissed him, but as alternatives went, presenting Lilly with sapphires wasn't half bad.

"Go on, then," Gideon urged. He handed her the box. "I'll meet you downstairs when it's time to leave."

*G*ideon watched Winnefred leave the room with sapphires in hand and asked himself, as he had a dozen times a day for the last week—

What the devil am I doing?

The answer was always the same. He was torturing himself.

There was no other possible explanation, no other plausible reason he could give for why he had ceased trying so hard to avoid Winnefred and had even begun to seek her out.

Why else had he not set his foot down when his aunt had insisted he be present for every lesson and shopping trip? Why else would he hand deliver a string of pearls to her chambers if not to see her, knowing he couldn't have her? It hadn't been necessary for him to pick out her gowns at the modiste's either. His aunt could have managed, and Winnefred hadn't cared one way or the other. It certainly wasn't necessary that he sit in the high-back chair in the library every night simply because Winnefred always sat on the green settee and the high-back chair afforded him the best view of her profile.

It was absurd, and it was the trip from Scotland that was to blame. He'd grown used to being able to talk to her anytime he wanted, and feeling the warmth of her pressed against his side, and seeing the details of her face with just the slightest turn of his head. He'd become so accustomed to having her there, right there next to him, that he found he could no longer go the day without needing to see her. Even the space of a few hours made him feel restless and dissatisfied.

The two days she had spent recovering in her chambers had been hell. Another day and he would have . . .

He shook his head and dragged a hand down his face. He'd not have made it another day.

And what did it matter that he couldn't go a day now?

There was nothing unseemly in his behavior toward Winnefred. Admittedly, he had a fair number of unseemly thoughts toward Winnefred, but a man couldn't be held responsible for a few—very well, quite a few—erotic daydreams.

Nothing he was doing harmed her. Nor did any of it

threaten his independence from responsibility. So, he stared a bit. A man was entitled to look. And he brought her trinkets from time to time. There was no harm in that. The woman needed spoiling—the Engsly estate *owed* the woman a bit of spoiling—and a gentleman could present gifts to a lady without becoming responsible for her. Too many gifts, or the wrong sorts of gifts, and he was honor bound to present an offer of marriage, but that didn't apply to wards and guardians.

The irony of using his questionable role of guardian as an argument *against* his responsibility for Winnefred was something he chose not to examine too closely.

He preferred to concentrate on his future plans. It would be months before the season was over, months before he would have to let Winnefred go, and if he was determined to spend that time torturing himself, so be it. He would stare, and buy her diamonds and pearls, and imagine her wearing them with nothing else. And he would do it as damn well often as he liked.

He tapped his cane against the side of his foot as a slow, determined smile spread across his face. If he was going to spend the next several months in torment, then he was bloody well going to enjoy it.

"Would you care to explain what you are doing in Miss Blythe's bedchambers, nephew?"

Gideon's head snapped up at the sound of his aunt's voice in the doorway. "Er . . . Just woolgathering. And now leaving."

"Not so quickly, if you please." Lady Gwen stepped into the room with a soft rustle of gold silk.

"Rebecca is in the sitting room," Gideon explained. "And Winnefred is with Lilly."

"Yes. I've just come from *Miss Ilestone's* chambers, where I was informed by *Miss Blythe* that she has no interest in obtaining a match this season."

He ignored her less-than-subtle reminder of her distaste for his use of first names. "Yes, I know."

"I presume this is the reason you were so adamant in your letters from Scotland that a dowry not be arranged?"

He gave a small shrug. "I see no point in making her a target for fortune hunters."

"There is still Miss Ilestone to match," she reminded him.

"Your expertise may not be needed in the case of *Miss Ilestone*." Because he wanted to draw the moment out, he leaned forward slowly before whispering, "She is Lucien's Rose."

It was a rare thing indeed to see the rigidly composed Lady Gwen visibly taken aback. Generally speaking, it was also a very brief thing. Lady Gwen's eyes widened and her mouth dropped opened in astonishment, but only for a moment. "Good heavens. Does he know?"

"I sent a letter to Italy. But I've not yet heard word back."

"Well." Lady Gwen tilted her head a little in thought. "It is possible Lucien has gone elsewhere in search of your stepmother. The letter may have missed him."

"It may have. In any event, he'll hear the news sooner or later." He pictured his brother reading the letter and smiled. "I'm happy for him."

"I am as well," Lady Gwen replied, before adding, "and irritated with you. You led me to believe Miss Blythe and Miss Ilestone were in need of my assistance."

"They are," he assured her. "Everyone is in need of your assistance, aunt. England would be a much finer place altogether if its people had the sense to fall in line with your opinions."

"Oh, rubbish." She studied him with suspicious eyes. "What other secrets are you keeping from me?"

"None from you. But since we are on the matter of secrets—Winnefred is under the impression she will be running Murdoch House on her own, and with strict financial restrictions. I would appreciate it if you said nothing to dissuade her of this notion."

"You wish for her to struggle and worry?"

"I wish to give her what she wants. She wants to work to make Murdoch House a success. She takes great pleasure in seeing the rewards of her labors, and I'll not rob her of that pleasure by robbing her of the work."

"But you mean to see she does not fail," Lady Gwen guessed.

"The amount of ten thousand pounds has been put aside in the event it becomes needed." He thought about that. "It won't be."

"Such faith in the woman," she said quietly.

"I have seen what she is capable of."

"I ought to reprimand you for encouraging your brother's ward to engage in such crass pursuits."

"But you won't," he guessed with a patronizing smile, "because you're fond of her."

Lady Gwen made a small scoffing noise in the back of her throat. "You ascribe a generosity I do not possess. I barely know the chit. It is you of whom I am fond. It is you I wish to see happy. Miss Blythe is nothing more to me than a possible avenue to your well-being."

"An avenue to my well-being? That's absurd."

"I have not seen you take such interest in and care for anyone or anything since before the war."

An uncomfortable knot formed between his shoulder blades. "My interests and cares have not changed."

"Deny it if you will, but remember that it is a dangerous game you play, nephew. Miss Blythe is an unmarried woman in possession of a clever mind, stubborn nature, and some very unusual ideas." She straightened a little, as if surprised by her own words. "Well. Perhaps you are right. Perhaps I am fond of her after all."

Chapter 27

*A*ccording to Lilly and Lady Gwen, Lady Powler's parties were neither the most extravagant nor the most fashionable events the London season had to offer. But to Winnefred, Lady Powler's ball looked a very grand affair indeed. Everywhere she turned she saw silk and jewelry, crystal chandeliers and gilded candelabras. And food, she thought, biting into a delightful confection of cake and strawberries she'd discovered at the refreshment table. There was more food present than she had seen in her life. The lively strains of a reel floated from the second-level gallery while the guests below danced and laughed and wandered about the enormous room in search of friends or introductions.

Despite her lingering nervousness, she had to admit that—the obvious wastefulness of it all notwithstanding— it was a rather pretty scene. Which was to be appreciated, because she and Lilly had done little more than stare at it for the last half hour.

Winnefred gave a quick look over her shoulder to be certain she wouldn't be overheard before leaning in her chair to speak with Lilly. "I did not agree to travel hundreds of miles just to watch you turn down opportunities to dance."

"I'll not leave you here alone," Lilly returned, calmly smoothing a hand over the skirts of her pale blue dress. She looked so lovely tonight, Winnefred thought. Absolutely beautiful. And more than one gentleman had taken notice.

"Lady Gwen is not ten feet away." She nodded her chin to where their chaperone was immersed in a conversation with a group of ladies her own age.

Gideon had been pulled into the card room by Lord Powler almost immediately upon their arrival, but Lady Gwen had remained in their company longer, making introductions and settling them in a quiet spot at the edge of the ballroom. Several gentlemen had since requested Lilly's hand for a dance. And Winnefred had watched her graciously turn down each and every one.

It was maddening.

She leaned a little closer. "I swear to you, Lilly, if you do not accept the next offer to dance, I will make such a scene that Lady Gwen will have no choice but to send us packing back to Scotland this very night."

"You wouldn't."

No, she wouldn't, but because it was imperative Lilly believe otherwise, Winnefred finished off the last of her treat, brushed off her hands, and sat back in the chair. Then she gave Lilly the same imposing look she had employed with Gideon when he had threatened to lock her in her chambers at Murdoch House.

"Do you remember the little ditty I learned at the prison?"

Lilly accepted the next offer.

And as Winnefred watched her friend being led to the dance floor, it occurred to her that, aside from having to bully Lilly into enjoying herself, and the brief moment upon entering the ballroom in which she seriously contemplated bolting back out again, the night was going remarkably well. To the best of her knowledge, she'd not yet made a single egregious error of manners. True, her glowing description of the Scottish countryside had been met with raised brows by the young ladies who had sat with them for a time. And probably, she should not have mentioned the specifics of her illness to the gentleman who had inquired after her trip to London. No one, however, had appeared to be overtly offended by, or even unduly interested in, her minor slips.

How silly she had been to imagine she would be the center of attention, that every guest would be watching her, meticulously appraising her every word and move.

Evidently, in the eyes of society, she was just another woman come to town. True, her connection to Lord Englsy made her a person of mild interest, but she wasn't a great beauty, an heiress, or even a legitimate member of the Haverston family. In short, she wasn't the sort of woman who warranted the ton's close inspection.

For the second time in her life, Winnefred was grateful for being the sort of woman others found easy to dismiss.

Better to be forgotten than despised, she thought.

And so much better to have her inadequacies ignored than have them reflect poorly on the people she cared about. All she had to do was refrain from any sort of behavior that was so monstrously inappropriate it couldn't possibly be overlooked—which she was almost certain she could manage—and Lilly would have her successful season.

She could feel herself smiling, then smiling broader when she caught sight of Gideon exiting the card room.

And when he is not about, do you miss him?

Apparently, she missed him even when he was only a room away.

She wanted to leave her little corner of the ballroom so she could go and tell him of the happy realization she'd come to about her visit to London, and how she had bluffed Lilly into dancing, and every detail of everything else that had occurred since they'd spoken last.

She decided she also wanted to reach up, take his face in her hands, and bring his dark head down for a nice long kiss, because, really, if she was going to indulge in ridiculous fantasies, they might as well be good.

Amused by the picture in her head of a well-kissed Gideon being forced to listen to every thought that had crossed her mind in the last half hour, she waited, almost patiently, for him to spot her through the crowd and make his way across the room.

"Miss Blythe," he said, bowing low, "may I interest you in a turn about the room?"

She rose to take his arm. "A turn would be lovely, my lord, thank you."

Gideon grinned at her as he led her away. "You look happy."

"Oh, I am." She gripped his arm tighter in her excitement. "Have you seen Lilly? She was dancing a moment ago. Plus, it's been near to an hour and I haven't scalded anyone, or offended anyone, or spilled anything. I can't remember the name of the lady in the bronze gown next to the potted palm, but she doesn't know that."

"Mrs. Carlisle."

"Ah."

"You won't be dining on my raw heart, then?"

"Not tonight," she said cheerfully.

Almost immediately, she wondered if she'd spoken too soon. A round of tittering came from the small group of women that had drawn Lilly into conversation after she'd left the dance floor. Tittering was never a good sign. She steered Gideon closer, but he held her back when she would have steered him directly into the group.

"Have a little faith in your friend," he advised and pulled her just far enough away to listen in without being noticed.

"A very interesting choice of gown, Miss Ilestone," one of the girls chimed. She tossed a quick, feline smile at her friends. "That style must be all the rage in rural Scotland because, I vow, I have never seen the like."

Fuming, Winnefred took a step forward with the vague and—she would admit later—ill-advised notion of breaking a nearby flowerpot over the brat's head.

Gideon grabbed her arm and shifted to block the view of his hold on her from the rest of the room. "*Faith*, Winnefred."

Clearly unaware of the scene taking place off to the side, Lilly tilted her head just a hair, smiled ever so sweetly, and patted the girl's arm in a sympathetic manner. "Of course you haven't, Miss Drayburn. It is a creation of Madame Fayette's. And she is a *little* particular in her choice of patrons."

The tittering stopped. Miss Drayburn opened her mouth but failed to produce anything beyond a splutter.

"But have no fear," Lilly continued, letting her hand fall. "We can be certain Madame Fayette will not hear of the slip from your friends. Now, do excuse me. I am promised for the next dance."

Winnefred watched as Lilly turned and walked away, a smug smile lighting her features. No, not just smug, but *amused*.

Gideon released her arm. "You see?"

"Lilly enjoyed that," she whispered.

"Does that bother you?"

"No, of course not. I'm just . . . I'd worried someone might be unkind to her. I never thought she'd like it."

"She liked winning," Gideon corrected. His eyes tracked Lilly across the room. "She belongs here."

Winnefred wanted to tell him he was wrong. Lilly belonged in Scotland with her. The words were on the tip of her tongue, but she bit them back, knowing them to be a lie. Murdoch House may have been Lilly's home for the last twelve years, but she'd never really belonged there. It had become increasingly clear over the last week that London was Lilly's world.

"I think . . ." She swallowed past a dry lump in her throat and forced herself to say aloud a fear she'd refused to acknowledge until now. "I think she means to stay."

Gideon looked at her and frowned. "You've been here a week. This is one ball. You can't guess at where Lilly will want to be months from now."

"You just said she belonged here."

"Amongst the ton, yes. But the ton only gathers in London twice a year. The other months are spent traveling or at country estates."

"That's true." And with a bit of imagination, she could picture Murdoch House as a small country estate. A very, very small country estate. "I suppose, if Lilly wanted to visit London now and then, that wouldn't be so terrible."

Not wonderful, not at all what she wanted, but not terrible.

"There you go . . . Feel better?"

"Yes. And no." Her lips twitched. "I still want to hit Miss Drayburn with the flowerpot."

"Is that what you had planned?"

"More or less."

"Try to make it less," he suggested.

"Oh, very well." She glared at the back of Miss Drayburn's head and whispered a particularly vulgar insult.

Gideon's shoulders shook with quiet laughter. "*Now* do you feel better?"

"Quite a lot, actually."

She sighed and turned to see Lilly glide across the dance floor once more, this time in the elegant circles of a slow waltz. It occurred to her that watching a graceful dancer in a pretty, candlelit ballroom was nearly as agreeable as being an uncoordinated dancer in the privacy of one's own home.

"Isn't that lovely," she said after a time. "Absolutely perfect."

"I'm sorry I cannot dance with you."

Winnefred looked over at the soft words from Gideon and found him frowning down at his cane. Regret and annoyance that he could not do as he pleased, she understood, but the apology baffled her.

"I am as well, as it troubles you."

"Of course it troubles me." The frown deepened to a scowl. "You shouldn't be standing here. You should have your pick of partners."

"I don't want a pick."

"You should be dancing." He turned his scowl in the general direction of several young gentlemen across the room. "Wait here. I'll see to it—"

"What? No." She whipped a hand out to grab his arm, then dropped it just as quickly when she realized the breach of manners. "I *beg* you, do not demand a dance for me from one of those men. It would be mortifying—"

"I wasn't going to demand . . . exactly."

She ignored the obvious lie. "Furthermore, I do not want to dance."

"Of course you do." He punctuated this bit of presumption with a nod and hard tap of his cane against the floor.

"Where on earth did you acquire such an impression?"

"In Scotland," he replied, as if the answer was obvious. "You had a splendid time dancing."

"Yes, but I was dreadful at it."

"But you've had more lessons, more time, more . . ." He trailed off, and his brows lifted in amused surprise. "You've not improved?"

"No." But she rather liked that he'd assumed she could. The dancing master had proclaimed her hopeless after the first dance. But Gideon, she remembered, had not been present for those lessons.

"Not even a little?" Gideon pressed.

She shook her head and leaned toward him in a conspiratorial manner. "Your aunt has instructed me to feign a touch of the headache whenever I am asked to dance."

He looked at her with patent disbelief. "For the whole of the season?"

"Either I am quite prone to them or exceptionally slow to recover."

Their shared laughter was interrupted by the arrival of Lady Gwen and a gentleman Lilly would describe as fashionably handsome—fair of eyes and hair, tall and light of build, a high brow, thin nose, and strong chin. Winnefred thought him not quite so handsome as Gideon, but she was predisposed to like him all the same because his eyes crinkled nicely in the corners when he smiled.

"Lord Gratley," Lady Gwen said, "may I present Miss Winnefred Blythe?"

Lord Gratley bowed as she curtsied. "Miss Blythe, would you care for a turn about the room?"

She'd rather have stayed with Gideon than take yet another turn about the room, but in the face of an open invitation, there was little she could do but agree. "A turn about the room would be lovely, my lord."

*G*ideon scarcely noticed that his aunt departed as soon as Lord Gratley escorted Winnefred away, and he certainly didn't see the knowing smile that briefly crossed her face before she turned and left. He was too preoccupied trying to ignore the seed of jealousy taking root in his stomach. And when ignoring failed, he attempted to reason his way around it.

It was just a turn about the room, he told himself. A brief walk with a man he rather liked. Lord Grately was a friendly, sensible sort with a keen sense of humor and an eye for seeing past the pretenses of the ton.

And therein lay the problem, Gideon thought darkly.

He didn't want another man seeing—*really* seeing— Winnefred.

Whether she was in a complicated ball gown or a simple dress, *he* was the only man who truly saw her. He knew that beneath the fragile silk was the steel spine of a woman who'd confronted a thief in her stable and beaten him to the ground. He knew that behind the soft smile was the unconquerable will that had kept two women alive on five pounds a year. Well-rehearsed manners hid a brash tongue, and the excuse of a headache would keep quiet the fact she was graceless as a lumbering army. Only he knew the simple, wild beauty of her. It was a treasure he wanted to hoard. She was a secret he wanted to keep all to himself.

He was being unreasonable and he knew it. But even as he berated himself for being a dog in the manger, he scowled as Winnefred laughed at something Gratley said. And he wasn't sure if it was better or worse when Gratley laughed at something Winnefred said in return. He only knew he didn't like it. This was not the sort of enjoyable torment he had promised himself in Winnefred's chambers.

Gideon felt the seed of jealousy sprout and grow as he watched them continue their slow tour of the room. By the time Lord Gratley returned Winnefred to his side, it had spread insidious little tendrils to his brain. And when Gratley bowed and took his leave, Gideon had the outrageous urge to trip the man up with his cane.

Some of his irritation must have shown, because Winnefred took one look at him and asked, "Is something wrong?"

"No, nothing." He succeeded in holding his tongue for all of two more seconds. "You should have a care, Winnefred. People will talk if you flirt overmuch with one gentleman."

"According to Lilly, some people will talk no matter . . ." She blinked and looked at him with a mixture of pleasure and confusion. "Was I flirting? With Lord Gratley, you mean? I'd no idea."

"You were smiling and laughing."

"*That's* flirting?" she demanded in a disbelieving whisper. "You can't be serious. How else would a lady react to a charming gentleman with a keen sense of humor?"

"A polite smile—no teeth—would suffice."

She gaped at him. "I'm to pretend I'm disinterested, even though I am not?"

He shifted his weight without realizing. "No. Yes. Were you very interested?"

She started a little at the question. And who could blame her, he thought? He had no business asking, no business even being curious. He *certainly* had no business sounding like a petulant boy when he asked the question he was so painfully curious about. He scrambled for a way to save his pride and, distracted, missed the quick light of comprehension in her eyes.

"I can speak with my aunt, if you like," he said, finding

an excuse for his behavior. "See if she can't arrange to find out which invitations he has accepted."

And make bloody well certain you aren't at a single one of them, a little voice whispered. He ignored it.

She peeked around his shoulder for a glimpse at Lord Gratley and studied the man with an intensity that had Gideon's hand curling tight around the handle of his cane.

"I think I should like that," she said after a time. "He was very easy to talk to, and he is handsome. Like a fairy-tale prince."

Gideon tried, and failed, to not turn around and give Gratley a quick and jealous assessment.

"His nose is flat," he declared, turning back to Winnefred.

"Is it? I hadn't noticed." She gave him a polite smile with no teeth that had him biting off an oath. "I suppose I only noticed his finer attributes."

He had no interest in and no intentions of learning of Lord Gratley's finer attributes. And after a closer look at Winnefred's features, he began to suspect she wasn't particularly interested in them either. Her lips were twitching.

"Are you goading me?" he asked, eyes narrowing.

"Yes. And quite successfully, I might add."

"Why?"

"Because you're being ridiculous. Don't smile and laugh," she scoffed. "I smile and laugh with you, and if it were inappropriate, Lilly would have mentioned it by now."

"Laughing with me is an entirely different matter." It wasn't really, because there was nothing wrong with her laughing with either of them, but it was too late to confess to that. "As your guardian—"

"Lord Engsly is my guardian, or *was* my guardian—"

"As the highest-ranking member of the Haverston family currently in Britain, and as the man who brought you to London, and as the—"

"Oh, please, let's not quibble over the matter," she cut in

with a small laugh. "Let me revel in my accomplishments awhile."

He considered and quickly rejected the idea of pressing the issue. In part because he knew he was being unreasonable, but mostly because he hadn't been at all sure where he was going with that last argument. "Accomplishments?"

"Oh, yes. It's been over an hour now and I've still not scalded anyone, offended anyone, or brained anyone with a flowerpot. And, according to you, I have even managed a flirtation with a gentleman of rank and wealth." She grinned and, apparently forgetting where she was for a moment, planted her hands on hips like a farmer surveying a fine harvest. "I am very nearly a success."

Chapter 28

$\mathcal{P}$lans to visit Hyde Park the following morning were cancelled when the weather turned cold and wet. Winnefred didn't mind. It gave her the chance to work on a task she'd been eager to tackle for weeks—planning a budget for Murdoch House. Gideon had promised her back allowance and a small bonus, and a fortune such as that required careful management. Though dreams of what could be done for Murdoch House had danced merrily through her head the moment the promise had been made, she'd been uncertain of Gideon initially and unwilling to plan for what she might not receive. That uncertainty had been put to rest well before they'd left for London, but she'd not had enough free time to attempt the job properly until today.

And she'd not have it again for some time. The next week of her life had been scheduled down to the minute—dinner parties, another ball, the opera, calls on the neighbors, and on the seventh day, Lady Gwen's grand ball. Which was, Winnefred had been informed by both Lady Gwen and Lilly, to be the highlight of the London season.

She doubted it could be nearly as engaging as her plans for Murdoch House.

Initially, she quite enjoyed making a tidy list of all the things the house and land needed, and accompanying each with an estimated cost of purchase or upkeep, but as the list grew longer, the pleasure began to fade. By the time she reached the end of her expenses, her lips were twisted into a grimace.

How was it possible she hadn't enough funds? She now had access to more money than she had ever seen. It was more money than she had ever dreamt of seeing. It had to be enough.

She tried running the numbers again, this time excluding luxuries like chocolate and new boots twice a year, but it made little difference. Then she tried spreading her expenses out over the course of two, and then three years, but that just made things worse. To keep the house running and the staff employed, Murdoch House needed to generate a goodly income, but for Murdoch House to generate a goodly income, it needed sufficient livestock and supplies and time. But once she paid for the livestock and supplies, there wasn't enough left over to keep the house running and the staff employed for the time it took for Murdoch House to generate its goodly income.

Damn it.

She tossed her pen down on the writing desk in her chambers and folded her arms over her chest. This was all Gideon's fault, she decided. He had been the one to bring twelve servants back from Langholm. *Twelve* for pity's sake. And all but a few of them house servants. She still had to hire more field hands.

"Blast."

She glowered at the list of numbers and made herself consider one option she had studiously ignored until now. She could sell the jewelry from Gideon.

Just the idea of it put a knot in her stomach, which was just enough motivation for her to consider, and accept, the only other option she had left.

She would ask Gideon for more money.

After a brief search, Winnefred found him seated behind the desk in a small study off the front hall. He'd taken off the morning coat he'd worn at breakfast and rolled up the sleeves of his shirt, revealing muscular forearms. His cravat retained the simple knot she'd seen earlier, but it had been pulled tight and the silk hung loose around his neck as if he'd been tugging on the material without realizing it.

She tapped lightly on the open door. "Gideon? May I speak with you a moment?"

Gideon looked up from a substantial stack of papers, a line of concentration across his brow and his hair sticking on end in several places. "Will it distract me from my current task?"

"Er . . . I think so, yes."

"Excellent. Take a seat."

She did as he asked, and because she wasn't quite ready to get to the topic at hand, she turned her attention to the papers on his desk. "What is all that?"

"Work from the Engsly estate. My brother's secretary has been taking care of things of late, but now he's gone and caught the ague."

"Inconsiderate of him."

"My sentiments exactly." He set his pen down. "What's troubling you, Winnefred?"

Her gaze shot to his and then away. She felt awkward all of a sudden—frustrated and ungrateful. Uncomfortable with the first and last, she focused on the middle.

"Mathematics," she grumbled and pointed a finger at him. "And it's all your doing. You shouldn't have hired so many."

"So many what?"

"People. Staff for Murdoch House." She threw her hands up in irritation. "I can't afford them. I know I asked Thomas to come, but he's only one. I can afford one, not several dozen."

"You don't have several dozen," he reminded her calmly. "Why don't you let some of them go if—?"

"Let them go? I couldn't possibly, not after so short an employment."

"Why not?" he asked, the question clearly academic from his standpoint.

"You know very well why not. They are relying . . . They need . . ." They needed her to keep them fed, housed, and safe. "I can't do it. I can't turn them out." She swallowed hard and forced herself to sit up straighter in her chair. "I need your help. I am asking you for additional funds to keep them employed. All of them."

"Certainly."

"It would only be a temporary measure," she rushed on. "Just until the land—" Finally, his response sank in. "Beg your pardon?"

"I said certainly. You may have whatever you need."

"But . . ." It couldn't be that easy. Nothing was ever that easy. "But the arrangement was for the allowance owed and—"

"The arrangement is changed," he broke in. "Do you want to argue the matter?"

She snapped her mouth shut and shook her head.

"Then it is settled," Gideon declared.

"Well." Apparently, it was to be that easy. "I suppose it is. Thank you."

"You are welcome." He held a finger up when she would have risen from her chair. "Another minute of your time, please."

She sank back into her seat, then rather wished she hadn't because he didn't say anything, he just sat there, silently observing her through curious eyes. And if she had been standing, she could have wandered over to the fireplace to inspect the clock or make a point of perusing the books on the bookshelf—something, anything, besides watch him watch *her*.

"What?" she finally demanded. "Why are you staring at me like that?"

"I cannot puzzle you out."

Puzzle her out? Hadn't he said she was simple? "What is there to puzzle out?"

"What you want," he replied.

"I just told you what I want." The man's mind moved in dizzying circles.

"No, you just told me what you want for someone else. If it hadn't been for the staff, you'd not have asked for more funds . . . You ask so little for yourself," he added softly.

She wasn't sure why that felt so much like an accusation to her. "That's not true. I've taken food, shelter, a wardrobe, a mountain of fripperies, a trip to London—"

"Because taking them meant giving them to Lilly."

"I asked you to bring me a pastry and chocolate," she reminded him.

"You offered me the coin to bring two pastries, one for Lilly and one for yourself, and you gave your last cup of chocolate to me." He tapped his finger against the arm of the chair. "Two errands, that's all you've demanded of me, the wealthy son and brother of a marquess."

"I demanded you take a meal a day with us."

"Again, because you thought it might benefit Lilly."

"Murdoch House—"

"I gave you Murdoch House. Why are you arguing again?"

"Because . . ." She searched for a way to explain her discomfort. "Because you would paint me a saint, and I don't think that's fitting." No more fitting than imagining her a true lady. "I don't . . . You needn't laugh quite so hard."

"A saint?" he echoed when his amusement faded. "I assure you, the thought has not entered my mind. Once."

A bit miffed he should agree with her so fervently, she steered the conversation away from the topic of her unlikely canonization. "Then why concern yourself over what I have and have not requested?"

He began tapping his finger again and looking at her as if she were a particularly fascinating riddle. It was, she decided, slightly preferable to being laughed at.

"I find it intriguing," he replied at length. "And frustrating."

She felt herself blush at the first and frown a bit at the second. "I don't see why you should become frustrated. If I want something, I will ask for it."

"Will you?" His voice was an incongruent mix of hope and skepticism. Suddenly, he stood and came around the desk. Before she could even think to ask what he was about, he'd taken the seat next to hers and shifted them both so they faced one another with their knees brushing.

In an abrupt change of mood, he grinned at her and leaned forward in his chair to take one of her hands in his.

"Ask me for something now."

Bemused, she looked down at their joined hands, then back at him. "What?"

"Ask me for something," he repeated. "Something just for you. Anything at all."

He was so obviously delighted by the idea, so adorably excited with his wrinkled cravat and mussed hair. She couldn't possibly deny him.

A thousand requests flew through her mind. Big things, little things, ridiculous things. A new stable. A pair of draught horses. A thousand pounds to spend on custard-filled pastries.

But then the sun broke out from behind a cloud and sunlight filtered through the windows into the room. She watched the effect it had on Gideon's eyes.

Lighter in the morning, she thought, and she spoke without thinking.

"You."

Gideon dropped her hand and reared back. "Beg your pardon?"

Oh, bloody hell. She hadn't meant to say that aloud. She'd barely been aware of thinking it.

She searched frantically for a way to cover her blunder. "*You* . . ." she began, drawing the word out, ". . . can buy me a draught horse."

That sounded lame even to her own ears. And to Gideon's as well, apparently. He was still looking at her as if she'd gone off and slapped him.

He grabbed his cane and rose to walk around the back side of his chair like a man in need of a shield. "That is not what you meant."

It certainly wasn't. And there was no way for her to backtrack now.

Very well, she would charge forward. It had to happen sometime. She couldn't go on wondering how he felt indefinitely.

"No," she said, "it is not."

Gideon swore under his breath. "I was under the impression Lilly instructed you on what a lady should and should not say to a gentleman."

"Certainly she did. But . . ." In for a penny, in for a pound, she told herself. "Well, you're not just any gentleman, are you? You're my friend. A friend who kissed me, and one I have found I very much like kissing back—"

"I apologized for that," he broke in. "And I will again. I am sorry."

"Why?"

He visibly started at the question. "What do you mean why?"

"Why are you sorry?"

He hesitated. ". . . Because it was a risk to your reputation."

She knew a badly delivered lie when she heard one too. "What nonsense. We were on a dark, rarely used road in the middle of Scotland the first time. Who in the world would have seen us? And—"

"Other people use roads," he pointed out.

"And make quite a lot of noise doing it," she retorted, growing increasingly annoyed at his evasions. "Did you expect a coach-and-four to sneak up when we weren't looking?"

"That's not the point."

"I fail to see that you have a point. Why are you sorry you kissed me?"

"Because . . ." He trailed off and leaned hard on the back of the chair. Winnefred waited for him to gather his thoughts, but when he lifted his face to hers again, she could see it wasn't his thoughts he'd been gathering, but a cold, hard resolve. "Because I cannot marry you."

He is the brother of a marquess.

Winnefred could have sworn she felt something inside her break.

There it was then, the reward for her risks and work and patience.

One more rejection.

$\mathcal{G}$ideon watched as the color drained from Winnefred's cheeks and anger, the kind that came from wounded feelings and damaged pride, flashed in her eyes.

"I've not asked you to marry me," she said stiffly.

She was so beautiful, he thought miserably. He'd only wanted to give her something for herself. Something from him. How had things gone so wrong?

His hand gripped the handle of his cane until his fingers throbbed. "There are certain attentions a gentleman pays only to the lady he intends to make his wife."

"Oh?" Her voice took on a brittle, mocking tone. "Are you a virgin as well, then?"

"I . . . No. Winnefred—"

She threw a hand up. "Don't. It isn't necessary for you to explain your decision. You are brother to a marquess, and I am the uneducated, ill-mannered daughter of a nobody." She stood up, her face a mask of barely controlled fury, and spun around toward the door. "Excuse me."

He caught her around the waist from behind before she made it halfway across the room. He couldn't let her leave, not like this. "Stop. Winnefred—"

"Let me go." She threw an elbow out and caught him mid-chest.

"Bloody hell." Ignoring the sudden loss of air, he shifted his weight to his good leg, dropped his cane, and wrapped both arms around her struggling form. "Stop. Let me explain."

Her only response was to bring her heel down, hard, on his toes.

"*Damn it*, Winnefred." He lifted her off the floor. "It has nothing to do with—"

She delivered a painful kick to the shin of his good leg.

"Son of a . . ." Eyes watering, he set her back down again. "*Listen* to me. I can't—"

She reared back and might have broken his nose with the back of her head if he hadn't twisted out of the way at the last moment and blurted out the only thing that might make her understand.

"I had powder monkeys on my ship!"

Chapter 29

*T*he room went still but for the rise and fall of chests and silent but for the sound of labored breathing. Winnefred could feel the hard pounding of Gideon's heart against her back, and his breath was hot and damp against her ear.

"Do you know what a powder monkey is, Winnefred?"

She wished she didn't care.

She hadn't expected a refusal from him to hurt so much, to cut so deeply. But it had, and it terrifed her, almost as much as it infuriated her, that he had that sort of power over her. She wanted to steal that power back. She wanted to tell him to take his powder monkeys and go straight to the devil. But the misery in his voice, the quiet desperation that had brought her struggles to an abrupt halt made it impossible to turn away.

"No," she whispered.

"Will you let me explain?"

No. I don't want to hear it.

She gave a small nod.

"Thank you." Gideon released her, bent down to pick up

his cane, and made his way to a sidebar for a small glass of brandy.

Watching him pour the drink sent a shiver up her spine. What sort of explanation required a brandy at eleven o'clock in the morning?

He turned around to face her, glass in hand and his features set in stone. She remembered being thirteen and hearing the news of her father's death from a stranger. The messenger had looked then as Gideon did now—reluctant, resolved, and detached.

"A powder monkey," Gideon began, "is a small boy who runs gunpowder from cannon to cannon during a battle. He keeps it under his shirt to protect it from sparks. There's at least one on every warship."

She licked lips gone dry. "You had one on yours?"

"I had six."

"Six? You had six boys on your ship?"

He laughed softly and without humor. "Oh, I had a great many more boys than that. Damn near a quarter of the crew was under twenty."

He stared at his glass for a long while, as if he might find an answer there, or simply a place to bury the questions.

"Gideon?"

"I had no business captaining a ship," he said softly. "No business being responsible for those boys."

"I don't believe that—"

"I didn't want boys on the *Perseverance*, but you take what you're given, don't you? That's what happens in war. You do the best with whatever you have . . . I thought it best to send them to the hold. In every battle, I sent the youngest to the hold to keep them safe." He shook his head, then downed the contents of the glass. "It didn't work."

She closed her eyes as the horror of what that meant washed over her. "I'm so sorry."

In a sudden burst of movement and noise that had her jumping back, Gideon threw the glass against the fireplace where it shattered into hundreds of bright and jagged shards. He whirled on her, his face hard and angry, his muscles bunched so tight she feared he'd shatter as the glass had. "*Children!* What the bloody hell did I know of *children*?!"

"Gideon—"

"I'll tell you what I know now! What I learned soon enough! It takes no more than a metal ball and the space of a heartbeat to rip through nearly a half dozen of them!" He dragged a shaking hand through his hair. "Just one ball. One ball and the captain responsible for placing them in the way of it."

"No. That's not true. You—"

She bit back the argument when a footman knocked on the open door. His eyes darted to the shattered glass, but as was expected of a man of his position, his face betrayed not a hint of emotion. "My lord? Are you or Miss Blythe in need of assistance?"

Winnefred watched, helpless, as Gideon struggled to pull himself together. "No. No, we are both well. Thank you."

"Shall I send for a maid?"

"That won't be necessary."

"Very good, my lord."

Winnefred listened to the sound of the footman's retreating steps but kept her eyes on Gideon. The flash of temper had burned itself out, and in its place had come resignation. She wasn't sure which was worse.

"Gideon—"

"No." He held up his hand. "I'm done discussing it. I only wanted to explain. I wanted you to understand why I can't . . . I will not be responsible for someone ever again."

Someone like a wife, she realized. Any wife. "But—"

"Let it go, Winnefred."

Afraid he would retreat again, she took an argumentative tone. "I'll not let it go. Because you are *not* responsible."

"You weren't there," he snapped.

"Did you ask for a young crew?" she demanded. "Pay a press-gang or buy their commissions? Did you fire the cannon that killed them? Build the ship that housed it? Start the war that required the ship?"

"No, I—"

"There is blame to be placed here," she pushed on. "But it is not yours. You did the best with what you had—you said that yourself. If politicians and royals and trumped-up tyrants who fancied themselves emperors had done *their* best to care for the people they were responsible for, we never would have had a war—or children fighting it."

"Men will always make war." He shook his head and turned from her to look out the window. "Always. There's little to be done about it but attempt to stay out of its path, and failing that, find the pleasure in life where and when you can."

Winnefred stared at his back, desperately racking her mind for a way to reach him, to help him. And then it occurred to her—

"Do you . . . Do you care for me at all?"

He threw a surprised glance over his shoulder. "What the devil has that to do with anything?"

"Answer the question." If she could find the courage to ask, he could damn well find the courage to answer. "Do you care for me?"

"I do," he said clearly. He turned and held her eyes as if to be certain she knew he meant it. "You must know that I do."

Her relief was so great, her legs turned to mush. She wanted to throw her arms around him and laugh. And she wanted to sit down. She ignored all three desires and nodded decisively. "And if we were on a ship right now, right this very moment, and a battle broke out—where would you put me?"

An instant of fear crossed his face before he could hide it. "I wouldn't allow you anywhere near a warship."

She ignored his evasion. "Knowing what you know now—where would you put me?"

"This is ridiculous."

He sidled away from the window, and her, as if to distance himself from the question. But she wouldn't let him run. She took two steps forward. "Where, Gideon?"

"Let it alone—"

Another step. "Where?"

He shook his head, pleading. *"For pity's sake."*

One last step to stand directly before him. "Tell me *where.*"

"I'd put you in the bleeding hold!"

She reached out to cup his cheek with one hand. "Because it's the safest place on the ship. Because you care for me, and it'd be the best thing you could do for me. What might happen after that would be out of your control."

"They were children," he whispered hoarsely. "They were innocents. I should have protected them."

"Even you cannot stop a cannonball."

"I should have—"

"No. There was nothing else you could do, Gideon. Nothing. It just was."

*G*ideon squeezed his eyes shut and shook his head. He didn't want to hear the words; he didn't want to admit that they might be true.

It just was.

He knew that there was a basic human desire to have control, to understand, to know the reasons *why.* He knew that the drive to discover meaning in the events of one's life—both large and small, beautiful and tragic—had led men to religion, philosophy, science. And greatness had come from those searches; comfort from the answers they provided.

But perhaps there were times when an explanation wasn't to be had, and maybe it was less frightening to blame himself than acknowledge his helplessness, and easier to shoulder the guilt than to accept that no one would be held accountable. But anything, anything at all, was better than contemplating the idea of six young boys dying senselessly in a hold of a ship and no one being held responsible.

Someone had to be responsible.

He drew her hand from his cheek and let it go. "I'm sorry."

She searched his face with her eyes. "I don't understand."

"This." He breathed past the knot of pain in his chest. "You and I. It cannot be."

"But you care for me," she whispered. "And I for you. Why—?"

"I cared for them too."

"But surely—"

"*No*, Winnefred."

She turned away and, for a long time, stared at the fireplace without speaking. He wanted to fill the silence, but he couldn't think of anything else to say. There was nothing left to explain.

Winnefred spoke at length, and without turning back to face him. "Is this . . . Is this your final say on the matter?"

"It is."

She looked at the ground and put her hands on her hips the way a person did when they were trying to catch their breath. "There is nothing I can say to change your mind?"

He wished she would look at him. "No."

She gave a nearly imperceptible nod of her head. "Very well."

This time, when she moved to leave, he didn't stop her.

Chapter 30

$\mathcal{F}$or a long time after Winnefred left the study, Gideon stood in the middle of the room and stared into the hallway.

He had told her. He had told her everything. He had shared with her the burden he had promised to carry alone. He wanted to berate himself for that, but there didn't seem to be any point. It wasn't possible for him to feel any worse.

This. You and I. It cannot be.

He'd always known that to be true, but he'd not spoken the words aloud until now. And he'd never intended to speak them to Winnefred. If he had been a little more careful, and a little less self-centered, he would never have had to. He'd known his interest was returned. He'd seen the light of desire in Winnefred's eyes and felt the way she had melted against him when they'd kissed. But he had willfully ignored what he'd known to be true so he could indulge in his own selfish need to seek her out.

Well, no more. It was too late to undo what was done, but he could repair what damage he could and make damn well certain he didn't cause more.

He would find a way to make things comfortable between them again, just comfortable enough for her to feel easy in his company . . . Which he intended to severely limit in the future.

There was no avoiding his duty of escorting the ladies to balls and parties, but his free time could be spent visiting friends or relaxing at his club. He could do that. He *would* do that.

To prove it, he grabbed his coat, shoved his arms through the sleeves, and left the study. He would spend a few hours at White's, he decided. He would give Winnefred a bit of time and himself a bit of space. Then he would see about making things easy between them again. Distant, but easy.

He was reaching for his hat and gloves in the front hall when the front door flew open with a crash.

Lucien stumbled inside, looking nothing like the proud and aloof peer of the realm their father had hoped he would become. His hair was windblown, the traveling clothes on his tall, lean frame were wrinkled and dusty, and there was a set edge to his sharp features that spoke of blind determination and not enough sleep.

Lucien's eyes snapped to his. "Gideon. Where is she?"

Suddenly, despite everything, Gideon felt the urge to smile. "Welcome home, Lucien. How was your trip?"

"Eventful. Where—?"

"I am quite well, thank you. You received my letter, I presume?"

"It reached me in Berlin. Is—?"

"Lady Engsly?"

"Dead," Lucian replied impatiently. "She succumbed to opium poison two months ago."

"Opium." Gideon blew out a short breath. "I hadn't realized she was an addict. But it would explain the madness, wouldn't it. Where is Kincaid?"

"He stayed behind to handle a few remaining details. For pity's sake, man, where is she?"

Gideon took pity on his brother. "Upstairs."

As if to prove his point, Lilly suddenly appeared at the

top of the stairs. She put her hand on the banister, looked up, and froze.

Lucien went equally still. *"Rose."*

Not wanting to intrude, and equally unwilling to miss what happened next, Gideon backed away to watch the scene unfold from the open doors of the dining room.

Lilly was the first to move. She resumed her walk down the stairs, coming to stop a few steps from the bottom.

"Lord Engsly. Welcome home." Her voice was smooth and calm, and so painfully polite, Gideon felt a pang of sympathy for his brother. "I trust your journey was a safe one?"

"It was . . . productive." Lucien took another step forward. "Are you well?"

"Quite, thank you. It was very kind of your family to allow—"

"You look just as I remember," he blurted out.

"I . . . I am headed to . . . to the library." She moved forward suddenly, down the last steps and past a stunned Lucien. "Excuse me."

"Wait." Lucien caught her arm. "Rose. Wait."

Lilly looked down at his hand and then slowly up to him. "My name is Lilly," she said coolly. "Miss Lilly Ilestone."

Lucien visibly started. His hand dropped. "Yes . . . Yes, of course. My apologies."

Lilly gave a regal nod of her head that Lady Gwen would have been proud to see and turned to resume her walk toward the library.

Lucien stepped forward, faltered, then growled something akin to "bugger this" and took off after her before she'd made it halfway across the hall. He grabbed her hand and pulled her toward the parlor.

"Stop." Lilly tugged at her arm. "What do you think—?"

"I think I haven't slept in days," Lucien practically barked. "I think I chased a madwoman across four countries." He threw open the doors to the front parlor. "I think I've waited twelve bloody years for this."

He pushed Lilly into the room, stepped in behind her, and slammed the doors.

Winnefred didn't like to think of herself as a selfish woman, but as she sat on her bed with Lilly and listened to the retelling of Lord Engsly's arrival, she was forced to admit that she was secretly grateful to have a distraction from her own troubles.

After leaving Gideon in the study, she'd spent a full hour pacing the floor of her chambers, berating herself and Gideon, and alternating between wanting to cry and scream and take the first coach back to Scotland.

Dealing with Lilly's woes was so much simpler.

Lilly plucked at the counterpane, her blue eyes filled with uncertainty. "Lucien . . . That is, Lord Engsly has agreed to stay at his own town house."

Which meant Gideon would have to continue staying here, Winnefred realized. "Is that something you asked of him?"

"Yes. I also asked that he acknowledge that a great deal of time has passed since we last met, and he agreed it is significant and promised to limit his references to our shared past."

"I see."

"He has also made it clear he intends to begin a courtship."

"Did he really?" Winnefred blew out a short breath when Lilly nodded. "Well. Is that what you want?"

"I didn't. I refused at first, but . . . Well, he did make concessions. It was only fair I do the same."

"What concessions did you make?"

"I agreed that it was, perhaps, unfair of me to criticize him for not seeking me out after hearing I had married. It would have been dishonorable for him to approach another man's wife in that manner." Lilly gave up plucking to tuck her knees up under her chest and wrap her arms around her legs. "I would never have thought so highly of him to start had he not been an honorable man."

Winnefred had thought the same thing, but she was glad Lilly had worked through the logic of it on her own.

"I agreed not to spurn the courtship. Winnefred . . ." Lilly shook her head. "I'd no idea . . . Gideon said his brother had feelings still, but . . . He traveled from Spain without rest. Because of *me*. He says . . . He says he is still very much in love with me."

"And you?"

"I don't know. I don't." Lilly's voice hitched, and her eyes filled with tears. "I made myself stop thinking of him so long ago. I *had* to. We were alone in Scotland with no funds and nowhere to turn. I was useless to you, heartbroken and grieving. You were thirteen years old, for pity's sake. You weren't supposed to be the strong one."

"We were both strong."

"I am glad you remember it that way," Lilly replied on a small, watery laugh.

"You should as well."

"Maybe. What I do remember . . . I remember that I loved him." Lilly's face crumpled. The tears streamed down her cheeks. "I loved him so much, Freddie."

Hurting for both of them, Winnefred wrapped her arms around Lilly and held on.

A fine thing indeed, she thought, for the pair of them to have their hearts broken by a pair of Haverstons.

Chapter 31

The only joy Winnefred found in the week before Lady Gwen's ball was in watching Lord Engsly dance attendance upon Lilly. True to his word, the marquess began a courtship, and to the considerable delight of the ton, he carried that courtship out with abandonment. He brought flowers and books and boxes of candy. He waltzed with Lilly at every ball, took her for drives in Hyde Park every sunny afternoon, and monopolized her attentions at every dinner party.

He made it clear to Lilly, to his family, and to anyone else who cared to listen that he intended to make Miss Lilly Ilestone his marchioness. In private, Lilly made it clear to Winnefred that while she didn't care about the elevation in status the attentions of a marquess afforded, she was not *wholly* opposed to the idea of making it permanent. Which Winnefred translated to mean she was falling in love all over again.

Even though a marriage to Engsly would put an end to the question of whether or not Lilly would return to Murdoch House, Winnefred was happy for her friend. She was not, however, happy in any general sense of the word.

Her friendship with Gideon had become distant and cold. It was as if a great wall had been thrown up between them and they were forced to deliver a volley of polite greetings and painfully formal exchanges over the barrier like a pair of armies firing over a battlement.

She wanted to place the blame for that squarely on his shoulders, but she couldn't. The distance was his doing— he had taken to isolating himself in his chambers once again and going to his club for most meals. He fulfilled his duty of escorting them about town, but he didn't seek her out in the parlor at dinner parties or engage her in conversation at Lady Hillspeak's ball.

He was avoiding her, plain and simple.

But the coldness was her doing. Initially, Gideon had tried to make the few minutes they spent together each day not friendly, exactly, but easier. He'd smiled at her and made little comments that were designed to entice a laugh. She had responded with an affected lack of interest.

She knew he cared for her. He'd made that perfectly clear. But her father had cared for her too, in his own way. That way had left her orphaned and abandoned in Scotland. She didn't want that sort of caring—the kind that was just enough to hint at, but never deliver on, the promise of more. Sometimes, hope could wound deeper than a rejection and damage more than just the heart.

Maybe if she tried harder . . .

Maybe if she put more effort into becoming a lady . . .

Maybe if she made herself into someone else, anyone else . . .

No. She wasn't going to make herself into someone else. And she wasn't going to sit about, waiting and hoping for Gideon to see she was perfect for him, just as she was, or chase after him, hoping for a kind word or sign of affection. She was done fighting, and waiting, and risking. She wasn't going to allow herself to be torn apart like some sort of foolish, spineless twit who . . .

Winnefred shifted in her seat in the far corner of Lady Gwen's crowded ballroom. She *was* sitting about, tearing herself apart like a twit, and she had been for the last hour. Ever since she had seen Gideon push his way through the crowd into the card room.

She turned her head to glower at the card room doors only to discover she could no longer see them through the mass of people. The ballroom, which had been fairly well crowded when she'd taken her seat, had grown absolutely packed while she'd sat, staring at the floor, lost in her thoughts.

For the first time, she noticed how hot she was and how close the other people were all around her. She was pressed up tight against the wall and staring at the backside of someone in a bright white gown. An elderly gentleman reeking of spirits was asleep next to her and slowly sliding off his chair in her direction. She put a hand out to slow his descent, stood carefully so as not to elbow the woman in front of her, and gently eased the old man's head onto her chair.

She needed air.

"Excuse me." She nudged her way past the women in front of her and moved forward into the room, determined to reach the terrace doors and the fresh air beyond. But it was slow going. The guests were packed in like cattle at market. People pressed into her from behind, jostled her from the side, and seemed oblivious to her need to move forward. They were laughing and shouting, calling to one another over the din. The air around her grew thick with sweet perfume and overheated flesh. She felt her nostrils flare and her stomach roll.

She looked back in the direction she'd come, wondering if she could return to her seat, where she'd been allotted at least a few inches of space in which to breathe, but the meager trail she had forged had been swallowed up by the crowd. And her chair had, no doubt, been taken by someone else by now.

She pushed forward again, into the noise and smell and great wall of people. She'd never seen so many people. She felt as if she were on the verge of being trampled.

Panic began to slither along her skin and creep into her lungs.

Out, she needed *out*. She couldn't breathe. She couldn't see. She tried to keep her eyes on the top of a door to the terrace, but the room kept moving, and there were so many people—too many stepping in front of her, pushing her off course. She wanted to yell at them, but she couldn't find the air.

Out! Let me out!

The room and its occupants shimmered, tilted, and spun in a disorienting roll.

A large hand gripped her elbow. "Slow breaths, sweetheart. You're nearly there."

Gideon. She wanted to laugh, weep, throw her arms around him, and punch him solidly in the nose.

Slow breaths? Was he mad?

"Breathe through your mouth."

She did, and the dense smells of the ballroom receded.

She followed him blindly through the path he created in the crowd, grateful for the steadying grip on her arm. Her stomach was no longer threatening to revolt, but the dizzying panic remained. There were just too many people. There wasn't enough air for all of them.

"Almost there," Gideon said again. He pushed his way not through the terrace doors but into a small chamber off the ballroom where a handful of servants were milling about. He ushered her past them, delivering orders along the way.

"Fetch Miss Ilestone, a glass of brandy, and a cup of tea."

He opened yet another door and pulled her into a sitting room. "You're all right now. There's no one else here."

He led her to a chair and sat her down. But she still couldn't catch her breath. She could hear herself struggling for air.

"Can't breathe."

"Yes, you can."

Gideon knelt in front of her and took her hand. He placed the flat of it against his chest where she could feel his heart beating, steady and strong beneath her palm.

"There now, do you feel that? Match your breathing to mine, Winnefred. A deep breath in . . . now out. There's a girl. Again . . . that's it . . ."

He kept her hand in place and murmured reassurances. She concentrated on the sound of his voice and the steady rise and fall of his chest. And slowly, she felt the panic recede and the air return to her lungs.

"Better?" Gideon asked at length.

She managed a jerky nod and let her hand slide away from his. "I don't know what happened. I only wanted to get to the terrace and then, suddenly, I couldn't find my way out." She gave a soft, unsteady laugh. "Perhaps I have a delicate constitution after all."

"Or perhaps," Gideon said darkly, rising from the floor, "my aunt invited too many people."

"I've never seen so many," she admitted. "I've never been so crowded."

"A crush like that can be too much for even a seasoned member of the ton." He spared a brief glance at the maid who arrived with the tea and brandy. The young woman set her burden on a side table and quietly slipped from the room again.

Gideon reached for the brandy and handed it to Winnefred. "A bit of this first."

"I've not had spirits before." She took a tentative sip and grimaced. "Oh, it tastes like . . . Like it would do a very thorough job of cleaning the floor."

He tapped the bottom of the glass with his finger. "Take a drink. A proper one."

She wrinkled her nose but complied. The liquid burned a path down her throat.

"Ugh. That's hideous." She frowned down at the remaining brandy in her glass as the burning turned into a pleasant warmth. "And strangely appealing. Should I drink the rest?"

He chuckled and took the glass from her. "That's enough for now. Try the tea."

She took the tea without looking at it. She realized

suddenly how comfortable she was with him, and how like their former selves they were behaving. She wasn't sure what hurt more, the longing to continue on in the same way or the idea that Gideon could.

He shouldn't be able to, she thought. It shouldn't be so bloody easy for him. It shouldn't be easy for anyone to hurt the person he cared about.

She wanted to tell him that, but the arrival of a visibly agitated Lilly forced her to put the anger aside.

"Freddie? Freddie, what's happened? Dear heavens, you're pale as wax." She rounded on Gideon. "What have you done to her?"

Winnefred rose to stand between them. If one of them was going to give Gideon a piece of her mind, it was going to be her. "Lilly, stop. I had a . . . a moment of discomfort in the crowd, that's all. He only sought to help me."

"Oh." Lilly's eyes darted from Gideon, to her, and back again. Finally, she sniffed and said, "Well. My apologies."

If Gideon was offended by that less-than-convincing statement of regret, it didn't show.

"Your concern for Miss Blythe is admirable," he returned politely. "I shall leave her in your excellent care."

Miss Blythe.

His voice echoed in her head as her heart twisted in her chest. He'd taken to calling her that now and again, as if he was slowly easing them further and further apart.

She watched him leave and wished she could call him back. If only to tell him to go to the devil.

Lilly stepped into her line of sight, a welcome distraction. "Tell me what happened."

"It was nothing." She gave a small shake of her head. "I tried to make my way to the terrace for a bit of fresh air and became trapped in the crowd."

"And?" Lilly prompted.

"And I grew overheated. And perhaps a bit dizzy. I might have become a little panicked." Or a lot, but she wasn't going to admit it.

"Oh, dear."

"Gideon found me and brought me here."

Lilly reached out to rub her arm. "I'm sorry I left you alone for so long," she said softly. "I only went to get something to drink and speak with Lady Gwen. The room filled so quickly. I couldn't find my way back to you."

"There was no need for you to come back. I wasn't doing anything of interest."

"Nevertheless—"

"You shouldn't be in here now, coddling me, instead of out there, enjoying yourself." She remembered suddenly that she had pushed and stumbled her way past a great many people in her attempt to reach the terrace. And she could only imagine what Gideon had done to get them through the crowd. Perhaps Lilly couldn't be out there, enjoying herself, now that her friend had behaved so poorly in front of two-thirds of society.

"Everyone saw," she said on a groan. "Everyone saw me leave the ballroom."

"Not everyone," Lilly replied, not sounding nearly as concerned as Winnefred really felt she ought. "But I should think quite a few."

"I'd been doing so well. Not a single misstep." Winnefred felt her shoulders slump. "Now I've embarrassed you."

To her surprise, Lilly merely laughed.

"It's not funny," Winnefred declared.

"Oh, but it is," Lilly insisted. "Embarrassed me? You had a fit of the vapors, Freddie. What could be more ladylike?"

"Oh." Her mood brightened, marginally. "I hadn't thought of that."

"It can be difficult to think clearly when one is in the midst of a fainting spell."

Winnefred winced at the comment and accompanying snicker. "You'll never let me forget this, will you?"

"Never. But I'll limit my teasing until you've fully recovered." Lilly walked over and opened a door that led outside. "A bit of fresh air is what you need."

Winnefred followed her onto a small private terrace with steps leading down into the torchlit gardens.

"I was trying to get to fresh air when Gideon found me. I don't know why he brought me . . ." She glanced over at the sound of a great many people talking over one another and saw that the main terrace was as crowded as the ballroom. "Never mind."

She took Lilly's hand and started them down a wide gravel path. The air and freedom to move about felt wonderful, and though there were others in the garden, strolling along the paths and milling about the fountains, their numbers were far fewer than in the ballroom. With the exception of the occasional passing couple, she and Lilly were left with relative privacy.

"It was fortunate Gideon was near you in the ballroom," Lilly said at length.

"I suppose it was."

"Surprising too. He's not been in your company much of late."

Winnefred hesitated before responding. She'd not mentioned her troubles with Gideon because she hadn't wanted to detract from her friend's new happiness with Lord Engsly. And, truth be told, she simply hadn't wanted to talk about it. She was trying so very hard not to think about it. But if the speed with which Lilly had turned on Gideon in the sitting room was any indication, her friend was already aware that something was amiss.

She sighed and resigned herself to the conversation. "We had a falling out of sorts."

"Over what?"

"Marriage. He won't marry me."

Lilly made some sort of choking noise in her throat and came to a stumbling halt. "Freddie, you . . . You didn't *ask* him, did you?"

"No, of course not. It came up . . ." When she'd propositioned him in a general sort of way. "It came up, that's all."

"Oh." Lilly blew out a long whoosh of air and looked up at the sky. "Oh, thank heavens."

"He doesn't want to marry anyone," Winnefred added, eager to move the conversation forward.

"Did he say why?"

"It's complicated," Winnefred hedged and started them walking again. "But the short of it is, he doesn't want to be responsible for anyone but himself."

Lilly pondered that for a time before asking, "Do you want to be married?"

No. Maybe . . . If it was to Gideon. "I don't know. And it's not relevant, really. He made it clear he'd not even consider the idea."

Lilly's response was to glance down another path and say, "Huh," and then look over her shoulder and add an equally distracted, "Hmm."

"That's not particularly helpful, Lilly."

"Lord Gratley is coming."

"What?" She turned her head to see the gentleman making his way down a path that intersected with their own. She rather liked Lord Gratley, but she was in no mood to talk to anyone besides Lilly. "Oh. Do you think we could slip away?"

"No." Lilly took her arm and brought them to an abrupt stop. "You're going to stay."

"What? Why?"

"Because Gideon is watching from the terrace."

She would not, absolutely not turn around. "Where Gideon is looking is no concern of mine."

"Of course it is." Lilly lowered her voice as Gratley drew closer. "You are going to stay here and flirt with Lord Gratley and prove to Lord Gideon Haverston that you don't care one jot what he thinks of marriage."

"But *why*?"

"Because it will make you feel better." Lilly's eyes flicked toward the terrace. "And Gideon strikes me as the jealous sort."

"Don't be—"

"Oh, look," Lilly chimed in a slightly elevated voice. "Did you know there was a fountain by the roses? How lovely. I must have a look. Wait for me here, won't you, Freddie?"

Winnefred didn't even try to call Lilly back. The fountain was only twenty yards away or so, and in clear view of the path. Strictly speaking, she was still being chaperoned.

And now that she thought on it, perhaps her friend was right. Perhaps a mild flirtation with another gentleman would provide a balm to her wounded pride.

Let Gideon see her enjoying Lord Gratley's company. Let him be reminded that he wasn't the only gentleman who might *care* for her, that there might even be a gentleman who wanted to keep her.

She turned and smiled at Lord Gratley with all her teeth.

Let Gideon see *that*.

Chapter 32

*G*ideon saw. With the exception of the red haze steadily creeping toward the center of his vision, he saw Winne-fred perfectly.

What the devil was Lilly thinking, leaving her alone with Gratley for so long? What could possibly be so fas-cinating about a bloody fountain that it warranted a half hour's inspection?

Winnefred had been near to fainting not a half hour ago. She ought to be sitting down, inside, *alone*.

He told himself he was being a fool, even as he shifted his position on the terrace for a better view. And he told himself he was being irrational, even as he decided the best view would likely be from the bottom of the ter-race steps.

Oh, yes, it was a much better view. He stood in the shad-ows between a set of torches—too far away to hear what was being said, but close enough for him to make out the shape of Winnefred's eyes, the strands of gold in her hair, and the bright smile on her wide mouth.

His hand clenched around his cane.

She ought to have been smiling at him.

Damn if he hadn't tried to make her. He'd made several overtures of peace in the first days after their falling out, and every one of them had been met with a cool rebuff. There'd been nothing for him to do but accept her feelings and stick to his plan of keeping a physical distance.

It had been bloody hard keeping his distance.

No . . . No, that wasn't right. It had been bloody hard in Scotland, catching sight of her about the house and sharing a moment or two of laughter with her before walking away. And it had been torment when they'd come to London and he'd sought her out, knowing he couldn't keep her. But *this* . . . This was hell.

He'd been so sure he could do it. He'd been so certain he could force himself to stay away from her. But he hadn't stayed away, not really.

He watched her from the edges of ballrooms and parlors. He came home early from visits to his friends and his club, telling himself he was tired, and knowing it was because he hoped to catch sight of her before bed. Even tonight, he'd not been able to sit through more than a single game of cards before going to look for her, and he'd come out to the terrace, knowing Lilly would insist Winnefred take a stroll in the fresh air.

He wished Lilly would stop staring at the damn fountain and insist Winnefred take a stroll back inside.

He also wished he could plow his fist into Gratley's nose. The man was standing entirely too close to Winnefred. And he had no business bending his head down to hers as if they were sharing some sort of secret. He already had her alone. Why the hell did he need to whisper?

Because whispering required a bent head, he thought darkly, and a bent head provided a better view down the front of a low-cut gown. Gideon wouldn't have guessed Gratley to be a rake and libertine, but the evidence was there now for anyone to see. Anyone but Winnefred, apparently.

She tipped her face toward Gratley's, laughing at whatever bit of stupidity the man had whispered, and reached out to touch him lightly on the sleeve.

That cut it.

*W*innefred wasn't sure what sort of reaction her little flirtation with Lord Gratley might garner from Gideon, but she certainly hadn't expected to see him leave the terrace and come marching down the path.

How interesting.

Gideon came to a stop before them and bowed.

"Gratley. Miss. Blythe." He turned in Lilly's direction and said rather loudly, and very pointedly, *"Miss Ilestone."*

Gratley bowed. Winnefred curtsied. Lilly gave him a small, cheerful wave. Winnefred wanted to laugh at the sight of it—her friend had grown fairly cheeky since becoming the probable future wife of a marquess—but Gideon looked sufficiently annoyed already.

"Something the matter?" Winnefred inquired.

"Your presence is requested in the library."

"Oh." That was considerably less interesting. "Lady Gwen, I suppose. Do excuse me, my lord."

"Of course." Gratley bowed again. "Miss Blythe, it has been a pleasure. Miss Ilestone!"

"My lord!"

Lord Gratley's lips twitched once before he walked away.

He really was a fine gentleman, Winnefred thought. He was clever and amusing, and he'd talked to her of fishing and not poked fun when she'd forgotten she wasn't supposed to know anything about fishing and offered her advice on bait.

Pity he hadn't been the one to come to Scotland.

"Did you just *sigh*?" Gideon demanded.

She threw him a cold glance and headed toward the house. He followed her in silence, up the stairs, through the sitting room, and into a side hall. But when she would have turned left to go to the library, he took her elbow and pulled her right toward a back stairwell.

She instinctively tugged at her arm. "What are you doing? I thought I was needed in the library."

"No."

"But you said—"

"I lied. I want a word with you."

She looked over her shoulder for Lilly, but her friend was nowhere to be seen. She tugged her arm again. "If you wish for my audience, you may ask for it."

Gideon stopped, turned, and glowered at her. "Will you come with me, or shall I—?"

"Yes, I will follow you," she said calmly and very, very quickly. If he'd finished that threat, she would have had to resist on principle's sake. She wasn't interested in resisting. Not now that it appeared Gideon had been affected by her flirtation with Lord Gratley after all.

She remained quiet as Gideon led her to her chambers, ushered her inside, and closed the door behind them. She would have spoken then, but Gideon didn't give her the chance. He turned from the door and gave her a smoldering look.

"What the *devil* did you think you were doing out there?" He bit the words out and she noticed for the first time that the hand gripping his cane was white at the knuckles.

Well, *good*, she thought. Let him be angry. Let him get well and truly furious. She could do with a good row.

"What I think," she began with careful poise, "is that I was having a perfectly innocent, perfectly lovely conversation in the garden with Lord Gratley."

"Lord Gratley."

"Clearly, you do not approve."

"I didn't say that."

"You didn't have to," she told him with a small shake of her head. "You repeat things when you don't approve."

"I do not."

She sent him a pitying look. "Prison. Highwaymen. Beat me with my own cane. Lord Gratley. You always repeat what I say when you don't approve of what I'm saying."

"I'm seeking clarification."

"Yes. Of things of which you do not approve."

She could have sworn she heard him growl. "You were flirting with Lord Gratley."

"I believe we've had this conversation before. And so what if I was? You've made your intentions clear." She made a show of straightening a velvet ribbon on her sleeve. "And so has Lord Gratley."

He took a few steps closer to her. "What are you planning, Winnefred?"

"Absolutely nothing." She plucked a piece of lint from her gown. "For now."

"*Explain,*" he ordered, every inch the naval captain.

She lifted one shoulder in a careless manner. "I made a promise to behave as a proper debutante for this season, and I will keep that promise."

"And after the season?"

"Well, I'll not be a debutante forever, will I? I'll not even be in London. I'll be enjoying the independence of being an old maid in rural Scotland."

"Lord Gratley resides here."

"Yes." She gave him a smile, as wicked a smile as she could manage. "But he often travels for sport."

She held her breath and waited for Gideon to explode. She waited for him to shout and storm and demand she never lay eyes on Lord Gratley again. It surprised her how badly she wanted that from him, how much she needed for him to show some sign, *any* sign of passion toward her.

But he didn't explode. He neither shouted, nor stormed, nor demanded.

Oh, he was livid; she could all but see the fury come off him in waves. But there wasn't a hint, not a whisper of lost control. He was in absolute command of himself— perfectly still but for the coiling of muscle in his shoulders and the slight, almost imperceptible lowering of his head.

He stared at her, unblinking, and suddenly, she knew she had lost the upper hand.

"Did you expect me to believe that?" he asked in a dangerously soft voice.

"I don't know what you mean."

"Oh, you do." He took a step toward her. "You most certainly do."

She began to back up without thinking, and he moved forward in return. Slowly, steadily he stalked her across the room.

"Do you think me a jester, Winnefred?"

"What?"

"A fool to poke fun at because I've made you laugh a time or two?"

"No. I—"

"Harmless then, because I kissed you in the moonlight and let you go?"

"I never—"

"Is it the limp? The cane?" In a move so fast it took her breath away, he swept forward and pinned her to the wall. "Did you think I couldn't catch you?"

Before she could even think of responding, his mouth swept down on hers and devoured it. It was nothing like the kiss he'd given her in Scotland. Nothing at all like the sweet meeting of lips they'd shared by the bridge. He used his body to keep her pressed against the wall and his hands to grip and tug her wrists over her head.

"Stop me, then," he breathed against her mouth. "Stop me. Show me why you thought it safe to play your little game."

For a moment insult and fear warred with desire. But then she felt it—the tremble in his hold, the hard crash of his heart against her chest, the quickened breath against her skin. He was struggling as she was.

She had promised herself she would not wait and hope, but she'd never promised not to take a chance. "I played . . . because I knew you would win."

His grip tightened, his eyes went black as night, and then his mouth slanted over hers again.

There was no time for her to sink gently into the heat as

she had in Scotland, no chance for her to find her way into the moment. She was pulled instantly, and willingly, into a battle of teeth and tongue and lips.

He shifted, sliding a knee between her legs. She heard herself moan in pleasure and press forward in a wordless plea to be closer. Her fingers flexed and un-flexed beneath his grip, needing to reach for him. But Gideon didn't relent; he kept her trapped and immobile against the wall.

The ache became a need as he dragged his mouth away to taste the line of her jaw, the lobe of her ear, and the column of her throat. She felt the rough scrape of his teeth and the soothing flick of his tongue. He nipped lightly at the sensitive spot between her neck and shoulder, and she gasped at the startling sensation.

He went still at the sound, his weight pinning her, the ragged catch and release of his breath hot against her skin. Slowly, his hands loosened and slid from her wrists, and for one terrible moment, she feared he would let her go completely.

He didn't. In a sudden change of mood, he slipped an arm around her waist and gently pulled her away from the wall. Then he was kissing her softly, languidly, as if he could spend hours just tasting her. His hands no longer sought to trap or take but to arouse through her gown with long, slow strokes and light, feathery brushes. As if he had suddenly decided to take care. More—that he wanted to take care.

Her last rational thought was that *this* is what she wanted. To feel needed and cherished, and loved.

Gideon had stopped thinking altogether. He reacted on feeling and instinct alone. His mind was blank but for thoughts of the woman in his arms. There was no ship, no battle, and no responsibility. There was no more anger or the wild need to brand what was his. There was only Winnefred . . . The feel of her fingers in his hair, the weight of her soft body against his, the sweet taste of her mouth, and the faint scent of lavender on her skin.

She overwhelmed him, drowned his every sense, and washed away all but the need to sink further into the feel and taste and scent of her. Almost of their own accord, his fingers began to work the row of buttons down the back of her gown. The material slipped from her shoulders. He nudged it further, down her slender arms and waist until it pooled on the floor in a circle at her feet. Firelight danced behind her, outlining her form through the thin white chemise and lighting her upswept curls.

"Beautiful," he whispered, reaching up to pull the pins from her hair. She was so beautiful.

He undressed them both in stages, stopping to touch each inch of her skin as it was exposed, and giving her a chance to do the same. She was both tentative and tenacious in her explorations, letting her fingers investigate his bare chest and arms, and her hands brush over his hips and waist. She hesitated when he removed his trousers, but only briefly.

His eyes closed on a groan when her small hand sought out the proof of his desire. He stilled, allowing them both the pleasure of her discovery, until that pleasure grew too keen. Keeping an arm firmly around her waist, he drew her hand away and walked her backward to the bed.

He followed her down to the counterpane and started the process of exploration all over again. She was a study in contradictions. So small, he thought, so fragile, but there was strength in her arms, and he felt the long, lean muscles of her legs as they moved against his. He dipped his head, tasting her neck, her collarbone, her breast. Her skin was impossibly soft, terrifyingly delicate, and yet he could feel the reminders of her calluses as she ran her palms across his back. She was both pale and flushed with passion. She was helpless and in command of his every thought, his every move, his every desire.

That desire grew sharp and ruthless as he watched her sigh and moan and arch beneath him. The need to take her clawed at him, and still he held off. He wanted her blind with need, lost to the demands of her body.

He took a nipple in his mouth, teasing it into a hard point with his tongue and teeth. He ran a hand down her side, over the subtle flair of her hip, and across the silken skin of her thigh to reach the softness between her legs.

She nearly came off the bed. "Gideon, *please*."

His name from her lips was more than he could stand against. He settled himself over her, struggling to be gentle, to take care as he pressed forward into the wet heat of her. She draped her arms over his shoulders and tilted her hips in encouragement . . . until he met the barrier that marked her as an innocent and, hoping faster might be better, pushed past it with a single determined thrust.

She tensed and swore. "Oh. *Ouch*."

He grit his teeth until the blinding pleasure of being inside her dimmed just enough for him to bend his head and kiss her brow. "I'm sorry, sweetheart. I'm sorry."

"This is . . ." She stared at him in shock and swallowed audibly. "This is *not* what I thought—"

"I know." He took her mouth in a long, deep kiss, only releasing her when he felt her nails recede a bit from his back and heard the breath she was holding flow out in a long sigh.

"I'm sorry," he whispered again. "Give it a minute more. Can you do that?"

She nodded and even managed a hesitant smile.

He wasn't sure he could do it. Every second, every heart-beat felt like an eternity. She felt like heaven, and every muscle in his body screamed at him to move, to sink into her again and again, until the need that had been clawing at him for so long was satisfied. He refused to listen. Keeping a tight leash on his own desire, he set about rekindling Winnefred's passion, his hands seeking out the places that had made her gasp and sigh before.

When she began to gasp and sigh again, he carefully withdrew and sank back into her, gauging her reaction. He groaned in relief when she met his thrust with a cautious movement of her own.

"Yes. Sweetheart." He thrust again, a long, deep stroke that drew a moan from her lips. "That's it . . ."

He loosened the leash then, letting instinct and desire take over. He lost track of time and place, of everything but the sweet sound of Winnefred's cries growing faster and higher in pitch and the biting pleasure that came from drawing out the moment of his release, waiting for Winnefred to find her own.

When she did, when her legs banded around his waist and she bucked and cried out in his arms, he plunged deep one last time, then pulled himself free with a ragged groan and spent his passion on the white linen of Winnefred's bed.

Chapter 33

Gideon stood in the library and scowled at nothing in particular. He didn't want to be in the library. He didn't want to be scowling, particularly, either. What he wanted was to go back upstairs, slip into bed with Winnefred, and pretend everything was fine, everything was as it should be. That's how he'd woken—with his limbs entangled with hers and the soft brush of her breath against his neck. For a few blissful moments, he had lain awake, steeped in the warmth of her and the memory of their lovemaking.

But all too soon, the reality of what he had done began to creep in, and with it came worry, remorse, and recriminations.

Naturally, he would have to marry Winnefred as soon as possible. It was the right thing to do. It was the only thing to do. And a part of him nearly crowed at the idea of it—at the knowledge that she was his now and that she would always be his. But the other part of him, the part that had driven him to leave Winnefred sleeping in her bed, berated him for his shortsighted selfishness.

It wasn't a simple matter of having her. It was a matter

of being responsible for her . . . And for any children they might have.

An image came into his mind of a small girl with amber eyes and light brown hair with golden streaks. She'd have his sense of humor, he thought, and her mother's laugh. He could almost hear that laugh.

The image faded away, only to be replaced by a likeness of Jimmy. Blond-haired, blue-eyed, armless Jimmy.

He dragged an unsteady hand through his hair.

There would be no children.

There would be no guarantees either, unless he meant to take a vow of abstinence—and he wasn't so damn short-sighted he could fool himself into believing that a feasible plan—but there were steps a man could take to lessen the likelihood of a pregnancy, and he meant to follow them. He didn't have a choice.

Winnefred might not care for it, but she was a reasonable sort . . . Well, no, she wasn't always. But she was practical. She would understand. She would have to. She bloody well didn't have a choice either.

*W*innefred didn't understand. She could not, upon waking, immediately puzzle through why she had fallen asleep to the sound of Gideon's breathing and woken to silence. Not complete silence, she amended, for she could hear the muted sound of voices downstairs and the soft shuffling of footsteps in the hall.

She turned over and looked at the window. Thin streams of sunlight snuck into the room around the edges of the drapes.

It was morning, she realized groggily. Late morning, by the looks and sounds of it. The servants must be up, clearing away the remnants of last night's ball. And Gideon had left because he'd not want it discovered he had spent the night in her bed.

Memories of that night came flooding back, accompanied by a warm wash of pleasure. Suddenly very much awake, she rolled out of bed and began to wash and dress.

Her mind raced with a thousand questions. What came next, a declaration of undying love and eternal devotion? That sounded a bit theatrical . . . It also sounded rather lovely. And closer to the truth of how she'd felt for some time now but hadn't been able to admit.

She loved Gideon.

She loved his dark eyes, his handsome face, his sense of the absurd, and his thoughtfulness and generosity. She loved the feel of his hands on her skin and his mouth against hers. She loved everything about him . . . Well, not his misplaced sense of guilt so much, but the rest, certainly.

Was she to confess that love to him now? Would he confess his back? And what came after? It wouldn't be marriage. He'd made himself perfectly clear on that issue, and she wasn't foolish enough to think he had changed his mind over the course of a few hours. Perhaps, over time, he would grow amendable to the idea. He was clearly *capable* of changing his mind. After all, he'd chosen to put his guilt before her . . . Until last night.

But what to do in the meantime? Were they to have a clandestine affair? They certainly couldn't have an open one. Lilly would never forgive her.

She spent some time trying to figure the problem out before giving up the notion of doing it alone. She'd just have to ask Gideon, she decided, and headed for her door. She couldn't very well plan their future without him, anyway.

After learning from a maid that Gideon was to be found in the study next to the front parlor, Winnefred made her way downstairs. She knocked softly on the study door as the sound of Lilly and Lord Engsly's mingled laughter floated from the dining room across the front hall.

Rather than wait for a response, she pushed the door open and stepped inside. Gideon was seated behind the desk again, but he didn't appear to be working on anything. There were no papers before him and no pen in his hand. What she saw instead was the same clothes Gideon had been wearing the night before, the shadows under his eyes, and the fact that he wasn't smiling when he said, "Good, you're awake. Have a seat, Winnefred."

A sliver of unease ran up her spine. She stepped up to one of the chairs in front of the desk but didn't sit. "Is something the matter?"

There shouldn't be anything the matter, she thought. Not this morning.

"Nothing the matter," he assured her. "I merely wish to discuss the arrangements of our marriage."

Winnefred sank slowly into her chair, caught somewhere between stunned, elated, and wary. Could he really have changed his mind overnight? It didn't seem possible. It certainly didn't seem logical.

"You told me you would never marry."

"Obviously, circumstances have changed. I'll see to it the banns are posted. My aunt will assist you in selecting an appropriate wedding gown and—"

"Wait." She held up a hand for silence and took in the set of his jaw and his hard, unsmiling mouth. And she came to the only reasonable, and heartbreaking, conclusion. "You don't want to do this."

He leaned forward and placed his elbows on the desk. When he spoke, his tone was gentle. But the words cut like knives. "It is true, I had not planned to take a wife, but this is no longer a matter of what was planned. I am bound by duty and honor to do what is right."

Bound by duty and honor.

She felt like a fool. A blind, lovesick fool. Of course Gideon would feel obligated to offer marriage. And of course he would view that marriage, and *her*, as a burden. He had not changed his mind overnight, only his objectives.

She breathed past a suffocating pain in her chest.

"Your offer"—*such as it was*—"is appreciated. But I must decline."

He straightened again, looking genuinely stunned by her response. "Decline? Why?"

"I should think that fairly obvious," she returned with as much composure as she could muster. It was hard to remain composed when the whole of her wanted to shake. "You do not wish to marry me, and I do not wish to marry you. We—"

"You don't?"

"Want to marry you?" *Not like this.* "No. I've no interest in sacrificing my freedom on the altar of marriage."

"I don't know it would be as bad as all that," he grumbled.

"Yes, it would." But it wasn't the loss of freedom that would make marriage to Gideon a nightmare. She was willing to relinquish some of her independence if it meant spending the rest of her life with the man she loved. But she had no desire to marry a man who did not love her in return—a man who viewed her as a yoke about his neck. And she'd be damned if she spent every day of her life wondering when he would find a way to break free of that yoke and forget her.

Tears pressed against the back of her eyes. She fought them back. "My personal feelings toward wedlock aren't pertinent at the moment. The simple fact of the matter is— You do not want a wife and I do not need a husband. There is no good reason for us to marry."

"There is *ample* reason." He leaned toward her and lowered his voice. "I stole your virtue, Winnefred."

If he leaned just a little closer, she thought darkly, she could reach out and strangle him.

Stole your virtue, indeed. As if she'd been some helpless maiden he'd ravished in the night and left a broken piece of rubbish in the morning.

She leaned in a little closer herself. If he wanted to be offensive, she could be offensive. "I have a great many virtues, Gideon. None of which have *ever* resided between my—"

"*Don't.*"

She sat back again and gathered her anger around her like a cloak. It was so much better than the hurt. "How easily you forget who I am. How *quickly* you would turn me into one of your pampered, incompetent, feeble-minded ladies of the ton."

"I've done no such thing."

"Haven't you? Why propose, then?" Without love. Without even a token of affection. "Why demand a marriage I've not asked for, if it's not to save me from myself?"

"Because that is the cost," he bit off.

Oh, yes, she could cheerfully murder him. "I decline payment."

He swore under his breath. "There are consequences, Winnefred. Things we must consider. You may be with child."

"I have bred Giddy," she reminded him coldly. "I know how new life is created. The differences between our species can't possibly be so dramatic as to allow a pregnancy without the male seed."

"The likelihood is decreased, but it is not a guarantee."

Even the armor of fury couldn't hold out the heartache now. A child with Gideon. It ought to be a beautiful vision of their future—the two of them smiling and laughing and arguing over who got to teach their son to fish. Instead, she saw only misery—a husband who felt trapped into marriage and forced into fatherhood.

It was unthinkable. And the fact she hadn't known a pregnancy could result even with measures taken to avoid it only served to illuminate how very blind she had been.

If she had managed to avoid the catastrophe of bringing a child unwanted by his father into the world, then she would thank her lucky stars, and make certain, absolutely certain, it never happened again.

"I see no reason to borrow trouble," she said eventually. "If I find—"

"It is not borrowing trouble to plan ahead."

"Then I shall plan ahead to revisit the matter if it becomes necessary." Why was he arguing with her? Why wasn't he accepting her refusal gratefully and allowing the excruciating scene to come to an end?

"Be reasonable, Winnefred. We—"

"I am being reasonable," she cut in. It had to end.

"You're being obstinate. We cannot, in good conscience—"

"The answer is *no!*" The murmur of voices across the hall ceased abruptly, but she was too furious to notice and too heartbroken to care. She stood from her chair. She couldn't stand it a minute longer. "Oh, what a hypocrite you are, with your grand speeches of finding the humor, the pleasure in every situation. And yet when you are handed something good and beautiful, you turn it into this . . . this revolting pile of onus and obligation and—"

"I am trying to do what is honorable," he snapped. "I have a responsibility—"

"I will not be your swiving burden to shoulder!" She bellowed this last and had Lilly and Lord Engsly rushing in the doors.

"Nor yours!" she added, rounding on Engsly. "Nor Lady Gwen's, nor anyone else's!"

Gideon rose behind the desk, and though he spoke to Lilly and Lord Engsly, his eyes remained fixed on hers. "You will excuse us a moment, Lucien."

"Oh, no, let him stay." Her voice was hard. She'd never known she could sound so hard. "I'm his cross to bear as well, aren't I? Or perhaps you prefer the image of suffering alone."

Gideon's fist came down on the desk. "That is *enough.*"

"It bloody well is." If she stood there a minute longer, just one minute more, she would crumble.

She spun around, blindly pushed her way past Lilly and Lord Engsly, and dashed across the front hall, intent on reaching her chambers before the tears came. Only they weren't *her* chambers, were they? It was Lady Gwen's blue room.

The tears came before she'd made it halfway up the stairs.

She didn't want the damn blue room.

She wanted her own bed, in Scotland. She wanted Murdoch House, and Claire, and the quiet solitude of her old life.

She wanted home.

Chapter 34

Gideon told himself he shouldn't be drinking. He should not be sitting in his chambers at three o'clock in the afternoon seriously contemplating the merits of becoming foxed.

Then he decided, yes, he should be drinking, but he should be drinking in celebration, not in . . . Whatever the hell he was drinking for now.

It felt like grief. His head hurt, his chest ached, and there was a sick feeling of helplessness crawling through his veins and twisting his stomach into knots. His mind moved sluggishly, despite the fact he'd had no more than a few sips of his brandy, and his limbs felt so weighted that even the small task of setting down his drink seemed like a chore.

But grief didn't make any sense. This was what he wanted, wasn't it? He'd escaped. He was free of obligation, of responsibility . . . of Winnefred.

How had it come to that? How the devil had he ended up drinking in the middle of the afternoon while Winnefred sat upstairs fuming . . . and quite possibly crying.

Bloody hell, he hoped she wasn't crying.

He'd *proposed*, damn it. There shouldn't be any fuming and crying at a marriage proposal.

He should have said something different, done something more. He should have made her stay and see reason. But he'd been so focused on what needed to be taken care of, so in dread of his upcoming responsibilities, it simply hadn't occurred to him she might argue. He'd not considered the possibility she would say no, and mean it.

Why had she said no? True, she'd made it clear from the very start she wasn't interested in obtaining a husband, but a general sort of dissatisfaction with the *notion* of a husband was different than an actual proposal from *him*. Or it ought to be.

She shouldn't have said no.

And it occurred to him now that he couldn't come up with a single reason why she should have said yes. He'd spoken of honor and responsibility, duty and . . . burdens. He'd spoken of burdens.

How the hell could he have been so thoughtless?

For all of her life, Winnefred had been treated like a burden. What was it Lilly had said—raised by a series of indifferent governesses hired by a careless father? And then she'd been pushed onto his father, who'd passed her off to Lady Engsly, who'd handed her to Lilly.

No wonder Winnefred was enamored with Murdoch House and so loyal to Lilly. It was the only place that had welcomed her in, and the only friend who hadn't abandoned her.

She'd been happy in Scotland, and might have gone right on being happy if Lucien hadn't discovered her . . . And begun the whole process all over again, Gideon realized with a sinking sensation in his gut. Lucien had passed the responsibility of Winnefred onto him, and he'd handed her to Lady Gwen at the first opportunity. Worse, he'd made it perfectly clear to her this morning he didn't really want her back.

But what the devil was he supposed to do? The responsibility of a wife and children—bloody hell, *children*—was something he had no business shouldering.

He would fail them, just as he had his men . . . his boys.

It just was was not an acceptable explanation for what happened aboard the *Perseverance*. It wasn't an acceptable explanation for anything that happened at war. Every man who fired a shot was responsible for the damage that bit of metal and gunpowder caused. And every officer was accountable for the orders that placed his men in danger. He couldn't pretend otherwise, nor did he want to.

He reached for his drink again, only to snatch his hand back.

Was he to cling to his guilt and fears to the exclusion of all else—to the exclusion of Winnefred? He wasn't sure he wanted that. He wasn't sure he could do it.

He wasn't sure he could not.

He still wasn't sure when, half an hour later, the long night, the grief, and the brandy took their toll and he slipped into sleep.

The sea was rough, tossing the frigate about like a dog playing with a bone.

Gideon tried to get his feet under him. He tried to focus on what he was supposed to be doing, but it was impossible to think with all the noise.

If the fighting would only stop for a minute, if the ship would just be quiet for one buggering minute, he'd be able to think.

In a heartbeat, the sea settled and the world went eerily silent.

His eyes flew to the open door of his cabin. The battle was still raging. He could see his men through the smoke and flame. He could feel the ship tremble under his feet. He watched as the end of a yardarm broke away and toppled to the deck.

But he heard nothing. Not the firing of cannons. Not the screams of his men. Nothing.

"Better. That's better."

He could think now. He could find them all a way out of this damnable . . .

And then he saw Winnefred, standing amongst the chaos, serenely feeding Claire bits of food from a napkin.

"No!"

He flew at the door, only to slam into a cold, hard wall. There was something blocking his way, an unseen barrier trapping him inside. He threw himself against it and beat at it with his fists.

"Get to the hold! Winnefred! *Winnefred, get to the hold!"*

"Don't know as I'd recommend the hold just now, Cap'n."

He whirled around at the sound of Jimmy's voice. Holy hell, his arms. Where were the boy's arms?

"No. *No.* What's happened to you?"

"Ball came right through the ceiling, debris flying every which way. But no more'n a body'd expect, what with you bringing a woman on board." Jimmy shook his head slowly, sadly. "They're bad luck, Captain. Everyone knows that."

"I didn't bring . . ." He whirled around and threw himself against the barrier. "Help me. You have to help me get out of here."

"'Aven't any arms, remember?" Jimmy peered around his shoulder. "She's a pretty one, isn't she? Doesn't much look like she belongs here."

"She doesn't. She shouldn't be here."

"A stowaway? Aw, c'mon, Cap'n, let it alone. You can't be responsible for every silly chit and goat what sneaks on board, can you?"

"That's right," a new voice called. "Ought to be helping us, I should think."

He spun from the door. There was Lord Marson and young Colin Newberry with Bill's dripping head.

"I can't . . . Look at you! There is nothing I can do for you."

"More'n you can do for the chit standing out there,"

Colin pointed out. He craned his neck to look out the door. "Ah. Here's the end of her, sure enough."

Gideon spun around again and watched in abject terror as a cannonball sailed toward Winnefred like a kite caught in a breeze.

She took a step back and let it sail right past.

Colin let out a long, low whistle. "There's a clever lass. No need to worry yourself over the likes of her, is there? She'll do well enough without you."

"She needs to be inside. She needs to be in here with me."

Marson dragged himself a little closer to the door. "She doesn't appear to need you at all, Captain."

"Not the point. I have to . . ."

Gratley suddenly appeared out of the smoke. He stepped in front of Winnefred, stripped off his coat, and draped it over her shoulders.

"Idiot. *Idiot!* What is he doing?"

"What he thinks best, I imagine," came Bill's reply.

Winnefred offered Gratley a bit of whatever was in the napkin. He accepted, took his time chewing, and then finally, *finally*, put his hand on Winnefred's elbow and began to lead her away.

"Ah, there they go," Colin called out. "That's nice, isn't it? And a heavy load off your mind, knowing someone else is responsible for the girl, eh?"

His breath came in sick, sharp pants. "Yes. Yes, it's a relief."

"Aye." Jimmy sidled up next to him and leaned up to whisper in his ear. "You a gambling man, Cap'n? Sixpence says he takes her straight to the hold."

The final slam of his shoulder against the barrier is what woke him.

He stared at the ceiling, waiting for his heart to resume its natural rhythm. As his mind struggled to orient itself, he had the irrational notion that if he turned his head, he would see Winnefred, watching him through golden eyes filled with concern and understanding, and love.

He willed it to be true. He ached with the need to see her. And he knew, down to very marrow of his bones, that the need wasn't going to pass with the dream. He didn't want to see her just this once or wake to her only when the nightmares came. He wanted to see her every time he looked.

He wanted her to be where he could always find her, touch her, smell the lavender and hay . . . He needed her to be where he could at least try to keep her safe, and happy, and . . . loved.

Slowly, he turned his head and saw only the empty room.

"Bloody hell, what have I done?"

Chapter 35

*H*ow the hell could you let her leave?" Gideon shoved his arms through his overcoat with enough force to nearly rip the seams. "What the devil were you thinking?"

Lucien leaned against the wall in the front hall. "At a guess, she left three hours ago. I believe, at the time, I was thinking of a gelding named Pockets. Handsome chestnut I saw at Tattersall's two days ago."

Gideon grabbed his hat and gloves from a waiting footman. "No one tried to stop her?"

"No one saw. We'd no idea she'd left until Lilly found"—Lucien held up a piece of parchment Gideon hadn't realized was in his hand—"this note."

He stalked across the front hall. "Why the hell didn't you say there was a note?"

"I tried when I woke you, but you were in such a hurry—"

Gideon growled and snatched the letter out of his brother's hand.

Dear Lilly,

> *Am gone to Murdoch House. Don't be angry. My apologies to Lord Engsly and Lady Gwen.*

Love,
  Freddie

"Left in a hurry by the looks of it," Lucien commented. He reached over to tap a finger against the paper. "Though she did spare a thought for Lilly and Lady Gwen, and *me*."

Gideon swore ripely, the only release for a growing swell of fear. "You find this amusing?"

"Enormously. Did you find it amusing when I came looking for Lilly?"

Because he couldn't say no, he shoved the note in his pocket and strode out the door as Lucien's voice called out behind him.

"Women travel alone every day, Gideon! She'll be all right!"

A groom was waiting for Gideon with his horse. He swung himself into the saddle, ignoring the sharp pain in his leg, and started his mount off at a gallop. He ignored everything now but the need to get to Winnefred. Lucien was right, women traveled alone every day. Lucien also knew that women were assaulted every day. That's why his own horse had been readied while he'd given the orders to the staff. Every able-bodied man in the house would be sent to look for Winnefred.

Gideon wasn't waiting on them. There wasn't a minute to spare. Winnefred would be an enticing mark, he thought darkly—young, pretty, alone, and likely ill.

Bloody hell, she made an *irresistible* mark. For a moment, the fear threatened to overwhelm him. If something happened to her . . . If he lost her completely . . .

He shoved the panicked thoughts aside. He would find her. He would find her, and she would be fine. She was an intelligent, self-sufficient woman—perfectly capable of taking care of herself.

He reminded himself of this again and again as he rode hell-for-leather through London and over the highway leading north. He kept reminding himself of it as he stopped at every coaching station he came to and questioned every innkeeper and servant. And still he thought of a thousand catastrophes that might befall a woman traveling alone, and every time his inquiries were met with blank stares and shaking heads, he imagined a thousand more.

He wouldn't be satisfied until he saw for himself she was safe. The heavy ball of fear and remorse in his gut would remain until he felt her in his arms, where she belonged. What an idiot he'd been to think it could ever be any other way. How could he have convinced himself that a distance from her would somehow render him less responsible for her, less in need of her, less in love?

*B*lack Ram Inn was not the finest coaching station to be found in England. Its wood was rotting and weathered to a sickly gray, shutters hung from single hinges or were missing altogether, and all three stories of it leaned precariously to the right. Winnefred figured it was one good storm away from toppling to the ground.

She couldn't have cared less. What difference did it make if the floor sloped and the stairs creaked and groaned under her feet? Who cared if the bed in her room looked as if it hadn't seen new linens in a decade and the single chair by the hearth appeared as though it might break under her weight? She could sleep on the rug in front of the fire.

So long as the rug didn't rock and sway beneath her, she would be happy.

No, not happy. She tossed her coat and bonnet on the chair and used the arm to leverage herself to the floor. She was miserable—sick and alone and hundreds of miles from home.

She'd barely made it out of London. Less than three hours in the coach and her skin had begun to grow clammy and her belly had churned and cramped. If she hadn't convinced the driver to stop at the inn, she would have heaved into her bonnet.

She closed her eyes on a sick groan.

How had things gone so terribly wrong? She wasn't supposed to be returning to Murdoch House in defeat, and she most certainly was not supposed to be returning alone.

Lilly should be there. And Gideon. High-handed, muleheaded, wonderful Gideon. She'd never admitted it, not even to herself, but a part of her had expected him to come back to Murdoch House with her. Or perhaps it was more accurate to say that no part of her had been able to imagine going back without him.

They were meant to be together. Why hadn't he been able to see that, instead of assuming he was better off without her . . . like everyone else?

What was it about her the world found so hard to stomach and so easy to refuse?

She inhaled deeply and tried to fight back the tears burning her eyes. She didn't want to think about Gideon. She didn't want to think about the ache in her chest that had nothing to do with the way the coach had been rocking.

She didn't need him. She didn't need anyone. She could be content with the staff for company at Murdoch House and happy with visits from Lilly. Besides, there were benefits to being alone. For the first time in her life, she had the freedom and the funds to do whatever she pleased. She could wear trousers to her heart's content and walk to the prison without a maid whenever she liked. She could play cards with Thomas, and she could drink scotch with highwaymen if it damn well suited her.

She had a home she loved and the funds to see it prosper. That was all she needed, she told herself, even as the ache in her chest tightened.

"It is," she whispered to absolutely no one, and the pain turned sharp.

"It has to be." Something inside her broke, simply shattered to pieces. This time, when the tears came, she made no attempt to stop them. She couldn't have managed it if she'd tried. The heartache washed over her in waves and poured out of her again in wrenching sobs that shook her frame. She cried until there were no more tears to be shed and the sharp pain had drained away, leaving her hollow.

Then she wiped her face with her sleeve, took a deep settling breath, and told herself she was done—done crying over Gideon and done pining after him as well. She had a spine, and she had her pride. She could and would stand on the strength of those until her heart healed. And it would heal. Maybe it wouldn't be the same, maybe it wouldn't be quite as open as it had been, but it would heal. She would make certain of it. She didn't have a choice.

She rose from the floor, brushed off her skirts, and set about making plans that did not involve Lord Gideon Haverston. She needed to get to Murdoch House, and she needed to get there in something other than the mail coach. The other passengers weren't going to approve of stopping every time she began to feel ill. Horseback would have been ideal, but she'd never been in a saddle a day in her life. She'd have to hire her own carriage and driver. There was nothing else for it. The expense would take a considerable bite out of her budget, but she would find a way to make it work.

Resolute, and feeling stronger than she had since she'd left Lady Gwen's house, she strode toward the door intending to set her plan into action. She made it halfway across the room when she heard her name being shouted from down the hall.

"Winnefred?!" The voice grew closer. Winnefred!"

Gideon.

It was instinct alone that had her striding to the door and flinging it open. He stood on the other side, looking rumpled and haggard and unbearably handsome, the rotter.

"Winnefred." He said her name like a prayer.

She slammed the door in his face.

* * *

*G*ideon stared at the closed door before him and listened to the loud turn of the lock. For one brief moment, when Winnefred had appeared, it had felt as if all the scattered pieces of his world had fallen into place. His entire body had sagged under the weight of relief. He'd found her. She was safe and whole and impossibly beautiful, and . . .

And then she'd slammed the door shut, scattering the pieces of his world once more, and neatly reminding him she was also still exceedingly angry. Probably, he should have given that inevitability a bit more thought during his search, but he'd been so anxious to find her, so overwhelmed with worry and remorse, he'd not been able to think of anything else.

And wasn't that at the very core of his sins? For too long he'd thought only of his own fear, his own past, his own wants and needs. Was he too late to make amends for that now? Had it taken him too long to come to his senses? Had he been so blind, so selfish that he'd lost her? He wouldn't accept that. He couldn't. She was the biggest piece of his world. If it took him the rest of his life, he would earn her back. Starting now . . . As soon as he figured out how to begin.

"Should I unlock the door for you, my lord?"

Gideon glanced over his shoulder. He'd forgotten the innkeeper was there. He shot the man a disgusted look. "Does the lady appear to want her door unlocked?"

The innkeeper shifted his considerable weight, rubbed at his balding pate as if trying to work an answer to the surface, and finally shrugged.

Gideon was tempted to snatch the ring of keys away for the safety of the other female guests. He pointed his cane down the hall. "Just go."

The innkeeper shuffled off, leaving Gideon alone with his thoughts. For several moments, he simply stood outside Winnefred's room, trying to find his footing and the right thing to say. Finally, he lifted a fist and knocked softly on the door.

"Winnefred?"

"Go. Away."

Oh, yes, she was furious.

"Are you well?" He needed to know for certain. "Are you—?"

"I've never been better."

He let another wave of relief wash over him before speaking again. "Will you open the door, please?"

"Absolutely not."

"I've come to apologize."

"How noble of you."

"You don't have to let me in. Just . . . open it a crack—"

"No."

"Then listen. Just listen." He placed the flat of his hand against the door and spoke through the wood. "I want to be responsible for you."

"Oh, go to the devil—"

"Wait. Let me finish, *please.*" When she didn't protest, he closed his eyes and spoke from the heart. "I want to take care of you. I always will. You could turn away from me now. You could bar me from your home. You could marry another man and excise me from your life completely. But I will always want to take care of you. I will always want to see to it you are happy . . . because I will always love you."

His confession was met with a silence. Gideon couldn't hear a whisper of sound coming through the door. He opened his eyes and dropped his hand. Had she stopped listening? Had she already made up her mind to believe nothing he said? Had she snuck out the window?

"Winnefred? . . . Are you there?"

His answer came in the form of the soft click of the lock as it slid free and the creaking of hinges as Winnefred opened the door. She'd been just on the other side of the wood, he realized, and he took a small step back to give her a little space. She'd been listening and was willing to hear more—both very good signs.

Her countenance was less encouraging. Her amber eyes held an ocean of skepticism, and the way she stood in the doorway, ready to bolt back inside, told him she was far from throwing herself back in his arms. But she'd been listening, and now she'd opened the door. It was enough to light a small flame of hope.

"You love me," she said, wariness evident in every word.

"Yes." He had to ball his free hand into a fist to keep from reaching for her. "I know I've given you little cause to believe—"

"You love *me*?" she pressed. "The woman you met in Scotland? The woman who wears trousers on occasion and sometimes—?"

"I know who you are. I know you better than I know the back of my own hand. I know you can't dance. I know you prefer custard to fruit. I know you learned to swear by visiting a prison and lost a sixpence to a boy so you could teach him to read. I know I hurt you by speaking of responsibility and duty." He bent his head in an effort to catch her eye. It was vital she understood, and believed, what he said next. "You are not a burden, Winnefred. You will never be a burden. I've no excuse for so disregarding your feelings by speaking so callously, except . . . Except I am so deeply in love with you, and it—"

"Do you want to be?"

"In love with you?" He straightened, took a chance, and reached for her hand. The flame grew a little brighter when she didn't pull away. "Yes. It terrifies me. The idea of children terrifies me. The thought that something might happen to you, that I might let something happen to you, *absolutely* terrifies me, and always will." He gave her hand a gentle squeeze. "I wouldn't be rid of that fear for any price. Because to lose it would be to lose you, and the possibility of our children. I . . . I want it—you and children and every moment of fear and happiness that comes with being in love. I want it. All of it."

The skepticism was fading. He could see the hurt and wariness retreating from her features.

"You love me," she repeated, and this time, she said it with confidence and the first hints of a smile.

"Yes." He pulled her closer slowly, until the front of her gown brushed against him. "Yes. With everything I am. If you believe nothing else I've said—"

"I believe you."

"You do?" Hope was no longer a small flame now; it was a blinding light that burned away the vestiges of fear and doubt. "And that you could never be a burden? And that I'm sorry? I'm so sorry, Winnefred. You've done all the work, had all the courage. I've been a blind and selfish—"

"I certainly believe that." Her smile grew. "All of it."

All of it. The good and the bad. He could no more fathom the extent of his good fortune than he could stop himself from asking for more. "I know I've done little to earn it, but I had hoped . . . Coming here, I had very much hoped that despite my blunderings, you might be willing to consider, at some point . . . bearing a similar responsibility?"

"That is a perfectly absurd way to ask if I love you."

"I know."

"It suits you." She slid her hand free to reach up and cup his face. "Yes. I love you."

All the pieces were falling back into place once more. He took a deep breath and found his own courage. "Will you marry me?"

She took a deeper breath and said, "Yes."

He heard his own shout of laughter over her own. He dropped his cane, wrapped his arms around her waist, and hauled her off her feet, intending to kiss her until they were both senseless.

"Wait." Laughing, she turned her head in a futile effort to dodge his lips. He kissed her cheek instead. Along with her brow, her nose, her hair—every part of her he could reach.

She batted a playful hand against his shoulder. "Wait! There's something else."

Momentarily defeated, he set her down but kept her tight in his arms. "What is it?"

Whatever it was, he'd find it, or fix it, or whatever it was that needed doing. In that moment, he swore he could hand the stars to her on a platter if she asked it of him.

"It's London," she explained, still laughing softly. "I know you've a home there, and it's a lovely city, but . . ."

"It is a lovely city," he agreed. He brushed her hair back from her face and, because he could, pressed a quick kiss to her lips. "We'll want to visit from time to time, I imagine. Particularly when Lilly and Lucien are in residence."

"Visit," she echoed, her smile growing even brighter. "Yes, I would like to visit from Murdoch House."

"On one condition," he agreed and watched her smile bloom. "We add to the house. I've grown accustomed to having staff again. And I want a large music room." He picked her up again and brushed his lips across hers. "I want to dance with my wife."

Epilogue

*T*he marriage of the Marquess of Engsly to Miss Lilly Ilestone was the talk of the ton. Not so much because of the groom's rank, or the bride's beauty, or the fact that their courtship had been the most elaborate London had seen in years, but because the couple, apparently rendered temporarily daft by their soon-to-be-wedded bliss, had elected to hold their nuptials on Lord Gideon Haverston's unfashionably small estate in the middle of the Scottish countryside. Some unlikely little *farm* called Murdoch House.

It was highly irregular. Members of society twisted their lips at the dreadful lack of taste exhibited by the pair, and whispered behind their hands at the absurdity of holding a country wedding during the little season, and carefully checked their mail with every hope and expectation of receiving an invitation.

They were collectively disappointed.

The only guests in attendance on the day of the wedding were family members, Thomas Brown, and a goat named Claire.

The goat came as a surprise to Winnefred. She was *certain* she'd closed the door of the stall tightly. But there Claire was, lying serenely in the grass between Lady Gwen and Thomas—who she rather suspected of having something to do with Claire's escape—while Lucien and Lilly stood before the vicar on the banks of the pond.

Winnefred sighed happily. She'd married Gideon in the same spot not six months ago.

Within a week of her return to Murdoch House with Gideon, Lord Engsly had arrived with a special license, and he'd been followed soon after by Lilly and Lady Gwen.

Rather than allowing the Howards to have anything to do with her wedding, Winnefred had sent to Langholm for another vicar, and she'd married Gideon the following day so she could watch his eyes lighten in the morning sun as they exchanged their vows.

He had promised to love and cherish, and she had promised to love, cherish, and obey.

She turned her eyes from the bride and groom to the man standing next to her. She couldn't imagine not loving Gideon, not cherishing him. Deciding that having kept two out of three promises wasn't half bad, she slipped her hand into his.

He looked down and gave her a warm smile that filled her heart.

She'd thought herself happy before Gideon had come. She'd believed she was taking care of the home she'd made for herself and Lilly. But she realized now she'd merely been making do for the both of them.

Now, as she watched Lilly laugh and kiss her new husband, and as she listened to the call of her cattle in the pasture, she thought that *here* was the light and sound and voices she had imagined the first day she'd come to Murdoch House. Here was the life and the laughter and the welcome.

She looked down to where Gideon's strong hand covered her own.

Here was home.

Turn the page for a special preview of
Alissa Johnson's next historical romance

An Unexpected Gentleman

Coming December 2011 from Berkley Sensation!

*M*iss Adelaide Ward was, by her own admission, a woman of unassuming aspirations.

In recent years, she had come to the conclusion that it was folly to seek more from life than what might reasonably be expected to materialize. And for an undowered spinster burdened with an eighteen-year-old sister, an infant nephew, a brother in debtors' prison, and seven-and-twenty years, what might reasonably be expected was very limited indeed.

She wanted a home, the company of those she loved, and the security of a reliable income. These were her dreams. They were few in number and simple in nature, but they were hers. She longed for them as any debutante might long to snare a peer, and she had fought for them as any officer might fight for glory on the battlefield.

It was with some disappointment, then, that on the very eve of seeing her efforts come to fruition, she found herself not emboldened with the thrill of imminent victory, but battling fear, nerves, and the surprising weight of reluctance.

Tonight, Sir Robert Maxwell would propose. She was certain of it. Fairly certain. It seemed a reasonable expectation. The courtship was reaching near to four months, which, in her estimation, was an excessive amount of time to allocate to romance. More significantly, Sir Robert had strongly hinted at the possibility of a proposal should she attend Mrs. Cress's house party. Well, she was in attendance, and had been for a fortnight. Surely tonight, amidst the music and drama of a masquerade ball, Sir Robert would present his offer.

Mind you, Sir Robert had no great appreciation for music, but he did seem to Adelaide to be inordinately fond of dramatics.

"I don't care for dramatics," she muttered.

Her feet slowed in the hall that led from her guest chambers to the ballroom. At best guess, the distance between the rooms required a thirty-second walk. She managed to stretch the first twenty yards into a ten-minute exercise of unproductive meandering. She stopped in front of the mirror to fuss with a rebellious lock of chestnut hair and wrinkle her small nose at the narrow features and light brown eyes she'd inherited from her father. Eyes that, she could not help but note, had begun to crease a bit at the corners.

A few feet later, she reached down to straighten her hem and pull a bit of lint from the ivory silk of her sleeve. Then she peeked into a room, fiddled with a vase, adjusted the low bodice of her gown, and stopped again to examine an oil painting . . . in minute detail, because art appreciation was not something one ought to rush.

And between each pause in movement, she literally dragged her feet. Her dancing slippers made a soft and drawn-out *woooosht, woooosht, woooosht* against the polished wood floor with every step.

Annoyed by the sound, Adelaide stopped to pull off her mask and fiddle with the feathers. This, she assured herself, was *not* another bid to stall. The mask required a considerable amount of fussing. She'd constructed the silly piece herself, and having no experience with—nor any apparent talent for—such an endeavor, she'd made a terrible mess of the thing. The feathers were unevenly spaced, sticking out where they ought to be lying flat, and bent in several places.

Sir Robert was certain to take note of it. She could envision his reaction well. His pale blue eyes would go wide, right before they narrowed in a wince. Then he would cover the lapse of manners with a smile that was sure to display his perfect teeth to best advantage. *Then* he would pronounce her a *most charming creature* in that awful, condescending tone.

"I don't care for that tone," she muttered.

She rubbed an errant feather with the pad of her thumb while the lively strains of a waltz floated down the hall and the scent of candle wax tickled her nose.

It was only a tone, she told herself, a minor flaw in a man positively brimming with things to recommend him. He was handsome. He was fond of her.

He was in possession of five thousand pounds a year.

The mere thought of so much money lightened the worst of her nerves with visions of a happy future. Her sister, Isobel, could have a London season. Little George could have a proper nanny. Wolfgang's debts would be paid. And the lot of them would have a roof over their heads and no shortage of food on the table. It was her dream come true.

"Right."

Ignoring doubts that lingered, she replaced the mask, securing it with a double knot and an extra yank on the ribbons for good measure. She set her shoulders, took a single step forward . . . and nearly toppled to the floor when a deep voice sounded directly behind her.

"I'd not go just yet, if I were you."

She spun around so quickly, she dislodged her mask and tripped on the hem of her gown.

"Easy," the deep voice continued with a chuckle, and a large, warm hand wrapped around her arm, steadying her.

She caught a glimpse of dark blond hair and light eyes, and for one awful moment, she thought she had been caught dawdling in the hall by Sir Robert. But by the time she righted herself and straightened her mask, that fear had been replaced by an entirely new sort of discomfort.

The man was a stranger. He shared the same light coloring and uncommon height as Sir Robert, but that was where all similarities ended. There was an air of aristocratic softness about Sir Robert; his frame was elegantly long and thin, and his features were delicate, almost feminine. There was nothing even remotely delicate or feminine about the man before her. He wasn't long, he was tall, towering over her by more than half a foot. And he wasn't thin, but athletically lean, the definition of muscle visible through his dark formal attire. He was handsome, without a doubt, with broad shoulders and a thick head of hair that was more gold than blond. But his features were hard and sharp, from the square cut of his jaw to the blunt jut of his cheekbones. Even his eyes, green as new grass, had an edge about them.

He put her to mind of the drawings her sister had shown her of the sleek American lions. And that put her to mind of stalking. And *that* made her decidedly uneasy.

Her senses tingled and her breath caught in her lungs.

She wasn't sure if she cared for the sensation or not.

"My apologies," he said quietly. His voice held the cadence of an English gentleman's, but there was a hint of Scotland in his pronunciation. "It was not my intention to startle you."

"Quite all right." She wanted to wince at how breathless she sounded. She cleared her throat instead and carefully withdrew her arm from his grasp. "I was woolgathering. Do excuse me."

She turned to leave, but he moved around, quick and smooth as you please, and blocked her path. "You shouldn't go just yet."

"Good heavens." The man even moved like a cat. "Why ever not?"

"Because you want to stay here."

He offered that outrageous statement with such remarkable sincerity that there could be no doubt of his jesting.

The act of silliness both stunned and intrigued her. He didn't look to be the sort of man who teased.

"That is the most ridiculous, not to mention presumptuous—"

"Very well. *I* want you to stay here." His lips curved up, crinkling the corners of his eyes. "It was unkind of you to make me say it."

She was surprised to find he had a charming smile. The sort that invited one to smile back. It did little to slow her racing pulse, but she liked it all the same.

She shook her head. "Who are you?"

"Connor Brice," he supplied and executed an eloquent bow.

She curtsied in return, then righted her mask when it slipped. "Miss Adelaide Ward."

"Yes, I know. Settle your feathers, Miss Ward."

"You've not ruffled them, Mr. Brice." She hoped he believed the lie.

"No, I meant . . ." He reached out and brushed the edge of her mask with his thumb. She swore she could feel his touch on the skin beneath. "Your feathers need smoothing. What are you meant to be, exactly?"

"Oh. Oh, drat." She reached up and pulled on the knot of ribbons at the back of her head. They refused to give. Sighing, she pulled the contraption over her coiffure and tried not to think of the damage she was doing. "A bird of prey."

"Ah." He grasped his hands behind his back, leaned down, and peered at the mask in her hands. "I thought perhaps you were aiming for disheveled wren."

The sound of her laughter filled the hall. She much preferred the gentle insult to the sort of compliment Sir Robert was sure to give. Mistakes were so much easier to accept when one was allowed to be amused by them.

"It's true," she agreed. "I look dreadful."

He straightened and his green eyes swept over her frame in a frankly appraising manner that made her blush. "You're lovely."

"Thank you," she mumbled. And then, because she'd mumbled it at the mask instead of him, she forced herself to look up when she asked, "And where is your mask?"

"I don't have one."

"But it's a masquerade." Had a mask been optional? She wished someone had mentioned that earlier.

"There is more than one way for a man to hide himself." He gestured at a door she knew led to a small sitting room.

"Is that where you came from?" No wonder he'd been able to sneak up on her so quickly. "Whatever were you doing in there?"

"Avoiding a particular lady. What were you doing out here?"

She wanted to ask which lady, and why he'd broken his self-imposed exile to speak with her—she was hardly the most interesting person at the party—but she was too busy trying to arrive at a suitable excuse for her dallying to devise a subtle way to pry. In the end, she didn't have to come up with anything. He answered for her.

"You're avoiding a particular gentleman."

"I'm not."

"Sir Robert," he guessed, and he shrugged when she sucked in a small breath of surprise. "Your courtship is hardly a secret."

She hadn't thought it was fodder for gossip either. At least not in . . . wherever it was Mr. Brice was from.

"I'm not avoiding anyone."

"You are."

Since he seemed immovable on that point, she tried another.

"Perhaps it is Mr. Doolin," she said smartly. She did make a habit of steering clear of the elderly man and his wandering hands, so it wasn't a lie, *per se*, but more of an irrelevant truth.

He gave a small shake of his head. "It's Sir Robert you're not eager to see, and you were wise to drag your feet. Last I checked, he was lying in wait for you right on the other side of the ballroom doors."

Her mouth fell open, but it was several long seconds before she could make sound emerge.

"Sir Robert does not *lie in wait*. I am quite certain he is not to be found crouched behind the doors like an animal." It was a little discomfiting that she could, in fact, easily imagine the baron doing just that. More than once in the past, she'd felt as if his sudden appearance at her side had been something of an ambush.

She sniffed, and with what she thought was commendable loyalty, she added, "He is a gentleman."

"Do you think?" Mr. Brice's smile wasn't inviting this time. It was mocking. "It is a constant source of amazement to me how little effort the man must exert to disguise his true nature. But then, the ton is ever ready to take a baron at his word and at his . . . five thousand pounds a year, I believe you said?"

Oh, dear heavens. She'd said that bit out loud?

Heat flooded her cheeks. This was awful. Perfectly dreadful. There was no excuse for having made such a comment. And yet she couldn't stop herself from attempting to provide one.

"I was only . . . What I meant by that is . . ." She told herself to give up the effort before she somehow made matters worse. "One cannot . . . There is no shame in marrying a man with an income."

And there it was . . . Worse.

Oh, damn.

Leave, leave now.

"Excuse me." She struggled to untie the ribbons of her mask. She'd put it on, go to the ball, and pray to every deity known to man that Mr. Brice's low opinion of Sir Robert kept the two men from speaking to each other, or about each other, or *near* each other, or . . .

"Allow me." Mr. Brice took the mask from her hands, his long fingers brushing across her skin. "You're right," he said gently. "There is nothing wrong with making a practical match."

"Oh. Well." That was very understanding of him, she

thought with a sigh of relief. Then she wondered if he might expand on that understanding a little. "You'll not repeat what I said?"

"On my word." He pulled the knotted ribbons free and handed her the mask. "The true shame is that you're given no other choice."

Was he speaking of the lack of opportunity for women everywhere to make their way in the world, she wondered, or was he referring to her shortage of suitors? She would have asked him, but she was distracted when his gaze flew to something over her shoulder.

She heard it then . . . Footsteps. The sound was muffled and distant, still around the turn in the corridor, but it was growing louder and more distinct.

She winced and stifled the urge to swear. It wasn't uncommon for two guests to meet in the hall and share a few words in passing, but it was generally frowned upon for a young, unmarried lady to converse with a gentleman to whom she'd not been properly introduced. At seven-and-twenty, she was no longer considered a young lady, but that wouldn't stop Sir Robert from chiding her for not making the trip to the ballroom in the company of a maid.

She didn't care for his chiding.

"*Please*, do pretend we've not been speaking," she whispered and took a step to move around Mr. Brice. Perhaps, if she put a bit of distance between them . . .

Mr. Brice had another idea. He reached over and opened the door he'd emerged from earlier. "This would be easier."

"Yes, of course." Hiding seemed something of an over-reaction, but it was preferable to having a marriage proposal turn into a lecture.

She brushed past him into the dimly lighted room. The door closed behind her with a soft click of the latch, and she stood where she was for a moment, taking a deep breath to settle her racing heart. It was fortunate Mr. Brice had so quickly interpreted the cause of her discomfort. It was even more fortunate that Mr. Brice had thought to shield her presence while he sent the passing guest on his way. Quite considerate of him, really. Very nearly the act of a knight-errant.

Having never before been the object of a gentleman's chivalry, the thought brought a warm slide of pleasure and a small, secret smile. But both began to fade as the hairs on the back of her neck stood on end. She turned around slowly and found herself staring at the small ruby pin in Mr. Brice's crisp white cravat.

"Good Lord," she gasped and stumbled back in retreat. "*What* do you think . . . ?"

Mr. Brice held a finger up to his lips, and she had no choice but to obediently snap her mouth shut. The unknown guest was approaching the door. She could hear his footsteps . . . or were they hers? She couldn't make out a click of a heel, and there was an odd rhythm to the gait, as if the person was shuffling down the hall.

The noise paused outside the door.

No. Oh, please, please don't.

She watched in mounting horror as Mr. Brice slowly extended his arm and took hold of the door handle. Surely he wasn't going to try to turn the key in the lock. *Surely* he wasn't stupid enough to open the door.

He wasn't. He kept perfectly still, his hand wrapped around the handle as if he meant to physically keep it from turning if necessary—which wouldn't seem *at all* suspicious to someone on the other side—until their uninvited guest resumed his leisurely stroll.

She let out a long, shaky sigh . . . then froze when the shuffling stopped and a loud creak issued from an old wooden bench not five yards down the hall.

He was stopping to rest. Who the devil actually used those benches to rest? An elderly guest, she realized, or a maid or footman neglecting their duties. It could be Mrs. Cress's mastiff, Otis, for all she knew. The dog was always climbing on the furniture.

Adelaide bit her lip and clenched and unclenched her hands. What was she supposed to do now? She couldn't be seen leaving a dark room without causing raised brows . . .

But Mr. Brice could. Gentleman could get away with all sorts of suspicious behavior.

She waved her hand about to catch his attention, then pointed a finger at the door and mouthed the word "go" as clearly as possible.

Apparently, she wasn't clear enough. He gave a slow shake of his head.

She pressed her lips together in frustration and jabbed her finger more emphatically.

He shook his head again.

Idiot.

He lifted a finger and pointed behind her. "*Go.*"

Glancing over her shoulder, she saw doors leading onto the terrace. The *dark* terrace that led down to the *dark* garden. The ballroom and lighted side of the terrace and garden were on the other side of the house.

She turned back with a scowl and shook her head.

He nodded.

She had the most ridiculous urge to shake her fist at him.

She fought it back. The silent battle of wills was getting them nowhere, and the longer they remained in the room, the greater the chance of discovery. With no other option left, she gave him a final resentful glare, then spun about and headed for the terrace doors.

The soft pad of his footsteps trailed behind her. Damn it all, he was following her. She would be in the garden, at night, with a complete stranger.

Without another thought, she grabbed a sturdy brass candlestick from the mantel. Instantly, he was beside her, his large hand covering hers on the candlestick. The scent of him filled her senses—the hint of soap on his skin, the light touch of starch on his clothes. His breath was warm and soft in her ear as he bent his head to whisper.

"It's the poker you want." His hand slid over hers until he grasped the top of the candlestick. He drew it away from her slowly and replaced it on the mantel without moving his mouth from her ear. "Longer reach."

She heard the edge of amusement in his voice and could

have cheerfully murdered him in that moment. At the very least, she would have liked to snatch the weapon back and take aim at his head. But ever the practical woman, she took the poker instead, slipping out the doors and into the garden.

Mr. Brice fell into step beside her. "There's a rarely used door around the back of the house. It opens to a short hall and stairwell that will lead you back upstairs."

"I know that." Her sister, Isobel, had an insatiable curiosity. She'd explored every inch of the house on their first day and given a detailed accounting of the building that evening. Adelaide made a mental note to apologize for the lecture she'd delivered to Isobel on the perils of snooping.

"Why are you following me?" she demanded.

"What sort of gentleman would allow a lady to traverse a dark garden alone?"

"The gentlemanly sort." Her eyes scanned the grounds for other guests, but their side of the garden was as still and silent as a tomb. "Why on earth did you come into the room? You should have remained in the hall."

"*I* should have? Why not you?"

"Because . . . you opened the door. I assumed—"

"That I opened it for you? There's a fine bit of arrogance."

She tried to remember if he had motioned her inside the room or not and was forced to admit he hadn't. "Nevertheless, you should have remained outside once I had gone in."

"You were not the only person hoping to avoid a particular guest," he reminded her.

How was it she could be walking in a dark garden while carrying a fire poker and fearing for her future—all because of the man beside her—and still feel as if she needed to apologize for the circumstances?

She was not apologizing. Probably. She would reconsider the matter when she was safely back inside. For now, she needed to concentrate on the best route through the garden.

The single path before her split into three. The one to

the right went to the front of the house. The path to the left led to the back, but it wound about the flower beds close to the house. It was visible to anyone who happened to look outside. The path in the center led deeper into the garden where they would be shielded from view by a hedgerow. She could make her way to the back of the house from that path, but she hesitated at the thought of going farther into the darkness with a near stranger for company.

"If I wanted to hurt you," Mr. Brice said conversationally, apparently aware of her line of thought, "I'd not have troubled to introduce myself first. Nor suggested a better choice of weapon."

Adelaide had to admit that he made a sound point. But, all the same, she readjusted her grip on the poker before setting off down the middle path.